[illegible]E

In their b[illegible]sed, Ricky felt as though s[illegible]n when Court took her in[illegible]e felt a slight resistance in[illegible] down at her.

"Well, Mrs. Wayne," he said, "aren't you glad to see your husband again?"

"You know that, Court. Only it's been so long. I feel a little strange. And I haven't heard from you lately."

"I was busy," he said rather shortly.

"Too busy to write a letter?"

He grinned at her.

"What is this, a catechism?" he inquired. "Where's the loving little woman I came home to? Can this be the girl I left behind me?"

She did not smile, however. "I've had time to grow up, Court. Can't you stop treating me like a child?"

He lit a cigarette and, sitting down on the side of the bed, eyed her.

At the look in his eye, she felt suddenly afraid . . .

MARY ROBERTS RINEHART

A LIGHT IN THE WINDOW

ZEBRA BOOKS
KENSINGTON PUBLISHING CORP.

The lines of A. E. Housman's poetry which appear on page 308 of this novel are from Last Poems by A. E. Housman, copyright, 1922, by Henry Holt & Company, Inc., and are reprinted by permission of the Housman Estate and MCA Management, Inc.

ZEBRA BOOKS

are published by

Kensington Publishing Corp.
475 Park Avenue South
New York, NY 10016

Third printing: December, 1988

Printed in the United States of America

1

Elizabeth got out of the limousine and spoke to the chauffeur.

"Pick up Mr. Wayne at the office as usual, Walter," she said. "I don't think we'll be going out tonight. With my son coming home so soon . . ."

Walter grinned.

"Sure be fine to have the captain back. The war's been over a long time."

She nodded impatiently.

"This occupation nonsense!" she said. "He should have been home a year ago."

She hesitated. She wanted to suggest that Walter get his hair cut. It annoyed her to sit behind him and see the fringe over his collar. But after all he had been a soldier too. He had been gassed. He had a bad cough, which he tried to smother when she or Matthew was in the car.

He coughed now, looking embarrassed as he did so.

"You ought to do something about that, Walter," she said.

"I'm all right," he said gruffly. "Smoke too much. That's all."

He let out the clutch and the high-powered car moved away. She still stood on the pavement with the wind from Central Park blowing her ankle-length skirt about her. Then she turned abruptly, a slight frown on her face, and crossed the pavement to the house, a small indomitable figure under her fur coat. To her left she could see the trees in the park, their bare branches swaying in the wind. On Fifth Avenue a few nurses were shepherding their children across the street. They looked cold, nurses and children alike, and the women looked irritable. Here and there a dejected dog pulled at a leash. When a policeman put up his hand they all stopped, as if they had abruptly run down, like machines. Like automatons, she thought.

She did not ring the bell at once. With a hand protecting her graying hair from the wind she stood and glanced up at the house. Always for years she had done this. It was a visible symbol of her own acumen and Matthew's success. It had been a ruin when she found it, and Matt thought she had lost her mind.

"It's a wreck," he said. "Who's going to rebuild it?"

"We are," she told him. "Bit by bit, of course. I want Courtney to grow up in a good neighborhood, Matt, and this is it."

They had done it too, but it gave her no pleasure on this raw November day of 1919. The war had changed everything. She had built and planned and hoped for her son, as well as for herself; then it had all been wiped away. In the twinkling of an eye, she thought, and realized the phrase came from the funeral service.

Nevertheless, she managed a smile when the butler answered her ring and opened the door.

"It's getting colder, Johnson. We may have snow."

Johnson permitted himself a polite smile in return. He closed the door behind her and helped her out of her coat.

"Mr. Courtney always liked the snow," he observed. "Will you have tea, madam?"

She glanced up at his impassive face.

"I think so. Yes. Where is—" She stopped. She hated saying Young Mrs. Wayne, but Johnson was helpful as usual.

"Mrs. Wayne Junior is upstairs in the drawing room. She had tea some time ago."

They exchanged glances. He knew she did not want to go upstairs to the girl waiting there. Not that she wasn't a pretty girl, and even a nice one, pleasant to everyone. But he knew Elizabeth too: her resentment of her son's hasty marriage two years ago, and the end of her ambitions for him.

"Perhaps if I bring the tea into the parlor down here . . ."

She nodded.

"Yes, please. Just plain tea. Nothing else. I'm half frozen."

She took off her hat and put it on the console table beside her. As usual there was a package of books there. And she thought distastefully of Matthew's library upstairs, crowded with books bearing the Wayne imprint. However, the house as usual was having a quieting effect on her. It had been a miracle and she had done it; the old high stoop gone, so that one went down a step or two into the marble-floored hall. The short but elaborate iron-railed staircase to the upper floors, the modern kitchen and service quarters to the rear. It was hers, her doing, for Matthew and herself and someday for Court. Only now—

She went slowly into the small reception room on her right and examined herself in the mirror there. The wind had not spoiled her stiff marcel wave, and a careful survey convinced her she had not changed much in the two years since Courtney went away. At fifty she was still slender, and her carefully massaged face was still smooth. Only her mouth spoiled her. It was set and determined, perhaps a trifle hard.

When Johnson brought her tea she sat down, and he placed the small tray on a table in front of her.

"Has—has Mrs. Wayne been out this afternoon?" she asked.

"I think not. No, madam."

She let that drop. "Early breakfast tomorrow, Johnson. Tell Katie, will you? The train leaves at nine."

"Very well, madam."

She sat back after he had gone. Usually the room amused her. The craze for Victorian furniture was only starting when she furnished it, and her women friends would stop and stare as they left their wraps in the small powder room behind it.

"What in the world, Elizabeth! What is it?"

"My mother's parlor. Isn't it quaint?"

She did not tell them that years ago her mother had sold the rosewood furniture to a junkman and bought a set of red plush. Or that the stuffed peacock had come from Third Avenue, as had the music box with its glass lid. Nevertheless, it was a fair imitation of the old parlor before her mother had done it over, even to the two conch shells on the hearth.

"Put it to your ear, Elizabeth. Can you hear the sea?"

"Is that the sea?"

She put down her teacup impatiently. She knew quite well why she was sitting there in what she called "Mama's parlor." It was because she was escaping into the dead past rather than face the future. Courtney, her son, was coming home, but not to her. He was coming home to the girl who was waiting upstairs; a girl who had not even cared to live with them, but had gone home to that wretched Ohio town after her brother had been killed in France. A girl she hardly knew, even now.

She had tried, she thought as she got up. During the time she had stayed with them she—Elizabeth—had introduced her to other young people, even given a party or two for her. But the other girls had grown up together, gone to the same schools, talked the same language. They had vaguely resented her, as though in marrying Courtney she had encroached on their own territory. And the girl herself did not fit into their scheme of life. Except with Matt. She and Matt got along famously. She would listen for hours to his talks about books and writers, or to his stories about the Spanish-American War.

"So, as I said, I went to the major. I was pretty cocky in those days. 'This water's not fit for hogwash,' I told him. 'No decent pig would touch it!' And the major—"

Elizabeth sighed and picked up her bag. After all, Courtney was coming home and nothing must spoil that. She glanced at the stuffed peacock on its pedestal, still smelling of mothballs after the summer closing of the house, and her eyes softened as she looked at it. Courtney had always called it Fanny, because its spread tail was like a fan. Now she went over and put a hand on it.

"Don't bring us any more bad luck, Fanny," she said. "And let everything come out all right."

She gave a final glance to her hair in the hall mirror, picked up her fur coat and went up the stairs.

The big drawing room that faced the street was growing dim. Fredrica Wayne was standing at the center window. In the fading light she looked shadowy and vague.

"For heaven's sake, Ricky, what are you doing in the dark?" Elizabeth said, and snapped on the high crystal chandelier.

The girl turned and smiled uncertainly at her.

"I like the twilight," she said.

"Johnson says you've had your tea."

"Yes, thanks."

In the strong light Elizabeth surveyed her, this girl who had married Courtney two years ago when he was lonely and bored in an army camp and already feeling himself a man. At twenty-four. How old was she now? Barely twenty, as against Court's twenty-six. Lovely to look at, of course. Most girls had a sort of beauty at that age, and she had been only eighteen when she married Court. A child! A pretty small town girl. She forced cordiality into her voice.

"I had tea downstairs," she said briskly. "It's cold outside. It may snow. I'm sorry to have been out so long, Ricky. I had a shampoo and a wave. I thought perhaps you would have a wave. It ought to suit you."

Ricky Wayne shook her head.

"I've never waved my hair. Courtney liked it the way it is. I hope he still does."

She came forward still faintly smiling.

"It's such a long time, isn't it?" she said. "And he hasn't written much the last few months. Lately he hasn't written at all."

"Nonsense," said Elizabeth, still briskly. "Naturally he's

been busy, getting ready to come home."

She sat down on the stool of the grand piano, and automatically ran her fingers over the keys for dust. They were clean, however. Indeed the big room with its French furniture and Aubusson carpet looked already garnished for the return of the son of the house.

"I do hope you aren't going to be difficult Ricky," she said. "We've tried to make you happy. Maybe we didn't go about it in the right way, but I wouldn't want Courtney to think we've failed you. He may wonder why you haven't stayed more with us. After all, it's almost two years."

Ricky stiffened slightly.

"Why should he wonder?" she said. "He knew Dave had been killed. He was there. And that my mother was alone. I've written all that to him. He understands you have been very kind, Elizabeth." She hesitated over the name. It was still difficult for her to call her mother-in-law by her first name as she had requested. "I haven't meant to be difficult. It's only . . ." She stopped, smiling again her faint disarming smile. "I think perhaps I'm frightened. It's been so long. It sounds silly, doesn't it?"

"Of course it sounds silly." Elizabeth's voice was sharp. "Frightened? Why should you be? I'll admit I thought you were both too young when you married. I still think so. People change as they get older. They want different things. But I am sure Courtney will do his part, if you will."

"I don't want him to have to do his part. It sounds as though he is trying to make the best of things. If that's the way he feels, or you feel—"

"Don't talk like a child," Elizabeth said impatiently. "I didn't mean that, of course. You didn't know each other very well or very long. That's all."

"He knew me well enough to want to marry me. And if he took me without knowing much about me, I did the same thing. Don't people in love always have to do that?"

"I wouldn't know," Elizabeth said dryly. "I suppose I went

through the usual adolescent romantic period. I simply don't remember."

She took a cigarette from the box—it was becoming smart for women to smoke—and lighted it. She was surprised to find that her hands were shaking with annoyance.

"Is that what you think of our marriage?" Ricky's voice was still quiet, but her color had risen. "That it was just the usual calf-love sort of thing?"

"Good heavens, don't twist my words around. I didn't say anything of the sort."

Ricky stood still. Elizabeth always made her feel young and immature. She was so sure of her place in the world, of her handsome background, of her perfectly groomed self and of Matthew, her husband. But now her own voice was firmer.

"It wasn't that on my part," she said. "I still love Court. It's only—I think we ought to have some time together as soon as he gets back. If we could go away for a little while—"

In spite of herself, Elizabeth's voice was slightly shrill.

"Aren't you forgetting something?" she said. "It's a long time since I have seen my son. And this is his home. He will want to come here. Why shouldn't he?"

She got up abruptly and put out her cigarette. She was flushed with indignation.

"I don't want to seem hard, Ricky," she said more quietly. "Certainly I have no idea of breaking up your marriage, but I still feel it was hasty and ill-considered." She glanced at the clock on the mantel and picked up her coat and hat. "It's time to dress for dinner," she said. "We're alone tonight. And it might be well to forget all this. Both of us have said more than we meant. There's no need of Court's coming home to a family row."

She made a fairly dignified exit, all things considered, but she was still flushed when she went up to the big front bedroom she and Matthew shared. The lights were already lighted, and in the bathroom the water was running. As she put down her wraps she smelled the strong scent of bath salts, and when the maid emerged a cloud of steam followed her.

"Thank you, Corinne," she said. "I'll lie down a few minutes after my bath. Don't wait."

Corrine disappeared and Elizabeth stripped and, putting a rubber cap over her hair, took her bath. She lay for some time in the water. It gave her body a spurious look of youth and freshness, and gradually she relaxed. When Matthew came in soon after, she was on the chaise longue wrapped in a warm negligee. He looked tired, she thought, tired and much older these last few years. He had lost some of his hair, too. But he smiled when he saw her. He bent down and kissed her lightly.

"Well, it's all set, Lizzie," he said. "He comes in at Newport News. It seems a long time, doesn't it?"

"Newport News!" she said resentfully. "They bring them in now as though they are ashamed of them."

"Court won't want a triumphal arch, my dear. He's got a wife to come back to."

She looked up at him, at his undistinguished face, his solid compact body, his steady eyes. She had almost lost him once to a girl in his office, but that had been long ago. Now he was hers, and she was safe. Thank God the passions of men die with the years. She sat up and looked at the small enameled clock on the table beside the bed.

"Seven," she said. "Better get ready for dinner, Matt."

He went out obediently to his small adjacent dressing room. She could hear him splashing there as he washed. He always splashed and snorted. But she did not get up at once. She lay there, defending herself against herself. All she had ever asked of the God she remembered once a week in her pew at St. James's was that her son grow up strong and well, and that he be kept safe.

Would he blame her now if things went wrong? That incredible conversation in the drawing room had left her with a blazing sense of resentment. This girl, this child, warning her to let her marriage alone. As though she was a jealous mother. As though she did not want Court to be happy. But she was frightened too. She had said too much. If Courtney ever learned, or even Matt—

Matthew was still splashing in the bathroom, and she tried to pull herself together. When he came back into the room she had taken off her negligee and was sitting in front of her dressing table, patting cold cream into her face.

He came over and put a hand on her still smooth bare shoulder.

"It's a great day, isn't it, Liz?" he said. "A great day for all of us." He looked a little sheepish. "I sent a check to the church today. Felt we ought to do something."

2

In the big room above, which had been Courtney's, Ricky too was preparing for dinner. Rather, having cried a little, she was holding a cold wet cloth to her eyes. Like Elizabeth, the scene in the drawing room had shaken her, but unlike Elizabeth, she had little or no experience to enable her to carry on in spite of it.

There was no dressing table in the room. Courtney had kept his brushes on a chest of drawers, and, having finished with her eyes, she went to it and gazed at the framed photograph standing there. It showed a tall young soldier in uniform, with a handsome head and a heavy, rather unruly shock of dark hair. The eyes too were dark, and they looked out from the silver frame with a disconcerting directness.

"You did want me," she said, under her breath. "You did, darling, no matter what she says."

But he was still unreal to her. The almost two years were a gap she could not bridge, and the last months when his letters had been so few had widened the gulf. He even looked strange to her, as though he had no reality, as though he had become merely something printed on pasteboard.

She forced herself to dress after that, putting on her stiff corset, knickers, and long full petticoat. As she combed her hair she wondered if she should have had it waved after all. But Courtney had liked it as it was. He would pick it up as it lay on the pillow and run it through his hands.

"How do you grow soft stuff like that?" he would say. "Eat mulberry leaves, like the silkworms?"

In the end she dressed it as she always had, letting it fall over her forehead and drawing it back over her ears into a loose knot at the back of her neck. At the last moment she put on a touch of lipstick. It was coming into vogue now, although rouge was frowned upon. Then she slid her feet into her narrow pointed slippers with their French heels and slid her dress carefully over her head. It was one Matthew liked, a blue velvet with a flat lace collar. She began to feel some of her assurance coming back.

When she went down the two flights of stairs to the second floor she heard Matthew in his library behind the drawing room. The library was Matt's room. It was lined with books to the ceiling, most of them bearing the Wayne imprint. And there was an overflow of them on the big desk. He was at the desk now, knife in hand, opening the fresh parcel. And he chuckled when he saw her.

"Got to hide these from Lizzie," he said. "She's threatening to move me to the warehouse as it is. You're looking very smart, Ricky."

She smiled at him. She was fond of him. In a way he reminded her of her father, the one who had reduced Fredrica to Ricky. Only her father had been young when he died. Young and gay and fond of laughter. Nothing at home had been the same after he went away.

"What have you got there?" she asked. "Anything interesting?"

"That's a fine question to ask a publisher!" He put down the knife and kissed her on the cheek. "Well, it's over at last, Ricky. All the waiting. Been hard on all of us, especially you, my dear. It's not a good idea, separating young married people. Doesn't give them much of a chance."

"Maybe he's forgotten me."

He snorted.

"If ever I saw a boy head over heels in love, it was Court.

Don't you worry about that. I wish you'd felt a little more that this is your home," he added, rather heavily. "It is, you know. Maybe Lizzie and I have been a bit old for you. But I'd sort of hoped to have a daughter around. Always wanted a girl of my own."

She heard Elizabeth coming down the stairs. And the click of her high heels on the hard wood sent a cold chill through her. But she had underestimated that indomitable person. Elizabeth came in as she always had, smartly groomed and pleasantly smiling.

"Good evening, Ricky," she said. "Matt, don't tell me those are more books?"

It was all as it had been since Ricky came back, a month or so before, and the sense of unreality persisted. It was only after Johnson had brought in the cocktails and Matt had proposed a toast that things became real again. Matthew stood, benevolently surveying them over his glass, and cleared his throat.

"Well," he said, "it's been a hard time for all of us. Only we are among the lucky ones. Our boy is coming back, thank God. So let's drink to him as well as to the others who"—he choked a little—"are staying over there."

Suddenly Ricky was back home, the day the Armistice was announced, standing with her mother in the town square. Her mother had been in deep mourning, a thin tragic figure, and Ricky had felt her trembling when down the main street had come the beat of a drum, and the band swung into action. It was playing "Over There," and in a few minutes it came down the street. The mayor's car followed it at a crawl, and behind it came other cars: the Town Council, the School Board. The men in the cars stood up and waved and the people on the pavements cheered and waved back. A procession began to form on foot behind the cars, men and women, black and white, young and old. The soldiers from the camp outside of town came in and joined. The parade took on form and dignity. It circled around the town park and finally, exhausted with excitement, it stopped in front of the Court House, and the mayor made a speech from the steps.

"On this grand and glorious day we give our thanks to Almighty God for the peace that at last has come to us," he had said emotionally. "Let us pray that never again shall war come to this great country. Let us rejoice that it is over, that—"

Ricky and her mother had stood together. Mrs. Stafford's body rigid, her face tight as she listened. All at once she had thrown off Ricky's arm and moved forward through the crowd.

"Shame on you!" she cried, suddenly and distinctly. Ricky flushed, and the crowd around them turned. But Mrs. Stafford stood there, her eyes blazing. "Shame on you all. Can't you remember the dead?" she said loudly. "What about the mothers whose sons didn't come back? How much rejoicing do you think I'm doing today?"

There was a stunned silence. Then she had turned and elbowed her way through the crowd while Ricky followed helplessly behind her.

It was only a flash. She roused to find Elizabeth's cool eyes on her.

"Aren't you drinking to Court, Ricky?"

"I'm sorry. Of course. I suppose I'm excited," she said. "Who wouldn't be?"

Matthew drank his cocktail solemnly.

"It's a great day. A great day for all of us," he said. "Let's hope the world has learned some sense at last."

Elizabeth was mild and conciliatory during dinner. She had said too much that afternoon and knew it. But the brief stimulation of the cocktail hour was over, and after the fingerbowls had been brought and Johnson had disappeared Matthew glanced soberly at Ricky.

"How about your plans?" he asked. "Yours and Court's, of course. Want to stay on here? It's your home if you want to. You know that. Only sometimes young people like to be by themselves."

Ricky glanced down the table, but Elizabeth's face was impassive.

"Of course, everything depends on Court, Dad," she said. "If he wants to stay here . . ."

Matthew eyed her.

"What do you want? You yourself? Speak up, Ricky. Want to be off by yourselves? In a small apartment, maybe?"

But Elizabeth did not give her a chance to reply.

"Good heavens, Matt," she said, exasperated. "Apartments cost money, and even with what Court has from your mother he can't afford one. Besides"—she hesitated—"we'd better see how he feels about things in general before we make any plans."

"What things in general?" Matthew demanded truculently. "They're married. They're in love. They have to live their own lives, don't they?" He rose abruptly. "Let's get out of here. And let the young people settle their own affairs, Lizzie. Time for all that later on. Come on, Ricky. Better go to bed early. We have a long day tomorrow."

But although Ricky went up to bed soon after, it was not to sleep. She lay in Courtney's wide bed, in what had been his room for most of his life. Elizabeth had kept it much as he had left it, his pictures of school and college, and one of a group at Plattsburg, with Courtney in the center and looking very young. Except for the framed photograph she had brought with her, and her own toilet things, it was still Courtney's room. But he himself still remained remote. And not only remote but for some reason alarming. As though she did not know him, or had never loved him, had never lain in his arms as his wife.

She did not understand it. She lay wide-eyed in the bed, her hair braided in two long pigtails over her shoulders, and began carefully to go back over the time they had been together. He had not been frightening then. He had been a charming and lovable boy with an engaging grin and an easy habit of getting his own way.

They met first at a dance at the cantonment. It was at the Hostess House, so called, and the camp band was playing. Her mother had not wanted her to go, although her brother Dave was going and offered to look after her. Dave was only a private, a big blond boy with a broad smile, but he could always get around his mother.

"I'll keep the roughnecks away, Mom," he said. "Let Ricky have some fun. She's not a baby."

So she had gone, and toward the end Dave brought up a young officer, trying not to look abashed as he did so.

"The lieutenant wants to meet you, Ricky," he said. "Wayne's his name. He's a good guy, in spite of what he's got on his shoulders!"

They danced the next dance together, and the next. She remembered that, and how he asked if he could call, and had written down her address in a notebook. It was, however, two days before he appeared at the house and rang the bell.

Beulah, their colored maid, opened the door.

"Well!" she said. "And who are you, soldier boy?" She gave him a white-toothed grin. "Seems like we get more soldiers than the camp out there. Come on in, if you can find a chair."

Evidently he was not the only one who had seen Ricky at the dance and learned where she lived. He found half a dozen other young officers scattered through the living room of the big frame house, being carefully chaperoned by her mother. And he looked rather sour.

"What is this? A town meeting?" he asked. "Maybe I'd better come back another time."

"You ought to stay while you've got the chance," one of the lieutenants said, grinning. "I've heard tell the general and staff are due tomorrow."

She introduced him to her mother, and later he found a place on the floor and Beulah brought him a glass of lemonade. But he had not stayed very long. Even then she knew he did not like competition.

He did not come back for a week. Other men came, sometimes officers, sometimes the privates Dave brought in. Beulah was enchanted, but Mrs. Stafford did not like it. She never left them alone with Ricky. She would sit in her chair, a thin austere woman, and keep an eye on all of them. But when Dave came she relaxed. She adored Dave, reckless young Dave who had played about with the town girls since he wore trousers. He was twenty then, and had been headed for trouble until the war came. Not until she learned that he was a private in Courtney's company had she paid any attention to Courtney.

Then she asked him to dinner, and, to Ricky's embarrassment, more or less placed Dave in his hands.

"He's a high-strung boy," she said, smiling nervously. "I'd like to think someone was looking after him."

Courtney had looked uncomfortable.

"I'm pretty new at this stuff myself," he said. "I'll do what I can, of course. Only this is a war, Mrs. Stafford. I can't promise to mother him."

There were fewer and smaller crowds at the house following that evening. It was gradually accepted that Ricky was Courtney Wayne's girl, and by the fall of 1917 they became engaged.

He simply took her in his arms one night and said he wanted her as his wife.

"It's a poor prospect," he said. "We'll be going off before long, and I may not come back. But I'm so terribly in love with you, darling. If I could carry you away with me, in my heart, as my wife—"

She was wildly, frantically in love with him by that time, but what followed moved so fast that it was difficult to remember. Her mother's dry protest, "How do you know your own mind, at eighteen? And what do you know about him or his people? It's like buying a pig in a poke." And then came Elizabeth's arrival on the scene, after a stormy talk over the long-distance telephone. According to the stationmaster, she was in a nasty humor when she got off the train. She surveyed the town with distaste. It was small and dingy in the morning light, and the nut and bolt factory below the track ejected masses of smoke and injected long lines of war workers.

"What a hole!" she had reputedly said.

They did not see her until evening. She went to the overcrowded hotel, filled with uniforms and young army wives with crying babies. She had no private bath, and the public one was a horror. She sponged off in her washbasin and went to bed while Courtney reported back for duty.

Ricky never forgot the dinner that night; her mother stiff and cool, and Beulah hovering over Elizabeth like a dark ministering angel.

"You eat this, Mrs. Wayne. That chicken's plumb fresh. My boy Joe brought it in from the country this morning."

There was almost a crisis when Elizabeth, watchful of her figure, declined the pie.

"You better try it," Beulah had insisted. "Mrs. Stafford's known all over for her lemon meringue. I'll just slide a teeny bit on your plate."

Ricky never knew what Elizabeth told Matthew on her return the next day. She could guess, however. "A typical small-town girl," she would have said. "Respectable, of course, or he needn't marry her. But he's made up his mind, and he's going to a war, Matt. What can we do?"

Ricky got out of bed and lighted a cigarette. She smoked only occasionally, usually with Elizabeth, but now she felt she needed to, if only to clarify her thinking. She put on a dressing gown and sat down in a chair by the empty fireplace.

From outside came the continuous soft roar of a great city settling for the night, the occasional sound of a taxi horn, the distant rush of an elevated train. And beyond the city lay the vast country itself, licking its war wounds and grateful for peace, while a defeated but unregenerate Germany watched the victors quarreling over the spoils.

It was in Germany that Court had changed. Until then his letters had been full of plans for their future, of a yearning desire to get back to her. Even during the decisive battles of that last summer, when Pershing decided to smash the enemy hinge rather than risk another winter for his men, he had written when he could.

Had she lost him? And, if so, how? She tried to face it, sitting in her chair in the dark, with an odd new look of maturity in her face. They had been like children, she thought, happy irresponsible children. His arms around her in the car when they left the church after their marriage. His air of pride when, at the reception afterward, he had stood beside her, tall and handsome in his uniform. His indulgent smile when his mother, ignoring the fruit punch and chicken salad, confided him to the care of his portly general.

"My only chick, you know, General, I'm counting on you to look after him."

And the general, looking somewhat staggered, saying, "My dear lady, I have the hell of a lot of *only chicks* in my division."

She asked Ricky that day to call her Elizabeth.

"I'm Elizabeth to all my friends, my dear," she said. "And I hope we will be friends. Anyhow, you have a mother of your own. It will be simpler all around."

"Thank you, Elizabeth," she said. "I'd like to."

Then they were gone, she and Court. They ran down the path to the waiting car, with the guests crowding the front lawn. And Dave threw an old shoe after them and to his embarrassment had neatly hit his lieutenant with it. Poor Dave, how queer he looked! But Court only laughed.

They were frightfully happy during the week in a hotel in Cincinnati. She was very young and ignorant, of course, but if the hot desires of his strong young body puzzled her, she was his, to do with as he wished. Only on the night his leave was up something had happened. It did not seem important at the time. He was awake beside her with a lighted cigarette in his hand. And he moved slightly away from her.

"Look here, Ricky," he said out of the darkness. "Let's get this straight. Just what do I mean to you?"

She was stunned with surprise.

"I don't know what you're talking about, Court. I love you. You know that."

"That's not what I mean," he said, almost roughly. "You let me sleep with you, but that's about all, isn't it? It's not really important to you."

"I wouldn't say that, Court. I'm your wife. Anything you want . . ."

"O God!" he groaned. "If that's the way you look at it . . ."

He never explained, and soon after they came back he was gone. One rainy night she was standing at the railroad station while silent lines of men in full equipment were loaded on the train. They looked frightening in their helmets, each man with his blanket roll and rifle. And Courtney himself seemed a strange warlike figure. She had promised not to cry, and she did not. She waved forlornly until the train disappeared into the darkness that was war.

When she went home she found her mother had drawn back the living-room curtains and put a lamp in the window. It stayed there until Dave was killed.

3

The Waynes wanted her to go east after the division left, but Mrs. Stafford was not well. Something was troubling her, although she did not tell Ricky about it. Now and then, however, she and Beulah were closeted in her bedroom, and Ricky could hear them arguing.

She was still worried about the last night in the hotel room with Court, but there was no one to whom she could talk. Her mother, Episcopalian as she was, still held the Calvinistic idea that sex was sinful, and Ricky wondered how her father had begotten two children. He had been a big jovial man who had owned and published the flourishing town newspaper. She did not remember him very well, except that on summer evenings he would take out the hose and sprinkle the front lawn, and when it was hot she and Dave were allowed to stand under the cool spray.

The days passed slowly after the division had departed. Most of the young men had gone. And in church on Sundays there was a flag beside the altar. There were stars in many of the windows, and as time went on some of them were gold. She had few visitors. Now and then Jay Burton dropped in. He had been in love with her since her high school days, and he would sit in the living room, a thin young man with sandy hair, watching her with hurt but shrewd eyes.

"Heard from Wayne lately?"

"He writes almost every day."

"Must be doing a hell of a lot of fighting!"

She felt sorry for him. The services had rejected him because of a football knee. Now he had passed his state bar examinations and was opening a law office.

"You can come to me when you want a divorce," he told her once. "I won't charge you for it. Free, gratis, and for nothing!"

"You'd like that, wouldn't you?"

"What do you think?"

Court had been gone four months when Matthew wrote asking her to come to New York.

"We are very lonely here," he said. "And after all, my dear, this is your home. I know Courtney would like to think of you in it. I am writing for my wife as well as myself, of course. She has gone to Maine for a day or two to see about the house there, but she sent you her love before she left."

Mrs. Stafford read the letter with an impassive face.

"They're your people now," she said. "It's only right they should take care of you."

"You're my people, Mother."

"That's as may be. A wife belongs to her husband. Don't forget that, Fredrica."

So she had gone, and Matthew met her at the station, looking rather anxious. He had kissed her warmly, however.

"Seemed like a good idea to be all together these days," he said. "Not that I expect anything to happen. But Lizzie's pretty nervous. A little young life around the place won't hurt either of us."

He seemed genuinely glad to see her. He informed her in the car that business was shot to hell, that Lizzie was staying in town instead of opening the place at Bar Harbor, and that the Democratic party always got the country into war. Having thus stated his credo, he lapsed into silence until the car stopped.

Elizabeth also seemed glad to see her. Here in her own domain she gained dignity. This was her background, the big house, the ordered service, even the framed photograph of a woman on the piano in the drawing room, wearing a handsome brocaded dress and plumes in her hair.

"Matthew's sister, Roberta," Elizabeth said. "She married an Englishman, you know. That was what she wore when she was presented at court."

"I didn't know," she admitted shyly. "I'm afraid I know very little about any of you, really."

"Well, that's what you're hear to learn." Elizabeth said briskly. "We want you to know us, and like us."

She knew they tried. With Matthew she got along famously. He was as friendly and hearty as a big dog.

"How's our girl tonight?" he would say when he came home. "Pretty as a picture, eh?" He would kiss her, his ruddy face smelling of soap and tobacco. But then it came. "Any word from Courtney?" he would say.

That colored everything they did, everything they thought. When any of them entered the house it was to look first at the hall table for a letter or—God forbid—a telegram. They were not living. They were waiting. And Ricky found herself waiting, too. It was like a contagion, this fear. At home she had not felt it so much, but here on the East Coast the war seemed nearer, the tension greater. Wounded men were coming home. Soldiers in uniform filled the streets or marched to some secret place of embarkation.

"We'll have to go on to Berlin and finish off the bastards" seemed to be the universal opinion.

So she like to be with Matthew, standing by as he showed her the war map on his library wall and moved the colored pins about. With Elizabeth, however, she was not so comfortable.

She did not fit into Elizabeth's world. She liked the evenings when Matthew brought home one of his authors and the talk was about books. But there were other dinners—Elizabeth's dinners—when the women who came were heavily jeweled and carried enormous feather fans, and when the talk was largely of people, or bridge at five or ten cents a point.

After the long elaborate meal the card tables were set up and she would slip upstairs to Courtney's room, which was now hers. But all of the Courtney she knew was his photograph there, and it began to have a remote, lifeless look. As though to bring him closer she would sit in the big chair by the fireplace and knit for him; the pitiful things women all over the country were knitting for their men, and which later were to litter the battlefields of France as they went forward, along with their blankets and even their letters. All the equipment that men abandon when they fight.

That room of Courtney's was her sanctuary. Not only from Elizabeth's parties. From the city itself, with its noise and extravagance. For what with high wages and war expenditures money was plentiful. Even the shop windows were dazzling; furs of all sorts, jewelry and flowers on display. One day Elizabeth brought home a gold-mesh bag. And Matthew scowled when he saw it.

"If you sold one of those bonds of yours to get that bit of nonsense you can take it back, my girl."

"Who said anything about a bond? I won the money at bridge."

"Fool women," he grumbled. "Some poor devil of a husband probably worked his head off to get that money."

But Elizabeth had her bag and kept it.

She was not unkind to Ricky. She did not even actively resent her. But they had nothing in common. And there were times when Ricky saw her alone and realized that much of her frivolity was an endeavor to throw off her anxiety about Court. She never entered the house without looking for a telegram on the hall table. Indeed none of them did, and as the fighting grew more and more violent that summer of 1918, there were times when they talked very little and none of them slept.

Ricky, going down to Matthew's library late one night to get a book, found him asleep in his chair, with Court's last letter on his knee.

Now and then she would have the car for a few hours, and Walter would stifle his cough and show her the city. He liked her, she knew. Probably he was sorry for her, alone in these strange surroundings.

"How about the Battery today?" he would ask over his shoulder. "There's an aquarium there, if you like fish." Or he would show her the Hudson, from an uptown street. "Must have thought he was seeing things, the first fellow who found it." Then he would cough and try to smother it. "That damned gas . . ."

Once or twice she asked him what it was like, at the war. He would shrug.

"Mostly sitting around and waiting to do something."

"But when was there something to do?"

"Well, you don't get much time to think. It's not so bad. I used to get excited beforehand. After that it was all right."

"All right? With people being killed all around you?"

"That's war, Mrs. Wayne."

It was after a drive like that that the telegram came from her mother. Dave was dead, killed in action. For the first time the reality of the war was brought home to her. Up to then she had not dared to think Courtney might not come back. Now she realized the sick terror that stalked men and women by day and by night. She had not cried. She had waited numbly for the train to take her home, dry-eyed and terrified, trying to remember Dave; a Dave lighthearted and gay, when he enlisted for the war.

"I'll bring a French girl back with me, Mom."

"You try it and see what happens!"

"Not a nice little mademoiselle? A nice little French wife who would know how to cook?"

"Get on with you. You and your girls."

For Dave had been like that, young as he was. On the night the division left she had seen him with his arms around one she did not know, and the girl had been crying bitterly.

The New York interlude was over. Her mother needed her. She was taking Dave's death badly. She said hardly anything but she ate little and slept less. Ricky, watching her grim still face, sensed a smoldering fury behind it. She did her best, but

Mrs. Stafford had built a wall, not only between Ricky and herself but against the world.

Only Beulah refused to recognize it.

"Now you eat something," she would say. "I ain't cooking good vittles to throw them away." Or: "You go right smack up to bed. I'll get a hot-water bottle for your feet. And you take that stuff the doctor left, or I'll give it to you myself."

It was a difficult time for Ricky. The New York interval was as though it had never been. The clothes Elizabeth had insisted on buying her were hung away, for she was wearing mourning now. Weeks went by, with Courtney in the middle of the fighting. And then at last no letters from him at all. She went almost wild with terror, and when one night long-distance called her she could hardly speak over the phone.

"This is Matthew Wayne speaking. Is that you, Ricky?"

"Yes. Is—is anything wrong?"

"Not much. Courtney's been in the hospital. A piece of shrapnel in his leg. He's all right now. Nothing to worry about. I just thought I'd let you know."

She was still trembling; but her breath had come back. She even had a moment of hope. "Do you think they'll send him home?"

"Not much chance, I'm afraid. They need all the men they can get. How's your mother?"

There was a letter from Courtney a few weeks later, forwarded from New York.

"It isn't serious," he wrote. "I'll be up and probably back on the old job before you get this. But I've had time to think. I want you to know how much I love you, and to hell with the censor. I can hardly wait to get back to you. And don't think I'm not coming! It won't be long now. The Hun is about through. Then we can start our life together, my sweet, and we'll make it a good one."

It was the most ardent letter he had ever written her, and some of her fear died with it. Now at last she could wait for him, and know he was coming back to her.

Little by little she drifted back into her old life, seeing Jay now and then, doing the marketing for her mother and watching the mail carrier as he came up the walk. Then one morning not long after the Armistice she received a letter which ruined all her hopes. Court was not coming back. He was being sent into Germany with the Army of Occupation.

"It won't be long, dearest. A few weeks or months," he wrote. "Then I'll be back and we can make some plans. I've been sick over the whole business, but what can I do? In this man's army . . ."

She went around rather dazed after that. Other men came home that winter. They drifted into the town, a few of them boastful, but most of them merely tired, content to be back, unwilling to discuss what was now past and gone.

"I declare," Beulah said, "they ain't got nothin' to say. Been everywhere and done everything, and so closemoufed they might as well never a been out of this town."

Only of course Courtney Wayne did not come. He was on his way into Germany, slogging along wet roads through Luxemburg, down a hill and across a hill to Trier and eventually on to Coblenz. In the towns the one-time enemy lined up to see their conquerors go by, their faces under their umbrellas merely stolid and expressionless. To Courtney they did not look defeated. They merely looked sullen.

He turned to the young officer beside him.

"Better not fool ourselves, Jim," he said. "We had them licked and then we quit. No wonder they think we're a lot of suckers."

To Ricky the winter that followed was endless. Outside of town they were tearing down part of the big cantonment. The long gray barracks were going, the big parade ground was bare and neglected. Only the administration building and the hospital group remained, and they would go soon. The hotel, crowded for two years, was back to its normal quota of traveling men, sitting in the windows and staring out boredly at the street. And somewhere in France the Graves Registration people had located Dave's grave and there was talk of bringing him back along with others, and burying them all in Arlington.

She still had no one to talk to. Her mother had shut herself and her bitter grief away, and at night Ricky would go to her tidy room, the toilet table draped in dotted Swiss and her narrow bed waiting, to lie awake for hours, wondering and uncertain. For now she had a problem of her own. Mrs. Stafford was blaming Dave's death on Courtney.

"All his fine promises!" she would say. "I notice he came out all right himself."

"That's not fair, Mother. He was wounded."

"A piece of shrapnel. What's that?"

It was the spring of 1919 when she noticed a change in Courtney's letters. They were less personal, and he had altered some of his ideas about the Germans. "They are not so bad when you get to know them. They don't like us, but at least they put up with us. And after the French at least they are clean. Good God, how clean they are."

In one of them he wrote that he had moved. He was now billeted in the apartment of an elderly college professor. There was a wife and two daughters, and one of them was almost blind. "She won't wear glasses, because apparently that would lessen her marriage chances." He did not mention the other. But also for the first time he did not mention coming home.

Then came the weeks and even months when there were no letters at all. She did not want her mother to know. She would meet the mail carrier down the street and pretend she had heard. There was no talk now of her going back to New York. Even Matthew had given up, although he still wrote to her.

But with the news that Courtney was soon to be on his way home there was no longer any excuse. He would expect to find her when he arrived. Nevertheless, while she was packing or, later on, lying sleepless in the train, she had a bitter sense of belonging nowhere, and to nobody.

4

Down in Virginia the transport lay out in the harbor. It had been a long stormy voyage, and the ship itself was not too seaworthy. For more than two weeks the men had slept in the steerage and even in the hold, coming up at messtime to cling to lifelines strung along the streaming decks, and in the end to get their rations of unpalatable food. For more than three weeks the endless poker games among the officers had gone on in the wardroom, broken only by the meals and such sleep as anyone could get.

Cigarettes had run out. The food—bad as it had been—was almost gone, but here and there a carefully hoarded bottle of liquor had been brought out for this last night aboard.

"Better drink it. The country's going dry pretty soon."

"Is that why we saved it?"

"Sure, my boy. What the hell have we been fighting for? Prohibition, of course!"

They felt defeated, a trifle anxious. Behind them was a war largely of smells and dirt, with only now and then the excitement of battle; a war which they knew now was neither won nor lost. Instead here they lay, unacclaimed and practically forgotten, with their dead on foreign soil and ahead of them no man could say what.

Their losses had been heavy. Courtney had been the only surviving officer of his company. The rest were replacements. But almost to a man they had liked Germany. He warned the company when it first moved in.

"Remember," he said, "this is the enemy. Don't fool yourselves. It is still the enemy. They'll be friendly when they get a chance, but don't let that influence you. They're looking to the United States for better terms, that's all."

He had warned them about venereal diseases too. And a lot of good that had done, he thought wryly.

He looked around the officers' wardroom. He had dropped out of the endless poker game that had gone on since they left Brest. Now he paid up and, taking his drink, left the table.

"God, this place stinks," he said. "I want some air."

As he stood under the lights of the wardroom there was little resemblance to the picture on Ricky's toilet table. He seemed taller. Certainly his shoulders had broadened. He was hard and fit and determined. And he might have been thirty or more when, still carrying his drink, he went out on the deck.

Standing there he could see the lights on shore. The small town had already lost its wartime importance and gone back to its former somnolence. Somewhere a locomotive blew its whistle, and here and there a car crawled along the waterfront. He had no real feeling of coming home. Rather a sense of anticlimax, of tension too suddenly relaxed, and of uncertainty ahead.

The other men had it too. Not that they said so.

"Going to be hard to settle down," they said. Or: "Going back to my job, I hope!" Only a few were cocksure and excited. "My girl? Sure she'll be waiting. She's a great kid."

But the older men were not so certain. "What's it going to be like anyhow? Think they'll get anywhere with the League? I don't trust the Hun. Never did."

"They treated us all right."

"Sure they did. Look what we gave them!" There was always a laugh at that.

It was, however, their personal problems that obsessed them. Many of them had been gone for two years. What about their wives? Had they been faithful? Most of them had had casual contacts with women during their long absence. Now suddenly they wanted their own, unsullied and loving.

"I've got a damned attractive wife. I only hope I still have her."

All of them wanted women, their own kind of women. The German prostitutes did not count. They had merely eased their tension for the time. They wanted American women, whether sweethearts, wives, or merely companions for the night.

"What's the first thing you'll do when you go ashore, Joe?"

"Get me a girl, same as you!"

Court leaned on the rail. There were no chairs on the deck. The transport had been stripped of everything movable to make room for the men. He himself had been sleeping on a mattress on the floor of the assistant engineer's cabin, while a major slept on the high bunk on top of a chest of drawers. Once as the ship rolled the major had been tipped out, and had spent the rest of the night swearing impartially at the army, the navy and the Atlantic Ocean.

He lit a cigarette, still gazing toward the shore. He knew they would all be there when they docked in the morning, his mother, his father and his wife, and once again he tried to reorient himself to remember his whirlwind courtship, and his wild determination to marry, to live at least a little before he went to a war from which he might never return. It had not been quite sane, he thought. He tried to recapture some of the excitement of the week he and Ricky had had together, but even this evaded him.

Standing by the rail and staring at the vague outline of the shore he tried to picture them all. But Ricky eluded him. So much had happened in that interval of almost two years. And she had been so young. Only eighteen. My God, he thought, people were still growing at eighteen.

He threw away his cigarette and went below. The colonel of his regiment was standing outside his cabin, looking rather lost.

"Well, this is it, Wayne."

"It looks like it, sir."

"You're about the last of the first crowd, aren't you?"

"Just about. We left a lot over there."

The colonel grunted.

"We're a little late for the excitement," he said dryly. "I don't imagine they'll have a reception committee for us over there on shore. Well, we've done our job. I didn't feel like sleeping," he added. "Couldn't settle down somehow."

"Same here, sir."

The colonel looked after him as he passed. There had been stories about him in Coblenz; that he had fallen hard for some German girl over there. And the boy—all his young officers were boys to him—had not looked happy tonight. He looked, if anything, rather apprehensive. Still he would get over it. He himself in Manila years ago—He grunted again and went below.

The poker game was breaking up in the wardroom. Men were going to their cabins, some of them not too steady on their feet. But Courtney did not go back to his quarters. Instead he went below to where some of his men were bunking off the engine room.

The air grew worse as he went down. On the last ladder it hit him like a blow. But at least the engine room was quiet. There was no longer the roar and beat of the long battle against the sea. An oiler in greasy overalls was reading the sporting page of a newspaper brought out by the lighter. He looked up as Courtney reached the steel deck.

"Evening, Captain," he said. "Those fellows sure been raising hell tonight."

"Can you blame them?"

"Well, they're home anyhow, whatever that means."

The hell-raising was over when he opened a door and passed into the men's quarters. Here the air was even worse, the smell of unwashed bodies, seasickness, and bad sanitation combined to make him gasp. But most of the men were asleep. They lay stretched out in tiers in their shallow coffinlike bunks, their faces wiped clean of all expression.

Here and there one was awake, however. He nodded to them as he passed. At one bunk he stopped. The boy in it was not asleep. He lay very still, his eyes open. When he heard Courtney he turned them toward him, without moving.

"How are you, Bill?"

"I'm better tonight, Captain."

He did not look better. Wayne reached out and touched his forehead. It was clammy with sweat.

"Look, Captain," he whispered. "Don't let them carry me ashore tomorrow. I can walk. The fellows will carry my stuff. I don't want to get home flat on my back. You fix it, Captain. I can make it."

"Let's see how you are in the morning, Bill."

"If I'd been wounded it would be different, but to have my goddam guts go back on me . . ."

Court stayed for a few minutes. He was fond of Bill Rogers. During the hard fighting before the Armistice he had been cheerful and uncomplaining. He had fought like a wildcat, too. Courtney had recommended him to the general for some sort of recognition, but nothing had come of it. The Army of Occupation had been forgotten. The time was over when crowds cheered the returning men. America had turned her back on the war, and was busy about other matters.

"You'll come back in the morning, sir?"

"Sure. Now get some sleep."

He had the cabin to himself that night. The major had been lightered ashore to see about the debarkation the next day, and the unaccustomed luxury of being along relaxed him. He took off his uniform, unfastening with relief the high stiff collar of the blouse and swearing when he found someone had borrowed the bootjack. He put on his pajamas and dressing gown, and going to the washroom took a shower. The place was littered with cigarette stubs and damp towels and smelled of disinfectant from the adjoining toilet. But the bath made him feel better. He whistled as he dried himself.

When he got back to his cabin he looked out the port before climbing to the major's birth. The ship had swung on her anchor, and the lights seemed nearer.

He lay for some time without moving. No use thinking about what was over and gone. Elsa was merely a part of the past. She had always known he could not marry her. He had told her about Ricky soon after he moved into the apartment.

"And is she very beautiful?" she had asked, in her good but accented English.

"Very beautiful."

"And you love her very much?"

"Of course. She's my wife."

He put Elsa impatiently out of his mind. He would have to tell Ricky about Dave, of course. Not everything. Not about the girls he found in the most unlikely places, but about the reckless courage that had caused his death. He had been brave to the point of rashness, had David Stafford. He had wanted to fight his own war.

"Watch me get those bastards," he would say.

They had never found him. Courtney himself had gone out at night to search for him, but with no result. Someone would have located him later, probably; have dug a grave and put a small wooden cross over it with his helmet on top and his identification disk nailed to it. They were scattered all over, those graves, all along the terrain where the Germans retreated, leaving behind them the neat headquarters where their officers had lived, with rustic furniture for their comfort and cement-lined dugouts for their safety.

He turned uneasily. He had meant to put the Germans out of his mind. But he could not. In spite of himself he was back in the apartment in Coblenz, with the little maid polishing the floor with felt slippers on her feet, doing a sort of rhythmic dance. With Hedwig reading without glasses, holding her book within a few inches of her eyes. With the big tile stove in the corner of the dining room, with the frau professor knitting and the old professor talking over his beer.

"An Armistice, Herr Captain, is not a defeat. The German people are not defeated. There comes a time in any war when the costs outweigh the advantages. This is the time to stop fighting, and that is why we stopped."

Only the Frau Professor in the family spoke little or no English. She remained for him to the end a mute, rather stolid figure. And Hedwig had never liked him. She had avoided him whenever she could.

He remembered the day he had arrived. They had been warned against fraternizing with their hosts, and he had been prepared to obey. He had climbed the stone steps to the apartment, followed by a soldier with his duffle bag, and with his German phrase book in his hand. It was bound in blue imitation leather, and the first pages were entitled "Easy Introductory Phrases." He had memorized one or two, but most of them had gone out of his mind completely.

The soldier with him had dumped his stuff on the landing and grinned.

"Not so bad, sir," he said. "We've been in a lot worse places. Remember that chicken coop?"

That had been Rogers.

He had rapped at the door, and a middle-aged hausfrau had opened it. It was cold. She wore a shawl over her shoulders and was obviously frightened. Perhaps it had been Roger's grin that relieved her, or his own youth. He had taken off his cap and held it in his hand.

"Spricht hier jemand Englisch?" he had inquired from the book.

"Ein wenig. Nicht viel," she said. "Bitte, kommen Sie herein."

The room was ugly. That was the first impression he had. It was cluttered with photographs and small souvenirs. In the center was a table with a red-and-white checked cloth, and in a corner a tall tiled stove. An elderly man rose and looked at him over his spectacles. He had been reading.

"My husband," said the woman, in German. "The Herr Professor Hans von Wagner."

No one had offered to shake hands. The room was chilly with the North German damp and filled with unspoken resentment. He had felt apologetic.

"I understand I have a room here," he had said, and was gratified to be answered in quite good if accented English by the professor himself.

"It is ready for you," he said. "I hope you will allow us the privacy of the remainder of our home. This is new for us. It is not easy." He glanced at Rogers. "What about the soldier?"

"That's all right," Courtney said hastily. "He'll be in and out, but that's all."

For a week he had not seen the daughters of the family. He had not even known about them. He was busy with the new problems of a peace which was no peace, and he hardly saw his hosts. His room opened on the rear hall, away from the living quarters, a comfortable enough place with the blankets buttoned inside the sheets, and the usual high pillows and half-sized feather comfort which usually ended on the floor. There was no stove in it. It remained consistently cold and damp all winter.

At first he had been wary and uneasy. Then one day he came home in the middle of the morning to find a girl there staring out the window, a small dark girl who looked at him with hot hatefilled eyes.

"Good morning," he said. "Not much of a view, is there?"

"What I see I do not like," she said coldly, and walked past him with her head in the air.

It had amused him at the time. Later it had become a sort of game, to make her speak to him, even to like him. Then it had ceased to be a game. Of course he had been no better and no worse than a good many of the others. Only Elsa had been a virgin that night he came home late to find her in his room. He had not counted on that.

After a while he dropped out of the berth and fished for his wallet in the pocket of his blouse. He took out a small snapshot and after looking at it for some time tore it into tiny pieces and scattered them out the open port.

The lights were still there on the shore. For almost two years he had waited to see them. Now he was not sure what they would mean.

5

The transport was being warped into the dock, her decks crowded with uniformed men in full equipment. But the dock itself was almost empty, except for a few officials. There was no band, no "Hail, the Conquering Hero Comes." Nothing but a gray November sky, long lines of waiting empty passenger coaches, and the silent men above looking over the rail of the ship.

Matthew was resentful. He pulled his overcoat about him and scowled.

"Makes me sick," he said violently. "If I'd known it I'd have hired a band myself."

"They don't care, Matt," Elizabeth said prosaically. "They're home."

"Not yet they aren't," said Matthew, still violent. "Not by a long shot. They'll be sent to a camp somewhere and left to hang around until the government sees fit to let them loose."

"They won't do that with Court, will they?"

"How do I know? I've pulled some wires, but I'm only a Republican."

Ricky said nothing. She was holding her fur coat—a gift from Matthew—around her and staring at such portions of the decks as she could see. But her knees felt weak and Matthew, seeing she was frightened, tucked her arm under his own.

"Get your smile ready," he said. "He'll want to find you smiling."

"I'm all right." Her voice sounded thin. "I suppose it's just excitement."

There was still no sign of Courtney, and it was cold and windy on the dock. The wind blew at her skirt, twisting it around her slim legs, and she had to hold her hat. There was no one around except the dock officials and a thin weather-beaten woman who sat patiently on a baggage truck and waited, as though she was used to waiting.

"Everybody expected they'd go to New York," Matthew explained. "Of course they had to choose this God-damned place! Well, here they come."

The general came down first, with his staff behind him. He looked like a tired old man. When the woman saw him she got up and took a step or two forward, and he saw her. His ugly face brightened and he smiled.

"So you made it," he said.

"I always make it, don't I?"

He kissed her and with an arm around her walked back along the dock. His work was over. He had brought his men back, or as many as would ever come, unless to lie in rows under neat white markers in Arlington. Matthew looked after them. He cleared his throat.

"Brave woman," he said. "Heard they lost their boy in the Argonne. These army wives . . ."

His voice trailed off. He was lost in admiration of all women, army wives and mothers, his own Elizabeth, and Ricky, standing there with her eyes like stars and her knees buckling under her. Then at last he saw his son.

Courtney did not see them. Two soldiers were helping another down the companionway. The boy was barely using his legs, moving them mechanically, but his face was proud. Court was behind them, watching and ready to help. Good God, Matthew thought, he's grown! He's bigger than ever. And he's a soldier, by God. Every inch of him.

He was bursting with pride, but none of it showed in his face. He stood stiffly imperturbable. He even moved to take a cigar out of its case. Then he remembered NO SMOKING signs and stopped. Courtney had not seen them yet. He watched young Rogers until he was safely on his way to the train. Then at last he looked around. They were standing as if caught in some sudden cessation of movement; his mother pale but smiling, his father stiff and erect, and Ricky—

He had an instant of panic. This girl with the grave face and wide eyes was his wife. He had sworn before God to love and cherish her, and for months he had not even been able to remember what she looked like. Even now she looked strange to him.

He broke through the line of slowly moving troops and reached them breathless.

"Hello!" he said. "And hello again. This is what I call a homecoming."

He caught up Elizabeth and kissed her. He shook hands with his father and slapped him on the back. Then at last he turned to Ricky, his eyes seeking hers. It seemed to him she drew back a little.

"Well, here I am, Ricky," he said, and put his arms around her. "Remember me? I'm your husband."

He kissed her then, and the wind caught her hat and blew it along the dock. He chased it and brought it back, grinning. The interval had helped, the first awkwardness was over. He gave them his old debonair smile while Ricky pinned on her hat.

"Damned nice of you all to come," he said. "Let's get out of here. It's freezing."

The general and his wife had disappeared. The men were still moving off the ship and being shepherded into line by military police. Young Rogers was not in sight. And for some reason none of them spoke. It was as though the two years had become an abyss which they could not cross. It was Matthew who broke the silence.

"How are you, boy?" he inquired. "How's the leg?"

"All right. Gets a bit stiff in bad weather. Nothing to worry about."

Courtney looked down at Ricky as they moved on. Her face was shaded by her broad hat, but he knew it was still grave, unsmiling. It was the hell of a welcome for a man home from a war, he thought. She had hardly spoken. Now as he took her arm he felt she was trembling.

"Not scared of me, darling, are you?"

She looked up then.

"No. I feel a little strange, that's all."

It was no time for a demonstration, with the eyes of the men on them. He released her arm.

"Well," he said, "if you all want to get on the train I have some things to do. One of my men is sick. I want to get him settled. And the colonel thought we'd have to go through the customs. He brought his wife a toilet set, and most of us are carrying a bit of it. The general has a hairbrush."

He seemed glad to escape, and it was an hour before they saw him again. They were settled in the train by that time. Outside the men filed slowly along. They looked cold and dispirited. Whatever they had expected it was not to land in an out-of-the-way place like this. But they were philosophical. They lit cigarettes with hands expertly cupped against the wind and edged along, gazing up without resentment at the officers' Pullman as they moved past.

Courtney rejoined his family as the first section pulled out. He pulled off his cap and wiped his forehead as he sat down.

"All set," he said gaily, "except for one gold-topped perfume bottle. One of the fellows left it on the ship. He's gone back for it." He reached over and took Ricky's hand, the one with the narrow wedding ring and the solitaire diamond.

"How about my girl?" he said. "Still like me?" She gave him her direct gaze, although she smiled.

"I have to get acquainted with you first," she said.

He appealed to the family.

"How's that for a welcome? Here's my wife, and she says she doesn't know me!"

"Well," said Matthew pontifically, "a lot of water's flowed

over the dam since you left, my boy. The Democrats have played hell with the country, Wilson's made fools of us all at Paris, and now with his League of Nations tomfoolery he's split us wide open. Makes me wonder what in hell you've been fighting for."

"Stop it, Matt," said Elizabeth. "That's no way to greet him. What are your plans, Court?"

"I've got twenty-four hours' leave. After that I don't know. I'll be demobilized along with the rest, of course. Maybe sooner. I'll try anyhow."

He still held Ricky's hand.

"I'm sorry about Dave, Ricky. We lost a lot of men that time. How's your mother? Still taking it hard?"

"It's changed her," she said evasively. "She can't seem to accept it. Dave—Dave did all right, didn't he? I mean, he wasn't afraid?"

"I wish to God he'd been more afraid."

But the barrier was there between them. They were like two strangers, making talk. Both of them had changed. He was twenty-six and looked thirty. Also she had the feeling he was acting a carefully rehearsed part and that he disliked doing it. After a while he released her hand and lighted a cigarette. She noticed he avoided her eyes.

"Got any plans?" he asked. "I suppose we'll have to settle down somewhere."

"I thought we might go away for a while. We hadn't much of a honeymoon. Unless you wouldn't care about it."

"I've been away. Or haven't you noticed?"

The train wound its way slowly toward Washington. In the dusty troop cars ahead the men were relaxed and quiet. The excitement of landing was over. They lolled back, each facing his own problem. Maybe they had saved the dreary country outside the windows, but no one seemed to know it. At one stop a small child waved a tiny American flag, and they waved back half-heartedly.

"Hope they'll let us have beer."

"The Huns could make beer all right."

"You bet."

They flocked to the ice-water coolers at the end of the car, thirsty with memories. The aisle was cluttered with their equipment, with German helmets and other souvenirs.

"Here, stop kicking that around."

"Why the hell don't you keep it out of the way?"

Courtney did not see Ricky alone until they were in their room at the Shoreham that night. He had been busy when they arrived, and after that there had been dinner. The dining room was almost empty. The war crowds had gone, the waiters who had been suspected of being spies, the foreign missions intent on getting what they could out of the country's riches. There was a sort of anticlimax, and even Matthew felt it. They were all relieved when dinner was over and the party broke up.

But in their big double bedroom, with the door closed, Ricky felt as though she was shut in with a stranger. Even when Court took her in his arms the feeling persisted. He felt a slight resistance in her. He held her off and looked down at her.

"Well, Mrs. Wayne," he said, "aren't you glad to see your husband again?"

"You know that, Court. Only it's been so long. I feel a little strange. And I haven't heard from you at all lately."

"I was busy," he said rather shortly.

"Too busy to write a letter?"

He grinned at her.

"What is this, a catechism?" he inquired. "Where's the loving little woman I came home to? Can this be the girl I left behind me?"

She did not smile, however. "I've had time to grow up, Court. Can't you stop treating me like a child?"

"I hadn't meant to," he said stiffly. "If I have I'm sorry. Look, I've had a long day. Can't all this wait?"

He unbuttoned his blouse and hung it on the back of a chair, but she made no move to undress. There was a sort of desperation in her face.

"You see," she said painfully, "I've been afraid there was someone else. If there is, I want to know. That's all."

"What on earth put that into your head?"

"I've felt it all day. As though you didn't really want me any more. Oh, I know. You're here. And I'm your wife. But it's been a long time. You've seen a great deal since you went away. Distracting things. But—"

"I've seen a lot of ugly things. What's that got to do with it? Look, kid, can't we forget all this? Maybe both of us feel strange. As you say, it's been the hell of a long time."

He lit a cigarette and, sitting down on the side of the bed, eyed her. She was lovely, he thought, lovelier than he had remembered, and more desirable.

"Look," he said. "I want you, Ricky. A man has a right to want his wife. After all, I had very little of you, my dear. A week in a hotel room."

"*Another* hotel room," she said, without bitterness. "I just want to get things straight, Court. It's almost two years ago, that week. Even then you didn't know me very well, did you? Perhaps I was just a girl who happened to be around when you were going to a war."

He stiffened and got up.

"That's a rotten thing to say, and you know it. God damn it, I was in love with you!"

"You were in love with me! That's the answer, isn't it? Even then I disappointed you, you know, Court. You as much as told me so, there in Cincinnati."

His nerves, rasped with war and the memory of things he wanted to forget, began to betray him.

"I don't know what you're talking about," he said roughly. "How can I remember what I said two years ago, Ricky? And if you're not going to bed, I am."

He made an abortive effort to take off his boots, failed, swore under his breath and got the jack from his suitcase. She watched him without moving. She was very pale.

"You haven't told me yet," she said. "Have you come back

to me, or have you just come back. If that's the way it is, you don't even have to pretend with me. You haven't really been in love with me for months. I know it from your letters."

"I thought you didn't get any letters?"

He had got one boot off and was working on the other. He did not look at her.

"Not for some time," she said. "And the ones I did get before then showed a change in you Court."

"Well, for God's sake, what about the change in you?"

"Maybe that's the trouble. I haven't changed enough." And when he said nothing, "I don't know what happened to you over there," she went on. "But something did. Maybe you simply forgot me. Or perhaps—"

"Plenty happened. What do you expect in a war?" He got the boot off and stood up. "Forget it," he said. "Maybe we'll have to pick up some of the pieces. It ought not to be too hard. Two presumably intelligent people—"

"Not if you have stopped caring for me, Court. We can't pick up the pieces in an hour. Or in a night."

Suddenly he was angry, furiously angry.

"Good God," he said, "do we have to keep on talking? Are you telling me you don't want to sleep with me tonight? That I'm to go somewhere else and leave you to your virginal bed? If that's what you mean, it's the easiest thing I do."

"I'm only saying—"

"You've said plenty," he said grimly. "I'll get a room at the Willard. And I'm not out of the army yet. You'll have time enough to make up your mind."

He stamped into his boots, caught up his cap and trench coat and slammed out of the room. Ricky waited until she heard the closing of the elevator door. When she got up she felt dizzy. She stood for a little while, steadying herself with a hand on the foot of the bed. Courtney's pajamas lay on it as he had laid them out. They were German pajamas, made of ugly ersatz cloth. She did not put them away. But she did not undress immediately. She went to the window and stared bleakly out.

The Capital was asleep. The war was over. Now it could go back to its old game of politics, of dinner and cocktail parties, of rebuilding the walls of isolation and smugness that had been so violently torn down. And Matthew and Elizabeth too were asleep. They did not rouse until the next morning when the telephone rang. Matthew answered it, to hear his son's voice.

"Sorry if I wakened you, Dad," he said. "I'm at the Willard. Ricky and I had a few words last night and I got out. Don't blame Ricky. It was my fault."

An hour or two later Ricky confronted both Matthew and Elizabeth in the sitting room of their suite, with an almost untouched breakfast on a table between them. She stood with her head high just inside the door and looked into their incredulous faces. Elizabeth, however, gave her little time to explain.

"What did you do, or say?" she demanded. "His first night at home, and you sent him away! How could you? How dared you?"

"He hadn't come home to me," Ricky said, her head still high. "He had just come home."

"You must have quarreled with him. He was happy enough yesterday."

"Was he? I wonder."

Matthew intervened.

"Let the girl alone, Lizzie," he said pacifically. "Why blame her? I told you Court says he was to blame."

"Of course he would say that," Elizabeth flared. "He's a gentleman. What else could he say?"

Ricky was still standing inside the door. Under her wide hat her eyes looked at them, uncertain and wretched. But her chin was stiffly set.

"I suppose I'm only another war casualty," she said, trying to speak lightly. "Only I don't know just what to do. I'm still his wife, even if he is different. I could go to Reno, of course, or he could."

Matthew stopped her irritably.

"What sort of talk is that?" he said. "Of course he's changed. So have you, Ricky. And even old married people have to get used to each other after a separation. That's all it is. You're coming back with us, of course. That's your home. And he'll be back too. Don't worry."

She wanted to cry then, to put her head down on Matthew's shoulder and cry her heart out. She had not cried all night. She had lain awake in the hotel bed with Courtney's bag still in the room and his dreadful ersatz pajamas on a chair. Lain awake, trying to reconcile the man who had left her with the laughing boy she had married. Feeling guilty too. Why not have taken him on his own terms, as other women undoubtedly did; accept his passion for love, and hope it would develop into something deeper?

"Where is your bag?" Matthew asked her. "Is it packed?"

"It's ready. In my room."

"Then we'd better be starting," he said, looking at his watch. "Ready, Lizzie? All right. Let's go."

But as they started out he put his arms around Ricky and held her a moment.

"He's been through a lot, my dear," he told her. "Give him a little time. He's probably feeling like a damned fool this morning. He sounded like it."

He released her, and she followed Elizabeth's small stiff figure out to the hall. To the train; and at last to her husband's home, where she felt she no longer belonged.

It was a week before Courtney came back; an endless week with Elizabeth coldly polite and Matthew friendly but anxious. Ricky wrote to her mother suggesting a visit home, to receive an uncompromising reply. "My dear Fredrica," she wrote, "I do not understand your wanting to come home at this time. It is a wife's place to stay with her husband, and if anything is wrong, remember you made the choice yourself. I am very busy too with my business affairs, and need time to straighten them out. Later on perhaps . . ."

People came and went during the week, chattering around

Elizabeth's tea table, the older ones having a glass of sherry, the younger drinking Matthew's carefully husbanded liquor. Ricky was uneasy before the sharp eyes of the girls and young women.

"But when *is* Court coming, Mrs. Wayne?"

"I'm not sure. He's very busy."

One afternoon a flamboyant young woman with short bleached hair eyed her shrewdly over her cocktail glass.

"I thought he was getting out right away," she said. "Are you sure he didn't fall for one of those pretty German fräuleins over there? It's been known to happen."

Elizabeth heard her.

"Don't be a fool, Emmy," she said sharply. "You know Courtney better than that."

"I know him all right," said Emmy, and had the grace to blush.

When Courtney did come back he did not announce his arrival, and as it happened both his mother and father were out when, his small tin army trunk on the pavement beside him, he rang the doorbell.

Johnson smiled when he saw him.

"Welcome home, sir," he said. "I'm sorry your mother is out. But your—Mrs. Wayne Junior is in, I believe."

He shook hands with Johnson and waited for him to bring in the trunk. Nothing had changed, he saw. It was all as he had remembered it a thousand times. In Mama's parlor the peacock still spread its tail and from the kitchen came the odor of cooking food. The very familiarity of everything relieved some of the tension of his return. He went back along the passage and shoved open the door to the service quarters.

"What's this I hear about Katie O'Malley running off with a policeman?" he said loudly.

There was a squeal from the kitchen, and a moment later Katie had her arms around him.

"My boy!" she said. "And it's coming home you are at last! Making fun of your old Katie, too." She held him off and looked at him severely. "It's time you got here, too," she said. "With that fine young wife of yours eating her heart out for you all this time. Not eating, the poor girl, and that thin—"

"Where is she, Katie?"

"Up in your old room. Where would she be?"

He went up the stairs, past the drawing room and the library, cluttered as always with Wayne books. His mother's room above was empty, but he paused a moment in the doorway to look at the array of creams and bottles on her toilet table, at the desk where she wrote her innumerable notes, and at the broad double bed in which he had been born and which his father had sturdily refused to part with. He had always disapproved of twin beds.

"Be less divorce if they'd never been invented," he would snort. "Twin beds and pajamas! Who ever thought up the idea of sleeping in a pair of pants!"

Courtney took the last flight more slowly. He was uncertain of his reception; even uncertain how he wanted to be received, for some small core of resentment still remained. Outside the door of his room he hesitated. Then rapped.

"Who is it?" Ricky said.

"It's your husband, if by any chance you still want him," he said, and a moment later she was in his arms.

6

Thus, at the end of November of 1919, did Courtney Wayne come home to the house his parents had bought early in the century, when the publishing business had begun to flourish. It had been a barn of a house in those days, with its high ceilings, steep staircases, and its small and dingy servants' quarters under the roof.

Elizabeth had endured it until bit by bit Matthew's finances had allowed her to change it. The old gas fixtures were gone, the stained-glass windows, the zinc-lined bathtubs. Matthew paid the bills under protest.

"Set on ruining me, aren't you?"

"Courtney's going to grow up in a proper home. At least it will be sanitary."

"People grew up all right here for a good many years. Even if they had oilcloth in the hall instead of marble."

In the end, of course, he was immensely proud of the house. He shouted when the bills came in but he paid them. And when as time went on they gave a dinner and he sat at the head of his table, with the women in low-cut dresses and the men in black and white, he would look across the flowers and candles at Elizabeth and grin, as if to remind her of their earlier days.

It was a changed Courtney, however, who had come home after that week. Also Elsa was a memory, as indeed was the war itself. No one wanted to remember it. As the men were demobilized they went home, putting on the clothes they had left behind, many of them too narrow now in the shoulders, and started to look for jobs. Some of the lucky ones got them. The others had no place to go. There were no saloons where they could meet, for wartime Prohibition had closed them, and soon the whole country would go dry.

They stood on street corners or in the drugstores, drearily drinking sodas or cokes or buying packs of cigarettes.

"Hello, Jonesy. Heard you were back. How did it go?"

"Not so bad."

"Lots of French girls, eh?"

They would grin sheepishly. Too many of them had reason to remember the French girls. But nobody really wanted to hear about the war itself. Anyhow, what could be told about it? A war wasn't strategy or tactics to them. It was the man next to you, the waiting for a hot meal, the letters from home, the mud and stinking dirt, and the whole bloody business of killing or being killed.

Contrary to his expectations, there had been no scene with Ricky. She had simply gone into his arms and he held her there.

"I was a fool, darling."

"We were both fools, Court."

"I went out and got good and plastered that night."

"I wish I'd thought of it!"

It was over. It was all right. If the rapture of his early marriage had gone, here at least was something permanent and dependable. He took her in his arms again. This time he kept her there.

He was very cheerful that evening, but she had rather a shock when he shed his uniform and put on his old dinner clothes. The jacket was too small for him. Even the sleeves were short, and he laughed as he stood in front of the long mirror.

"You must have married a kid!" he said gaily.

He did not notice that she had gone slightly pale. She had never seen him out of uniform before, and he did not look funny to her. He merely looked different. He stood in front of the long cheval glass and chuckled again.

"Mama's little boy's been growing up," he said complacently.

"You don't look like yourself at all."

"Well, you don't look like the little girl in the gingham dresses I used to know, either. Don't you like me this way?"

She had to fight the feeling that this was still another man, and an even stranger one.

"Of course," she said. "Just don't expect me to rave over the way your wrists stick out. That's all. And you might take off your watch. Your father still thinks a man who wears a wrist watch is a sissy."

But Matthew made no comment on the watch when, after dinner that night, he and Courtney were in the library. Matthew lit a cigar, but he did not sit down. He went to a window and stood looking out. When he turned he looked uncomfortable.

"I don't want to meddle with your affairs, son," he said, "but that night at the Shoreham—what in God's name got into you?"

Court put out his cigarette.

"Nothing much. She felt strange with me. That's all."

Matthew eyed him shrewdly.

"She's no fool," he said. "I thought myself there was something wrong that day. Look here, Court, you haven't made a fool of yourself over some girl over there, have you?"

"We were ordered not to fraternize, Dad."

"That meant a hell of a lot!"

Matthew did not pursue the subject. Times were bad, he said, and getting worse fast. A lot of country banks had opened on a shoestring during the war. Now they were loaded with mortgages, chattel and otherwise, and the farmers who had overexpanded were going broke. So were the banks. So were a lot of industries. There would be the devil to pay. As for Prohibition—

"They've put it over on us," he said heavily. "I've got a room in the basement with a steel door, and I've hired space in a warehouse. But it's a mistake, Court. A bad mistake. And look at the taxes. The government's got its hands in our pockets now for sure, and we'll never get them out. What about these Germans, Court? You've had a chance to study them."

"Not a fair chance. They'd been instructed to be careful of us. They've been pretty well starved, of course."

"So you're sorry for them!"

"Not at all," Courtney said carefully. "I don't like them as a race. I don't trust them either. But there are some decent ones, of course. They're not all tarred with the same stick. I liked a few of them. That's all."

Matthew eyed him over his cigar.

"I'd advise you not to say that openly. It's liable to be misconstrued," he said dryly.

When Courtney went upstairs he found Ricky waiting for him. She had thrown a rose-colored negligee over her nightgown, and she looked shy but no longer frightened. Later he realized she had not greatly changed, but she still did not understand or reciprocate his passion. But she was tender and warm, and when she turned over to sleep he threw an arm over her and held her close.

He lay awake for some time. He was still lost in his new civilian status. Up to now his thinking had been done for him. There was always someone higher up to do it, and to take the blame when things went wrong. But sooner or later he would have to make some plans. Outside of his army pay he had never earned a dollar in his life. The few months between his graduation at Harvard and his enlistment the following April had been spent, the summer at Plattsburg, the winter at Palm Beach with his mother. Elizabeth had not been well that year.

He had a modest capital, left him by Matthew's mother, but it would not support them both. He would have to take a job of some sort. His father would want him to go into publishing, of course, but he did not want to sit at a desk day after day.

After a while he released Ricky and cautiously lit a cigarette. By the flare of the match he looked down at her, small and somehow helpless in the big bed. He would have to take care of her. But he was no longer the passionate reckless boy who had married her. What he felt for her was tenderness rather than love. Yet there she was, his wife.

The cigarette meant nothing in the dark. He put it out and resolutely went to sleep.

After years of early rising he was awake long before the household the next morning. He got up and putting on slippers and a dressing gown went down the stairs to the lower hall. The paper was in the vestibule. He took it into the small parlor and looked over it. Woodrow Wilson was still ill, a sick man shut in behind a wall of silence and secrecy; Bolsheviks from Russia were said to be invading the Pacific Coast. The stock market was down, while food and clothes were going up, and there was no mention whatever of the return of troops from the occupation of Germany. The country had apparently forgotten them.

He went back to the kitchen, with its French range, its odor of good food, and its dumbwaiter to the pantry above. Katie was just coming down. She looked flustered when she saw him.

"What's wrong?" she said. "What are you doing up at this hour, Mr. Courtney?"

"Habit, Katie. The army believes in getting up early."

She had been there a long time, a big motherly Irish woman. At prep school and college it had been Katie who packed his boxes: the raisin bread and cakes and cookies, even the homemade candy. Now she was bustling around to hide her excitement.

"I'll have some coffee in a jiffy," she said. "That lazy kitchen-maid! I had to stop and wake her."

When she put the coffeepot on the stove he saw she was crying. He went over and put his arms around her.

"What's all that for, Katie? Anything wrong?"

"Nothing. I'm just Irish, that's all. The Irish cry easy.

There's been a good many times, Mr. Court, when I never thought to see you here again. Your father, he never gave up hoping, and your mother the same. But that fine little wife of yours, she was scared. When she was lonely she'd bring her knitting and sit here in this kitchen with me. She was afraid, all right."

"Lonely? Why was she lonely?" he asked sharply.

"Well, you know how it is. We're not young folks here. Anyhow she wasn't here much. You know about that, I guess." She was busy making coffee, and she avoided his eyes. "Not that everybody wasn't kind to her, Mr. Court. Don't get that in your head. But they were busy. You know how it is."

"In other words, she's had the hell of a time," he said shortly. "I don't suppose it was much better when she went home either. Her brother being killed, and if I know her mother—"

He did not finish. He ate his breakfast at the kitchen table with its clean red cloth, but without appetite. He was still there when he heard his father ring for his breakfast, and found him in the dining room, shouting for the paper. Courtney put it in front of him with a grin.

"Up early, aren't you?" Matthew said, mollified.

"Yes. I've had breakfast. I've just been wondering, Dad. Does mother want us to stay on here?"

"I think she hopes so, Court. For a while anyhow. Unless you have other plans. Of course you know there's a place for you in the business."

"Mind if I take some time to think about it?"

"No, but I won't live forever," Matthew said dryly. "You could start at a fair salary, Court. That and what you have of your own ought to be enough."

"Money!" Court said with some bitterness. "After you've seen money wiped out the way I have you begin to wonder about it. What's the use of struggling to get it? Oh, I'll work, of course. You needn't look like that. But this chase after the dollar—"

"Dollars helped to win this war. I don't know but that they did win it." Matthew's voice was grim.

"The chase after them helped to make it, all over the world."

Matthew looked at him sharply.

"What sort of ideas have you brought back anyhow?" he demanded. "Don't tell me you've gone red."

"Oh, red! That's patter, Dad. I've been in a democratic army, that's all. There are no classes in the trenches. Or in the graveyards," he added soberly.

The talk ended on rather a sour note, Courtney intimating that publishers were parasites who fattened on the other fellows' brains, and suggesting time to look around for something else. As a result it was an indignant and badly upset Matthew who drove behind Walter and his cough to the office that morning. When his secretary came in with the mail she found him staring blankly at nothing. After twenty years she knew his every expression and could draw her own deductions. She was a spinster of forty, efficient to the nuisance point, but this morning after a brief "Good morning" she left the mail and went to her small office next door.

Matthew did not look at his letters. Beyond the mahogany partition he could hear the rattle of many typewriters. And beyond them in his mind he could see his expensive staff, his editors and their associates, his sales manager and his advertising director, his art department and his manufacturing department. And outside of the office were the compositors and printers and shipping men, all the vast machinery that went into the making of a book.

He could close his eyes and see what he had built over the long years. If Courtney didn't want to come into the business—

After a while he called in his secretary again. He knew he could trust her.

"Sit down, Angela," he said. "No, don't open your book. I'd like to talk to you. Court doesn't want to come into the business, Angela. And I need him."

She stirred. From behind her glasses she glanced at him. "Have you told him that?"

"Not yet. I suppose I'll have to."

She said nothing. Of all the office force, probably she alone knew the whole picture, the rise in costs, the end of the demand for war books, the slump in business, and the huge stocks in the warehouse bins which would have to be written off at a loss. She knew too that he had borrowed to the limit of safety from his bank, and that he was paying outrageous taxes. He had fallen into the habit of discussing his affairs with her as he did not with his own treasurer. Now she played nervously with her pencil.

"What about Mrs. Wayne's bonds? She has a lot of them."

"I'm not touching them," he said firmly. "They are hers. Or my insurance. That's for her too."

Angela said nothing. She was not fond of Elizabeth. For twenty years she had sat in the small cubbyhole she called her office and watched Matthew put his savings into bonds for his wife. Had made out the checks to pay Elizabeth's bills. They had grown as time went on, but she knew to a dollar the cost of the big house, even of everything Elizabeth wore, and what she had in her box at the bank.

"He may change his mind," she said finally. "He's just back. It's rather soon."

She had a way of comforting him, this unattractive woman who years ago had replaced a girl who had almost broken up his marriage. He sat back and smiled at her.

"He may at that," he said, and proceeded to dictate his mail.

Nevertheless, when she had gone he sat for some time pondering his problem. He had inherited a moderate fortune from his parents, one of those Boston fortunes accumulated by stern living and even sterner saving. He had received only part of it, however. Another part had gone to his sister Roberta, who had married an Englishman, and a moderate sum had been put in trust for Courtney until he came of age.

With his own portion Matthew had bought an interest in

what was now his own business, and he was proud of what he had done with it. He had worked hard, always with the idea that Courtney would join him when he grew up. Now for the first time he was uncertain. He had sent a boy to the war and got back a man; a dissatisfied, unsettled man at that, he thought unhappily, with God knows what ideas in his head.

He grunted and asked the switchboard operator to send in Mather, the firm's editor in chief.

Mather was a tall thin man, almost bald at forty. He had a way with authors, keeping them at work and smoothing down their grievances. He was convinced that all authors had grievances. Usually they wanted more publicity, although Mather did not believe advertising sold books. They sold because people liked them and talked about them. This, however, was an opinion Mather carefully concealed from his writers.

"Now I'll show you the layout, Smith," he would say. "It's more than good. It's excellent. Look at this, and this, and this. Matter of fact, we've spent more than we had allocated to the book."

Matthew valued Mather, even if he did not always agree with him. But Angela Ellis detested him. When she saw him in Matthew's office she got up and closed her door.

Mather grinned.

"On the rampage again?" he inquired genially.

"She's busy."

"What about Courtney? Coming to work soon?"

Matthew cleared his throat.

"That's why I sent for you," he said. "He may need some time. The boy's tired. I expect he'll find it hard to settle down at once. And," he added rather irritably, "he hasn't been back twenty-four hours."

"Well, just so he's coming," Mather said. "I could stand some help. Stuff's pouring in now. Just why authors think war is romantic I don't know. That's what we're getting anyhow. Always thought it was a dirty business myself."

Matthew faced the remainder of his day grimly. The manufacturing department brought in estimates of costs which made him purple with fury. The sales manager reported a rise in the expenses of the salesmen. The switchboard operator became ill and went home, and even the bootblack who made a daily round of the office gave his shoes what Matthew called a lick and a promise, and disappeared before he could shout him back.

He went home that night to find Emmy Baldwin in the drawing room with Court and Ricky. He went upstairs irritably to Elizabeth, resting on her chaise longue before dressing.

"What the hell's the Baldwin girl doing here?" he demanded.

"Why shouldn't she be here? She's one of Court's oldest friends."

"She made a fool of herself about him, if that's what you mean. Still crazy about him, probably. Her kind doesn't let go."

"I think you're being silly, Matt. She married Billy Baldwin, didn't she?"

"And where is he now? She got rid of him fast enough. And I mean fast."

Emmy stayed a long time. He could not get into his library to read the paper or look over the proofs he had brought from the office. From upstairs he could hear her voice.

"He hadn't a stitch of clothes, but he had a small towel. So he wrapped it around his head . . ."

Matthew snorted. Emmy and her dirty stories! He could hear Courtney laughing, but Ricky seemed to be quiet.

7

The days following Courtney's return always had a dreamlike quality to Ricky. There were times when in his arms she felt the barrier of time and absence had been broken, when her love for him seemed at last to have brought him back to her. There were others, however, when he seemed not so much to hold her off as to have forgotten she was there.

As a matter of fact he was fighting a vast discouragement. Life suddenly felt stale and flat, as though he had given two years of his life to no purpose. And there was no drive in him, no real urge to go to work. Sometimes he sat for hours in the cold on a bench in Central Park. When he found an ex-soldier he would talk to him. Otherwise he merely sat, not even thinking.

One night he frightened her. She wakened to find him in the darkness leaning over her in the bed and shaking her.

"Dave!" he said thickly. "Is that you, Dave?"

She never told him. He grunted and lay back, muttering but still asleep.

He had been home ten days when he disappeared one afternoon. By midnight he had not come back, and Ricky was frantic with worry. She did not go to bed. She sat in his big chair and waited, listening for footsteps on the stairs which did not come. At dawn he found her there, asleep, and stood looking down at her. He bent over and touched her.

"Sorry, Ricky," he said. "Better get to bed."

"Where have you been, Court? I was terrified."

He did not reply at once. He was still staring down at her, his face gray, his eyes tired.

"To think," he said slowly, "the poor devil had never even had a woman."

She was wide awake by that time. Awake and alarmed.

"What poor devil? What are you talking about?"

He was taking off his coat now, deliberately avoiding her eyes.

"Just a kid," he said. "One of my outfit. He died in the hospital tonight. Name was Rogers."

He undressed and followed her to bed, but she knew he was awake. Wide, staring awake. She made no move toward him. He was more completely detached than she had ever seen him. After a while she spoke.

"What did you mean, Court? That he'd never had a woman?"

"What do you think I meant?"

"You mean a prostitute?"

"Any woman. What's the matter with prostitutes? If a man needs them—Good Lord, Ricky! Don't you know what war is? You may have a week, a life, or only a day. And you're a man. Don't you know a soldier would be accosted by tarts half a dozen times in any block in Paris? Or in any other French town?"

"I see. So that's war."

"It's a good many men's idea of a war."

"And it happened to you?"

"Why not? I was American, so I had money. I wasn't picking them up, if that's what you mean. I happen to be a fastidious sort of bloke. So was young Rogers. He was a virgin. The men used to kid him about it."

"And Dave? Was he—?"

"Dave's dead," he said. "Let him alone, for God's sake."

They never reverted to the subject again. One afternoon he was gone for hours, she thought probably to young Roger's funeral. He came home silent and depressed, but apparently with young Rogers gone at last he was prepared to settle down to work. Matthew had been right, however. There were few openings in the business world, and none where he cared to risk his capital.

His father had said nothing more about the office. Then one night Courtney himself gave him the opening. Matthew found him in the library, looking over some of the recent Wayne books. He said nothing. Courtney looked up at him and grinned.

"Funny," he said. "I've seen books with this imprint all my life, and I haven't an idea how it's done."

Matthew drew a long breath.

"Better come down and look us over," he said. "How about tomorrow? I've something to talk to you about, anyhow."

He went obediently enough the next day. He found his father alone in his office, with Angela shut out and some notes in his own hand on a paper in front of him. It was the first time Courtney had been in the office since his return, and he came in smiling.

"Same old boiler factory!" he said. "Why don't you get an office where you won't hear that racket?"

"That racket, as you call it, enables us to eat," Matthew said grimly. "And that's not so amusing as it sounds."

Courtney looked at him.

"What's wrong? Business bad?"

"We went in the red during the war, and we can't seem to get out of it. We still sell plenty of books. We're getting more for them, too. My God, Court, when we put fiction up fifty cents I didn't sleep for weeks. And the public simply took it in its stride! Didn't seem to care. It's not that."

The plain fact, he went on, was that like most other businesses they had overexpanded during the war. Now with taxes, high costs, and strikes they couldn't seem to catch up. They had had a backlog of good titles, but the public wanted romance now. It couldn't get enough of it. It was sick of war.

And good romantic writers were scarce as hen's teeth.

Court had listened attentively. Now he grinned across the desk at his father.

"What do you want me to do?" he inquired. "Write a love story?"

For the first time in years Matthew longed to lay violent hands on his son.

"Don't talk like a fool," he said irritably. "If this doesn't mean anything to you it does to me."

Court's smile died. There was nothing frivolous about him now. He eyed his father.

"It's as bad as that, is it?"

"It's pretty bad. I haven't told your mother. I'll have to soon. We can't go on living the way we do."

There was a brief silence. Courtney broke it.

"How about my money? Would it help?"

Matthew drew a long breath.

"You might lose it. You'd have to take that chance, Court, and you have a wife."

"I'd be willing to take the chance, Dad, if you are," he said soberly. "I don't suppose that would mean you'd want me here, in the firm?"

"It will be your investment. You ought to look after it."

"And if I lose it?"

"We're both sunk," said Matthew flatly.

It was a little time before either man spoke. Then it was Courtney.

"We can't very well let the business go," he said rather unwillingly. "The imprint's valuable, I take it?"

"We've got a good name. What's valuable nowadays nobody knows. The war's changed everything."

"I'm no publisher, Dad."

"You can learn. I did." Matthew cleared his throat. "We need new blood here, at the top. We've got in a rut, and I'm too old to change. Not"—he added—"that I want any of the newfangled ideas you seem to have brought back with you.

There's a lot of radical nonsense in the air. If it's the last thing I do I'll fight it."

Courtney smiled.

"New ideas aren't necessarily radical," he said. "It's not a new world. It's only a different one." He saw Matthew's face and got up. "All right, that's settled. I can try it anyhow. Or you can try me. I don't imagine I'll be any good. When will you want me to start?"

Matthew did not answer at once. He was unlocking a drawer of his desk. Now he produced a box of the expensive cigars he kept for emergencies—such as indignant authors—and seldom smoked himself. He was surprised to find his hands shaking. His voice, however, was steady.

"You'd better get the hang of things as soon as you can. Look over the place. After that, George Mather's yelling for help in the editorial department."

"Good God, Dad, I'm no editor."

"Editors aren't born, they're made," said Matthew, and felt unreasonably pleased with himself.

Courtney walked the streets for hours that afternoon. He was shocked and bewildered by his father's statement about the publishing house. It had always been there, as much of his home life as his mother herself or Fanny the peacock. He could remember the talk at the dinner table with famous foreign and American authors, the long discussions of this and that literary subject, and his mother's pride in having what she felt was a salon of sorts. The war had changed all that, he imagined.

But he did not anticipate going to work with any particular pleasure. He never had worked, except in the army. On the other hand, he ought to be damned glad, he supposed, to have work to go to. A lot of men were still milling around, unable to get jobs. He knew too that Ricky would be pleased.

He told her that night, and was annoyed at the look of relief on her face.

"What did you expect?" he asked. "That I'd loaf the rest of my life?"

"We can't go on living on your parents. At least I can't, Court. After all, you've been on the loose for a good while. I'm glad you're going to work. Your father will be pleased."

"What do you mean, on the loose? If you think a war—"

"The war's been over for more than a year," she reminded him.

It was the nearest to a real quarrel they had had since their new rapprochement. Ricky knew the strain had been telling on her, his wandering about the city, his occasional remoteness. And Courtney himself felt guilty. He went over and kissed her lightly.

"Sorry, darling," he said. "How about dinner and a dance tonight? It's a long time since we danced together."

A long time since Dave had brought him up to her at the hostess house. "The lieutenant wants to meet you, Ricky. Wayne's his name. He's a good guy—"

"I'd love it," she said.

She looked very beautiful that night at the Plaza. Courtney was proud of her. But they were not long alone. Other men discovered her. And once when he found himself abandoned he saw Emmy Baldwin. She beckoned to him and he went over.

"Looks as though your wife has snagged my man," she said. "Sit down, Court. I'm not very happy tonight."

"Why? What's bothering you?"

"As if you didn't know! I don't seem to get over it. That's the trouble."

"Get over what?" he looked puzzled.

"Over you, you idiot. I was crazy about you. I still am. When I heard you'd married someone else—"

"You married too. Remember that?"

"What was I to do? Go around eating my heart out?"

"What happened to Baldwin?"

"I couldn't stand him. That's all."

"I suppose he's paying you alimony." He grinned at her. "That ought to help."

"Not any more than he can get away with. Are you still in

love with her, Court?"

"Look at her. What do you think?"

He did not take her seriously, but she represented the world he had known, the lost world of summer vacations, of sailing and dancing and mountain climbing, of Christmas holidays from college and dances in his first evening clothes. And when he asked her to dance she felt soft in his arms, as though she wore no corset. He held her closer.

"It's like old times, isn't it?" he said. And felt relaxed and comfortable again.

Father and son went downtown together the next morning, Matthew to his office, Courtney to sit in Mather's room and learn the rudiments of the new job.

Mather was explicit, if somewhat cynical.

"We get several thousand manuscripts a year," he said. "Each one is somebody's baby, so we're pretty careful. They're recorded on a card file as they come in. Then they're read and sorted. A lot go back at once. You don't have to eat all of an egg to know it's bad. The possibles go to one of the assistant editors for reading, and the good ones come to me. That's all there is to it."

"It sounds all right. Where do I come in?"

Mather smiled dryly.

"You'd better start with the possibles," he said. "After that I imagine you'll work with me.

Courtney lit a cigarette and looked at the man across the desk.

"How am I to know they're possible? I read one of the Lockwood books the other night. I thought it was horrible."

Mather looked alarmed.

"For the Lord's sake, Court," he said, "be reasonable. We don't like all the books we publish. That's unimportant. We give the people what they want. That *is* important. And they like Lockwood."

Courtney said nothing. For less than an hour he had been a part of the staff, and already he knew he disagreed violently with its policy. But he had taken orders and kept his mouth shut for a long time. He did it then. But he knew that here was a whole new world, of new ideas, new hatreds, new fears. And as far as he could see his father was ignoring it. He went back to the office that was now his and sat before his empty desk. No wonder business was bad. If they sat here in their ivory tower and let the world go by—

But as time went on he found the work absorbing. He read manuscripts all day; some of them neat, the work of the professional writers, others slovenly and almost undecipherable. The more promising ones he took home to go over at night, often to go yawning to bed, and sometimes to find Ricky already asleep.

She was finding her life singularly pointless. When Courtney wanted her she was there, but her days were endless. Once she suggested again to Elizabeth that they take an apartment somewhere, and Elizabeth reported it indignantly to Matthew that night. Matthew, however, failed her. She could hardly believe it.

"Why?" she asked. "They're comfortable here. And with Court working hard—"

"I have an idea they'll get along better alone."

"Get along better? I don't know what you mean."

"Look, Lizzie," he said patiently, "when we were married we knew each other through and through. You'd been my secretary. You knew all about me. Even then we had the hell of a time getting adjusted, but we did. Those two have been married a few weeks, with a long interval between. Court has seen a lot of women in that time. I'm not saying he slept with them—but, well, he's not the same man she married. Give them the same chance we had."

But Courtney had settled down into a comfortable rut of business and occasional pleasure, and he saw no reason for changing it. Now and then there was a dinner party, or they went to the theater. They saw Ina Claire in *The Gold Diggers*, Frank Bacon in *Lightnin'*, and Drinkwater's *Lincoln*. It was a new world to Ricky, new and glamorous. But *The Gold Diggers* startled her. She was still thinking about it when they got home.

"All women aren't like that, Court."

"The hell they're not!"

"So I'm one too! I feel like one, you know, living here the way we do. If we had a place of our own—"

He laughed and kissed her lightly.

"What's the hurry?" he said. "Let's go down and see what Katie has in the icebox."

It was always like that. It was still like that when in the late winter Matthew received a letter from his sister Roberta, Lady Truesdale, in London.

8

Matthew brought the letter home from the office and handed it to Elizabeth without comment.

"Dear Matt," Roberta had written. "I am coming back to America for a visit. Things here are in a dreadful muddle. Poor Arthur left me almost nothing. Anyhow, the estate is entailed and I must live on my small American investments. This perfectly sickening war! Everybody is poor, and you have no idea how prices have gone up here. I have a girl to raise too, and girls are expensive.

"I hope you can take us in for a while. Sheila is twenty, poor child, and not a beauty, but she might make an American marriage. All our best men are gone, of course. And she'll have my bit of money someday. That ought to help. We are sailing next week."

Elizabeth looked stricken.

"I can't have her, Matt. I can't."

"Well, she's my sister," Matthew said heavily. "She's had a bad time, with Arthur's being killed and all."

"Why not a hotel? Or an apartment?"

"You've read the letter. She's got very little money."

"She has the income from your father's estate. And besides, with Court and his wife here . . ."

Matthew looked at her. He loved her. He was the faithful sort. With one exception he had been faithful all his married life. But just then he was coldly angry.

"So long as I have a home, my sister is welcome in it. If it crowds you, let Court and Ricky find a place of their own. We both know Ricky wants it."

"This is Court's home," Elizabeth said doggedly. "Just because Roberta married a tuppenny baronet is no reason for putting him out."

"He's a man, isn't he? A man with a wife, at that. Why shouldn't he get a place of his own? I'm damned if I understand you women," he went on irascibly. "You want your boys to be men, and when they are you try to make babies of them again."

She gave up then. Matthew was usually easygoing, but his family feeling was strong. He had a way of saying that blood was thicker than water, which set her teeth on edge. She had to accept Roberta. Nevertheless, there had been no change in the situation when Roberta and Sheila arrived. The guest room behind Elizabeth and Matthew's bedroom was prepared for them, and Ricky found herself expected to remain.

On a gray day in February Matthew met the ship and brought the visitors home, a rather shocked Matthew who had had difficulty in recognizing his own sister in the tall gaunt figure in black he saw coming down the gangplank. Good God, he thought, she's an old woman. He greeted her warmly.

"Well, Roberta my dear," he said. "Welcome home."

Sheila trailed behind her, a mildly pretty girl, shy and silent and badly dressed. Like her father, he thought. Like Arthur. She looked frightened at the noise, the loud greetings, the general confusion on the dock, and she seemed surprised when he kissed her.

"You've shot up like a weed," he said. "The last time I saw you—"

He stopped at that, because the last time he had seen her had been in the house in Cadogan Square in August of 1914, and Arthur had just been recalled to the army. Matthew remembered her as a long-legged weeping child with bad teeth, hanging onto her father's uniform blouse, and begging him not to go.

He got them through the customs and to the waiting car. But none of them had much to say, and they drove home almost in silence. At the house Elizabeth was waiting, and she put on a good act of making them welcome. Roberta, however, was not fooled.

"I don't suppose you wanted us much," she said. "Why should you? But we had to go somewhere."

Elizabeth's smile stiffened.

"Of course we want you, Roberta. We'll do all we can to make you happy."

"It's a little late for that," said Roberta forthrightly. "But I'd like Sheila to find a husband. There are hardly any men left in England."

It was not a particularly auspicious beginning, but it solved itself by both the newcomers resorting to the guest room and Roberta going to bed there, with Johnson carrying up a tray for both of them. Ricky, offering her services, was politely but firmly repulsed.

"No, thanks," Sheila said in her high British voice, "we're doing very well. Just tired, and mother was seasick."

The fact that Roberta was "her ladyship" to the servants excited them. To Matthew, however, it was an old story. It was more than five years since he had seen her. Then it was in her tall English house which, save that it had only one bathroom—and that at the turn of the main staircase, was not unlike his own New York one. Matthew had grumbled about the bathroom. He even offered to put in some extra ones. But Arthur Truesdale, who was a tall, thin, casual man with no occupation since he had left the army, said he thought they could manage.

Matthew had not thought much of him. Then one day while he and Elizabeth were still there war was declared, and soon after he saw Arthur's thin figure in an ill-fitting uniform drilling an awkward squad in Hyde Park. Matthew had got his family home finally, in a one-class steamer on which women nursed their babies openly on the decks, children threw banana skins everywhere, and stewards closed the portholes at night and blacked them out with circular pieces of cardboard.

He remembered this voyage when they had all gone to bed that night and he was alone in the library. It had been a nightmare, for there was already talk of submarines. Also he had felt the bad air and the sense of being shut in. And he had considered the war unnecessary and absurd.

"All this stuff about Belgium," he had snorted. "Nobody likes the Belgians anyhow. They're not decent either. Look at the fountain of theirs in Brussels!"

The fountain, which was the famous one of a small boy relieving himself into a basin below, was Matthew's symbol of a decadent Europe. He was having no truck with it.

Now Arthur was dead. He had been killed rather soon, as a matter of fact. And his widow, a thin and haggard copy of her former self, was installed in his house. And Sheila.

But aside from early morning tea and a disconcerting habit of leaving their shoes outside at night to be cleaned, Roberta and Sheila made little change in the household. The rents for apartments had shocked them both, however. When she was tired of house hunting Roberta would go to the park and sit there, watching the pigeons and the squirrels. She had a good many bitter memories to keep her company; the desperation of Arthur's death, the frantic war activity that had followed it. She had gone to France, to find no hospitals, no trained nurses; men lying in stinking bandages on the cement floors of railway stations, or newly wounded, so that her skirts were often covered with blood to the knees.

There were no surgical dressings, there was no morphia. She had made endless trips across the Channel to get drugs, to raise funds to buy them. The Channel was dangerous. She would stand on deck, clutching the rail with her hands and staring out. She did not mind for herself, not with Arthur gone, but the morphine had to get across. And there had been one dreadful night at Folkestone when they would not let her get on the boat. The Germans had said they would sink any ship which crossed that night, and the authorities refused to stamp any passports. She went into the shed on the wharf to expostulate with them.

"But I have morphine for our wounded."

"Sorry. No passengers tonight."

She had stood still. The men around the table had forgotten her. The long line of disappointed people had dispersed. She clutched her bag and went out. It was very dark, but not far away she could see the dark shadow of the boat. There was no one on deck. Her heart was pumping hard. She even felt a little sick. She did it, however. She got on the boat and locked herself in a cabin. It was as simple as that.

There had been a row the next morning, of course. The captain was furious.

"I have no right to let you off," he said. "I should take you back. That means arrest."

"That's not important," said Roberta. "But I must hand this morphine over to somebody."

He looked at her. He knew her well. She had made many such trips with him. Then he reached out and put a hand on her shoulder.

"You're a damned nuisance," he said, "but you're a brave woman, Lady Truesdale. Now I've got to fix it up with the French. Maybe they'll jail us both."

The French did not, however. Now she was here, watching the squirrels and the pigeons. Watching too, with her acquired British detachment, Elizabeth and Matthew; and because she liked Ricky, watching her also.

"She's a nice child," she told Matthew one night. "She'll make Court a good wife, if she has a chance."

"What d'you mean, a chance?" said Matthew, eying her sharply, her thin neck, her tired face, her long slim white hands. Like the other women of her adopted country she looked better in her black dinner dress, and he saw she had managed to save her pearls. She was not beautiful, but he had never underestimated her intelligence. "What do you mean?" he repeated.

"She's not happy, Matt. Don't look as though you wanted to bite me. What's wrong between her and Court? Is he sorry he married her?"

"Good God," said Matthew, "of course not. He's busy. He's learning a new job. And he's like his mother. Sound as a nut, but not demonstrative."

Whatever opinions Roberta had about Elizabeth she kept to herself, but not long after that talk she went upstairs to Ricky's room. It was March by that time, and a brisk cold day. But Ricky had not gone out. Roberta found her with a book, looking listless and tired. Roberta sat down and, picking up a cigarette from a box, lit it.

"Is this what you are going to do the rest of your life?" she inquired. "Sit around feeling sorry for yourself?"

Ricky flushed. She shut the book.

"I'm not sorry for myself. I just feel useless."

Roberta eyed her.

"How old are you?" she asked abruptly.

"Twenty."

"My God, you're the same age as Sheila. Only Sheila has an excuse for being what she is. She's had rather a thin time, and she's been through a lot you'll never know about. You've at least got a husband."

Ricky gave her look for look.

"I haven't had him very long," she said. "Or very much."

Roberta knew the story by this time. She shrugged her thin shoulders.

"People don't just get married," she said. "They make a marriage. It takes time and patience and compromise."

"But a war marriage—"

"There's nothing wrong with a war marriage. I married Arthur just before the Boer War. He came back skin and bones from fever, poor dear, and it was months before I could bear the sight of him. It worked out all right in the end."

"It takes two people to do that," Ricky said. "I can't do it alone. Court's not the same person I married. He's kind, I don't mean that. But he's different."

"You mean there's some other woman?" Roberta asked, out of a long experience.

"Not here. But he was in Germany a long time. I've wondered if there was someone over there."

"Possibly," said Roberta practically. "Men always need women. I suppose he's had his experiences. I wouldn't worry about them. If they happened they were an episode, and now he's back. That's what matters. You have him."

She put out the cigarette and got up.

"You haven't had a chance to be a wife, have you?" she inquired. "To darn his socks and sew buttons on his underwear. That's all done for him here. Of course if that's the way you want things, go on as you are. If you don't, why not get out of here? Unless you like this featherbed living. I do not."

She went out, closing the door firmly behind her, and Ricky got up and surveyed herself in the mirror. It was all well enough to tell her to put up a fight. She was not the fighting type. She remembered years ago a little girl who had slapped her. They had been walking home from school, carrying their books, and all at once the child had hit her. She had not hit back. She had merely been stunned with surprise.

She felt as though she had been stunned for a long time, and as though Roberta had roused her at last. She smoothed her hair and went downstairs to confront Elizabeth.

As it happened, Elizabeth was in a bad humor that day. She had learned that Court had been seeing Emmy Baldwin now and then, buying her a drink in some speakeasy or other, and once or twice a lunch. She had tackled him about it that morning.

Court had merely laughed at her.

"Why shouldn't I take an old friend to lunch? God knows I take our lady authors out, and a rum lot some of them are."

"Emmy Baldwin's not a rum lot," Elizabeth said sharply. "She's dangerous. She'd like nothing better than to break up your marriage. And I want no scandal in this family. And another thing, Court, I wish you'd let my employees alone. Just because Walter has a cough—"

He stopped smiling.

"All right, if you want murder on your hands. He's a veteran. He can go to a hospital in Colorado and have a chance. Otherwise . . ."

It had ended in a rather bitter quarrel, what with Walter and Emmy both as issues. And Courtney had slammed out of the room. So she was still upset when Ricky rapped at her door. Elizabeth was at her desk writing a check for a bridge loss, and she raised her eyebrows when she saw who it was.

"Yes?" she said. "What is it, Ricky? If it's not important—"

"I think it is," Ricky said. She came into the room, closing the door behind her. "It is to me, at least. I don't want to hurt you. Please understand that."

It *was* Emmy, Elizabeth thought wildly. There was a new determined look in the girl's face. She—Elizabeth—braced herself.

"I don't know what this is all about," she said. "If it's anything about Courtney—"

"It is," Ricky said. "About Court and myself."

Elizabeth stiffened in her chair.

"I don't know what you've heard," she said, "but it's natural for him to see his old friends. Emmy Baldwin is only one of them."

"Emmy Baldwin?"

Oh, damn, Elizabeth thought bitterly. It wasn't Emmy, after all, and she had made a fool of herself.

"He took Emmy to lunch not long ago," she said. "They met on the street and lunched together. I thought it was bothering you. It's quite usual, you know, in New York. Perhaps back home it wasn't done. I hope you're not being silly about it."

"I didn't know it, but I don't mind," Ricky said simply. "He has a right to his friends. That's not what I want to talk about."

She drew a long breath. "I think we ought to have a home of our own. Just a small place probably, but our own."

Out of sheer relief Elizabeth drew a long breath. And Ricky drew up a small slipper chair and sat down.

"I hope you won't object," she said. "I'm very grateful for what you have done for us. But Court's able to stand on his own feet now. And—well, I don't want to lose him."

"That's absurd. You're his wife."

"There is more to being a wife than sharing a room and a bed with a man."

Elizabeth looked shocked.

"You needn't be crude. There are some things well-bred people don't discuss."

Ricky smiled faintly.

"You sound like my mother. She never mentioned sex either. She thought it was sinful. She still thinks so." And while Elizabeth struggled to control her inner fury: "I want a home and a husband of my own. I'm not letting my marriage go on the rocks if I can help it."

She got up. Elizabeth did not frighten her any more. In a way she felt sorry for the small exasperated figure before her.

"What kind of talk is that?" Elizabeth demanded. "You have every comfort here, every luxury. I've tried. You'll admit that. And Courtney is contented here. That should mean at least something to you."

"It does, of course," Ricky said calmly. "Only I think I'm the one to make him contented. Either that or I don't belong at all."

For the first time in her long, ambitious, determined life Elizabeth faced defeat, and knew it.

"Do as you like," she said coldly, and turned back to her desk. . . .

It was unfortunate that Courtney was short-tempered when he came home that evening. He had had a hard day. In spite of Mather's easy synopsis of the new job, he was finding it complicated and trying. In spite of all his efforts too, he still remained the boss's son. Mather was friendly but condescending, and Courtney's reading of a script was largely a matter of superrogation. He had come in that morning with a report Courtney had written and a patronizing smile on his face.

"See you liked this stuff, Court."

"I didn't like it. I felt the fellow had something to say that needed to be said. That's all."

"Still sorry for the world, are you? Well, this fellow isn't. He's only sorry for himself. But maybe you like the Russian idea."

"Hell no," Court said shortly. "I just don't believe in government by politicians instead of by the people."

"Try and get it," Mather said, and left him fuming.

He was still rankling when he came home to wash up for dinner. Ricky was already dressed. She had put on a dinner dress he liked, and some of his bad humor left him.

"What's up?" he inquired. "Are we going anywhere?"

"I hope we are. Permanently."

He came out of the bathroom and surveyed her.

"And what does that mean?" he asked.

She explained while he changed his shirt, and at first he was merely annoyed.

"I don't get it," he said. "I come back from a rotten day to find you on the rampage."

"Is it a rampage to want a home, Court?"

"What the hell do you call this?"

"It's your home, not mine. Look, Court, I don't mind your seeing your women friends when you want to. I don't mind a lot of things. But we're married. I'd like to stay that way. I even want a family. You'd like a son, wouldn't you? Most men do."

"Why?" he said lightly. "To be cannon fodder for the next war?"

But she confronted him gravely.

"I don't know how you feel about our marriage, Court. I'm

not even sure how you feel about me, or about anything. But I would like to have children. I want a home of our own and a family. If you don't, it's time to realize that we haven't enough in common to stay together.

He stopped dressing and stared at her.

"Do you know what you're saying?"

"I've been spending hours thinking how to say it."

"I don't get it, Ricky. Is this an ultimatum? Are you saying you'd leave me and go back to that God-awful town? It's absurd. It's childish."

"I'm not a child any more. People do grow up, you know."

He stuck his hands in his trouser pockets and inspected her as if he had never seen her before. Some of the indignation died out of his face.

"I've been pretty rotten, I suppose, since I came back. Maybe we're not the same kids we were, but I don't want to break up, Ricky."

"Why?" she asked. "Let's have this out. You're not in love with me any more, are you?"

"In love!" he said impatiently. "People don't go on indefinitely being in love. Not romantically. But I care enough to want you here, in my life. Isn't that an answer?"

"Not quite," she said steadily. "You might want a mistress, without being in love with her."

"That's a filthy thing to say." He lit a cigarette savagely. "What on earth are we quarreling about anyhow? Because you want an apartment? Go on and get it, for God's sake, if that's the trouble."

He went back to his dressing. His dinner shirt was ready for him. Johnson had seen to that. And by the time he had finished he went over and kissed her, as he might have kissed a naughty child.

"All this about a few rooms and baths and janitor service!" he said mockingly. "Bless your little heart, do what you like. Only you'll have to fix it up with Mother. That's an issue I won't face."

"I've already talked to your mother."

He whistled.

"What did she say?"

"Does that really matter, Court? It's our marriage, not hers."

"So it is," he said soberly, and took her in his arms.

9

It was into a new and not too happy world that Ricky and Court moved that early spring of 1920. The brief joyride was over, and America was settling down to postwar depression, to strikes, to Prohibition and unemployment. Worst of all, at least to Matthew, capitalism itself was under attack.

"Not that it will go far here," he told Elizabeth. "Every man who owns a setting hen is a capitalist. Or a life insurance policy, or a share of stock, or even his own home," he would go on, flushed with anger. "These damned Russians . . ."

He suggested cutting expenses at the house, now that the young people were leaving and Roberta had at last found an apartment within her means. But Elizabeth received the idea coldly.

"I might save forty dollars a month for a housemaid," she said. "If that means anything."

It never occurred to her or to the people she met socially that their old overlordship was finished or that, even if it revived for a time, as a world order it was ended. True there was a new and disconcerting feeling in the air. When she took the big limousine downtown nowadays men idling on street corners gave it ugly looks. Walter was gone now. Courtney had sent him to a veterans' hospital in Colorado, and the new man, a brash and cocky youth, had no idea of the decorum of his job. He would wave at all and sundry.

"Hi, Joe! How's the taxi business?"

"Rotten. Looks like you fell into something soft, Al."

One day on her way to a fitting Elizabeth carried down and handed Albert a new and inconspicuous radiator cap to replace the former one. He grinned as he took it.

"Just who do you think you'll be fooling?" he inquired.

But she had come a long way since she had been Matthew's secretary thirty years ago. She was not going back.

To Ricky that early spring was one of unadulterated happiness. She had found a six-room apartment in the East Sixties, with one window which gave a rather restricted view of the park. Now she was furnishing it. Matthew had given her a check for the purpose, and with Sheila to help her she haunted auction sales and antique shops outside the fashionable area. Sheila had lived with good English furniture all her life. Now she showed a keen sense for a bargain and even a flair for decoration.

Together they went gaily through the days, coming home at night exhausted but contented. There were long secret conclaves in Ricky's room too, for no one, not even Courtney, was to see the apartment until it was finished. Ricky was planning to do her own housework, and one evening she confronted Courtney with a budget.

"You see!" she said triumphantly. "We can manage beautifully."

"You've left out the doctor bills."

"Doctor bills! For what?"

"For my indigestion. From your cooking."

"I'm a good cook. Wait and see."

What she called the grand opening was to be a family tea party. Roberta from her furnished walk-up apartment sent her a mass of early spring flowers that day, and Matthew sent her a box of American Beauties. But as she had hoped, it was Court who came first. He rang the bell and inquired for her formally.

"I understand Mrs. Courtney Wayne lives here. If she's at home—"

She dragged him in, and watched him eagerly as he looked

around. The lamps were lighted, the tea table set and drawn up before the long sofa under the windows. He stood still, saying nothing.

"Don't you like it, Court?"

"Like it! What did I marry? A decorator?"

He was very proud of it. Proud of her too, as the family gathered. She showed a new young dignity as she poured the tea, and he saw that even his mother was impressed.

"I must say it's very nice," she admitted. "Did you say you made these muffins yourself?"

They wandered around, to the dining room and the kitchen, to the unused maid's room, to the main bedroom and to the small guest room beyond it. But it would not have been Elizabeth had she not found some faults. The kitchen was absurd, hardly more than a closet. And as to the bathroom—

"You'll never get into that tub, Court."

"It has a shower too. Only women sit in tubs."

"Your father has sat in a tub ever since he was born."

"Him and Diogenes!"

He was happier that day than he had been for some time. It was only the business, with Mather and himself differing on its policy and the fact that they had missed out on some of the books they should have had; Sinclair Lewis's *Main Street*, and Wells's *Outline of History*, both coming out that year. There was a youngster named Fitzgerald who was promising and Edward Bok was writing his autobiography. Even Matthew was thumbs down on this last.

"Fellow who runs a woman's magazine!" he said. "What's he got to say that anyone wants to read. I hear he carries a pocketful of unset jewels in his pants pocket. Sounds like a sissy to me."

"Bok's no sissy, Dad."

There was another point of contention between them, his own liberalism against his father's conservatism. Anything that opposed the established order was treason to Matthew.

"I'm not publishing sedition," he said flatly. "These

lunatics want to change the world."

"Not entirely, and only for the better, Dad."

Matthew stuck out his lip.

"We've got a responsibility, Court. Any publisher has. Books over our imprint are honest books. I'm no Bolshevik. I believe in the Republic and I'm sticking by it. These young fools drinking rotgut whisky and sprouting new ideas don't belong in it. They've even got the loose Russian ideas about women, too. As though chastity didn't matter. Look at this story about the lions in front of the public library getting up and roaring whenever a virgin goes past!"

The difference was between his father and himself, with George Mather more or less a bystander.

"I'm an editor," he told Court. "I'm a pretty good one too, if I do say it. But I'm up against a stone wall in your father. After all, if he wants to think we're still back in the last century or that all sex is indecent, it's his business, not mine."

"That's being completely pusillanimous!"

Mather grinned.

"Don't pull Harvard words on me," he said. "I only went to Yale, my boy."

But aside from the business Courtney was having his own problems: Soon after he came home from Germany he had sent a Christmas parcel to Coblenz. It had been carried by an officer going there on a mission.

"They're a decent lot," he explained. "I owe them something for the way they looked after me."

He had felt better for sending it—much-needed soap for them all, a pipe and tobacco to the old professor, a warm sweater coat for Frau von Wagner, and a reading glass for Hedwig. To Elsa he had sent a small wrist watch, and with the package a small covering note. But it was spring before he heard from them. Then it was the professor who wrote in his careful English.

"How can we thank you, dear friend, for your kindness to us all? And how forgive me for this long delay? But I have sad news to tell you. My dear wife died a week ago after a brief illness, and I need not explain my anxiety and grief. You who were so good to us will understand. You provided us with so much we badly needed.

"Things are very bad here. We have lost much territory, as you know, and this has been a sad year. Coal and food are more scarce than ever. And the people are surly and unhappy. I am afraid it will take a strong hand to control them.

"You will understand, my friend, that my daughters do not write. Hedwig is prostrated with grief. Later they will do so, of course. Have I said that Elsa has married? You may remember Hans Reiff, who came to see us on occasion? He has been much attached to her since childhood, but I admit her marriage was a surprise and a disappointment to me. I do not agree with him politically, and he is filled with hatreds.

"They live in Munich, where so much mischief is hatched, especially among the students. I have sent there your so handsome gift. And she will write her gratitude."

The letter came to the office, and he sat for some time looking at it as it lay on his desk. She had lost no time, he thought wryly. Vaguely he recalled Reiff, a young ex-private who had sat, sulky and taciturn, in the living room of the apartment, regarding him with hostile eyes. Once he offered him a cigarette. He refused as if it had been an insult.

"I do not smoke Amerikanisch tobacco," he said rudely.

Courtney felt vaguely shocked. The image of Elsa had faded during the last months, but now he saw her clearly. She had packed his small tin trunk for him before he left, folding the garments carefully. But there had been utter tragedy in her face.

"Don't look like that, darling."

"How must I look?"

"I'd like to remember you smiling."

He sat back in his office and closed his eyes. Outside, the infernal hammering of the typewriters went on, but his office was quiet as though the business was still detoured around him. And for a few minutes he was back in Coblenz, a nervous young officer who had been carefully warned against fraternizing with his new hosts. Once more he saw the frau professor with her shawl around her shoulders, and behind her the sitting room, with the checkered cloth on the table, and the tall cold stove; and once more Elsa at the window of his room the day he had arrived, stiff and resentful of him.

His brief infatuation for her was over, but the news of her marriage had hurt his pride. On his way to the Harvard Club he decided to send her a wedding present. Something ironic, he thought. But the stores were fresh out of irony. He settled finally for a pair of silver candlesticks and tried to put something on the card about how rapidly the candle burns. This failing, however, he fell back on an old verse:

Yet Ah, that Spring should vanish with the Rose!
That Youth's sweet-scented manuscript should close!

She would not recognize the familiar quotation, but at least she would know its meaning, and he left it to her to translate it to Reiff. The idea rather amused him.

10

They were barely settled in the apartment before Ricky realized she was not well. She did not tell Court, busy and tired as he was, but it was all she could do to get his breakfast. Then she would crawl back into bed, too ill to take away the dishes or clean up the living room.

It was on one of her bad days that Elizabeth came in. She had to wait for some time before the door was opened. Then she gazed at Ricky in amazement. She was pale, and although it was late afternoon she wore only a bathrobe over her nightdress.

"I'm sorry," she said. "Come in. I've been sick all day. The place is a mess. I haven't—"

She clapped her hand to her mouth and disappeared; left alone, Elizabeth went into the living room. It was untidy, with cigarette butts in the ashtrays, the couch pillows rumpled, and a thin film of dust over everything. She looked around in distaste. Then she emptied the ashtray in the fireplace and straightened the pillows. She was still doing so when Ricky reappeared.

She had run a comb through her hair and looked somewhat better. But the crushing truth had struck home to Elizabeth. She was to be a grandmother. She felt a hideous sense of distaste.

"I suppose you're pregnant," she said dryly. "You might have told us."

"Pregnant!" Ricky stared at her. "Is that what it is?"

"Good heavens," said an irritated Elizabeth, "what did you think it was? Poison?"

She got no further. Ricky reached out for a chair, missed it, and fell flat on the floor in a dead faint.

Elizabeth was shocked to the point of terror. She got some water and sprinkled it on the girl's face. Getting no reaction from that, she telephoned to the family doctor. He was out, but his nurse was there, a calm young woman who soothed her into reason.

"Pregnant," she said. "Well they do faint now and then. Just keep her head flat. She'll come out of it."

She did, of course. She did not say anything at first, merely lay there while a badly shaken Elizabeth slid a blanket over her and looked remorseful. When she did speak it was to apologize.

"I'm sorry," she said. "Things just went black."

"I'm the one to be sorry," said Elizabeth valiantly. "I should have seen how ill you were. Can you stay there while I fix your bed?"

She nodded and closed her eyes. When Elizabeth came back she was sitting up, her color rather better.

"I didn't know it was like this."

"Well, it's no fun, but someday you'll think it was worth it."

They were closer together that day than they had ever been before. Elizabeth got her into a clean bed, made her a cup of tea, which she managed to keep down, and was running a carpet sweeper over the living-room floor when Court came back. He stood with his jaw dropping inside the door.

"What's up?" he said. "Taking on a new job?"

"In case you don't know," she said sharply, "you're having a baby. It's a pity men can't have some of the nastiness of it."

He looked stunned.

"A baby! Good God!"

"Don't stand there with your mouth open," Elizabeth said, still sharply. "What did you expect? And you need somebody here to look after her. She fainted this afternoon."

He tiptoed into Ricky's room. She was awake but still pale.

He leaned over and put his arms around her.

"Why didn't you tell me, darling? You've scared the life out of Mother. Me too."

"I didn't know. I just felt sick. Are you glad?"

"Of course. What do you think I am, a monster? I like it. I'm proud as hell."

He smiled down at her, and she smiled back.

"I won't be like this all the time, Court. Only three months."

"Well, we're getting a woman here to do the work tomorrow. We'll get a nurse too if you need one. Nobody is going to say that the new Wayne baby isn't coming under the best Wayne imprint. Now shut your eyes and take a nap. Mother and I will get the dinner."

He sat on the edge of the bed later on and fed her, the charred lamb chops, the underdone peas, some sips of black coffee. Because he was there she choked it down, only to lose it after he had carried out the tray. But nauseated or not she was happier than she had been since his return. It was as though he had been in a far country and had only now come back to her.

"When's it arriving, darling? Or is that a secret? After all, I have a bit of stock in it myself, you know."

"Sometime in December, your mother says."

"That's a long time to wait. Think you can take it?"

"Of course. Other women do."

Matthew was excited over the news. He insisted on babying her, although by the end of June she was much better.

"Sit down, girl. Let me fix my own drink."

"But I'm all right, Dad."

She knew he hoped for a boy, although he did not say so. A boy who would be a good Republican, she thought. For by now the party had held its convention and nominated Warren Harding; a compromise supposedly suggested by a dying man named Penrose in a Washington hotel; a man who left his bed only for a wheelchair and who was surrounded by telephones on thirty-foot cables as a spider is surrounded by its web.

Matthew was very cheerful. At least it meant an end of

meddling with Europe.

"We could elect a cigar-store Indian," he boasted. "Don't fool yourself, girl. The people are fed up with the Democrats. As for the Reds, we'll show them where they get off."

In Matthew's political lexicon he classed them both together, Democrats and radicals.

Out of his new hopefulness he even agreed to open the Bar Harbor house that summer. He could stay with Courtney or at his club, and the sea air would be good for Ricky. But Ricky did not go to Maine that year. A letter from Beulah had worried her, and against Courtney's protests she left for Ohio early in July.

She had not sent any message beforehand, and she left her bag at the station to be delivered later and walked to the house. The town seemed dead. The factory below the track was closed and boarded up, and early as it was groups of men were lounging in the streets. Perhaps she had her first realization of what was happening all over the country at that time. New York had been different, the pace still rapid, the streets still crowded. Here an air of idleness and neglect hung over everything. And when she reached the house the same impression prevailed. The lawn was uncut, the porch steps broken.

She let herself quietly into the house and, hearing Beulah in the kitchen, went back there.

Beulah was on her knees scrubbing the old linoleum. She looked up in amazement, and getting to her feet, took her in her big arms.

"So my girl's come back," she crooned. "My own little girl. How are you, child? You sure look grand in your fine clothes."

"I'm all right, Beulah. I got your letter, so I thought—"

There was no time for more. Her mother was in the hall, and Ricky turned to meet her. Mrs. Stafford stared at her, and at first she looked alarmed.

"Why, Fredrica!" she said. "How on earth did you get here?"

"By train, darling. I didn't walk."

The frightened look had gone. She came in and kissed Ricky, but there was no great warmth in the kiss. Over her shoulder Ricky was conscious that her mother was looking at Beulah, that something had passed between them.

"Aren't you glad to see me, Mother?"

"Of course. I hope we can make you comfortable. You're used to luxury by this time."

"Not much luxury. We're all right, but Court only has his salary. I did all my own work until not long ago. I want you to know, Mother, I'm having a baby in December."

But Mrs. Stafford's detachment accepted this as she had accepted Ricky's arrival, without enthusiasm.

"That's very nice," she said. "I'm sure the Waynes are pleased."

"Aren't you, Mother?"

"I am if you are. You raise them and then you lose them. That's life. Stop goggling, Beulah, and get Fredrica some breakfast."

Ricky said nothing more, and they ate together amicably enough. It was plain that her news had excited Beulah, but she said nothing. And now and then Ricky found the big colored woman's eyes fixed anxiously on her mother. There was something wrong, but she did not know what it was. Beulah in her illiterate scrawl had written that Mrs. Stafford was not well, but except for her curious apathy she seemed normal enough.

It was obvious, however, that something—the depression probably—had hit her badly. There seemed to be little or no money. The house looked shabby. It needed painting, and there were loose boards on the front porch. It was clean, of course, trust Beulah for that. But the chintz covers in the big living room were worn and faded.

She questioned Beulah when she had the opportunity.

"There's something wrong, isn't there? We always used to have enough."

But Beulah was evasive.

"She ain't never been the same since Mr. Dave's death," she said.

"Are you being paid, Beulah?"

"Don't you worry about that none, Miss Ricky."

"But are you?" Ricky insisted.

"Sometimes she's a little late, but I get it. Trouble is she don't eat enough to keep a bird alive. If my boy Joe didn't bring in a chicken now and then . . ."

"You're not *feeding* her?" asked Ricky, shocked.

"No, ma'am, I jus' tempt her now and then."

She got no further, then or later. After a few days she accepted her mother's disinterest in herself and her affairs. She was not unkind. She was merely abstracted. But she had developed certain unnatural quirks which puzzled Ricky. For example, the July nights were warm, but Mrs. Stafford refused to sit on the porch with her. She would argue:

"Why not? It's such a nice night."

Then one evening her mother turned on her sharply.

"Why should I?" she said. "With those gossiping creatures watching everything I do."

"What on earth would they gossip about?"

"How do I know? I've been a decent woman all my life. I've given my son to his country, ungrateful as it is, and I've paid my bills and owe no one anything. But they sit out there and talk. I've heard them."

It made no sense to Ricky. She went out and sat alone on the porch. The tree-shaded street was cool and quiet, and here and there a householder was watering his lawn. Just so years ago her father had taken out the hose and on hot nights let Dave and herself stand under it. Queer that this was what she remembered best about him. His standing there, and people stopping to talk with him over the white paling fence.

"Hello, Stafford! Giving the kids a bath?"

He had been there and then he was gone. Like Dave, she thought. He had died when she was twelve, a genial stoutish man who had one day in his office felt a pain and died of a ruptured appendix a week later.

She turned her head and looked through the window into the living room. Her mother was sitting in her chair, with a lamp at her elbow and a photograph album on her lap. Ricky recognized it, the old snapshot album of herself and Dave as children. She was running her hand softly over one picture.

When Beulah slid around the porch and called softly to her she found she was trembling. In the darkness, only Beulah's white apron showed, and the whites of her eyes in her black skin. She got up carefully and went down the broken steps. But Beulah did not speak at once. She took her by the arm and led her around the corner of the house.

"Don't you worry, honey," she said in her soft voice. "She ain't like this all the time. It's seeing you has took her back."

"It's crazy, Beulah. People aren't talking about her."

"That's just one of her ideas. Her mind's all right. Only she can't forget Mr. Dave. She's as smart as the rest of them, aside from that. Smarter, far as that goes. Don't you go thinking your ma's crazy."

Ricky began to cry. She put her head on Baulah's shoulder, her slim body shaking.

"I'm frightened, Beulah."

"Don't you be scared. I'm here. I'm looking after her, honey."

But more than this Beulah would not say.

Ricky made the best of it after that. Her mother was often away, spending her time in the cemetery. They were bringing back the bodies of the men who had died abroad, to bury them in Arlington. But Mrs. Stafford resented the idea.

"If Dave comes back, he comes here," she said. "Beside his father, where he belongs."

She was preparing the lot with her own hands.

It would have been better had any of her friends been in town. Most of them were away, however, at the camps on a lake not far off, or at other resorts. Even Jay had gone on business relating to the factory. For the good of the child she carried

Ricky took long walks, and now and then she went out to the site of the old cantonment where Courtney's division had trained. It looked abandoned and desolate. Some of the buildings were down. On the others the paint was peeling, and the parade ground was covered with weeds. She would sit there on a pile of old boards, trying to recapture some of the old rapture.

She found it difficult. That Court loved her after his own fashion she knew. He had cared even more since he knew about the baby. But she was not essential to him, as he was to her. He could go on, living his man's life without her, while she—

At least the child would need her, she thought, and felt warm and comforted.

One morning while she was in the drugstore a plane landed on the old parade ground, and a blond boy got out and trudged into town. Ricky saw him come into the drugstore, the straps of his leather helmet loose and a bundle of placards under his arm. Old Mr. Wilkins was behind the counter and the boy grinned at him and touched his helmet.

"Afternoon, sir. Mind if I put one of these in your window?"

He held out a card. It said "AIRPLANE RIDE $2" and Mr. Wilkins scowled.

"Want to kill somebody?"

The boy laughed.

"Safest thing on earth," he said. "I've been flying all over the country. In France too."

He saw Ricky and grinned.

"Like a ride sister?" he said. "Take you for half price. I need some dinner."

He was shabby, she saw. His flying clothes had seen hard wear, and he had been in the war. On impulse she held out her hand.

"I won't go up with you," she said, smiling back at him, "but I can ask you to have a soda with me. My brother was in France too. Only he didn't come back."

They sat together at one of the small tables, and he talked

cheerfully and gaily about himself. His name was Eric Graham, but he was generally known as Buddy, and he was in the flying game to stay.

"Someday we'll have ships as big as Pullman cars."

"And you'll be flying them?"

"Flying them! I'll be building them."

To her astonishment Buddy and his enterprise were a success. He made ten dollars the first day. And after he had given an exhibition of stunt flying he made even more. He looped, barrel-rolled and zoomed down over the treetops, to emerge cheerfully and grinning from his little contraption of canvas, wood and wire. She had gone to the field that day to watch. She was pale with terror, but he only laughed at her.

"Nothing to it," he said. "She's a tidy lady. She knows her business."

It had been a shock to him to learn that she was married.

"What's the idea? A kid like you?"

"I'm twenty-one. I've been married three years."

"Still like him?"

"I do. Why?"

"Just wondered. Where is he?"

"Back in New York. He's a publisher."

"Well, everyone to his taste, as the cow said when she licked her nose."

She liked him, his reckless courage, his cheerful grin. He had a hundred dollars in his pocket when he left in his flimsy little airplane, and so helped to begin something which was years later to change the very face of the earth. She stayed two or three weeks longer, but she felt that Courtney needed her and her mother did not.

One day she got on an eastbound train and started for New York. Her life was there now. Her life and her love.

11

Elizabeth was largely alone in the big frame house by the sea that summer. She had left Katie in New York for Matthew and Courtney and as there were few dinners that year she managed very well with a local cook. Also she had taken Albert and the car. Automobiles were now allowed on the island. Its long isolation was ended, but the roads were still poor and often dusty.

The house was ready when she got there. The winter shutters down, the small fountain with its pool uncovered. But it was still cold. She had the furnace lit and set about resolutely to pick up the dropped threads of her social life. It was not easy. Some families had not come at all. The ones who had were concerned largely with Prohibition, the election, taxes, and the depression. It was difficult after dinners to get the men out of the smoking room. They stayed there over their cigars and brandy, the latter bootlegged from Canada, puzzled and angry. Business was bad, and what the hell did these riots mean? Where were the police? Where was the government? But they knew the answer to that. The government was in bed in the White House.

"Wait until Harding gets in," they said. "He'll put an end to these damn-fool ideas."

Only to a few did it matter that a man who had been the hope of the world two years before lay dying and repudiated. Or that his great scheme for world peace was to lie quiescent for another quarter of a century.

One day Matthew wrote that he would have to go abroad.

"It's time to see our people over there," he wrote. "I haven't been over since 1914. But I will be home by the time you come back. I have promised Roberta to try to locate poor Arthur's grave. But I think it unlikely, after six years. Why don't you ask her up? I think she is lonely."

She was not fond of Roberta, but she was lonely too. And a title was always useful. She drew the line at Sheila, however, but this proved unnecessary. It developed that Sheila had found a job with a decorating firm. Roberta came, rather to Elizabeth's surprise.

She refused, however, to be a social asset.

"I haven't any clothes," she said. "Anyhow, I've been away too long from that sort of thing."

She was no trouble. She seemed content to sit on the terrace for hours at a time, with her thin hands folded in her lap and her eyes fixed on the sea. Over there somewhere Arthur lay and all the best that England had had. What was it in men that made them fight wars? she thought. Nobody gained anything, not even the victors. Once she looked up from her preoccupation to find Elizabeth beside her.

"I suppose there's not much hope Matthew will find Arthur, is there?"

Elizabeth was moved to impatient pity.

"I wish you'd forget all that, Roberta. It's over. Why live in the past?"

"The past is all I have," she said quietly.

It was true. She had lost Sheila. They still lived together, but Sheila was away all day, and she had made friends by that time, so she was seldom at home evenings. Roberta never inquired about the friends, or even the nights when Sheila slipped in at all hours, sometimes a little unsteady in her movements.

The past, tragic as it was, was safer. She thought about it, there on the terrace, with the sea gulls strutting about the lawn and Elizabeth endlessly busy elsewhere. She had never fooled herself. She had been an unpromising girl, all legs and arms, and made an unhappy debut. Elderly Boston had accepted her, but she had gone to her first parties shivering with terror. Matthew never went to dances, so she went alone or with her mother. When she had no partner she hid in the dressing room, pretending a tear in her ball gown, fixing her hair, anything for an escape.

Then, during a weekend at Newport, she met Arthur, a tall, thin Englishman with a military mustache who seemed to like her. At first she had been afraid to hope. He would sit in the Wayne parlor and, since neither of them was a talker, there were long painful silences.

One day he told her she had beautiful hands. It was the nearest to a compliment he had paid her. But after two months of sitting, he went to her father and said he would like to marry her.

"I have a modest income, not much," he said. "But it's time I married. And I'm fond of Roberta, sir."

That was all he had ever been, fond of her. It had been all she asked in return for her own love of him. He had never been faithful. He would wander off with some woman or other, be gone a month or so, and then come home with his money gone but his manner to her impeccable as always. Once he had even gone to the Boer War, where the Boers had captured him, stripped his long thin body of his uniform, and set him free under a broiling sun. But always, war or women, he had come back to her.

"You're looking well, my dear."

"I'm all right. Tea will be ready in a minute or so."

Only, of course, in 1914, he had not come back.

She was not fond of Elizabeth, but she admired her. The family was shocked when Matthew married her. Elizabeth had been his secretary, and of no family anyone had ever heard of. Yet she had made him a good wife, hard and driving and ambitious, but faithful and devoted. Perhaps Matthew owed some of his success to her. She did not know.

The two women were largely alone. Elizabeth had hoped for a visit from Courtney while Ricky was away, but he did not come. Mather's wife had had a baby, a son, and he was taking his vacation to be with her. But there was another reason, which neither woman suspected.

Alone in New York Courtney was finding his days long and his evenings longer. The town seemed deserted, and there was only a skeleton staff at the office. He was bored and often irritable. Then one afternoon, walking to the Harvard Club, he ran into Emmy Baldwin.

He did not want to see her. The heat was intense. His clothes were sticking to him, his collar wilted. What he wanted was a plunge in the club pool and a long cool drink, but Emmy stopped him.

"Hello," she said. "Stinker of a day, isn't it?"

"You look cool enough."

"Well, I'm not. How about buying me a drink?"

He looked down at her. In the bright sunlight her hair looked brassier than ever, but she was smiling, and his annoyance faded.

"I'll do better. I'll buy you a dinner. How about Claremont?"

She agreed, with a slightly malicious look in her eyes. He did not see it, however. He managed to get a bottle of Scotch, and they rode to the inn on the top of a bus. Emmy was at her gayest. Claremont was cool. There was a breeze from the Hudson, and before he knew it they had finished the Scotch he had brought.

He began to feel relaxed, and when Emmy put her head on his shoulder on the bus going back and told him what a dirty trick he had played on her, he put an arm around her and kissed her.

"I was so terribly in love with you, Court."

"All over it, are you?"

"You know better than that. Come on back with me, Court.

Surely you can spare me a little time."

Sure he could spare her a little time. Time was all he had these days alone in town. He began to feel sorry for himself. For Emmy too. Poor Emmy, making the best of things, living on her scrap of alimony in that awful apartment, and still crazy about him.

They had more drinks at Emmy's, and because it was still hot she got into something cool and loose. After that everything was pretty hazy. He awakened the next morning in her bed, with a terrific thirst and a considerable bewilderment. Emmy was still asleep, and not looking at all attractive. He slipped out and went home to bathe and shave.

He had not meant it to happen. He merely felt a sense of disgust, not only that it had happened but that it had happened while Ricky was carrying his child.

Ricky came home a day or two later. He had a feeling of guilt when he met her at the train, and when she came toward him smiling. Forget it, he thought. Here's your wife and you're glad to see her.

He was, rather to his own surprise. He had not realized how he had missed her. He went toward her limping slightly, for the heat had ended with rain. She saw it at once.

"Court, darling, you shouldn't have come."

"Why? Oh, the leg. It's nothing. Tired after the trip?"

"A little."

He took her home and, still guilty, insisted that she go to bed. He carried a tray in to her himself, and when she insisted later on, with his hand on her abdomen he tried to feel the movements of his child. It was too soon, of course, but he pretended to do so.

"Going to be a husky kid, isn't he?"

"What if it's a girl, Court?"

"Who says I don't like girls?"

It was all right, he thought. Every man made a fool of himself once in a while.

His father came home early in September. He looked worn

and dispirited when Courtney had a talk with him in his library that night.

"Things are pretty bad there," he reported. "But they're getting better. They have plenty of guts, the British, and I managed to sell Roberta's house. Never did like the place anyhow."

Nevertheless, he was rather excited over the English writers, Maugham and Walpole and Rebecca West, although some of them puzzled him.

"Little thin book of poems called *Leda* by a fellow named Huxley, Aldous Huxley. I turned it down, Court. It didn't amount to anything, and there's no market for poetry. As for the Bloomsbury group—"

"What about them?"

"When they have meetings they read their own stuff through a megaphone or something to their friends! That's the story, anyhow. I always said the British had no sense of humor. As for the French, they aren't doing much. Gay enough on the surface, but too many mutilées on the streets—and too many women in black. I didn't find Arthur's grave. After all, it's a long time."

There was a slight change in his voice when he spoke of his trip to Germany.

"They don't know where they are or where they're going. We can't stay there forever. Some of them want the monarchy back. It mightn't be so bad. They're used to discipline, and the republic's not going well. They're still in rotten shape. No cars on the streets, and not enough food or coal. When people are as badly off as that—"

He did not finish. He was looking at Courtney, standing at the hearth.

"I'm wondering," he said, "if you left any obligations over there. I'm not asking you any questions, and I don't want to interfere. It just happens I met a man in Coblenz who knew about you. He was a German. He seemed to think you were pretty well tied up with a girl over there." And when Court said nothing: "He was a friend of the family. He intimated that things had gone rather far."

Courtney felt himself flushing.

"Look, Dad, what did you expect? Of course there were girls. You could get them for a bar of soap or a package of cigarettes. I never claimed anything else."

"I'm not talking about that. I'm referring to Elsa von Wagner. That was her name, wasn't it? What about her?"

"She wasn't a prostitute, if that's what you mean."

"I gathered that," Matthew said dryly. "What I'm asking is how far you were committed to her?"

"I've never heard from her since I left. That's the truth. I sent them some little things for Christmas last year. They'd been damned good to me. Her father wrote and thanked me. That's all."

"Then you didn't get her into trouble."

"Good God! No!"

Matthew looked relieved.

"I didn't like to mention it," he explained. "But if you had any obligations I wanted to know. I might have helped."

He leaned back in his big chair by the empty fireplace and relaxed. He had been worried all the way home, for he knew men. He even knew something about war. And two years was a long time for a boy to do without women. But a married man was in a different category from the others. He had no business fooling around.

"Well, I had to get it off my chest," he said. "We'd better forget it. I gather you thought a lot of the girl, but it's over." He paused and looked up at Court towering above him. "Ricky was smarter than the rest of us at that, Court. She knew there was something wrong when you came back."

Court smiled sheepishly.

"It's finished, Dad. She's married."

"Yes. So I understand."

He walked home the few blocks to the apartment that night. The talk had shaken him. Yet Elsa had known all along that he was married. Known too that she would lose him eventually. But he remembered the last hour or so before he left, the tin trunk being packed and the look of sheer tragedy on her face. He had said he wanted to remember her smiling. Well, she had not smiled, but she had consoled herself very soon. With that pimply Reiff. Funny. He had never thought she liked him.

He forgot her after that. He was learning more and more about books and their manufacture. The linotype machines, setting up the type for the galleys which came back to the editorial staff at the office for correction. The master number on each manuscript which went all through the plant, from editorial department to finished book. The page proofs, the final making of the copper plates.

One day that fall he went into the foundry. It was a warm day, and the men working over the molten metal were half naked.

"Hot in here, isn't it?" he said.

"Not like midsummer. Goes to a hundred twenty-five."

He began to understand his father's belief that each book they published was a minor miracle: a miracle of printing, collating, and sewing, of trimming to size, of smashing to flatness, of truing and rounding and backing. And after all this, of casemaking and stamping, of casing and jacketing. And that one book-manufacturing firm alone, working double shifts, had produced nine hundred thousand books the month before. Each manuscript after it left his office had gone through at least twenty different operations before bound books were ready for the warehouse.

People read books, but what did they know about them? Or even about the people who made them? He himself—

In October a new Lockwood romance came in, and soon Mrs. Lockwood herself appeared. She was a tired-looking youngish woman, badly dressed, but Mather was busy and so Courtney took her to lunch. She surprised him over her cocktail.

"I suppose you detest my stuff," she said. "You're Harvard, aren't you? One of Copey's men?"

"What's that got to do with it?" he said stiffly. "The reports are all very good."

She smiled.

"Meaning it will sell!" she said. "Someday I'm going to write what I want to. Then nobody will buy it. Just now I've got a family to support. Four children and a husband with t.b. contracted in the army. He won't go to a hospital, so—I do my best."

The story depressed him, although she was cheerful about it. But he wondered that day what lay behind the writers who came and went in the office: the successful ones, well dressed and self-assured; the unsuccessful, timid and anxious. He had been impatient with many of them: the ones who wanted to spend hours talking about themselves, the ones who wanted advances on royalties, the ones who resented their poor reviews and brought in their grievances to him.

Writing was not only a profession to many of them. It was a method of living, often of sheer survival. No wonder they tried to see Matthew when they could. Court could understand that. In a way Matthew was a father to them. They could take their problems to him, their personal troubles, and he would listen and help when he could.

Probably he had known about Anne Lockwood all along. That was why they had pushed her books.

12

Young Jeffrey Wayne was born early in December. Courtney called a taxi when Ricky's pains started, and stayed with her until she was taken to the hospital delivery room. He found the palms of his hands sweating after she had gone. She had looked pathetic, poor kid. She had clung to him as long as she could, and she had made as little fuss as possible.

He felt frightened and guilty, like all husbands at such times, but he had no sense of approaching fatherhood. The child was still unreal to him. All he wanted was that the thing be over. He stayed in the room, pacing the floor and counting the hours as they passed.

Outside in the visitors' parlor Matthew and Elizabeth waited. Matthew paced the floor, looking at his watch every now and then. The hospital was quiet. Outside a fine hard snow was falling. A sharp gale blew it against the windows and screamed around the building. The storm worried him, as though it meant something; he did not know what.

"Kind of slow, isn't she, Lizzie?"

Elizabeth moved. She had been remembering the long agony when Courtney was born. Only at the end they had put a few drops of chloroform on a towel, and she had grasped it frantically. Perhaps they did things better now. The Germans had something they called "twilight sleep," but doctors in America were slow in approving it. Perhaps if she had spoken about it—

"Of course it's slow, Matt. Give her time."

"Be a good thing for them to have a child. Hold a marriage together."

"There's nothing wrong with their marriage," said Elizabeth firmly.

They were still there at dawn when Ricky was brought back from the delivery room. They saw her being wheeled from the elevator, but neither of them moved. This was Courtney and Ricky's hour, not theirs. They felt like intruders just then. But the nurse beside the stretcher looked calm and cheerful. It was all right then. Matthew got up and stretched.

"It's over, Lizzie. I wish to God I had a drink."

Inside the room Courtney stood stiff as Ricky was brought in. She looked tired and pale, but she was smiling. "You have a son, Mr. Wayne," said the nurse. "A fine boy, and a brave young mother. Shall I go out and tell your family?"

To his amazement Courtney found a lump in his throat. He leaned over and kissed Ricky.

"Everything's fine, darling. I'm proud of you."

She reached out and caught his sweating hand.

"I'm glad," she whispered, and was instantly asleep.

His first view of his son shocked him, however. He looked up at the nurse's placid face.

"Roll it up in a blanket and give it to me," he said. "I want to leave it on somebody's doorstep."

The advent of young Jeffrey changed their lives somewhat. Ricky was absorbed in the child, while during his early months at least Courtney regarded him with a detached pride.

"What on earth is he crying about?"

"He's perfectly all right. He wants to be picked up."

"Then why not pick him up?"

"He has to be trained, Court. The nurses at the hospital are very particular about it."

So the thin wail would go on increasing in volume until both their nerves were on edge. At last Court would fling down what he was reading and go sulkily to bed, the baby would give it up as a bad job and go peacefully to sleep, and Ricky with both ears and the nursery door open would get what rest she could.

Yet Courtney was proud of the boy. In the office he and Mather compared notes on their offspring.

"Uses his little pot already, Court. Smart kid."

"What do you mean, smart? Young Jeff walks to the bathroom!"

They would grin at each other, the two fathers of sons, and go back to work. If Courtney felt that he now had second place in Ricky's heart he had little time to think about it. For America was at last pulling out of the doldrums. Harding was in, and Matthew was cheerful.

"What did I tell you?" he said. "The Republicans know something about government. They should after almost fifty years."

But he still resented the few liberal books Court had managed to get on the list, although to his surprise they sold. He did not realize that an intellectual revolution was taking place, or that the old laissez-faire years were over.

"Lot of young radicals," he grumbled. "They're against capitalism, but I notice they watch their royalties same as anybody else. What's all this talk about the common man? Who is he anyhow? You can bet it's always the other fellow."

Courtney realized that young Jeff's advent had changed some of his own ideas. What he wanted now was a safe secure future for his son. And the boy was growing fast. In spite of Matthew, Ricky had refused a nurse for him. She loved caring for him. In the morning she would pick up his warm damp little body and hold him to her with possessive firmness. Courtney, bathing and shaving, would watch her face.

"Don't like him, do you?"

"I didn't know it would be like this, Court. I never used to like babies much."

"Don't spoil the brat. That's all."

"I wish you wouldn't call him that."

"He's mine too, isn't he? If I choose to call him names . . ."

The baby had drawn them together. If there were times when he felt that he held a mother in his arms rather than a wife he never let her know. Such passion as she had was still for the child, not for him. Yet she had never been lovelier. Maternity suited her. On Sunday mornings while he loafed he watched the ritual of the baby's bath, her young face grave as she tested the water in the rubber tub, the powder and fresh clothing warming by the radiator, the bath blanket on her lap, even the folded paper with which she cleaned young Jeffrey's tiny fingernails.

"I think his eyes are going to be brown, like yours, Court."

"That's wishful thinking. I have very fine eyes."

"But look. There *are* little brown flecks in them."

There were, as a matter of fact. By spring young Jeffrey was a brown-eyed baby, fat and ridiculous in his small ermine-trimmed bonnet and going to the park daily in his English perambulator. Ricky would find a bench and sit there, among the nurses and governesses, proud and complacent. She took peanuts for the squirrels, and young Jeffrey on her knees would wave his arms with excitement. Or as Courtney observed, at least he waved his arms.

He seldom saw Emmy. Now and then when he and Ricky went out to dinner—the maid watching the baby—he met her, but she made no effort to see him alone. He had no feeling about her whatever, although once he thought she was watching him with mockery in her eyes. Then one night he played bridge with her and she lost twenty dollars.

"Sorry, Court," she said. "I'll have to give you a check for it."

His secretary sent it to the bank with other checks for deposit, and it came back marked "Non sufficient funds." He tore it up, but it worried him. It had never occurred to him that she could be in financial straits.

Now and then that spring of 1921 Roberta came to dinner

with them, taking a bus from her small walk-up flat but meticulously wearing one of her old black evening gowns. She liked to argue with Court.

"We have real democracy in England. When the government ceases to represent the people it goes out."

"What do you mean by 'we'? You were born here. You're living on American money, aren't you? As for democracy, they're still feudal over there, and you know it."

Other people came to dinner. Court brought home some of his authors, and there was good talk over the table. Like his father before him, he would look at his wife across the candles and be proud of her. For Ricky was growing up. She was no longer the girl from a small town, shy and timid. Now and then he gave her a manuscript to read, and was surprised at her critical ability. Only once did they differ, but then it was profoundly. It was over a book called *Purple Haze*, and Matthew refused to publish it. However, he agreed to see the author, and so one day he found a boyish-looking youth sitting across the desk from him.

"I am going to be frank, Mr. Nelson," he said. "I don't care for books like *Purple Haze*."

"So I gather," said young Mr. Nelson cheerfully.

"You're rather young, aren't you? I'm wondering how you came to write it.

Young Nelson smiled, showing fine white teeth.

"I just looked over the market," he said pleasantly. "It seemed to me there were only two sure-fires, crime and sex. I happen to know more about sex."

Mather was resentful of Matthew's attitude.

"What are we, a lot of fuddy-duddies?" he demanded of Courtney. "We have to move with the times. I don't want dirty books. I hate them. But there's a difference between that and honesty. After all, people do sleep together."

Courtney grinned.

"Only in connubial beds, according to M.W."

Matthew had become M.W. to the staff since Courtney came in.

"Well, hell, we're here to sell books. If the public wants sex, I say let them have it."

The company was out of the red, although as time went on it became clear that the Republicans were performing no miracle. It was not their fault. The country had overexpanded during the war. Not only industry. The farmers had bought more land, on the cry of food for the world. Now in the West a long dry summer with bad hay had been followed by an interminable winter. On the ranges as the snow began to melt, the cattlemen had ridden over their pastures, tailing up those animals which could be brought to their feet and shooting the others. And bookstores continued to close.

One day Mather brought in a manuscript and put it on Courtney's desk.

"Another sexy one," he said dryly. "We could stand a bestseller. See what you think of it."

He read it that night. It was tripe, but he had to admit that it held his interest. If the public really wanted that sort of thing, this was it. When he had finished he looked across at Ricky knitting a sweater for Jeff. If she could take it—

Ricky, however, could not take it. She told him so the next evening when he came home.

"It's a nasty book," she said. "Whoever wrote it has a nasty mind."

"There's nothing dirty about sex, my dear."

"He makes it dirty. Are you going to accept it?"

"If I can put it over on Dad, yes."

He was shaking cocktails, but his voice was irritated.

"Would you want your child to read it, Court?"

"Oh, for God's sake, Ricky! Sex isn't shameful. It isn't sinful. What on earth did your mother tell you about such things?"

"We never discussed them," she said simply.

"Then it's a damned shame you didn't."

Sometime in the night it occurred to him to let Emmy read it. She was worldly enough, and she represented innumerable other idle worldly women. And women were the book buyers.

He called her on the phone the next morning and asked her to lunch with him. At the table he picked up his brief case and laid it before her.

"I wonder if you'd do something for me, Emmy?"

"Short of letting you shove me under a taxicab—"

"No, I'm serious. I want you to read this manuscript for me."

She burst into shrill laughter.

"That's the funniest thing I've heard in years, Court. Me read a manuscript. I don't read much of anything. You know that."

"You'd get twenty dollars for it. Can you do it tonight?"

She laughed again, but the fee obviously interested her.

"Emmy the bookworm!" she said. "It's not exactly what I'd planned for the evening, but—well, anything for you, Court. You know that."

She read it that night in bed, lying with the pages scattered about her, her bleached hair brassy in the lamplight, her rose-colored silk sheets kicked to the foot of the bed. At three o'clock, with her eyes burning, she gathered it together and put out the light.

The next morning she called Court.

"It's a knockout," she said. "I couldn't put it down."

"Anything you thought should be cut?"

"Well, if you start with the premise that the girl's a nymphomaniac, why try to go prudish with her? And when am I going to see you again?"

"I owe you a lunch and the check for the job."

That, however, was all it turned out to be. Emmy grinned at him mischievously when she saw him, but she could take things or let them go. In the meantime she could afford to wait.

The next day Matthew read the manuscript of *The Passion Flower*. He read it at his desk, with Angela keeping out of his way. When she heard him fling it across the room she sent for Courtney.

"I'd be careful," she warned him. "He's having a fit."

Actually it was a flushed, almost apoplectic Matthew who stared at him when he went into the office. The pages of the script were scattered all over the floor.

"What the devil are you fellows trying to put over on me?" he demanded. "Since when did we take to selling aphrodisiacs? I wouldn't even let your mother read it."

"I think she might like it. I know she's fed up with our old romantic stuff."

"Very well," said Matthew grimly. "Send someone in here to pick it up. I'll take it home with me."

A night or two later he had a shock from Elizabeth. He had not dared ask her about the manuscript until after dinner. He sat waiting through the inevitable soup, roast, salad, dessert and fingerbowls. When at last Johnson had gone he looked across the table.

"Well, what about it?"

"I don't see what all the fuss is about, Matt. I've read worse books."

"Oh, you have, have you?"

"Certainly. I hope I'm beyond adolescence and puppy love."

He stared at her.

"Puppy love! Is that what you call it now? For God's sake, Lizzie, don't tell me that it was puppy love that made us get married. It was romance, whether you like the word or not."

She wiped her fingers on her huge damask napkin.

"I don't remember feeling particularly romantic about you, Matthew. I cared for you a lot more after we'd been married a few years."

She got up, but he did not move. He sat looking at her. She was her usual cool well-set-up self. He didn't understand women. He never would understand her.

"So you didn't care about me at first?" he asked.

"I was fond of you. I thought we'd go places together. But romance . . ."

"Well, I suppose I wasn't a particularly romantic figure," he said heavily and got up, to relapse later into bewildered silence in the library over his coffee.

13

Late in the spring of that year Courtney received a belated note of thanks from Elsa. He had never seen her writing before, an English version of German script. The letter, however, was legible as well as prim.

"My dear Captain Wayne," she wrote. "My husband and I thank you greatly for your so beautiful gift. I assure you we will use it on our table when candles are available. Just now they are very rare, as is much here in my country.

"My father has told you of our mother's death. We miss her greatly. I fear he is lonely without her.

"With many thanks from us both, dear Captain, I am faithfully yours,

Elsa Reiff"

It read as though she had got it out of a book, he thought disgustedly. He reread it, then he tore it up and threw the scraps in his wastebasket. So that was that. Nothing about the lines from Omar he had sent. And her husband thanked him too. Damn it, he hadn't sent the candlesticks to the pimply Reiff.

But he felt only annoyance. His life was well organized by that time. *The Passion Flower* had been accepted and promised to do well. And Emmy Baldwin, to her own amusement—and financial gain—was doing some further reading for the firm.

She had a hard shrewdness which was useful, although Mather disliked her.

"Keep that bleached floozie out of my office," he told Court. "I don't want even my boy's picture to see her."

He kept a snapshot of his son on his desk, a blond curly-headed baby with a dog beside him.

But Courtney was restless. They had their own group by that time, Ricky and he, of young married people like themselves. They all carried flasks, and sometimes he drank too much and felt rotten the next morning. But the quiet evenings at home palled on him. He would wander around like a caged animal.

"Let's get the hell out of here and go somewhere, Ricky."

"Again?" She would lift her eyebrows.

"What's the matter with you? I sit at a desk all day. I need some sort of relaxation."

She would agree, but she was not greatly interested. The crowds and the noise bothered her, for this was the start of the roaring twenties, with their lowering of standards, their preoccupation with sex, their jazz, their short skirts and bobbed hair for women; and with their headlines of graft in high places and their unemployed veterans. The beginning of the great American insanity.

Nevertheless, she would go, to be held too tight by her dance partners, too often unsteady on their feet, and occasionally amorous.

"For heaven's sake, do you have to crack my ribs?"

"I'm crazy about you, Ricky."

"Then stop tramping on my feet."

"Hell, you're cold. Beautiful but cold. Come on, be nice to me. How about lunch tomorrow?"

Now and then Courtney had to rescue her.

But he was twenty-nine that spring. He was no longer the boy who had wooed her in such desperate haste before he went overseas. He was not even the man who had cared so desperately for Elsa von Wagner. There were times when even the thought of going home irked him. He had taken to stopping in at the club for a highball and a rubber or two of bridge in the afternoon instead. He was playing two cents a point now, but he was a reliable player. And on Saturday afternoons he played golf at the Sleepy Hollow Club, driving himself out in the roadster he had bought.

Ricky did not play, and so sometimes when he could not get a foursome, he took Emmy with him. She played well. In her short skirt and loose blouse she swung like a man. But she was careful not to alarm him. She still kept her easy half-mocking attitude.

"What's the hurry? Have to get home to mama?"

"I have to get home. It's dinnertime."

But one day she slid her arm through his on the way back to the clubhouse.

"You're not really a domestic creature, are you? Babies and bottles and diapers—that's a queer sort of life for you."

He pulled his arm free, not ungently.

"Look, Emmy," he said, "let's get this straight. You live your own life and I live mine. I happen to like mine."

"Except for a little escape now and then?"

"Forget it, Emmy. We're good friends. Let it go at that."

If Ricky resented the fact that her own life had settled to a domestic pattern she did not let him know. In the morning while the baby slept she marketed on Madison Avenue. In the afternoon she wheeled him in his pram to the park. When Courtney came home at night the apartment was neat and cheerful, and she herself carefully dressed. She wore now, instead of the old stiff corset, a tiny girdle of pink moiré ribbon and a tight brassière over her small breasts. Childbirth had not changed her figure. She was still slim-waisted. But she had not cut her hair.

They had urged her to do so, at the beauty parlor.

"Madam has a lovely head. It would be chic and becoming. And new."

She had refused, however. Courtney had always liked her hair as it was.

Her days were fairly monotonous, the baby growing, Courtney going to the office, cocktail parties for authors, and Sunday lunches with Matthew and Elizabeth. Matthew going down to the basement and unlocking the steel door to bring up gin and vermouth for cocktails, and a bottle of wine. Then after the cocktails the roast beef with Yorkshire pudding, the ice cream or meringue, and the going home again stuffed to the eyes and comatose.

But she was aware that her relationship with Courtney was slowly altering. She had always taken it for granted that married people loved each other, and theirs was supposed to be a happy marriage. But was it really? Perhaps they had missed something in the early days. They had had a week or so together and two years of separation. By the time he came back they had both changed, grown, developed. It had been impossible to recapture the early ecstasy of their engagement and their brief honeymoon.

It never occurred to her, however, that he could be unfaithful to her.

Jeffrey was almost a year old when Harding called his Disarmament Conference. Along with it was to go the dedication of the great white amphitheater at Arlington on the Virginia hills overlooking Washington, and the burial of an unknown soldier who was to typify all the men who had died overseas.

To Ricky it meant the end of war, a safe world, a safe Jeffrey. But to Courtney and Matthew it meant something else. One day in November Courtney came into his father's office, his face set.

"There's an extra out," he said grimly. "Harding's decided to sink our battleships."

Matthew glared at him.

"Don't talk nonsense. Sink our ships!"

"That's the bright idea, apparently. We'll do it too, like the fools we are."

"But why? So we can build a new lot?"

He sat there while Courtney paced the floor and told him what he knew, and what all the world was to know before nightfall, while Matthew listened in explosive silence.

"Why, the damned idiots," he shouted. "We'll do it. Of course we'll do it! But watch the rest! They won't. Not on your life they won't. It's Never-Never Land. The Mad Hatter's Tea Party. No ships, so no war. For God's sake, what are the British doing?"

"The last I heard they were fainting, all over the place."

In the end the devastating plan was accepted, tongue in cheek by some, with pleasurable surprise by others. The greatest navy in the world was to destroy itself, to sink its best ships while others sank theirs not so good. To kill its first line of defense, and so end war.

It was into this new world that Ricky was to bring her second child, a girl. A new world, with Matthew savage and Courtney cynical. With the pacifists starry-eyed and the navy incredulous. And in the tall brick house in Washington Woodrow Wilson dying, his dream of a unified world dying with him.

A new world, with Matthew refusing to publish Wilson's letters to a woman friend, harmless as they were, because the dying and the dead have their rights. And later turning down a book about Harding which was not harmless; because Matthew was a man first and a publisher second.

Ricky began to suspect she was pregnant again in Bar Harbor the following summer. She said nothing about it at first. She had taken little Jeff with her, and the boy was flourishing. Also he provided her with an excuse for not going out, which was a relief. For with the return of the Republicans to power the season was the gayest in years. There were more dinner parties, more cars, more yachts in the harbor. Roads were being paved, houses painted, and New York businesses had opened shops on Main Street and were showing extravagant clothes, laces, silver, and what not.

Elizabeth, however, was beginning to show a possessive interest in Jeff as he emerged from babyhood. To her amusement he called her Liz.

"Come and sit on Elizabeth's knee, Jeffrey."

"Don't want to, Liz."

He would shake his dark head, and Elizabeth would catch him up and hold him while he wriggled.

"He's as stubborn as his father," she would say proudly.

He was a tall child for his age, and already self-sufficient. He liked to go to the cove nearby where Captain Trimble kept his fishing boat. The old man liked the boy.

"Like bo'," Jeff would say. "Get on bo'."

Sometimes the captain would lift him on. The boat smelled fishy, but Jeff liked it. But one day a lobster pinched his finger, and Elizabeth was furious.

"You ought to have better sense," she told Ricky sharply. "That boat's filthy. Come to Elizabeth, darling. How's the poor little hand?"

It was useless to argue with Elizabeth.

Ricky was certain of her pregnancy before she left, but she did not tell Courtney. His letters had been infrequent, and he had stayed in New York all summer, on the plea of business. Also she was not certain how he would take it. Another child meant more expense, and they were still living on his salary. Perhaps it would have been better if she had, for one day Elizabeth heard from Roberta.

"I trust you to keep this to yourself," she wrote. "I don't customarily interfere with other people's affairs, but I understand Courtney is seeing a good bit of the Baldwin girl. There is some talk about it. Perhaps Ricky might come home. I suppose he is lonely. And all men are not like Matt."

Elizabeth scowled, and tearing up the letter flushed it down the toilet. She wrote a bitter note to Courtney that night, but by that time it was too late. He had become pretty thoroughly involved with Emmy. She had become a regular reader for the firm, and she was in and out of the office constantly.

At first it had been a sort of game. She would sit across his desk, smoking his cigarettes and making her shrewd reports while the sharp eyes of the clerical force watched his door. But she exuded sensuality like an aura. He was not in love with her. There were even times when he actively disliked her. Nevertheless, he was lonely, and the bars were down, had been down since the dinner at Claremont.

To give him credit he did not suspect that Ricky was pregnant again. And he was careful, very careful. He never spent the night in Emmy's small airless apartment. He would go home late, to hear his father's voice.

"That you, Court?"

"Sorry, Dad. Got in a bridge game at the club."

There was no question of money between them. Now and then he sent her a box of flowers. And once—on her birthday—a gold cigarette case, which she immediately sold. She told him, to his annoyance.

"What on earth do you do with your money, Emmy?"

"Clothes, rent, liquor. Especially the rent. You wouldn't believe how it piles up."

He suggested that he pay her rent for a while until she got things straight. Both of them understood it was a purely friendly gesture. And she kept a record in a small black book. He would put seventy-four dollars in an envelope and give it to her.

"It's damn nice of you, Court. Let's see, what do I owe you now?"

She was very careful, and not only about money. She simply made him comfortable and let it go at that. She had no hope that he would ever care for her, or that this was more than a brief episode. And although he agreed to pay her rent until she caught up, he let her know quite plainly that the situation had to end when Ricky came back.

She took it calmly.

"I'll miss you, Court," she said. "I suppose I'm a damned fool about you. But what's over is over."

He meant it to be over. He was very gentle with Ricky when she came back, gentle and remorseful, especially when he heard her news.

She had brought back a nurse for Jeffrey, a true New Englander, dour at times but always efficient. Her name was Hilda and Courtney smiled when he first saw her.

"Where did you get old pickle-face?" he asked.

"She's not sour at all. Jeffrey adores her."

Hilda was a great comfort to her in the months that followed. Courtney was kind enough, but the thought of another child so soon rather appalled him. It was Hilda who carried the trays when Ricky was unable to get up, who kept Jeff away from her and conciliated the procession of general houseworkers who came and went in the kitchen.

She had a sharp tongue too.

"Why didn't you telephone you were going to be late, Mr. Wayne? The dinner's spoiled."

"I have a business, Hilda."

"You have a club too. I called it up. You'd just left."

But toward the end he felt sorry for Ricky, as well as guilty about the months of her absence. At night he would walk with her around the block, her swollen body hidden under a cape and his arm supporting her. And one day he brought her a new gadget, something he called a crystal set. He put earphones on her head and far away she heard faint music.

"What on earth is it, Court?"

"Radio, darling. What did you think it was?"

After that she listened as often as she could. Courtney maintained later that Peggy came into the world by radio. But as a matter of fact the birth was hard and long, and she had a post-partum hemorrhage. The doctor looked grave."

"She'd better not have any more, Mr. Wayne. It would be a risk. We almost lost her this time."

Courtney was profoundly shocked.

"Then she won't have any more, doctor," he said. "I promise you that."

He went in to see her after that talk. She looked white and exhausted, and he pulled up a chair and when he had kissed her, he took one of her long braids of hair and kissed it too.

"I'm sorry, Ricky. Terribly sorry. It was bad, wasn't it?"

"Pretty bad. I'll be all right."

"You're not going through it again, darling. Never again."

She smiled weakly.

"I'm glad she's a girl. If there's another war—"

"There won't be another war," he said confidently.

14

The baby was three months old when they had a brief visit from Mrs. Stafford. David had been brought back to Arlington after all, and lay there under his neat white headstone, along with rows of others, so thick that they seemed to be marching.

She inspected Peggy without any particular enthusiasm.

"She looks healthy," she said. "Why didn't you nurse her? I believe in breast feeding, myself."

"I had no milk, Mother. I wanted to."

"No wonder, the life you live."

She expressed no particular gratification over the fact that the child had been named Margaret for her.

"I know names I like better," she commented.

"Like mine?" Ricky teased her.

"Fredrica was your father's choice," Mrs. Stafford said stiffly. "His father was named Frederick."

She approved of little Jeff, however. She even made shy overtures to him once or twice.

"Who are you?" he inquired, standing with his legs apart and staring up at her.

"I'm your grandmother."

"Liz is. Not you."

"You see, Mother?" Ricky said. "He doesn't even know you. You should come oftener."

"I have other things to do."

She was remote rather than unfriendly, but she disapproved

of Ricky's housekeeping and detested New York. The crowds worried her, the rapid pace. And she was shabby. Ricky tried to buy her some clothes, but she resented it.

"I've stood on my own feet all my life," she said firmly. "I don't want charity now."

She was on her way to Washington, and Courtney sent flowers to her hotel there for David's grave. She carried them with her, and knelt dry-eyed on the ground before the small white marker. But there was nothing there to remind her of the smiling boy for whom she had kept the light in her window. After a while she got up and walked over to the Tomb of the Unknown Soldier. There was as yet no move to protect it. It stood stark and bare and white next to the cement drive, and all day cars drove by it, and dirt and cigarette butts lay all around it.

She found a family eating a picnic lunch beside it and stalked over to them.

"Get out of here," she said fiercely. "This is the grave of a dead soldier. Get out or I'll have you thrown out."

"Sez you!" said the man.

But she stood there watching them with a set face and at last they got up sheepishly and moved away.

Her visit left Ricky singularly unmoved. It was as though now at last her early life had been cut off, or hardly existed. As though she had always been Ricky Wayne, learning to drive in city traffic the roadster Courtney had given her as a bonus, he stated, for Peggy; finding herself cramped in the small apartment now with two women and the children; and going out again with Courtney to theaters and dinners and dances where the men and even the women drank too much—as though drinking, having become the forbidden sin, had gained a new attraction.

She was not entirely cut off from the past, however. Once she read in a paper that Buddy Graham had formed an aerial circus and was barnstorming the country with it. It took her back to the time before Jeffrey's birth, to the blond boy in the drugstore with a handful of placards, and his statement before he flew away that he would build planes someday.

If there was any change in her, any dissatisfaction, Courtney did not notice it. For the office was a madhouse now. The old reliables were still selling, but from 1920 on there were new names to conjure with, the saturnine Lewis, big hairy Hemingway, Scott Fitzgerald, Hergesheimer, Heywood Broun, and many others. The newspapers were giving extra space to books. Had not the New York *Times* given two whole front pages of the book section to *Three Soldiers* by Dos Passos? They were all men, of course. But that young Englishwoman whose pen name was Rebecca West had written her *Return of the Soldier*, a slim blonde girl called Elinor Wylie was already scribbling verses on the backs of old envelopes and trying nearsightedly to read them, Dorothy Parker was wielding a pen sometimes dipped in gall but always in sheer brilliance, and Edna St. Vincent Millay was about to win the Pulitzer prize with her poetry.

Wayne and Company was doing well. *The Passion Flower* had sold enormously, against indifferent or indignant reviews, and had been followed by one or two other, almost equally frank about sex. Matthew had, as he said, washed his hands of the whole dirty business, and even George Mather did not wholly approve.

"When is the Privy Council going to meet?" he would inquire.

But Courtney stoutly defended the new independent. Many of this iconoclastic group stemmed from the war, a few from *The Stars and Stripes*, the soldiers' paper abroad. Always critical, as newsmen are, they had come back with no illusions but profoundly American. And what they were leading—whether they knew it or now—was a revolt against the English domination of American reading and American thought. The serious reviews had previously been dedicated to British authors. They had even invaded the lecture market, patronizing home talent and earning huge amounts. Now at last

America was to develop a literature of its own.

Not that there was any great change in the public taste as yet. All sorts of books were selling. They poured into the office, the neatly typed ones, the slovenly ones, some even written in pencil; to be entered on cards, rejected or held over. On Monday mornings the editors conferred. They sat with either the manuscripts or their own informal notes before them and made their decisions.

But Matthew no longer attended these meetings. He was getting on, in his sixties now. The financial end of the business was his, the rest he left to others. And his doctors had cut down on his smoking. Angela watched him like a hawk, counting the cigars in his box morning and night.

"For God's sake, Angela, let me alone. Stop nursing me."

"You'll not commit suicide while I'm around," she would say tartly.

Little by little he was relinquishing the actual business to Courtney. Some of the war problems were solved by that time. There were still strikes, but there was more paper, some of the pulp from Sweden. And Courtney was glad to take over. It was to him now that final decisions were brought, the size of the books, the grade of paper, the number to be printed in the first edition. Even the advertising layouts. A new man now rode herd on Mather, watching that he did not hold up manuscripts, and there were staff meetings in the directors' room with Courtney presiding, and the big table littered with drawings and reports.

Now it was Courtney who carried home the books as they came out. Already the apartment was crowded with them. He would pick one up and examine it carefully, almost affectionately, the binding, the jacket, the imprint.

"Got a fine review for this in next Sunday's *Times*," he would tell Ricky. Or perhaps the reception was not so good, in spite of the suave letters he or Mather had sent out. He was still young enough in the business to be resentful. "What's the matter with these fellows?" he would ask indignantly. "It's a damn good story."

True to his resolution he was seeing little of Emmy. He saw her only in the office, and as often as not she made her reports to George Mather. If Mather disliked and distrusted her, at least he admired her shrewdness. He would lean back in his chair and eye her.

"Lots of brains under that bleached thatch of yours, Emmy," he would say.

She would tilt her eyebrows at him.

"What's wrong with my hair? Better men than you have liked it."

Once or twice she suggested he take her to lunch or buy her a drink but she never got very far with him.

"Look, Emmy, don't waste any time on me. I'm an old married man."

She would laugh good-humoredly.

"It never hurts to try."

But there were times when he felt rather sorry for her. Once in a while she would come in looking yellow under her make-up, to borrow some aspirin and carry it to the water cooler to swallow.

"Had a big evening last night."

"A girl has to relax now and then."

He suspected that she had been in love with Courtney for a long time. And that he was now avoiding her. But one day he saw an envelope addressed to her on Court's desk and picked it up.

"She's been paid, Court."

"I know that. She's in trouble about her rent."

Mather stood looking down at him, at his harassed face and big sagging shoulders.

"See here, Court," he said, "that's not very smart of you."

"What the hell am I to do? Let her be evicted?"

"I hardly think it will come to that," Mather said dryly.

Matthew, shut off at the other end of the long floor, knew nothing of all this. To him Emmy Baldwin was merely one of their readers, a bleached-blonde hussy whom he saw occasionally at a distance smoking and swinging her hips. He was uneasy, although not about her. Already with Harding's death there was threat of an oil scandal, and Matthew's old friend Doheny was involved in it.

"Anyone with sense knows what the navy's game is," he told Elizabeth. "They want to store oil on the West Coast in case of trouble with the Japs. Only of course it has to be secret, so it won't upset the dirty bastards."

He never realized that the reverberation of the Teapot Dome scandal had sounded the death knell of the Republican party in the years to come. And the thing was not over. One day Courtney came into his office and, lighting a cigarette, sat down.

"How would you feel about a book on Harding, Dad?" he inquired.

"My God! Can't they let the dead rest?"

Courtney grinned.

"I understand this one is to be different. It seems he has an illegitimate daughter."

Matthew looked profoundly shocked.

"And that's coming out in a book!"

"We've been offered a look at the manuscript."

"I wouldn't touch it with a ten-foot pole. But it's bad news anyhow," Matthew added heavily. "The Democrats get us into war and raise our taxes but we Republicans are supposed to wink at graft and the Ten Commandments. No wonder those Communist friends of yours are hopeful."

15

There was no doubt that the apartment was crowded. What had been more than adequate for two was now impossible for six people. By the time Peggy was two and Jeff five the situation had become urgent, and Courtney, coming home tired, would find the children still awake and underfoot.

"They ought to be in bed."

"You try it. They've been put there twice."

Young Jeff was both mischievous and headstrong, but he was a truthful child. When caught in some trouble or other he never denied it.

"Did you do that, Jeff?"

"Yes, Daddy."

"Then say you're sorry."

"But I'm not sorry."

"Do as I tell you. Say it."

"I won't."

Once Courtney smacked him, smacked him hard.

"Now are you sorry?"

But Jeffrey only gave him a cold stare.

"I don't like you, Daddy. I want my mother."

In the end Elizabeth proposed that they buy a house.

"Every woman ought to have a real home," she said didactically. "I know I did. And look what a comfort our house has been, Courtney. Get Ricky a house. She'll love it."

Ricky, however, did not love a house. She wanted an

apartment, a larger one if necessary, but an apartment. In the end it became almost a family fight, with Sheila supporting Elizabeth, Roberta determinedly neutral, and Courtney intrigued with the idea. Only Matthew was on Ricky's side.

"Why saddle her with a house if she doesn't want one?" he demanded truculently of Court.

"I notice you and Mother get along fine in yours."

"Yes, and the hell of an expense it is."

Ricky knew though that sooner or later they were going to have a house. A city house, not in the country where the children could run and grow rosy. A house as like Elizabeth's as Elizabeth could produce. In sheer resentment of having her life blocked out for her she took her car one afternoon and drove out to the country club. It was a brilliant day, and the course was dotted with men and caddies. Above the purr of the engine she could hear the sharp click of clubs against balls, the calls of "Fore," and over near the huge clubhouse there were tennis games going on, the girls in short white skirts, the men in flannels.

On the wide veranda a half dozen middle-aged women were patiently rocking. She parked her car and walked over to the building, but she did not join the women on the porch. Some quick revolt made her turn away. She would never be like that, middle-aged and waiting for Court: for Court to play golf, for Court to come home to her or to decide her life for her. She was not like that. She was Ricky Wayne, with her own life to live.

It was a revolt against all patient waiting women, although she did not know it. Against her mother in her dreary quiet house. Against Roberta, lying awake and listening for Sheila to come tiptoeing in. Even against Angela at the office, alone at night in her small apartment, and making a vicarious life out of the keys of a typewriter and the neat letters for Matthew to sign.

She went into the women's part of the club to clean up after the trip, but the girl there was like the rest. She was standing waiting in her neat uniform, and Ricky eyed her as she leaned before the mirror to powder her face and touch up her lips.

"Isn't it pretty dull in here?" she asked.

"It gets livelier about lunchtime."

"I should think you'd want to yell your head off. You can't even see out the window."

"I don't mind it, Mrs. Wayne. It's a job. I'm glad to have it."

Well, maybe that was what life was. A job. You did it as best you could, and what was the use of yelling anyhow? Her brief rebellion was over. When she joined the women on the porch later she was smiling, or giving a good imitation of a smile.

"Isn't it a wonderful day? Like summer."

They agreed, looking around as though discovering the weather for the first time.

"That's a lovely hat, Mrs. Wayne."

"I'd hate to tell you what it cost. I ought to have bought it on the installment plan."

The greenness about her rested her eyes. She felt peace stealing over her again. And when at last she saw Courtney coming in with the other men of his foursome, she waved at him. He looked pleased to see her.

"Hello," he called as he passed. "Been playing over my head today. How about a drink?"

She nodded. It was all right. He could have his mother and his house and his business. In the times that counted, when they were alone together and he held her in his arms, he was hers and she was his. She was no immature child now. She was a woman, fully ripened.

Yet her revolt was not entirely over. In the car on the way back to town he brought up the subject of the house again.

"I need more space," he said. "I need a room to work in, for one thing. The way it is now, with the kids always around—"

"They're in bed and asleep when you're working, Court. If you need more space, why not a bigger apartment?"

"I'm a house liver," he said rather sulkily. "I like to change floors. I like to go upstairs to bed. And you need a real home. Every woman does."

"That sounds like your mother," she told him, and he lapsed into resentful silence.

The house matter, however, was not immediately settled. In May she took a flying trip home to see her mother. She had finally had a letter from Beulah, scrawled on ruled paper with a lead pencil.

"Your ma is letting me go. I have begged her not to but you know her. She says she is hard up and will get a room somewhere. I think you ought to come out and see her and talk her out of it, as she is used to this house and to me. Anyhow, she acts queer sometimes. Seems like shes never been the same since Mr. Dave."

For the first time in a long time Ricky thought of Dave; that he was gone, that he would have no more girls, that he would not eat innumerable hot cakes at breakfast any more, or get her to tie the tie of his dinner jacket for parties. He had been an usher when she was married, walking shakily up the church aisle in his private's uniform, with the general and some of his staff in the front pews. And he had got rather tight at the reception later. Somebody had brought a bottle.

"You be good to her or I'll knock your block off," he had told Court before they left.

Matthew had promised him a job, she remembered, when he came home from the war.

"Come and see me, son. We'll have to take care of our soldiers."

Well, they had taken care of him. They had brought him back and put a small white headstone over him. On Memorial Day they would add a tiny flag. There would be thousands of such flags fluttering in the wind. Nearby would be the Tomb of the Unknown Soldier, and the monument to the dead of the Confederacy, facing South. And not far away the fighting top of the *Maine*, with the names of the men who had died on it.

She left for Ohio the next day, leaving the children with Hilda. She had not been back for a long time, but things looked much the same when she got out of the train the next morning.

The wooden station was shabbier and needed paint. The whitewashed stones that had spelled out the names of the town in the small garden beside it were no longer white. But the stationmaster knew her. He looked old and dispirited. And she remembered he had lost a son in the war.

"How are you?" he asked. "You sure look fine."

"I'm all right. How are you?"

"Oh, so-so. I'm getting on, of course. Town's not in very good shape. They say times are better, but we don't see it here. Too many fellows loafing around. No jobs. Well, we had our bit, I suppose. The camp brought a good bit of money in while it was here."

He got her a taxi and she drove out home. From the street she could see part of the old cantonment where Court and Dave had been trained and where later Buddy Graham had landed his ramshackle plane. It was a desolate waste, with here and there a pile of old lumber.

She had not wired her mother and as before it was Beulah who welcomed her.

"Well, for Gawd's sake, Miss Ricky!" she said. "Why didn't you let us know?"

She stepped inside. The hall was the same, clean and tidy, but like the outside it showed wear. The carpet was worn threadbare, and the small red Peruvian silver tray that had been her mother's proudest possession was gone. Beulah was eyeing her with concern.

"Your ma's out," she said. "She's looking for a room this very minute, and she's just about breaking her heart about it."

"What happened, Beulah?"

"Bank's taking over this house for the mortgage, and her so stiff-necked she wouldn't let you know. If it wasn't for Joe I don't guess we'd be eating much. You got my letter?"

"Yes. Thanks, Beulah. I had no idea it was like this."

"How's them babies of yours? Ain't I even goin' to see them, Miss Ricky?"

"They're fine. I've written to Mother about bringing them out, but she didn't seem to want them. Or any of us. I see why now. Things are pretty bad, aren't they, Beulah?"

The colored woman hesitated. Then without speaking she picked up the bags and carried them upstairs. Ricky took off her hat in what had been her room until her marriage—and after it, while Court was in Europe—and before her mother could return she proceeded systematically to go through the house. It shocked and surprised her. The piano was gone. It had been bought years ago when she was so short that her feet could not reach the pedals; bought so she could have the music lessons she detested. Now too she discovered that even the silver tea set in the dining room had disappeared, and both the pantry and the old icebox on the back porch were practically empty.

She was appalled. She turned on Beulah almost savagely.

"Why didn't you write sooner?" she demanded. "How could you let me go on living the way I do with things here like this?"

"She'd about killed me if I did, Miss Ricky. And don't you go tell her now, either. Just say you came for a visit, won't you? And if you've got some spare change I'll slip around to the store and buy me something for lunch."

Ricky gave her twenty dollars, and alone in the house she sat down to think. There was no use offering her mother a home with her. She would not accept it. Something had to be done, however, although she had no idea what.

She was still bewildered when her mother came back. She did not see Ricky at once. She stopped in the hall and took off her hat before the mirror there, and it was through the glass their eyes met. She did not turn at once. She seemed visibly to brace herself. When she did move she was apparently her old self, cool and dignified but not unwelcoming.

"You surprised me," she said. "What brings you here? You haven't left your husband, have you?"

Ricky laughed and kissed her cheek.

"Can't a daughter visit her mother? Aren't you glad to see me?"

"I'd have liked some notice," Mrs. Stafford said grudgingly. "Of course I'm glad to see you."

She was hoping, Ricky saw, that she could still keep up her pitiful pretensions. She inquired for the children, looked dutifully at the photographs Ricky had brought, and blandly ignored the smell of cooking meat drifting in from the kitchen. Not until the meal was over did she bring up her problem, and then obliquely.

"I'm getting on," she said. "Now with you gone, and Dave . . ." She drew a long breath. "I don't need this house any more. It's too big."

"Why don't you let me help you, Mother?" Ricky asked gently.

"I wouldn't take your money," she said. Her face flushed, her voice rose. "The kind of books you publish! You ought to be ashamed. Sex and more sex. And all this stuff about socialism or worse. I got up one day and walked out of the Reading Club, and I never went back. If that's what our boys fought and died for . . . !"

She was flushed with resentment. She was even trembling.

"I hate to think of your living on that sort of money. It's pandering, that's what it is. I wouldn't take a cent from you."

Ricky was left stunned and uncomfortable as her mother went up the stairs and closed her bedroom door. She remembered the old tolerant days when the house had swarmed with young people, and she found it difficult to reconcile her mother as she had been then with the elderly shaking woman who had climbed the stairs.

She did not reappear, and as Beulah said she usually lay down in the afternoons, Ricky got her hat and went out. She had no plan, except that things could not go on the way they were.

She still had no idea what to do when she reached the center of town. It too seemed dispirited. The street corners were full of idling men and boys who eyed her as she passed. She hardly noticed them, and if she had not seen Jay Burton's sign in an upper window she would probably have gone home again. But there it was: "J. C. Burton, Attorney-at-Law." She had not seen Jay since her last visit, and she felt rather uncertain as she started up the dusty uncarpeted staircase to his office. When she opened the door with his name on it there was a girl sitting at the typewriter, and Ricky suddenly remembered her.

"Why, Bertha!" she said. "I haven't seen you for years. Do you remember me? Ricky Stafford."

Bertha smiled and got up.

"I've seen you. I went to your wedding. Or rather I stood on the pavement and watched you go in. You were a lovely bride."

"It's funny. I was thinking about you not long ago."

"About me? What on earth—"

"We were just kids, and you slapped my face. I was wondering just why you did it."

Bertha was amused. She began to laugh.

"Me?" she said. "And you remembered it! Good gracious, if my folks ever knew I'd laid a hand on one of the high and mighty Stafford kids I'd have had my bottom spanked for sure." Then she sobered.

"I'm sorry about Dave, Ricky. I was away at business school when it happened. I used to be crazy about him, like all the girls."

"Yes. I'm afraid Mother's not over it yet. Maybe she never will be."

Bertha gave her a quick look, and she realized then that her mother's situation was probably well known to everyone in town. She flushed slightly.

"I wonder—is Jay in?"

"The boss? Sure he is. He's not busy. He'll want to see you."

She rapped on the inner door and then opened it.

"Mrs. Wayne's out here," she said. "Can you see her?"

Jay came to the door himself. Save that his sandy hair was somewhat thinner he looked about the same. Older than Court, she thought, as though things had not been too easy for him. Obviously she had taken him by surprise. His smile was somewhat forced, but he held out both hands to her.

"Well, well," he said. "You're a sight for sore eyes, Ricky. Coming to see me about a divorce, I hope!"

"I don't know exactly why I came at all."

Behind his desk, however, with her in a hard straight chair across from him he eyed her shrewdly.

"Maybe I can guess. It's about your mother."

"Yes. I—we—had no idea things were as they are. She won't take any help from us. Now she's losing the house. I don't understand it, Jay."

"I suppose the bank's held off as long as it could. But they can't carry the whole town, or the county either. You know the way we've been hit out here."

"I see." She sat back while he lit a cigarette and after hesitating offered her one. "No thanks. I smoke, but I don't care to just now. Listen, Jay, what do you hear about Mother? She seems changed to me."

He did not reply at once. He stared at the old linoleum on the floor beyond her, and whistled soundlessly to himself. When his eyes came back to hers they were full of pity.

"She never got over Dave's death," she said evasively. "She's shut herself off too much, for one thing. I understand she won't see people when they call, and she seems to resent a lot of things."

"Have you any idea what she has to live on? She never talks to me."

"Well, I think the sale of the paper brought her considerable capital. I don't know how much or what's happened to it. Of course she got Dave's insurance money."

"How much is the mortgage, Jay?"

"I've heard it's five thousand. The property is pretty well run down."

But she was certain he was keeping something back. His frank friendliness had turned to caution, and he obviously did not care to discuss the matter with her.

"I wish I could help you, Ricky," he said. "How about seeing old Jim Butler at the bank? He's an old friend, isn't he? They might compromise. The house won't be much good to them. There's nothing doing here in real estate."

He was relieved when she agreed. It was too late to go to the bank that day, however, and when she made no move to go he sat back, relaxed, and told her the small and simple annals of the town. He revived old memories too.

"Remember my old Model T? You drove it now and then, and were you a rotten driver!"

"It was fun, wasn't it? We used to take picnic lunches. It seems ages ago!"

"Only a hundred years or so." His voice was dry.

"You haven't married, have you?"

"No. There was only one of you, you see." His voice was light, but his eyes on her were steady. "As a matter of fact I had my mother until a couple of years ago. And a lawyer in a town like this doesn't make a lot."

When she finally left he sat for a long time behind his desk, gazing at nothing. He had been certain it was over, a boy-and-girl affair, to be smiled over and forgotten. But that day he was not so sure. When at last Bertha came in, she eyed him shrewdly.

"She hasn't lost her looks any, has she?"

He roused and got up.

"No. I guess that's all, Bertha. Better go home."

"Not divorcing the wonder boy, is she?"

"Certainly not. What put that into your head?"

"I didn't think she looked what you might call joyous," said Bertha. "But maybe that's none of my business."

She went out, to straighten her stockings and put on powder and fresh lipstick before she swaggered out of the office and down the stairs. On the street she stuck out an aggressive chin as she passed the men on the next corner. So, once she had slapped Mrs. Courtney Wayne, the town girl who had made a rich marriage! After she had passed the loafers she permitted herself a grin.

16

Ricky went to the bank the next morning, making the excuse to her mother that she wanted to wire about the children. The telephone was gone, along with so much else, and Mrs. Stafford made no comment.

She looked very lovely that day, even in the long waist and short skirt in fashion that year, and Mr. Butler greeted her warmly.

"Well, how's my girl?" he asked after he had kissed her. "They must treat you well in New York. You're a picture, Ricky. Hard to believe you have a family."

When she spoke of her mother, however, his cheerful expression changed.

"In a way she's a war casualty," he said heavily. "Only we don't have hospitals for people like that. If only these boys of ours—" He checked himself and glanced at her. "I suppose you found the house in bad shape."

"I'm not worried about the house, although I hate to see her lose it, Uncle Jim."

He grunted.

"Well, my dear, a bank is not an eleemosynary institution. Matter of fact, I'm a little puzzled, Ricky. What has she done with the capital your father left her? It was a sizable amount, according to our ideas out here."

"Wouldn't you be in a position to know?"

He looked slightly embarrassed.

"Not for the last few years, Ricky."

"I don't understand."

He tapped on the top of his desk with his fingers, as if debating with himself.

"I'd better tell you. We lost her account not long after Dave's death. She'd been making pretty heavy withdrawals even before that. I had an idea too that when she went back into the vault it wasn't always to cut coupons. One day I asked her in here to talk things over, and I got the tongue-lashing of my life."

"And you don't know what she did with it?" she persisted.

"Not actually. There's been talk, of course. I'd rather not repeat town gossip. Get her to tell you, Ricky. She's up against it now. She'll have to get help somewhere."

When she was outside again the sunlight made her dizzy. It shone against the brilliant red of the five-and-ten, and against the old-fashioned colored bottles in the drugstore windows. She had a feeling that the people she met looked at her with disapproval, her smart citified clothes, her broad hat, her high-heeled shoes. What could she do? she wondered. And what was the talk Uncle Jim had mentioned?

She tried that night to get her mother's confidence, but without result.

"I'll hate to see the house go, Mother. It's the only house I remember."

"You've got a place of your own now."

"It's not the same," she persisted. "Can't you somehow manage to stay on? Father left you something, didn't he?"

"Not much. It was gone long ago. I spent most of it on you and Dave." There was a brief hesitation before she mentioned Dave. "Then I gave a bit to the war memorial in the square. His name's on it."

"But even that—"

Mrs. Stafford's color rose.

"I'll thank you to mind your own business, Ricky," she said shortly. "I've managed my own affairs without help for a good many years."

She rose abruptly from the table, as she had the day before. Only now Ricky thought she looked almost frightened. She went up to her room, banging the door behind her, and Ricky turned to find Beulah at her elbow.

"I couldn't help hearin' what you was sayin' to your ma," she said, her voice low. "I'd just about made up my mind to tell you anyhow. Only don't you go and let her know I said anything."

"I won't, of course," Ricky said impatiently. "What's it all about, Beulah? Where's her money gone?"

Beulah told her then. Dave had got into trouble before he left. It was a girl on a farm—and she claimed the coming child was his.

"Not that I believe her," she said. "The way that girl carried on it could be anybody's."

Whatever the truth was, according to Beulah, her no-account father had made Dave marry her before he went to the war, and Mrs. Stafford had been blackmailed ever since to keep the secret.

"You know how your ma is about Mr. Dave's memory. It's like it was holy. Lots of folks know, but she doesn't think so."

Ricky sat down at the table, her untouched coffee before her. So Dave had had a child, or so the girl claimed. Poor Dave, going to war and wanting to live before he left. Dave at twenty-one married, and a father! Beulah put a heavy brown hand on her shoulder.

"Don't take it so hard, Miss Ricky. He was a man, young as he was. Maybe he knew he wasn't coming back. Them boys, they were all excited, and the girls were worse. That Annie Stewart was a hellion."

Ricky looked up at the wide brown face with its gentle eyes. "Even so, Beulah, it couldn't have taken all she had."

The woman listened. There was no sound from above.

"It took plenty," she said grimly. "It was a plain holdup. They came here one night before Dave left. There was a lot of shouting. The girl, she was bawling to beat the band, and her father was threatening to bring some sort of lawsuit. You was out with the lieutenant somewhere. Anyhow they got Dave in and he didn't deny it. He looked scared to death."

"So he married her."

"He married her all right. The baby came about five months after he'd gone. But it seems like that was only the start of it."

"Why? What else could she do?"

"Maybe you don't know about the war memorial, Miss Ricky. It meant a lot in this town. I guess she was afraid they wouldn't put Dave's name on it if this came out. She got that notion anyhow. And before long she had to buy them a farm to raise the boy on, and farms cost money. She even put a bathroom in it, although Gawd knows who uses it. And they were no-good farmers. They let the barn burn down. Maybe Annie was smoking in it, or maybe she had a fellow there. It's just been one thing after another, and your ma paying. Now she hasn't got anything left, they're raising all sorts of fuss. They got a nerve too, them Stewarts," Beulah added. "They named the boy David. They call him Pete, but David's his name all right. David Stafford."

Ricky slept very little that night. It had turned very warm, and she got up and sat at the window, smoking and trying to think. She could not tell her mother what she knew, but the blackmail must end. She knew now where Dave's war insurance money was going; to his widow, of course. And there was still the doubt Beulah had expressed that the boy was really Dave's.

But she never doubted after she saw Pete Stewart the next day that he was Dave's son. He had Dave's blue eyes, Dave's wide mouth and blond shock of hair. But the appearance of the farm startled her. It was run down and neglected, with the skeleton of the burned barn still standing.

She had asked Jay to take her to drive that day, and once in his car—no longer the old Model T—she had asked him to go to the Stewart farm.

He eyed her shrewdly.

"So you know?" he inquired.

"Yes. Beulah told me last night."

"Well, God knows it's no secret. Dave wasn't the first with that floozie, nor the last either. Cities are fairly decent compared with the country districts sometimes. Only the poor damn fool had to marry her." He glanced down at her set face. "What good can you do by going there? They're a rough lot."

"I want to tell them it's all over, Jay."

"Don't they know that already?"

"They've kept Mother terrorized for years. I suppose there's no hope of getting the farm back."

He shook his head. He had had the title searched and seen the deed signed. He had fought Mrs. Stafford over the affair until he saw it was useless. Of course she had sworn him to secrecy, and so far as he knew the Stewarts had kept to their part of the bargain.

"Outside of naming the boy," he added. "There was talk, naturally. Everybody in the neighborhood knew Jake Stewart hadn't a thin dime of his own."

They did not talk much after that. Ricky was immersed in her own thoughts. And Jay was remembering the old days when he had hoped to marry her. But she had chosen Courtney Wayne instead. And now he was a small-town lawyer, he thought wryly, making an occasional furtive visit to a girl in Columbus and spending his days behind a desk in a shabby office.

Once, however, he slowed the car and looked at her.

"I've got to ask you this, Ricky. Are you happy? Are you glad you married Wayne?"

She turned candid eyes to him.

"I wouldn't change anything, Jay. It was strange at first. Court was gone so long. I felt as though I didn't know him when he came back. It's all right now."

"And you're happy?" he persisted.

"Yes," she said, after a brief hesitation. "He's very good to me, and I have my children."

"That's a hell of an answer," he said, starting the car again. "Maybe it's not my business, but there was a time when I thought making you happy might be my job someday. Of course he's good to you! Why shouldn't he be? You're still in love with him, aren't you?"

"I love him very dearly," she said quietly. "And it *is* your business, Jay. You're one of my oldest and best friends."

He did not look at her again until they were near the farm. When he did he saw that she was pale.

"I didn't mean to bother you, Ricky."

"It's not that, Jay. If the father is there . . ."

"I'll be around. And it's a good day. The men will be outside. At least they ought to be. There's a brother or two. Maybe I'd better go in with you?"

"No. Thanks a lot. I have to do this myself."

They turned into a narrow lane, and the farm buildings stood before them—such as they were. An open shed was evidently used for the two cows in a field near at hand. Farm machinery, rusted and broken, lay in the yard, and a few chickens were penned in a wire enclosure, with the earth dry and bare. The house had been a good one. It was still good, for that matter. But the curtains at the windows were torn, hanging in rags, and some of the glass panes were broken.

A small barefooted boy in overalls was standing on the narrow front porch staring at them as the car stopped. Ricky put her hand on Jay's arm. He could feel her trembling.

"It's Dave's boy," she said shakily. "Dave's boy! He's exactly like him."

The child was calling into the house.

"Hey!" he shouted. "Somebody's here. Come on out."

Ricky never forgot her first view of Annie Stewart. She came out, wiping her hands on her apron, a thin, youngish woman who still had the remnants of former prettiness. Her red gingham dress was dirty and her feet thrust into run-down slippers. But Ricky's anger had died, as well as her fright. She got out carefully and smiled at the child.

"Hello there," she said. "You're a big boy, aren't you?"

He clung to his mother's skirts, staring up at her shyly. But by that time Annie Stewart suspected her identity. Her face set.

"If you're Ricky Wayne, he's your brother's kid. And don't make any mistake about it. He's no bastard. I married Dave. If you don't believe me—"

"I do believe you," Ricky said coolly. "Even if it was a little late. Can't we go inside?"

"If you like." Annie's voice was indifferent. "It's a mess in there."

But she opened the sagging screen door, and Ricky found herself in an uncarpeted hall, dirty with the mud brought in by men's boots, and with a bare staircase equally filthy. The farm parlor was somewhat better. To her surprise she saw her piano there, and Annie smiled unpleasantly.

"Yeah, that's where it is, in case you wondered," she said. "Your mother thought the boy might learn to play it. It gave me a good laugh when it came."

Ricky sat down on a dusty chair. She had stopped trembling. There was a picture of Dave framed in red plush on the mantel. It had been taken in his uniform, and he looked young and gay and heartbreaking. Annie followed her eyes.

"He did me a dirty trick," she said without feeling. "Got me in a jam and tried to leave me. My father about killed me."

"I'm sorry. But he made it all right later, didn't he?"

"The hell he did! They had to make him marry me. I was only a kid, and I was crazy about him. Then he had to go and get killed!" Her lips trembled, and she picked up a corner of her apron and wiped her eyes.

The boy had come forward now. He stood close by Ricky, his blue eyes fixed on her.

"Who're you?" he inquired.

"She's your aunt," Annie said, truculent again. "Now get out of here. Go and wash yourself. You're a sight." And when he had gone: "What brings you here anyhow? If you're just curious, you've seen the brat."

"I wasn't at all curious," Ricky said with dignity. "I came to explain some things to you. I didn't know about the child until yesterday."

"We wasn't advertising him. Not that I was ashamed. It was your mother's idea."

There was a stir outside and a man came in. Ricky knew at once that it was Jake Stewart. Annie's father. He was a towering figure of a man, unshaved and untidy like everything else, but also in a rage.

"What's Jay Burton doing outside in his car?" he demanded.

Then he saw Ricky. He looked at Annie.

"Who's this?"

"It's Dave's sister."

It took him a moment to recover. When he had he loomed over her, tall and almost terrifying.

"What do you want?" he inquired. "Ain't it enough that your brother ruined my girl? Ain't it enough that I've got his boy to keep? What's Burton mixed up in this about? I want no lawyer sticking his nose in my business."

Here, however, was something Ricky could face. She had been sorry for the child, for Annie too. But she felt nothing but anger at the bully before her. She got up.

"I came here to say that it's finished," she said crisply. "You've had all from my mother you're going to have. There's nothing more to be had."

"That sounds fine, coming from you! D'you want this story all over the town? I thought your mother—"

"It's all over town already," she said. "Everybody knows about it. I'm not denying the boy is Dave's. I'm sorry about that, but he married Annie, didn't he? She's getting his insurance money, I imagine, too. But I am saying that there is to be no more blackmail of my mother. You've had all she has."

He was taken aback. For a minute or so he could not find

words. Then:

"And what about you? You've got plenty. You married money. You want this boy raised right don't you?"

"I'm sorry," she said. "My husband and his people are not interested. My mother is completely impoverished and I have no money of my own. I would like to help Dave's boy, but it just isn't possible. You have a good farm here. You can afford to raise the child. After all, he isn't only Dave's. He's your daughter's too."

There was a quiet finality in her voice which enraged him.

"It's not as easy as that, my girl." He was threatening again. "I've had to mortgage this place. There's no money in farming now. If I'm to keep the boy—"

"You might try doing some work!" she told him quietly. "This place is a disgrace. My mother gave you a good property. Now look at it. And I'm serious about the end of things. You can shout about the boy from the rooftops. It won't change anything."

Just then Pete decided to throw some stones at Jay's car, and there was a noisy altercation from the lane. She picked up her bag and looked around her, at Annie, looking frightened, at Jake, angry and uncertain.

"You are to let my mother alone in the future," she said firmly. "If you bother her I'll see if there isn't legal protection for her. You've worried her long enough. Now she has nothing left. And I mean nothing."

Nobody went with her to the door. She left behind her a silence, broken by a string of oaths from Jake as she reached the porch. She found Jay examining scratches on the roadster and also swearing under his breath. She did not begin to tremble again until she was settled in the car and they were on their way back.

"I almost went in," Jay said, glancing at her frozen profile. "It sounded like trouble."

"At least I told them." She began to cry, tears rolling down her face. "But it's Dave's boy, and I feel dreadful. To leave him with those people . . ."

"He looked healthy. Well fed too, Ricky. I wouldn't worry about him. He's better off than a lot of other war orphans, my dear. Just remember that."

He would have given a good bit to have been able just then to put his arm around her and let her cry on his shoulder. In years past he would have done just that. Now all he could do was to give her a fresh handkerchief. When she had dried her eyes she smiled up at him.

"You're a great comfort, Jay," she said. "You're so solid and substantial and dependable."

And not glamorous, he thought dryly, or romantic, or rich. Just a fellow who sits on his backside all day waiting for some other fellow to get into trouble so he can get him out.

Ricky had a trying scene with her mother before she left that night. Mrs. Stafford was sitting in the living room, inert and detached, and Ricky drew a chair close to her and reaching over took her hand.

"Isn't it time we had a real talk, Mother?" she said. "You've had a dreadful time. I didn't know how bad it had been until today."

"I don't know what you are talking about."

"About Dave, darling. And Dave's boy."

Mrs. Stafford gave her a terrible look, of fear and almost hatred.

"What do you mean, Dave's boy?"

"I saw him today, Mother. He *is* Dave's boy. And it's not a secret. I know you've tried, but people *do* know. They don't hold it against him, either. After all he was very young, and he did marry her."

Mrs. Stafford was ablaze with resentment and indignation.

"You and your snooping around!" she said. "You'd bring out a scandal against your own brother, and him dead and unable to defend himself! To have to marry a girl like that—"

It was no use going on. Her mother flung herself out of the room, leaving her there alone. When Beulah came in she told her she had seen the Stewarts and she was not to let any of them in the house again. Beulah eyed her admiringly.

"You're sure growing up, Miss Ricky," she said. "Used to think you was kind of spineless. But no more, Miss Ricky. Not me."

Jay took her to the railroad station that night. Both of them were rather silent. They shook hands almost formally, and he stood waiting until the train had pulled out. After that he drove back to his apartment over the bank building. He parked his car in the alley as usual and went upstairs. The rooms were dark, and even after he turned on the lights they looked hopelessly dreary. His small sitting room had been furnished by the Bon Ton Furniture store, a couch, two chairs, a lamp and table. By the window was the desk where he sometimes worked at night, when he had work.

He took off his coat and, going to the kitchen, poured himself a drink. After that he picked up the telephone and called a number in Columbus.

"That you, Clara?" he said. "How about my coming over tomorrow? All right with you?"

Apparently it was all right with Clara. He poured himself another highball and, sitting down in one of the Bon Ton chairs, forgot to drink it.

17

Court had seen little of Sheila during the past year or two. Once, when the question of a house was being debated, he had sat by, amused to find her so changed from the shy girl who had been like a wraith in the house when she and Roberta first arrived. She was smartly dressed, with her hair shingled and her small breasts held flat in the new boyish form. Smart and assured, and doing well in the decorating business, he understood.

She had never come to the office, so he was surprised, the morning after Ricky left, to look up and see her standing in the doorway.

He was feeling rotten. He had spent the evening before with a group of young writers, starry-eyed revolutionaries who would have been scared to death to see their theories put into practice. They sat in a darkish room, on benches or the floor, listening to melancholy Russian gypsy music, and trying to drink Russian vodka, the taste of it not altered by the pinch of salt and sucking of a lemon that seemed to be part of the formula. But Courtney had staggered out at midnight, fed up with Russia, which he considered a bloody mess, and with vodka, which was even bloodier.

"Well, hello," he said. "Come in. I've got a rotten hangover. What can I do for you? Don't tell me you've written a book."

"I might some day at that," Sheila said equably. "I get a lot of material in this job I've got." She sat down and took out a cigarette. "I think I've found a house for you, Court. It's a bargain for a quick sale."

"Ricky doesn't want a house. You know that."

"She'll like this one. It's in the East Sixties near the park. It would be fun to do it over. I've got the key if you want to look at it. But I've only got it for twenty-four hours. Other people are after it."

She got out the key and put it on his desk, littered with promotion stuff, with the proofs of the fall catalogue, with cards, posters, and suggestions for window and counter displays. He eyed it without speaking.

"I'm telling you, Court. It's hurry-up stuff. And there's a string to it." She put out her cigarette and got up. "If you take it I'd like to do the decorating. After all, I found it."

He laughed for the first time.

"Quite the businesswoman, aren't you, Sheila? Well, why not?" he added lightly. "You're supposed to be good, aren't you?"

"I am good."

He was still amused after she had gone. But the idea of the house intrigued him. Apartment living was not good for children, in spite of Ricky. Also he wanted a library like his father's, where he could look up and see Wayne books around him. He put the key in his pocket, and that afternoon he took his mother to see it.

In spite of the warm weather the house was cold and dark, and the scrap of cement-paved yard behind it was bare and unattractive. Elizabeth, however, was enthusiastic.

"It's a bargain, Court. With a little remodeling it will be just what you want."

"I'd have to mortgage it up to the roof."

"I'll help you, if you need help."

"Thanks, I'll manage it myself, Mother, if I take it."

He did take it. When Ricky came home a day or so later he had signed up for it, and even made a down payment on it. He was still excited when he met her at the train. She was touched when she saw his tall figure and rather rakish soft hat in the distance. Here at least, after the past days at home, was something solid and dependable. She felt a warm revival of her early pride in him, of the days when he had towered above the other uniformed men, and of the days of their honeymoon when the clerk at the desk of their hotel had looked up at him with a cheerful grin.

"All ready for you, Lieutenant. And the little lady too. Hope everything will be all right."

He pushed his way through the crowd to her and caught her by the arm.

"Hello, darling. God, it's been lonely without you."

She was safe again, and secure. This was her life, Court and the children. Nothing must spoil that. He was still holding her when he called the taxi. He always seemed able to get cabs and headwaiters and clerks in stores without difficulty. And once inside he put his arms around her and kissed her.

"I have some news for you, Ricky," he said jubilantly. "I've found a house. You'll love it."

"A house?" she said faintly.

"What do you think I mean, darling? A barn?"

She tried to hide her dismay. To buy a house now meant they could not help her mother. All the way back she had been planning how to tell him the situation at home. Now she could not. And in his enthusiasm he did not notice. He was full of plans, the old high stoop to go and an English basement to be installed.

"It's pretty high," he said. "Five stories. I think we'd better have an elevator. Can't have you trotting up and down the stairs all the time."

"It sounds as though it will cost a lot," she managed.

"It will be worth every penny, and more, Ricky."

Just so years ago Elizabeth had talked to Matthew. Like mother, like son.

"You haven't bought it, have you, Court? You know I don't want a house. It means a big staff. We can't have a furnaceman, and a butler, like your mother and father."

He had had an arm around her. Now he withdrew it and sat stiffly upright.

"I don't expect you to run the furnace, if that's what you mean."

"Then you've already bought it?"

"I have, subject to the usual delays."

"You knew I was coming home. Couldn't you at least have waited until I saw it? I have to live in it, you know."

"Damn it all!" he said sulkily. "I bought it for you. It was to be a surprise. If this is the way you're going to take it—"

She was still bewildered when they got home. Courtney was still sullen, but the children were wildly excited when they saw her. Jeffrey ran whooping at her and almost knocked her down. And Peggy—who had refused to walk for her first two years, with an iron determination inching her way along the floor on her small bottom—held up her arms and rushed at her to be picked up.

Something which had been frozen in her for the past few days and in the cab with Courtney melted as she held them close to her.

"I thought maybe you wouldn't come back," Jeffrey said shyly, looking at her through his long lashes.

"As if I'd ever do a thing like that, darling!"

It was Peggy who struck the practical note. She wriggled off Ricky's knee and ran to where the bags had been dumped.

"I want my present. Where's my present?"

Ricky's glance at Courtney was stricken.

"Daddy's bringing it," she said after a moment. "One for you and one for Jeffrey. I had so much to carry. Just wait and see."

Courtney grinned at her, his good nature restored.

"Wait until tonight, kids," he said. "Let's guess what they'll be."

She saw the house that same afternoon. It daunted her completely, as did Courtney and Elizabeth's plans for it. They amounted to a practical rebuilding; and before long Courtney was bringing home blueprints of all sorts, laying them out on his desk in the den and holding them flat at the corners with ashtrays, books or whatever came handy.

"Look," he would say, "if we pare a little off this bathroom we can deepen this closet."

She tried to show an enthusiasm she did not feel. The size of the house appalled her, the high flights of stairs tired her, and the cost frightened her. Sometimes the architect came to dinner. He was a veteran too, a good-looking man, somewhat older than Courtney and with an engaging smile. He was apparently trying to hold down the costs.

"Now look here, old man, that's expensive. Better make the plans and stick to them. Changes after we start cost money."

In a sense, however, it was a relief. There were fewer nights when they went out to dance and drink, fewer nights when Courtney took writers out to see the town. If in a way he had substituted a house for a wife, there were times when he came back to her, passionately loving and needing her. She was maturing during those months, too. Perhaps he was a more experienced lover, or perhaps she was merely growing up. He was still careful of her, however. She was to have no more children.

It was when she realized finally the extent to which he was committed that she took her problem about her mother to Matthew. She hated going to him, and she was shivering with distaste and anxiety when she found herself across from him at his big desk. As usual he eyed her with his friendly smile.

"What's the trouble, Ricky? You look like a scared rabbit."

She tried to return his smile.

"I am scared," she said. "I hated to come."

He sobered immediately.

"If it's about Court—"

"It's not Court, or the house," she said quickly. "It's about my mother. I don't know what to do. She's in trouble, money trouble among others. Maybe you can think of a way out. I can't. She's losing her home, for one thing."

He looked relieved, rather to her surprise. For a moment he had thought the old German story might be coming out at last. Or even—for he was no fool—that Emmy Baldwin might have been making trouble.

"Well, better tell me all about it, my dear. If I can help I will."

She felt encouraged. At least she stopped trembling.

"I can't ask Court," she explained. "He's tied hand and foot with the new house. And I can't do anything myself. I have a dress allowance and enough to run the apartment. That's all. I thought maybe if you would buy Mother's house I could pay you a small rent for it. You see, it's all she has left. My father died in it, and my brother Dave was raised in it. To think of her in one room at her age, with no one to look after her . . ."

He looked increasingly thoughtful as he listened. The business was prosperous, but he had been trying to build up reserves against any future emergency. Also the expansion of the past few years had been expensive. Still, only five thousand dollars! And the girl across the desk was looking at him with eyes which were at once hopeful and desperate.

"I gather you haven't told Court."

"No. He can't help anyhow. I know that."

"What's happened to your mother's money, Ricky? I thought she was at least comfortable."

She had to tell him then, about Dave's marriage and the child, about the Stewarts too, and the farm. He listened incredulously.

"Why on earth didn't she go to a lawyer? After all, he married the girl, didn't he?"

"She's been trying to protect his memory," she explained. "Small towns are queer, you know. And she adored Dave. All the time he was gone she kept a light in the window for him. Even after she knew—"

She broke down then and began to cry. Matthew got up and coming around the desk put a hand on her bent shoulder.

"Now, now," he said sturdily. "There's nothing wrong about what your mother tried to do. Nothing shameful about the whole business for that matter—except in her mind. How old is the child?"

She dried her eyes and sat up.

"Seven, nearly eight. It's a bad environment, but I can't help that. The farm's all right. It's neglected, but he looks well nourished."

He sat back and lit a forbidden cigar. But for the grace of God, he thought, I'd be paying for some German child of Court's. He was sure there had been more to that episode than Court had ever acknowledged.

"So it's a boy," he said. "Queer how many boys are born in wartime. Well, let's hope they grow up in a peaceful world. I think I can fix it, Ricky. Give me the name of the bank out there. They may take less to get out of it. And this is just between ourselves. You're not to bother about any rent."

When she had gone Matthew sat thoughtful for some time. In some obscure way he felt he was compensating Ricky for the girl in Coblenz, and even possibly for the blonde hussy he saw around the office now and then.

Elizabeth eyed him suspiciously when he came home that night. She was dressing when he came in, and he bent down after his habit and kissed her bare shoulder.

"You must have had a good day," she said.

"Only so-so," he said. "Just clearing some things up. Always feel better when I can wipe something off the slate."

A few days later he called Ricky on the telephone.

"Everything's fixed," he told her. "They found a piece of land out there she didn't know she owned. It brought in enough to pay off the mortgage."

"She didn't own any land."

"She did since last week," said Matthew cheerfully, and cut off her thanks by putting down the phone.

18

That early summer Courtney was surprised to receive a letter from Professor von Wagner. He had retired, it appeared, and was now living on his small pension in Berlin.

"You must realize, my friend, that affairs here are still bad. Worse, I fear. The Republic no one pleased, and this man Hitler, of whom you know, is inciting the people to revolution. Now he is free from prison and well of his wound. He is supposed to be hiding, but his work goes on. I saw him once at my daughter Elsa's home in Munich; a small man in a cheap blue suit and a trench coat. He carried a dog-whip, for what reason I do not know. But Hans, Elsa's husband, tells me with pride that when he goes to have his teeth attended some friend always stands by him with a Luger pistol pointed at the dentist. So greatly he fears assassination.

"Otherwise all is well with us. Hedwig has married. Or have I already written this to you? My memory is not good as I grow older. Elsa's son grows fast. She calls him Otto. But I find myself to be lonely, with my dear wife gone and both of my daughters with other interests.

"I understand the times are very good in America. It has been my dream sometime to see your great free country, but I have no hope at my age. Now and then at the cinema I see your tall buildings. They look as though America having conquered the land is reaching toward the skies."

He answered the letter and forgot it. The fall list was large, and although demand continued there were many problems to face. A million books a year was roundly a million pounds of paper. And he had to find the paper. Sometimes it was scarce. The mills did their best, took in the pulp, bleached and rolled it. Then in freightcar loads it was shipped to the printers. But in this long and complicated cycle, from manuscript to completed book, a single cog might slip or a strike hold up production.

The public did now know this, but Courtney had learned it. He knew now that promotion was to sell books to the booksellers. Publicity was to sell them to the public. Wayne and Company was spending a fortune each year on both.

But as the professor had written, times were good. Coolidge and Mellon had managed to both cut taxes and reduce the war debt. And with returning prosperity, or what looked like it, there was excitement in the very air. All over town building was going on, apartment houses, office buildings. Crowds stood around the excavations while the drills bit into the rock below. Along the streets moved rivers of cars, dammed by red lights, released by green ones, and the pavements were crowded with pedestrians, going somewhere or nowhere in particular, but always hurrying.

The shops were filled with luxury goods, and with extravagant buyers. Now the war was far behind, the navy sunk, the army cut to a thread, and peace was not only here. It was wonderful.

It was America at its best, and at its worst. Sheila spent her weekends in Long Island swimming in private pools in the daytime, playing bridge for high stakes at night. Ricky took golf lessons, making her practice swings under the professional's eyes, trying to keep her head down, her wrists flexible. She would hit the ball, only to see it dribble a few yards on the fairway.

"Topped it, Mrs. Wayne."

"I hate to dig up the grass."

"Don't worry about that, I'll put it back."

When occasionally she played with Courtney she seemed to

be all over the course. He waited for her patiently while the caddy located her ball, and she would come in tired and hot.

"I'll never learn the fool game."

"You'll learn all right. You can't play a fiddle overnight."

But she knew he was glad when it was over and he could go back to his Saturday foursomes.

She was reconciled to the house by that time. On Hilda's day out she walked the children past it. It was only the shell of a house now, a thing of brick and beams, and old wallpapers. It looked bare and exposed, its privacy invaded, its secrets open to the world.

"That's our new house, Mother?"

"It will be, Jeff."

"Gee, it looks funny."

One day she asked Courtney about the cost. He was evasive. "It's more than I'd expected, but I'll handle it all right. Don't worry."

She did worry. With the dismantling finished, the shell of the house looked enormous, and now the cement in the small yard was being dug up for some planting there. It was Elizabeth's idea, an Elizabeth still in town and too excited to leave for Maine until later.

"But why a garden? We won't use it."

"My dear girl, your dining-room windows look out that way. That hideous bare yard made me shiver."

She felt sometimes that it was really Elizabeth's house rather than her future home, and a climax came when one day Sheila came to see her.

"I thought we'd better have a talk," she said. "How are you, Ricky?"

She sat down, jerked off her tight cloche hat and shook her head in relief.

"Aren't we crazy," she said, "to wear these ridiculous things? And look at our clothes. I've just had a fitting for an evening dress, the skirt to my knees and a ribbon for a train."

"You have nice legs, Sheila."

But Sheila said nothing. She fitted a cigarette into a holder and lit it.

"I suppose you know I'm going to do your house," she said.

Ricky stared at her.

"I didn't know," she said. "Of course I have some ideas of my own." She smiled. "I don't imagine we'll quarrel over them."

Sheila expertly blew a smoke ring.

"I wonder!" she said. "You know who's paying for the furniture and decoration, don't you?" And when Ricky said nothing. "It's Aunt Elizabeth, of course. She has all sorts of plans, mostly bad. We'll probably end with the devil of a fight."

"Elizabeth!" Ricky said, fighting to keep her voice down. "I had thought—well, after all I have to live in it, Sheila. I'd like to have something to say about it."

"Try and get it! You know her as well as I do. It's to be a secret from Uncle Matt. So don't say I told you."

"Does Court know this?"

"I imagine so. I don't suppose he could do it himself."

Ricky felt frozen inside, frozen and helpless. She walked to the window and looked down at the street. The children were coming home from the park. She could see their small figures, with Hilda shepherding them. When she turned her face was set.

"I can't go on, Sheila," she said. "I don't want the house. I never did. Now it isn't even mine, or even Court's. It's his mother's. Let her live in it. I won't."

Sheila shrugged and got up.

"That's your business, Ricky. After all, she's doing a kind thing. She means it that way. Anyhow, I'd go slow with her."

She went back to her shop on Madison Avenue, and to the layout she and Elizabeth had planned. She was good, as she had told Court, and she had brought in a lot of business. In the shop she carefully preserved her British accent, and the people whose houses she decorated knew she had belonged to the aristocracy over there, and got the impression that only the war had impoverished her.

"The old families are all going," she would observe sadly. "War and taxes, of course. It's the end of the old regime. When I think of my poor father . . ."

She seldom thought of her father, as a matter of fact. She left that for Roberta; a Roberta sitting much of the time alone in the small walk-up flat she shared with her daughter. In the mornings a woman came in to make the beds and clean the place. Otherwise she merely sat there, surrounded by the photographs of her lost life; the one of Arthur in his uniform, the earlier one of herself in court dress when she had been presented, and one of a small Sheila in their Sussex garden, laughing and showing the bands on her teeth.

To her Sheila told the story of the afternoon, and Roberta was troubled.

"Why should Elizabeth try to dominate her life? Ricky is no child."

"She means all right."

"The world is full of people who mean well and destroy whatever they touch."

She went around to Courtney's apartment that night after Sheila had dressed and gone out. But Ricky was shut in her room and the whole atmosphere was strained.

"We've had the hell of a row," Courtney told her. "Ricky went to Mother's this afternoon and raised the devil about the house."

"Whose house is it, Court?"

"Don't *you* start that, Aunt Roberta. If Mother's putting up the money she has a right to some say about what goes into it."

"So has Ricky."

"Well, she will have," he said impatiently. "Look, Aunt Roberta, let's both keep out of this. It will settle itself. Ricky got excited today. That's all."

In a sense it did settle itself. Now and then Elizabeth consulted Ricky. Rather, she showed her the plans, the marble floor in the entrance hall, the iron railing to the staircase, the wall fountain in the hall at the head of the stairs. Ricky especially disliked the idea of the wall fountain. Elizabeth had picked it up at an auction, a hideous yellow marble bowl supported by two fat and ugly bronze cherubs. But it had already been bought.

She had no one to consult. Courtney was busy and irritable, for he and his father still differed at times over the policy of the firm. Matthew was ruggedly nationalist.

"We made a mess of Europe. Now let's keep out."

"People want informative books."

"All right, let them read about America. What's the matter with loving your own country? We used to call it patriotism and be damned proud of it. What's the matter with being an American? To read some of these fellows—"

But now and then when it rained he would see Court's faint limp, and look up at his tired face.

"All right. Go ahead son," he would say. "I guess I'm getting old."

To his rage and disgust, however, he learned belatedly one day that they had lost Anne Lockwood. Emmy Baldwin had read her last manuscript, and instead of her usual report had merely written "This stinks" in large letters on the box and brought it back.

It caught both Courtney and Mather at a bad time. The spring day was warm, and a new strike was holding up production. Courtney looked at Emmy's indictment and pushed the box over to Mather.

"What about her? Do we need her?"

"Hell, we don't need anybody. We ought to get rid of some we've got. Anyhow, I looked over the stuff. It's the usual thing, neither worse nor better."

Nobody consulted Matthew. Courtney wrote a polite letter.

"My dear Mrs. Lockwood: We are sorry indeed to return the manuscript of your last book.

"We have been proud to have you among our authors, and

we hope you will continue so. But the readers are rather disappointed in the last story. It seems dated. After all, we have passed into a new era. The war . . ."

He suggested that Anne come in and talk to him about other work, but she did not do so, and when Matthew learned about it the mischief was done. Angela brought him the news.

"I thought you'd better know," she said. "You always liked Mrs. Lockwood."

Matthew blew up.

"Who did it?" he roared. "Who turned it down?"

"Well, I hear Mrs. Baldwin didn't like it. She didn't even write a report on it. She—"

"Go on. What about it?"

"She just wrote 'This stinks' on it," Angela said happily. She detested Emmy, and this was her chance.

"She did, did she!" Matthew's voice was choked with fury. "Get out of here. I'll fix this. Get Court in here. Get George Mather too. And don't look so God-damned pleased."

The two men came in, Mather uneasy, Courtney ready to do battle. Matthew glared at them.

"You fellows turned down the Lockwood book?"

"We did, Dad," Courtney said firmly. "What about it? It was a rotten book."

"Who said it was rotten?"

"The report was bad. Just the usual pap, Dad. I read it myself. I couldn't take it."

"*You* read it? What about me? I'm still the head of this business, in case you forget it. I built Anne Lockwood myself. You didn't, either of you. Besides she's a damned fine woman and she sells."

"She did sell, Dad. Times have changed."

"Her sort of people haven't. I'll take a certain number of your highbrow books. I'll even publish poetry, although God only knows what they call poetry nowadays. But I won't have this sort of thing happen if I have to read every script that comes in. Who made this report, anyhow?"

"It wasn't only Mrs. Baldwin. We all saw it."

"All right. The Baldwin woman is out. And keep her out of this office. I don't want to see that bleached head of hers around the place."

He wrote a long apologetic letter to Anne Lockwood that day, doing it himself in his cramped almost illegible hand. But it was too late by that time. She had already sent the manuscript to another publisher.

She had to sell it somewhere. For years she had carried on, raising her children, caring for her husband, alternating between housework and her writing. At first she did not tell Tim, fighting tuberculosis on the porch of their small home upstate. Summer and winter he stayed there in his pajamas, struggling for air, seeing his children but not letting them come too close to him, and hearing Anne's typewriter going hour after hour. He was losing the battle and knew it, but he never spoke about it.

He was not bitter. But there were times when he wanted the typewriter to stop, when he felt he could no longer endure Anne's terrible industry. Nor was he fooled about the manuscript when it came back. From his porch he could see the expressman deliver it.

It was an hour or so before she came out to him. She was calm and smiling.

"What about the book? Wayne like it?"

She knew he had seen the parcel. She leaned over and touched his dank hair.

"Don't worry about it, darling. I guess I'm a bit dated. Maybe I can fix it up."

She brought her mending to the porch that day, an overflowing basket of small undergarments, stockings with the toes out, little girls' dresses which needed buttons.

"I'm taking time out to catch up on this," she said cheerfully. "The kids are in rags. You need some buttons yourself."

"On what?" In spite of himself his voice was bitter. "I don't wear clothes any more."

He lay there watching her sew, and wondering about what would happen to her after he was gone. He had been one of the first to go to the war. He had had no political opinions, no burning desire to help the French or the Belgians. All he had felt was that the thing had to be stopped. It had never occurred to him that he might get sick.

Now he was coughing his life away, and what good had it been? Now and then when he was able he sat up and made some notes for a book he had meant to write himself someday. He was going to call it *The Drifters*, and it was aimed at America. Because sure as hell the country was drifting. It had no leadership. What faith it had had was destroyed by Harding and not revived by Coolidge. So where, America?

He found himself in a cold sweat.

"What did they say about the story, Anne?"

"We're in a new era, Tim. No one wants romantic love any more. Not my idea of it anyhow."

"Who told you that?" he said truculently. "What about the ten million or more young unmarried people in this country? They're not all reading Dos Passos and Hemingway. They're still falling in love, aren't they? That's your audience. It always has been." He managed to smile. "Even some of the old boys and girls like to remember."

He drew a long breath of relief—or as long a breath as he could draw—when her book was accepted elsewhere. And once again she was working. The tap-tap of her typewriter went on, hour after hour. Sometimes he held his hands over his ears to cut it out, but she never knew this. She would stop to get the children lunch and send them off to school. Then she would go back to work again to pay the rent, the doctor's bills, the grocer and the butcher. And to escape for a little into the Never-Never Land of her own creation.

He knew now he would never write *The Drifters*, to warn the world where it was going. The only world he had was the small space of his bed, with his sputum cup beside him and the urinal on the floor.

That scene with Matthew had disturbed Courtney, although it brought with it a sense of relief. In recent months there had been some difficulty with Emmy. It had become an accepted thing that he continue to pay her rent, although he had not gone to her apartment for a long time. Perhaps he could get out of it now. It annoyed as well as worried him, for the house was costing him almost double what he had expected. It was being done on a cost-plus basis, and each week he had to meet the contractor's payroll. There had been strikes too, which held up the work. He was short tempered and impatient, and Matthew was not surprised when he came to him one day for a substantial loan.

"I could put up my preferred stock in the company as collateral," he suggested. "That is, I could turn it over to you, if you'll take it. I'm rather pressed for cash just now."

His father eyed him.

"Gone in over your head, haven't you?"

"Labor costs are higher than I'd counted on, Dad. But the way things are the house will be a good investment. Real estate in that neighborhood is booming."

In the end Matthew lent the money. He sold some stock and gave Courtney a check. And the next day he saw in the morning paper an announcement by another firm of Anne Lockwood's new book.

He swore and, crumpling the paper into a ball, thrust it into his wastebasket.

He was tired, and in September he joined Elizabeth at Bar Harbor. The season was over, and he spent most of his time merely sitting on the terrace and looking at the sea. Like Roberta. He watched the gulls too. Now and then they would stand by the fountain on the lawn, surveying the goldfish in the pool, but if he moved they would tuck up their feet and fly away.

The town was practically empty by that time. Labor Day saw the end of the season. In September children had to be taken home, to the dentist, to get clothes, to be prepared for the school year. Now the leaves were beginning to turn, to red and yellow. Soon the whole island would be a tapestry of color. The yachts were gone, the floats towed away to be stored against winter storms and ice. Now and then someone called to say good-bye, but Matthew spent part of his time down by the little cove where Captain Trimble kept his boat. It was quiet there.

He had bought a copy of the new Lockwood book on his way up, and one day he carried it there and read it. The paper jacket showed two lovers, chastely embracing under a lilac tree in bloom. He eyed it sourly. He could do better color work than that. But he liked the story. Perhaps it was dated. If so, he was dated too. Maybe Courtney was right, and that damned Baldwin woman too. Anne was writing about a static world, a peaceful world, safe and secure. Not one which had vanished with the war.

19

The house was almost finished by November. Elizabeth had installed the wall fountain almost over Sheila's dead body. Now they were quarreling again over Elizabeth's desire to furnish it after the new modern fashion and with Sheila holding out for copies of Chippendale and Sheraton. Between them Ricky was helpless. She was beginning to loathe the whole business.

Then in November she received a letter from Beulah.

"I guess I had better write to you, only don't worry too much, honey. We got Mr. Dave's boy here. His mother ran away with a fellow, and them no-good Stewarts have lost the farm. The boy ain't bad, but he swears something awful, and it takes a fight to get him into the bathtub. He is right good looking, like Mr. Dave, but he was in rags when your ma brought him here. She had to buy him clothes, and it makes it hard to manage with what we have. But your ma thinks the sun rises and sets on him, so don't you worry. We'll get along."

Ricky sent her a check, and that night she read the letter to Courtney. His reaction surprised her.

"Well, if she wants the boy, why not? There's plenty of room in that house. She may be lonely too."

"She has no money, Court. Just enough for the two of them. And she's not well. She oughtn't to try to raise a child."

"What can you do about it? She's got him. I'd say she has a right to him if she wants him."

She hesitated. Then: "I can't go to your father again, Court. He's done enough."

"What do you mean?"

She told him, mincing no words, and he listened incredulously.

"Five thousand!" he said. "And you went behind my back to get it. What does that make me, for God's sake?"

"You couldn't have done it. The house—"

"So it's the house again! I knew it would come back to that. It doesn't seem to occur to you that I'm doing it for you."

"You think so. Actually you're doing it for yourself, Court. I never wanted it. You know that."

He did think it over that night, shut in the little room he called his den. He did not want Ricky going to his father again, and there was some justice in what she had said. He decided that if he stopped Emmy's check he could send Mrs. Stafford perhaps a hundred dollars a month. He had continued it because he had lost her her job with the firm, but after all he was not keeping her. He seldom even saw her.

He called her on the telephone that afternoon and arranged to buy her a drink at a speakeasy. She met him without rancor. She knew it was Matthew who had dismissed her, not Court. He saw, however, that she was wearing a new fur scarf, which made him wonder.

He had taken a table and she sat down and pulled off her gloves.

"I suppose the business is going to the dogs without me," she said.

"We manage," he said dryly. "I'm sorry, of course. You know how it was."

"Sure. The dear old pater!" Her voice was ironical.

"Matter of fact you were wrong on the Lockwood book. It's doing fine."

"I only gave you my opinion. It's not my fault we have a hundred and thirty million morons, is it?"

He did not mention the object of the meeting until they had

had a couple of drinks. She talked idly. She'd made a killing at roulette at a house party in Westchester. Hence the scarf. But her eyes were wary.

"Now look," she said. "I don't suppose any sudden passionate desire to see me brought you here today. What is it? Don't tell me you want me back."

"No. As a matter of fact, it's rather the reverse. I'm in a mess. Emmy. The house and all the rest of it. Now Ricky's mother has adopted a child. I have to help her."

She cocked her head at him.

"Not yours, by any chance?"

He was annoyed.

"Of course not. Her son's boy."

"And so?"

"I'm as sorry as hell, Emmy. I've been glad to help you out but the plain fact is I can't do it any more."

"I see." She was not shocked. Perhaps she had expected something of the sort, but she did not like it. "I'm sorry too, Court. It's been a comfort. At least I knew I had a roof over me."

"You talk as if I'm putting you out on the streets."

"Well, aren't you? More or less?"

"You managed all right before, didn't you?"

"If that's what you call it."

She got up, pulling the scarf around her neck.

"You ought to be glad I'm the sort of woman I am," she said. "I could raise hell about this, you know. Only I happen to care about you, you big lug. Don't worry. I'll get along."

She left him at the table and went out, nodding to people she knew, flaunting her short skirts and new scarf. But she left only relief behind her. He went back to the office and sent a check for a hundred dollars to Ricky's mother, with a pleasant covering note.

When he told Ricky that night, he was astonished to see her burst into tears. She seldom cried. He pulled her down on the arm of his chair and held her there.

"I'm sorry, darling," he said awkwardly. "I didn't know you felt like this."

"I'm sorry too. I was beastly, Court."

"I suppose she'll take it? I wrote a nice letter."

"Not for herself. She will for Dave's boy."

They were closer that night than they had been for a long time. Emmy was out of the way at last, and Court felt warm with generosity and relief. He picked up Ricky's slight body and carried her into the bedroom.

Only a day or two later his mother called him up.

"Can you come in on your way home?" she asked. "Before your father gets here?"

"Of course. Anything wrong?"

"Nothing. I just want to talk to you."

There was suppressed excitement in her voice, however, and he felt uneasy. He felt even worse when she took him into Matthew's study and closed the door. He mixed himself a highball before he turned and surveyed her.

"All right, I'm here. What's up?"

"Court, I want to make some investments. There's a boom on, in case you haven't heard."

He had heard, of course. Wherever he went there was excited talk about it. America was at last at the beginning of a new era. Never mind dividends, take increment instead. Look at the country's resources. Look at steel. Look at oil. Look at copper, or radio, or automobiles. Look at the movies, now that talking pictures have come. Men at the club would scan the papers for the closing quotations or call their brokers.

"How'd things go today? Good, eh? Well, I was thinking, Bill—"

"You mean you want to buy on margin?"

"Of course. Everybody's doing it."

He whistled.

"It's dangerous, Mother. And what about Dad? He won't like it, if you mean using your bonds."

"I've sold some of them already, Court, to furnish your

house. Your father doesn't know it but if I can make some money and buy them back I'd feel a lot better."

He did not whistle this time. He sat down and eyed her soberly.

"I didn't know," he said. "So that's how it is! I'll have to pay you back somehow. It will take time."

That, however, was not her idea. She wanted to sell the rest of her government bonds and get into the market. She even produced a list, already prepared. Court inspected it while she watched him.

"I got it from a friend of mine," she said. "She got it from her broker."

"Not her butler, by any chance?"

She ignored that.

"It's a good list, Court."

It was. There was nothing wrong with it. He stuffed it in his pocket and smiled at her.

"I'll consult someone about it," he told her. "After all, I owe you the money, and if you want to take a flier and have a little fun, I can't stop you."

"Part of what I make is to be for you, Court."

"If and when," he said, and kissed her good-bye.

When Matthew came home he found her still in his study, her eyes snapping with excitement. He eyed her suspiciously.

"What's up, Lizzie? You look like the cat with a saucer of cream."

"Nothing's up, as you call it. Don't stare at me, Matthew. You make me feel like an old hag."

"You're always lovely to me, my girl," he said, and lacking a bare shoulder to kiss, bent over and kissed her cheek. He knew her, however. He smiled down at her.

"Just you mind your p's and q's," he added. "Lots of lunatics in this world. Don't let 'em fool you. And keep out of this market. Leave it for the easy-money crowd, my dear. Someday we'll sit back and watch them hunting for cover." He eyed her, but her face was expressionless. "Keep your bonds,

Lizzie. This is a balloon ride, that's all. Coolidge had better do something to stop it, or there'll be hell to pay."

She had made a small paper profit by the time the house was finished. As a result it was as nearly a copy of her own house as she could make it, from the marble-floored foyer to the short iron-railed staircase, from the elaborate bathroom fixtures to the equally elaborate kitchen. Sheila had won out on the drawing-room floor, with Courtney's library behind it and the long dining room overlooking what Elizabeth called the garden. But the bedrooms above were modern, shiny polished surfaces, angular but comfortable furniture.

Except for the red-painted door in the English basement, however, and the automatic elevator, it was only a smaller edition of the other house, and Ricky found it both familiar and strange. Yet she had to admit it was comfortable, even beautiful. Only over the daybed in Courtney's dressing room had she registered a protest. Sheila had grinned.

"For fights," she said cheerfully. "For the times when you never want to see each other again. It's a handy arrangement sometimes."

And she had not liked the idea of having the children on the floor above her.

"I want them near me, Sheila. Not so far off. They're used to it. They like to run in and out."

"They don't want to be under your thumb as they get older, my dear. I know. I was raised in England and they have the right idea. Nurseries off by themselves. It was fine. I could make all the noise I wanted, and when I was washed and sent down for tea . . ."

Ricky found it difficult to prepare for the moving. There was no room in the new house for the accumulation of the last years of strenuous living, and one by one she saw battered but treasured pieces of furniture going to the secondhand man. Then a day or two before the actual shift to the new quarters she went down to the basement storage room and found Courtney's battered old tin trunk. She had not seen it since it had been put there. Court himself had shown no interest in it.

"Nothing but old uniforms in it," he said. "Throw it out or stick it away somewhere. I'm sick of the sight of it. I came home in a duffel bag."

She had sent it upstairs, and the next morning she asked him for the key.

"Lost, I suppose," he said indifferently. "Why bother about it? What's the use of lugging it around?"

"Someday Jeffrey may want to see your uniforms. I'd like to myself."

He grinned at her.

"To remind you of the way I looked when you married me! Romantic, aren't you? Probably full of moths by this time. I feel a bit like that myself sometimes."

Now and then during the day, while she packed trunks and the drawers of chests and chiffoniers, she passed it as it sat in the hall. By the middle of the afternoon, however, when the children and Hilda were out, she found a box of old keys and sat down on the floor beside it. She did not try to open it at once. She was back to the night when she had stood on a station platform and watched a train full of excited men in uniform moving out; seeing Court's young face as he waved to her, feeling again the rain on her face and the tears she had not let him see.

Eight years ago, and here she was, his wife and the mother of his children. Some of the old feeling came back, a bit of the old ecstasy. She leaned over and touched the trunk with caressing fingers. He was hers. He was alive. Dave was gone. That could not be helped. But Court had come back to her. She was filled with gratitude, for him, for Jeffrey and Peggy, for all that life had brought her.

She was still somewhat exalted when she found a key to fit and threw back the lid. The trunk had been carefully packed. Contrary to Court's expectations, there were no moths in it. It looked indeed as though it had been freshly packed, his uniforms pressed and folded, the boots polished. She laid them out on the floor beside her, going through the pockets of the blouses automatically as she did so. It was not until she had almost reached the last of them that she found the letter on thin foreign paper and merely addressed "Courtney" in a foreign hand.

It had not been sealed. It was merely there, like a bomb or a hand grenade, only dangerous if exploded. Not that she so regarded it. It was simply something he had overlooked or forgotten. He was always careless about such matters. Only when she had slid it out of the envelope and glanced at it did she realize its importance. Then it was too late. She was already reading it.

"My dearest," it began. "I am putting this where you will find it on the ship, or when you are far away in your own country. It is my farewell, which I cannot speak before my family. Also it is my prayer that I have made you happy and not lonely. I know you have loved me. Women always know. And—now I tell you, as I could not before—I shall have something of yours to keep you in my heart always. Do not worry. I am proud and happy about it. And I am always yours. Elsa."

She sat staring at it dazedly. All the long bitter waiting for him to come home, and this girl, this German girl, comforting and loving him. And being loved. The tone of the letter was too assured to doubt that. She remembered his homecoming, the almost remote look he had given her on the pier after he left the ship, her own feeling of strangeness, as though he was not the boy she had married, as though something had come between them.

Now she knew that it had.

She was no longer the ignorant girl of those days. She knew men were often unfaithful. Probably Court had been no virgin when he married her. And in a war the bars were down for many of them. But this had been no casual affair. That was implicit in every word. This Elsa had loved and been loved. And what had been the thing she could not tell? A child, of course? A German child, coming to Court and this girl, like Dave and Annie Stewart. A child like the dirty little boy who had thrown stones at Jay's car that day. But then, of course, it would be clean. The Germans were clean people.

A child. Court's child.

All the life had gone out of her. In the kitchen she could hear Carrie, the cook, packing her pots and pans, and the children would soon be home. She got up dazedly and carried the letter into their bedroom. She should have known, she thought; the change in his letters after the war ended and he moved into Germany, and the odd constraint she had felt at the Shoreham in Washington when he came back. The coldness in his voice that night.

"Good God, do we have to keep on talking? Are you telling me you don't want to sleep with me tonight?"

And her own reply, that she still felt strange with him, which in the end had sent him slamming out of the room and the hotel. Perhaps he was thinking of this Elsa even then.

She had no idea what to do. She hid the letter in her jewel case and locked it there. Then, feeling lost and despairing, she put on her hat and coat and rang for the elevator. The apartment was in chaotic confusion, but she left it as it was. She never remembered later just where she had gone, except that she had walked endless city blocks, trying to clear the confusion from her mind. It was a bleak winter day, with now and then a flurry of fine snow. It fell and melted, and after a while it turned to rain. The buildings she passed looked dingy and ugly. The pavements were wet and after two hours or so she discovered she was wet too.

It was quite dark and still raining when she found herself near Roberta's apartment house. It was raining hard by that time. Passing cars clicked their chains along the streets and her fur coat was soaking. On impulse she went in, climbing the stairs slowly, and rang the bell.

Roberta was alone. She was sitting with a teacup on the table beside her when the bell rang. She got up, unfolding her thin length deliberately, and opened the door. When she saw Ricky she knew at once that something was wrong. The girl's face was white and her lips almost blue.

"What's happened? Come in and get that coat off you. You're soaked. Do you want pneumonia?"

Ricky let her take the coat and sat still while she brought her a cup of tea.

"Take that. It's hot," Roberta said. "And I've put some brandy into it. Don't talk. Just get it down."

The tea or the brandy helped her. She slipped off her sodden pumps and managed a smile.

"Why do I come to you when things go wrong, Aunt Roberta?"

"Because I'm always here," Roberta said practically. "And because I've had troubles of my own, probably. What's the matter now? The house? I told Elizabeth you'd hate it."

Ricky shook her head.

"It's Court. I've just learned he had some sort of affair with a girl while he was in Germany. A German girl. It rather shocked me."

"And she turned up?" Roberta inquired prosaically.

"No. It's not that. I don't know, but I don't think so."

"Then why worry? After all, that was years ago, wasn't it? He's probably forgotten her name by this time."

"Not if she had a child. I think she had. She put a letter in his army trunk. I suppose she packed it. She as much as said she was having a baby. His baby."

These fools of men, thought Roberta viciously. Court and the German girl. Court and Emmy Baldwin. Arthur and God knows how many women. She saw Ricky's eyes on her and rallied.

"I doubt it," she said emphatically. "Don't tell me Court's supporting an unknown offspring all these years. And being German you can be sure they'd be after him for money if there was one. In the second place, what if there is? They'd like it over there, especially if it's a boy. They don't mind illegitimacy, if that's worrying you."

"But what am I to do?"

"Do? Are you going to make a fuss over what's over and done with long ago? Don't you suppose I knew my old Arthur had his pretty ladies for years? I remember once he had to choose between one of them and a decent bathroom in the house. He chose her."

"And you knew about it?" Ricky's eyes were wide.

"I knew Arthur," Roberta said placidly. "He was fond of me, you know, although I was nobody's beauty. He always came back to me, especially if one of them had been nasty and gone around with someone else. He needed comfort and I saw he got it."

Before this matter-of-fact attitude of Roberta's, Ricky's semi-hysteria began to look childish and immature. She made another effort, however.

"He wasn't in love with them, Aunt Roberta. Court *was* in love with this girl."

"Of course Arthur was in love with them; one after the other. He used to be quite desperate, poor dear."

She was very late getting home. The rain was over, but the street lamps shone down on shining wet streets. South of her as she waited for a taxi the tall office buildings showed row on row of lighted windows reaching up toward the sky, as though the night had not a thousand but a million eyes. The city looked unreal, like something out of a fairy tale, and the houses too had lights in the windows, as though to welcome home some tired wayfarer.

She was going back. She knew that, back to her husband and her children, and tomorrow to her own house. But in the cab she realized that something had gone out of her marriage—her faith in Courtney, her sense of security, for herself and hers.

Courtney was already at home when she got there. He was sitting on the floor beside the trunk, with his bad leg stretched out as though it bothered him—as it did in bad weather—and with the children crawling over him. They had had their supper and been bathed. Now in their nightclothes covered with diminutive bathrobes they were clean and sweet as they rushed to her.

"Daddy's showing us his uniforms! Come and look. He's got a helmet too. A German helmet with a hole in it."

Court was smiling.

"I'd clean forgotten this old stuff," he said. "How about a kiss for your soldier boy?"

She hesitated only a second. Then she bent down and kissed him. He looked happy and excited, with his children swarming about him and the stuff spread out around him.

"Don't touch that gun, Jeff. Give it to me."

No, she would never spoil things for all of them. It was over, long over. She looked down at the things on the floor.

"Do you want to keep all that, Court?"

"It doesn't take up much room. I'll bet I couldn't get into these uniforms now."

He got up carefully, picked up a blouse and pulling off his coat put it on. Or tried to. It was too small, however; too tight in the waist and too narrow in the shoulders. He eyed himself in the hall mirror, as the children laughed.

"Great Scott," he said. "What a kid I must have been! And I thought I'd kept my figure pretty well!"

Ricky watched him. Of course he had been a kid. The German episode had been a part of his youth, of the reaction after the war, of the very loneliness the girl had mentioned. Young and alive, terribly and grimly alive, after seeing death all around him for so long.

The hard tight band around her chest relaxed.

"You *have* kept your figure, Court. You've grown up. You're a man now. That's all."

He stripped off the blouse, with its high constricting collar, and dropped it into the trunk.

"Remember, hands off the gun, kids," he said. "Someday I'll teach you to shoot, Jeff. When you're a big boy."

"And me too." This was Peggy.

"You too, of course. Now here's Hilda. Off to bed, both of you. Tomorrow night you'll sleep in the new house. That will be fun, won't it?"

Ricky went in to change for dinner. She took off her wet pumps and stockings and put on a negligee, since most of her things were already packed. The letter was still in her jewel case. She would get rid of it as soon as she could. But Court kept coming in, for this or that. Once he brought in a ragged dirty book from the trunk.

"Did you look at this?" he inquired excitedly. "I'd forgotten I had it. It's the diary from an advance observation post, marked not to be removed. I found it on a hill as the Germans retreated. It's one of ours and it's seen plenty. Look at the last entry, Ricky. 'November 11, 1918, A.M. Artillery fire ceases.' The end of the war, darling. Look, the boy's hand was trembling when he wrote it."

He even brought the cocktails into the bedroom before their sketchy final dinner. He was in high good humor, and she tried to meet smile with smile. She saw he was still limping slightly.

"Last drink here," he said. "To the new house, my darling. And to the loveliest girl in town."

She drank obediently. Like the boy in the observation post her hands were not quite steady.

"To the new house," she said. "And to all of us, in it together, Court. God willing."

20

Courtney cleared out his desk in the den that night, putting his papers in a box on the floor beside him. Now and then he wandered in to where Ricky was finishing her packing.

"Remember this old picture of you?" Or: "That's old Jenks, at camp. Forgot I had it. He was killed in the Argonne, poor devil."

Back of one of the drawers he found a letter from Walter, the chauffeur who had gone to Colorado years ago after being gassed, and he sat looking at it, wondering if he had answered it. It was dated three years ago.

"Dear Mr. Wayne: I am all right now. Have been doing odd jobs out here for some time. But I don't care for the West. I wonder if you know of a place for me. They say I ought to be in the open, and if your mother needs a driver I would like the job again."

Courtney felt guilty as he read it. He was sure now he had forgotten to reply, and after three years it was unlikely the address was any good. Nevertheless, he stuck it in his pocket. They could use him somehow, he thought. He had always liked Walter.

It was a distracting evening and it was late when they prepared for bed. Both of them had been busy with last-minute preparations for the morning. When he had taken a shower he came in to find Ricky already settled, the room filled with packed trunks, and his chiffonier already empty.

"Where are my handkerchefs, Ricky?"

"I left two out for tomorrow. They're on the bureau."

But they were not on the bureau. He wandered around, jerking open drawers without result.

"D'you suppose the kids took them?"

"They may have. They've been excited all day."

She got out of bed and pulled on a kimono. "I'll go and look," she said worriedly. "I hate to open your trunk again."

The handkerchiefs were in the nursery, folded to resemble vaguely a pair of rabbits. They were not too clean, either. She was apologetic as she carried them back. But she did not give them to Court. She stopped abruptly in the doorway, putting out a hand to steady herself.

Her jewel case was on the top of her toilet table and Court had the letter in his hand. He looked up when he heard her, his face set hard.

"Where did you get this?"

"It was in the trunk, Court."

"You've read it, of course."

"It wasn't sealed. I didn't know what it was."

"Well, you know now. That's what took you out in the rain this afternoon, I suppose. Where did you go? To Dad?"

"No. I had to think things out. That's all." Her throat was tight. "I meant to burn it tonight but I've been so busy, and you kept coming in—Don't look at me like that! I wasn't going to tell you about it."

"You had no business reading it. Letters are private property."

Her own face set.

"I have a right to know you were living with another woman after you had married me. I'm not on the defensive, Court. Oh, I know all the answers," she said wearily. "You were young. You'd been away a long time. You'd been through battle and sudden death. I told myself all that today. That's why I wasn't going to show it to you, even if she—"

"If you mean if she was going to have a child?"

Her temper suddenly flared.

"What else can I think?" she said bitterly. "That's what matters, isn't it? I could understand the other. What about this child? Are you supporting it?"

"There is no child, Ricky."

She stared at him.

"But she says—"

"I hear from her father now and then. She's married. He's worried about the way things are going over there, but he's never mentioned anything else. He would have if it had happened. Be sure of that."

She said nothing. He came over and stood near her, looking down at her gravely.

"Do you mind if I tell you about it? It's been over for a long time. I haven't even thought of her for years. And you'd have to know about conditions over there to understand. The awful boredom of the occupation—I almost went crazy. And she and her family had been through a lot too. I—well, I felt sorry for her. For them all, for that matter."

"Didn't you make them a poor return? To seduce their daughter?"

"It wasn't like that. It just happened. The man she'd been engaged to had been killed. Most of the young men had been. There wasn't much future for her. She got in the habit of talking over her problems with me. Then one night— Look, I don't want to talk about it. There's no real explanation. Certainly there's nothing to wreck our marriage about."

"No," she said slowly. "I know that. But I know you were still in love with her when you came back to me. That was hard to take, Court."

"From the minute I saw you it was over, darling."

She did not answer. It had not been over, and she knew it. But it was over now. In the back of her mind she knew that this German girl had been only a substitute for the early romantic years of their marriage, the time together they had lost and would never recapture. This tall sober man looking down at her was her husband, tied to her not only by the children or by habit and the thousand and one small things which unite a family, but by something more. Perhaps marriage was always like that. It began in passion and ended in the undemonstrative love and mutual dependence.

Court was tearing up the letter. He walked into the bathroom and flushed the fragments down the toilet. When he came back he went straight to her.

"That's that, Ricky. Let's forget it, shall we?" He stooped down and kissed her. "My poor darling," he said softly. "I'm sorry. I'm sorry as hell. You know that, don't you?"

She knew it. Her hysterical shock of the afternoon was gone and she lay content and tired in his arms. Tomorrow they would begin again, in the new house. But she could not sleep. Finally she got up, and going into the dismantled living room, lit a cigarette and sat in the dark. Just so, she remembered, had she sat in his room in the big house before his return.

He had not wanted to come back to her. She knew that now. He had come off the ship with his mind full of another woman, and she had been there on the dock waiting for him. She flushed with shame in the darkness . . .

She was never to forget the confusion of the first day in the tall house near the park. It was still raining, and the movers dripped over the furniture and the new carpets. She had brought the things she mose cared for, but so completely had Elizabeth and Sheila done their job that there seemed little or no place for them.

She had two new servants now, a parlormaid and a housemaid, who stood around useless and bewildered in the confusion. Elizabeth's old cook Katie had got them for her, but Katie was not there to order them about. She had been retired on a small pension. Elizabeth now had a Frenchwoman who never left her kitchen, and who served what Matthew termed fancy stuff.

"Good God, Lizzie, can't I have a plain beefsteak any more? Or a boiled egg for breakfast?"

The children ran wild that day. Hilda could not restrain them. They were up and downstairs, getting underfoot everywhere, with Peggy following Jeffrey in whatever he did. Ricky caught her with one fat leg over the banister and hauled her off howling.

"I'll put you to bed if you can't behave."

"You can't. My bed's not fixed."

Courtney had escaped early.

"Better send them to Mother's," he said. "She wants them and this is no place for them."

It would have been sensible, she knew. Yet she wanted them to have this first day in the new home, and somehow after the scene last night she was holding to them as part of her readjustment. It was not only a new house. It was a new life. Not a simple life, either, she thought, ordering by telephone the food for her enlarged household. There were four now in the smart little servants' hall adjoining the kitchen.

She was very tired when Shiela arrived at lunchtime; a Sheila who jerked off her hat as usual, shook out her hennaed hair and surveyed the mess critically.

"You'll have to feed me," she said. "Just an egg or something. I have to watch my figure. What on earth did you do to Mother yesterday? She said you'd been in."

She eyed Ricky curiously. But Ricky had herself in control.

"I stopped in to see her. That's all. Why?"

Sheila lit a cigarette and dropped onto the sofa by the drawing room fireplace.

"I thought she was upset. She likes you, you know," she said reflectively. "And she doesn't like many people. I suppose it's because you're all I ought to have been. You're by way of being a beauty, for one thing. She never had any looks, so she admires them." She glanced around the room. "I had my way on this floor, at least," she said. "The rest of the house is a bastard combination of fight, compromse, and Aunt Elizabeth's money. The money usually won," she added ruefully.

By the time Courtney came back there was at least a

semblance of order in the house. He stopped in the entrance hall and looked about him, with a fine sense of possession. Of relief too. He had taken Professor von Wagner's letters from his files and studied them carefully. They were purely friendly. He was anxious about a changing Germany, but nothing else.

The parlormaid had heard him, for she came forward to take his raincoat and hat. She was a pretty little Irish girl and he smiled at her.

"Like it here?" he asked.

"It's a little early to say, sir. But the house is grand."

"What's your name?"

"Rosie, sir."

He went on up the short staircase to the second floor. The drawing room was already in order, the lamps with their heavy silk shades lighted and a fire burning, and in the hall at the head of the stairs Sheila had turned on the wall fountain. It splashed gaily into the basin below, fringed with ferns and hanging vines. He stopped to inspect it, and he was still there when Ricky started down from the floor above. He looked up at her, his eyes wary and anxious, but she was smiling.

She had dressed carefully, and he watched her with pride as well as relief. It was all right. He caught her in his arms and lifted her from the lower step.

"Hello, beautiful. Love me again?"

"I never stopped, Court. You know that."

"How about the house? Kids like it?"

"They haven't stopped long enough for me to know. Hilda's exhausted. So am I."

He was boyishly happy all evening, boyish and lovable. She did not tell him how alien she felt in the house or even in his arms. And that night for once he forgot his worries. To his amazement his mother had sold all her bonds. They amounted to almost two hundred thousand dollars. She had handed him a check for that amount.

"Your father has given me some every Christmas for twenty-five years," she said gaily. "Now let's go in and make a killing, Court."

He put her out of his mind. The house fascinated him. He wandered about, taking Ricky with him and trying out the elevator, examining again the oil burner in the basement, even the new electric refrigerator. He took ice cubes from it and mixed them a drink.

"To us all, my dear," he said.

"To us all," she replied, valiantly smiling.

Later he lit a fire in the library behind the drawing room, and as though the last barrier between them was down, he talked about the war for the first time since his return.

"It was bloody hell, darling. That boy in the post writing that the damned thing was over couldn't believe it any more than I could. He was lucky too. There were a lot of men lost that morning. Everyone knew it was over, but the Germans had to send back to Berlin for men important enough to sign the Armistice, while the fighting went on."

But he did not mention the occupation. He filled a pipe—he was smoking a pipe now at home—and shifted to the business and his father's refusal to move with the times, or to expand.

"We need another floor in the building," he said. "But he yells murder if we spend any money. He's getting tight in his old age."

"He never seems old, and it's been his business for a long time."

"Too long, if you ask me."

She was indignant.

"You can't mean you want him to get out. I don't believe it."

"He could still be Chairman of the Board. It would let him take things easier. He sits in that chair of his day after day with that damned snooper Angela on the watch for fear I put something over on him."

She did not say anything. In the silence she could hear the fountain splashing in the hall. It made her nervous. She longed to turn if off, but she did not move. When Court spoke again it was to talk about the literary crowd he knew, of the enormously fat Ford Maddox Ford, of Carl Van Doren and Bill Benét, of John and Margaret Farrar, and of Heywood Broun, writing his brilliant book reviews in a bed in the center of his room, surrounded by bookcases and ashtrays. Doing his best work, according to his own statement, when "stimulated by the toxins of exhaustion."

Court was at his best that night, proud and happy and contented, there by his fireside. Nevertheless, they both felt self-conscious when Matthew came in. He looked tired, and when Court mixed a whisky and soda for him, he barely touched it.

"Your mother's at the opera," he said. "Can't take it myself. So I came to see how you're getting settled. Like it?" he asked Ricky.

"I have to get used to it, Dad. It's still strange."

"So is the world we live in," he said. "How long is Coolidge going to let the stock market balloon go up? He could stop it if he had the guts, raise the rediscount rate of the Federal Reserve Banks, do something."

"*We're* doing all right, anyhow," Courtney said pacifically.

"And how long is that going to last? Look at this new book club! I never expected to see a man in the publishing field break down and cry, but I did the other day at a meeting. Don't fool yourself, Court. It's a direct invasion of our business. Are the people so dumb that they have to have their reading chosen for them? It's an octopus, that's what it is."

He left them after that, but not to sleep. He was still in the library when Elizabeth came home. He heard her walking up the stairs in her stiff silver-brocade dress, and when she came in he saw she was wearing her pearls and her ermine coat. She glanced at him.

"Have a good time?" he inquired.

"Yes. Everybody was there. Have you been here all evening?"

"I walked around to Court's for a while."

"How are they? Getting settled?"

"Pretty well, I didn't stay long. Lizzie, do you think Ricky is happy?"

"I don't know what you mean," she said sharply. "Why shouldn't she be? She has everything."

She picked up her feathered fan and went out, but he did not follow her immediately. It seemed to him that what he had seen in Ricky's lovely face that night was a touch of heartbreak.

21

Elizabeth found the months that followed exhilarating. The market continued to rise, and she only laughed when Courtney warned her.

"It won't go on forever, Mother," he told her. "And remember this. We can't expect to buy at the bottom and sell at the top. I don't want to risk anything. We'll get a decent profit and get out."

But it was all new to her, new and exciting. When she went out to bridge parties she was one of a group of women most of whom were gambling in stocks. Sometimes the player who was dummy got up and went to the telephone to come back with the news.

"Off a little today. Nothing to worry about." Or: "Average is up two points. Very active market."

The vernacular began to come easy to her, and she learned how to read the stock list in the papers. Not that she let Matthew see her do it, of course. She waited until he had gone to the office or was asleep in bed. And one day she checked up with her list, sitting at the French desk in her boudoir, a smallish indomitable figure, adding as easily as she added her bridge scores. She was thirty thousand dollars ahead already. More than enough to pay for the furnishing of Courtney's house.

She seldom read anything else in the press, but Matthew snorted over the fine and friendly Japanese, the good neighbors the Germans had become, and the fact that bootleggers were making fortunes and paying no income taxes.

"How the hell do they do it?" he demanded. "Let me try to get away with ten dollars and see what happens!"

By fall at his own request he became Chairman of the Board. He sat at the head of the long table putting motions as they were made, taking the votes, and watching his business gradually ooze from under his hands. It had changed in the last few years, and he felt incapable of coping with it. The old methods had gone. Now the firm dealt as often as not with agents.

"I used to know my writers," he grumbled to Angela. "Now I never see them. I might as well be buying a new overcoat."

He missed the men and women who for years had sat across his desk from him and discussed their problems. He had known them well, their troubles and their successes. But now he hardly recognized the world some of them wrote about; a world where the young drank to excess, where sex seemed the end and aim of existence, where the underworld and the slums were more glamorous than the polite civilized existence he had always loved, and where new radical opinions were opposed to everything in which he believed.

To Ricky the change made little difference, unless to increase her own domestic problems. They were entertaining more, for one thing. One day, out of sheer annoyance with the long hair that made her dressing a problem, she had it cut. It made her look very young, but Courtney scowled when he saw it.

"What on earth have you been doing to your hair?" he demanded.

"It was a nuisance, Court."

"Not to me," he said sharply.

She had brought the long braids home in a paper bag. She put it away in a drawer and forgot about it.

The house and the children took most of her time. When they went out it was sometimes to a formal dinner, or she might find herself on the floor of some slightly darkened room, the silent center of a cyclone of furious talk.

"What do you mean, the state supreme and still opportunities for everybody? How do you get that way? Look at Russia!"

"The state could see everyone had an equal chance. The way things are now—"

"So you want to destroy individual rights."

"I want to destroy individual privilege."

"What is privilege? Hasn't a man the right to pull himself up if he has the brains to do it? This leveling of yours makes me sick. It wouldn't last more than a year or so. Then the smart ones would be ahead again."

Sometimes Ricky was dizzy with the noise. They made her feel ignorant too. They would throw Stalin and even Aristotle around like shuttlecocks. Apparently Aristotle had said that the function of the state was a good life for its people. Aristotle! Don't give me that! The old fool didn't know anything about the modern state. All right, what was the modern state?

"What do you really believe, Court?" Ricky asked after such an evening.

"Damned if I know," he said, grinning. "I used to have a lot of theories. I guess that's all they were, theories. I'm a peaceable gent, Ricky."

Now and then Courtney saw Emmy. She apparently held no resentment against him. Sometimes he even played a round of golf with her when Ricky was not available. She was still showily attractive, her brassy hair bobbed and carefully waved, her short skirt flying as she swung her club. They played a dollar a hole, but when she lost it was only a matter of bookkeeping, as the rent had been.

"That's three I owe you. Wait until I put it down."

Out would come the book. They would walk back to the bar and have a highball or two. After that he would drive her back to town, go home and take a shower, to doze over a manuscript after dinner while Ricky sewed, the fine hand sewing her mother had taught her.

He had no feeling about Emmy, except a sense of relief that she had gone out of his life. One day she made a surprise visit to his office. She swaggered in under the eyes of the girls and kicked the door to behind her.

"Look, Court," she said. "I've got some money. Not much, and don't look like that. I didn't sleep with anyone to get it."

He half expected she would pull out the black book but she did not.

"I've made a cash settlement with Bill Baldwin," she told him. "Twenty thousand and no more alimony. I'm going to invest it."

"Fine," he said heartily. "How about some bonds."

"Don't talk like a fool. I'd get six hundred a year out of bonds. I'm going to buy common stocks."

"Then why come to me, Emmy? Go to a good broker."

She laughed.

"I don't want a broker. Why should I? You've done pretty well with your mother, haven't you?"

He knew it then for what it was, a bit of more or less polite blackmail. He was annoyed at her mention of Elizabeth. How much had his mother been talking?

He put up a fight, or as much a one as he dared. He couldn't be responsible for her money. She remained insistent, however.

"You owe me something," she said. "I've behaved pretty well, haven't I? I lost my job here, I lost—well, some other things. If this is my chance I'm taking it."

It ended by his giving her a list of Elizabeth's stocks, as carefully selected as possible. She tucked it into her purse and got up.

"We'll call it even now, Court," she said. "And watch me go!"

When his secretary came in with the mail to be signed she found him deep in thought at his desk. He looked up, startled.

"I didn't hear you, Adele," he said.

"You looked as if you were asleep."

She was a small pretty girl. Secretly she adored him, but she would have died before she let him know. He signed the letters and checks, while she blotted them. Then he looked up at her, smiling.

"You're not in this market business, are you?"

She flushed.

"I have ten shares of General Motors, Mr. Wayne."

"Well, sell it and get out."

It was different with his mother It was useless to tell her that general business was not really good, that there was still plenty of unemployment, and that there was nothing under the market but hysteria. She was drunk with excitement.

The market kept on rising. Even Coolidge's statement that he did not choose to run for another term did not stop it. The papers showed pictures of his shrewd sober face, under an Indian bonnet; in a Stetson hat, fishing in the Black Hills, and fishing for trout with worms. But Coolidge did not matter. Look at the financial page. Look at Radio. Look at International Nickel. Look at anything you like.

To add to his worry he was certain that his father was suspicious. Matthew was, indeed. He knew his Elizabeth; knew this febrile exaltation of hers was not normal. But the real shock came in the fall of 1927, for that was when she had her face lifted.

She had not told him. She went to a private hospital "to be looked over," and she asked him not to visit her.

"I need a rest," she explained. "I've never seen this town so gay. I'm going to read some books and just rest."

He was worried about her. She had not been sleeping well, and she had been pushing herself—and him—too hard. Almost every evening for the past year or two he found himself in tails and a stiff white shirt either going out or entertaining at home. She was using more make-up than usual too, and he began to feel that she was showing her age. Always she had seemed young to him and certainly she was still her active energetic self. But it startled him to realize that she was in her late fifties.

So he was glad she was taking a rest; although the few days in the hospital extended to two weeks and more. He dutifully sent her flowers, and called her every morning.

"How are you, Lizzie? Feeling better?"

"I'm fine. Thanks for the roses, Matthew. They're here beside my bed."

"Still in bed, eh? I miss you, you know. Kind of dull in the house without you."

"Why don't you go out? An extra man's a godsend these days. I know you're being asked."

"I'm all right. Just you get rested and come home, old girl."

On the day she was to return he was back at the house early, to be there when she arrived, and he went down to the front door when he heard the car drive up. Johnson was already there, but Matthew went out to the curb and opened the door himself. It was late afternoon of a November day, and all he saw was Elizabeth in her mink coat and muff as she got out. He gave her a quick husbandly kiss.

"I was about to go up to the hospital and ask you to move over in the bed," he said. "Feeling better?"

"Fine. How are you, Johnson? I hope everything's been running smoothly."

"Very smoothly, madam," said Johnson, and gave her a strange look.

She preceded him up the stairs so it was not until she had taken off her hat that he realized what had happened. He stared at her in horror.

"Good God! What have you done to yourself?"

For there was Elizabeth, smiling carefully—she had been warned about smiling—with a blank expressionless face and the outer corners of her eyes slightly tilted upward.

"Don't you like it?" she inquired. "They're very proud of it at the hospital. I looked so dreadful, Matt. I did it for you."

That was what hurt. He knew she had done it partly for him. Of course, there were other reasons. She had her own vanity, like other women. But this mask was not his Lizzie's face. It was terrible, dreadful. It was as though he was in a familiar bedroom with a strange woman.

"I suppose I'll get used to it," he managed to say, "if you like it, my dear."

Then he did the bravest thing he had done in a long time. He went over to her and kissed her cool, unwrinkled, unfamiliar cheek. He could have wept. In fact he almost did. But if she had been anxious, the gesture reassured her. She slipped off her coat and went to her dressing table, laden with the gold set he had given her bit by bit over the years. She turned on the light over it and surveyed herself.

"Don't bother about my eyes," she said. "That's only temporary. I really should have had my neck done. They wanted me to. But that can wait for another time."

He left her as soon as he could and went downstairs to the library. There he closed the door and looked blankly around him. The fire was burning, the evening papers were on the desk; there was even a package of Wayne books. It was all the same, only upstairs— He did not look at the papers. He sat down heavily in his old red-leather chair, where he had sat on Court's first evening home from the war, where he and Lizzie years ago had wrangled over manuscripts, where later he had studied Court's reports from prep school and examined his bills at college.

He felt like a man who comes out of an anesthetic to find he has lost a leg.

He never grew entirely reconciled to his new Lizzie, although after a time he accepted her. Her eyes were less tilted, for one thing, as time went on. Nevertheless, he was as self-conscious as a debutante at her first party when they went out together. He could see the startled looks of the people they knew and hear whisperings behind Elizabeth's elegant slim back. It remained for Court to come out flatly when he and Ricky went to see her, the first night of her return.

"For God's sake, Mother! You look like a plaster cast. What on earth made you do it?"

But Ricky—you could always trust Ricky, Matthew thought—kissed her warmly.

"You look years younger," she said. "Don't mind these men. Did it hurt much?"

Elizabeth accepted the kiss, but her eyes were on her son. She made a face at him, or as much a one as she dared.

"Your wife understands, if you don't. And if you think it was any picnic—"

Matthew was grateful to Ricky that night, and later he realized that this had been the beginning of a new rapprochement between the two women. Whatever she felt privately, Ricky had risen to Elizabeth's defense that day.

Nevertheless, for months to come it was only at night, with the lights out and when he lay in the big double bed beside her, that she seemed anything but a stranger. Then in the dark he would lean over and kiss her good night.

"Had a hard day, Lizzie?"

"Much as usual, Matt."

Sometimes she wanted to yawn, but she was afraid to. She would put up her hands and desperately hold her jaws together.

He had other worries too, had Matthew. Court had purged their lists of the more radical writers but the thing was insidious. One day Angela told him they had a Communist in the office. He sent for the boy—he was hardly more than that—and stood him up in front of his desk.

"How do you like your job, Mr. Elwood?" he inquired politely.

"It's all right, Mr. Wayne."

"How do you like this country?"

Elwood flushed.

"I was born here. It's my country, sir."

"Is it now? That suprises me. I got the idea somehow you didn't care about it."

"If you mean I'm not satisfied with the way things are run, I'm not alone in that. A good many of us believe that there are certain inequities—"

"Sure there are," Matthew said. "That's the reason you're standing there and I'm sitting here behind this desk." His voice softened. "That's the inequity, son. You don't make men equal. They're born different. Some want to work and some don't. Some have brains and some don't. Think it over, boy. I don't want to lose a good man."

He wanted to go on, to tell him communism did not exist. That it was only another name for iron discipline, hard work, and bloody punishment; that it was a tyranny of terror, controlled by a small group of men shut off in the Kremlin and guarded day and night from assassination. But he looked at the boy's blank face and let him go.

What did he know of the churches, their icons gone and instead huge posters showing the former priests with their feet on the bent backs of the peasants? Matthew seldom went to church himself, but he was a profoundly religious man, and the new war against Christianity shocked him. His sense of property was outraged too by the liquidation of the middle classes, and the slum livers moving into the great houses, hanging their bedding out the windows to air.

It comforted him to think that his family was safe. He was not in the market, and if Lizzie was taking a small flier it was her money, after all. It never occurred to him that she had risked all she had.

He paid the premium on his insurance that day with deep satisfaction. No matter what happened to him it would take care of them, of Lizzie first and Court's children after her. He was smiling when Angela brought him the check.

"I hope you fired that kid," she said.

"He'll grow up," he said. "He'll grow up, my girl."

She snorted as she blotted the check.

22

By the fall of 1928 Jeffrey was almost eight and Peggy five. Already the boy was going to St. Bernard's; but to his disgust not in the school bus. In his fear of kidnaping, Courtney had hired a chauffeur to take the children about.

"That's silly," Jeffrey protested. "I'm no baby. I like the bus."

Courtney had been firm, however.

"You'll go the way I send you, Jeff."

He had sulked for a while, then accepted it. He was still a stubborn child, but a lively one. There was nothing quiet about him. He was everywhere, knocking things over, shouting down the stairs, bringing other small boys in to risk life and limb in boisterous play. Only Peggy remained much the same, small and fat and coquettish.

"She'll be a heartbreaker some day," Matthew would say, watching her.

Neither of the children had liked Elizabeth's new face. Peggy indeed had not known her.

"Who is it, Mum?" she asked in a whisper.

"It's your grandmother. Don't be silly, Peggy."

But Peggy had let out a howl and had to be banished.

Sometimes Matthew wondered if he had imagined the look of heartbreak on Ricky's face the night they had moved into the new house. Whether he had or not, he could not find it now. At twenty-eight she was still slender, her face as lovely as ever, with its short straight nose, its wistful mouth and broad forehead. Sometimes he thought she looked tired, however, and he worried about her. One day he asked her about her mother. She gave him her quick smile.

"She's all right, thanks to you and Court."

"Like to go and see her?"

"I can't leave the house very well. Anyhow I don't think she wants me much. She has Dave's boy now, you know."

Then something Roberta said to him one day made him wonder. It was apropos of something or other. He never remembered what.

"She's a brave girl, Matthew," she said in her dry crisp voice. "There was a time when I thought it was all over with Court and her; but she took that particular fence without a tumble."

"What fence? What on earth are you talking about?"

"Never mine what it was. It's none of your business now, or mine either. All men act the fool now and then."

So it was the German affair he thought. And the girl was a thoroughbred. If he had lost Lizzie—and he was not yet reconciled to the face he kissed night and morning—he had this little group to love and care for. He was realizing that as sons grow up and marry parenthood changes. Now he was only nominally Court's father. He was his partner—he hoped—his friend. But in his grandchildren he saw the fulfillment of all his hopes, his years of effort.

"Too big to sit on the old man's knee a minute, Jeff?"

"I'll sit on a chair, Grandfather."

"Well, well; growing up, aren't you?"

Peggy, however, loved to be cuddled. She craved affection. She would crawl on his lap where now his portly abdomen made a cushion for her, and look up at him with Ricky's candid gray eyes and with their heavy black lashes.

"Tell me a story about Fanny."

Fanny had by now developed a history. He was a notable peacock out of a king's garden.

"So," Matthew would say, "when it was a hot day Fanny would spread his tail and make a breeze. The king would be cooled off and all his courtiers—"

"What are courtiers, Grandfather?"

Life for Ricky had fallen into a pattern. True, it was an expensive one, now that there were five servants to be paid, including the chauffeur. In the mornings she did her marketing and shopping; and attended to the thousand and one details of her complicated establishment. If she felt more mother than wife sometimes she could do nothing about it. Mother and housekeeper, she thought, watching Courtney at the table to see if his food pleased him, or hesitating before she gave him the huge bills which her allowance never quite covered.

She was reconciled to the house by that time. She would never like it. She had never grown accustomed to the shiny surfaces and planes and angles of the modernistic bedrooms. And sometimes when the children were out and everything quiet, the drip of the wall fountain would get on her nerves so that she wanted to scream. She would turn it off; and when Court came back at night it was the first thing that greeted his eyes as he reached the head of the stairs. If it was not running he inquired the reason.

"What's the matter? Anything wrong?"

"No. I—it seemed so noisy—I forgot to turn it on."

"Noisy! That little drip!"

Because he liked it he would start it again.

But he was a good father. He loved the children devotedly. When they were sick he hung around their rooms, driving Hilda into a frenzy.

"She's all right, Mr. Wayne. It was that party she went to. She got excited and ate too much. That's all."

They went to a good many parties, Jeffrey and Peggy. The wave of extravagance had reached the children. Even the gifts they brought home represented the new factitious prosperity. And in return they gave parties of their own. Sometimes they had a paid entertainer, or a magician, to hold their bored attention.

"I slipped behind him," some mite would say. "He had that bowl of goldfish fastened to his coattail."

There were the nurses and governesses to contend with too. They sat like a coroner's jury watching the entertainment, the food, the favors. Ricky often felt she gave the parties for them. When they were gone she would go over her wrecked house, wondering if all this was good for the children and remembering her own childhood, with Beulah turning the freezer on the back porch and her mother watching the oven.

"For goodness' sake, Ricky, stop jumping. You'll make the cake fall."

She would pay off the hired butler and watch the caterer's chairs being carried out. Then she would take a couple of aspirins and try to soothe Hilda's feelings.

"You heard what the French governess said, Mrs. Wayne? She said Peggy was fat like a pig."

Ricky would have like to raise the children more simply, but even her own life was complex in the extreme. They went out to dinners, with bridge to follow, to the theater, to this and that. She was fitted for the expensive clothes Courtney liked her to wear, she had manicure appointments, and—now that Elizabeth had a box at the opera—she often had to sit with her there since Matthew refused to go.

It looked as though her life would go on like this forever. Certainly she and Courtney had settled down into the conventional married couple. He was gentle and even tender with her. And she had given up all hope of anything more. There were times of course when he wanted her, but he was an experienced lover now, and on this common ground at least she could meet and respond to him.

Some of his anxiety about his mother's stock gambling was gone by that winter, for the market was still going up. She told him one day she had almost three-quarters of a million dollars.

"On paper," he reminded her. "Isn't that enough, Mother?"

It wasn't enough by that time. Nothing was enough for Elizabeth, with her new face, her new car, her box at the opera. Nothing was enough for millions of other people too. Even the skyline was changing. Real estate was changing hands with dizzy rapidity and at fabulous prices. Jewelers were selling everything they had. Installment buying was filling garages and houses with gadgets of every sort, to be paid for in the indefinite future.

"How much is that Panama hat?"

"Forty dollars, sir."

"My God, what does it do—whistle?"

But the hat was bought. Furs were bought. Buildings were bought. At auctions, paintings, furniture, and silver brought far more than their value. One day Elizabeth bought a Raeburn for Matthew's library, a hard-faced English squire in a wig and a red coat, which Matthew detested on sight.

Matthew was still worried. "The world's gone crazy," he said. "How long will this sort of thing keep up?"

He still said nothing to Elizabeth, however. He had no idea how heavily she was involved. But one day when he learned that Johnson his butler was in the market, along with some of the other servants, he called them all in and threatened to fire them unless they sold and got out.

But the dam was still holding. Hoover had been elected in November of 1928, and Courtney gave Ricky a string of pearls for Christmas that year. He stood by the tree after they had trimmed it and pulled a flat case out of his pocket.

"Here's something I got at Woolworth's," he said. "See if you like it."

She was a little pale as he put it around her neck and kissed her. He picked up his highball and held it up.

"To my wife," he said, "and to us, my darling, here in our own home at last. To us, and to the children and the future."

She was happier that night than she had been for a long time. Happy even when he asked her not to tell Matthew they were real.

"I've made some money in the market," he said, "but you know how the old boy is. Fine as they come, but a bit behind the times."

He bought a limousine too that winter. In the evening now when they went out she wore her pearls and the chauffeur tucked a fur rug about her knees. There was a sense of unreality about it, but all their world was doing much the same. And down in Washington a sturdy, heavy-set man now sat behind the President's desk and watched the insanity of the country with apprehension. There was nothing he could do, however. It was too late.

Matthew knew Hoover and admired him. He knew he was a conscientious man; that at night he took his work from the Executive Offices to the Lincoln Study and worked there until his wife drove him to bed. But the floodwaters had been piling up since the World War. Now the walls were cracking, and he knew it.

That year Courtney put Jeffrey into the Knickerbocker Grays. Thereafter twice a week he put on his quaint gray 1812 uniform and went to drill. Ricky had lost her baby son. She knew it when Jeff began to walk and talk like a miniature soldier, and when on father-and-son day Court and Jeff marched together in the big drill hall of the armory she had all she could do not to cry. For Court too was once again a soldier, his head up, his shoulders square, his feet keeping time to the band with its corpulent leader.

But she was uneasy too. All those little boys, working at being soldiers. So small, so serious, stiff and straight! Did they know what it meant? Had Dave known, or Courtney, or all the others? Going off laughing to war, waving to the girls they left behind them on station platforms, and then—

One evening that winter Court came home looking amused.

"We've got a new bootlegger, Ricky," he said, as he shook

the cocktails in his study. "You'll never guess who it is."

"Not Aunt Roberta, I hope!"

He laughed.

"No. It happens to be Walter. You remember him, don't you? Used to drive for Mother. He was gassed in the war but he looks all right now. Doing pretty well too, he says. Has his own boat. Works off Cape Cod, or somewhere up there, then trucks the stuff down."

Certainly she remembered Walter; Walter trying not to cough, Walter showing her the Aquarium, and the Hudson and Central Park.

"That's the Flatiron Building, Mrs. Wayne. Way it's shaped, you know." Or: "Imagine the way the fellow felt when he discovered the river! Must have been something those days; trees in the Palisades and—well, just the water. Nothing on it."

Now he was a bootlegger. She felt rather shocked.

"It doesn't sound like him," she said. "It's dangerous too, isn't it?"

"He doesn't seem to think so. Says they play poker with the Coast Guard between shipments. Then they go out and chase each other around."

She still did not like it. Walter had done his best for her during that unhappy time before Court came back, a boyish-looking man who always forgot to get his hair cut, and smiled at her when Elizabeth's back was turned. Once when Elizabeth was dressing him down for some brief delay he had winked at her.

"He had a bad cough," she remembered. "Is it gone?"

"No cough, and he's better dressed than I am! He says his liquor is good. None of the synthetic stuff they sell around here or the Italians make out of stills in their cellars in Chicago for Al Capone. Not that Capone's stuff is bad. He has a graduate from Columbia to analyze it. But of course it's not the same. I sent him around to see Sheila. She has to have liquor for some of her customers."

Both of them would have been astonished could they have seen Sheila and Walter that same night in an Italian restaurant on Fifty-third Street. Walter did not drink, but he had brought a flask of Scotch and poured some for Sheila in a coffee cup.

"How is it, Miss Truesdale?"

"Wonderful. How on earth do you get it, Walter?"

He told her, over a minestrone and spaghetti with meat sauce. It was a game to him, but a lucrative one. "After all, if people are going to drink, get them decent liquor," he said.

He sat beside her, debonair and smiling and carefully dressed, and Sheila's gray-green eyes snapped with excitement as he talked. He did not eat a great deal. Mostly he talked—and watched her.

"You know you scared me to death when you first came over," he said.

"I did? Why?"

"Well, you see, I'd never known any people with titles before. Your mother was Lady Truesdale. Maybe you were something or other too. I didn't know. This aristocracy stuff—"

"Mother was an American, and forget the aristocracy, Walter. It didn't mean a thing. Mother brought me here to find a husband."

He looked surprised then amused.

"How's it worked out?"

"I preferred a job."

"Still free, are you?"

"Certainly."

"Maybe you haven't met the right kind of man."

She gave him a long sideways glance.

"Just possibly," she said.

23

By the spring of 1929 Matthew was definitely suspicious of Elizabeth. He had managed to accept her new face. After all, her eyes at least were normal again. But her excitement and her wild extravagance had him puzzled.

One day he spoke to Ricky about it.

"Look here," he said, "do you think Elizabeth's in this damned crazy stock market?"

"I haven't any idea," she said honestly. "I think Court was, but he got out."

"Well, maybe she did too," he said, his voice heavy.

He said nothing more to her, or to Elizabeth either. Years ago he would have demanded to see Elizabeth's bonds, have cracked down on any nonsense about what he called her nest egg. But this new Elizabeth rather daunted him. After all, the money was her own. If she wanted to play the fool with it— He lighted his after-dinner cigar and looked at Ricky, her shining head bent over some sewing.

"What about your mother? How is she?"

"She seldom writes, but Beulah says having Dave's boy has been good for her. It gives her something to do. But I worry about her. She's not very strong."

He smoked for a moment. Then he eyed her. "That's a nice string of pearls you've got. Real, I suppose?"

In spite of herself she flushed.

"They are why I think Court's out of the market."

"They look very nice on you, my dear," he said. "You deserve them."

It was foolish to try to keep things from him, she thought. He was old and wise and kind. They were both silent. Even the street was quiet. Only the splashing of the fountain in the hall could be heard, and she did not mind it when Matthew was there.

"Do all these things make you happy?" he asked after the pause. "That's the only use of things, you know. We don't need much to exist. Only food and shelter and enough clothes to cover us. The rest is trimming."

She smiled at him.

"I suppose I'll always be a small-town girl, Dad. All this grandeur bothers me sometimes. But I have Court and the children. Yes, I'm happy. I wouldn't change anything."

So it was over, he thought. Whatever had hurt her was gone. He drew a long breath of relief.

In early June of the year Ricky went home to see her mother. Later she would take the children to Maine as usual, but she went home alone. She had not liked leaving Courtney. He was worried about something, but he did not confide in her. So far as she knew the business was prosperous. Indeed all the world seemed prosperous. Even the town when she got out of the train. Her first view of it astonished her. Apparently only the station agent remained the same.

"Thought it was you," he said. "You wouldn't hardly know the place, would you? It's got rich overnight. But we haven't got a new station yet," he added. "Railroads ain't allowed to speculate. I'll take your bag."

A new taxi took her home. Main Street had been repaved, the drugstore at the corner had a fresh coat of paint, and next to Jay Burton's office a sign in a window announced a brokerage firm. The taxi driver looked at her in the small mirror in front of him and grinned.

"Old town's waking up for sure," he said. "Been asleep ever since the war. Now look at it!"

She was relieved to find her mother's home unchanged. It looked rather more weather-beaten, if anything, but at least there had been some attempt at repairs. The real indication of what had happened was a bicycle at the front steps and the sound of a boy whistling from somewhere in the rear. She put down her bag and walked around to the kitchen door.

Young Pete was sitting on the steps. He was wearing a pair of clean but patched overalls, and he was whittling at a piece of wood which bore a vague resemblance to a plane. As she appeared his knife slipped, and he let out a yelp.

"Jeez!" he yelled and flung the knife to the ground. "The God-damned thing—"

"You stop that talk, Pete," Beulah called from the kitchen. "You want more soap in your mouth?"

He saw Ricky then, but he made no move. She smiled at him.

"Hello," she said. "You're Pete, aren't you? I'm your aunt Fredrica. Don't you remember me?"

Aside from the fact that his chin was small and pointed like his mother's he was even more like David than before. He had the same eyes, the same unruly hair, even the same grin. Now he grinned at her in derision.

"I haven't got any aunt."

"I'm your father's sister, Pete."

"Haven't got any father either. He was killed in the war. And my mother was a bad woman. She's gone too." He sucked a finger, picked up his knife and resumed his whittling. "I'm making a plane," he said matter-of-factly. "It's going to be the best God-damned plane around here."

He had raised his voice somewhat, and Beulah's angry voice came from the kitchen.

"You talk like that and I'll get my Joe to whale the life out of you. Who you got out there?"

"She says she's my aunt," he replied indifferently. "I haven't got an aunt, have I?"

The visit had a nightmare quality after that, what with Beulah's excitement, her mother's restrained greeting, and

Pete. Always Pete. She saw at once that the household revolved around him. And while the boy was rough and tough, she did not think he was vicious. She noticed that his language was more restrained when her mother was around. But even Beulah spoiled him badly.

"He's all right, Miss Ricky," she said. "He's picked up them bad words at home, that's all. He likes your mother all right. As for her, you'd think she'd got your brother Dave back."

"What about *his* mother?"

"She don't never write. Old man Stewart's dead and the rest is scattered hither and yon. He's got nobody but us."

But Mrs. Stafford did not look well. Climbing the stairs left her breathless, and now and then she complained of a pain in her chest. It annoyed her to have Ricky mention it, however.

"Only indigestion," she said. "For heaven's sake, don't fuss over me. I won't have a doctor. I'm all right."

The house was still shabby. And a good many things were broken. The boy had a way of barging into the furniture and throwing himself into chairs. But before her mother he was at least careful not to swear, and his table manners were not bad. Only now and then she found him watching her warily, like some young wild creature.

"Kids around here say you're rich," he observed the second day of her visit. "I say they were liars."

He had been shoving the lawn mower around in a desultory fashion while she sat on the steps, and he had stopped in front of her.

"My husband works," she said, smiling. "That's the way to get along in this world, Pete. To work."

"I don't like work. I'm going to fly a plane someday."

"Flying is work too."

He only grinned at her and went back to the mower.

She stayed only three days. On the afternoon of the day she was to leave, Jay Burton came in to see her. She was surprised to see that his hair was turning gray. He was friendly and smiling; and his light kiss was a brotherly one.

"Let's look at you," he said. "I only just heard you were here. Bertha, of course. You look as though the world's being kind to you."

"I'm fine, Jay. And you?"

"Things are picking up. I suppose you've noticed. Even a lawyer gets some pickings these days. Not in the market yourself, are you?"

"I don't know anything about it."

He did not stay long. He said he had some work at the office, and got up. Then hat in hand he stood looking down at her, not smiling.

"I've missed you, Ricky," he said. "I guess you know I never got over you. Now it's too late for me to change."

"I like to think you're always here, Jay."

"I'll always be here when you need me."

He turned quickly and went away, and she watched him getting into his car. He was the faithful type, she knew. Like Matthew. She did not know why she did not put Court in the same category.

The limousine was waiting for her when she reached New York the next morning. As she stood at the curb she became aware of a woman in black standing beside her and realized that it was Anne Lockwood, whom she had met once or twice not long after her marriage. Anne had not seen her, however. She was staring ahead as though she was not seeing much of anything. She did not move until Ricky touched her sleeve.

"I'm Ricky Wayne, Mrs. Lockwood. Can I take you somewhere? I have a car."

Anne Lockwood did not start. She merely turned her head, her eyes still blank.

"I'm all right, thank you. I've just been taking Tim home."

"Tim?"

"My husband. I took him down to Arlington. He'd earned his place there. It's quiet, you know. He won't have to listen to my typewriter any more."

She got into a taxi and left Ricky, stunned and shocked, on

the pavement.

She told Matthew about the encounter that night. The next day he took a train and went to the small town upstate where Anne lived and worked. Tim's bed was gone from the porch now but Anne's typewriter stood uncovered on its table. As though she had only been able to take time out to bury her husband, he thought.

He felt guilty and ashamed. When she came down, he put his arms around her and held her.

"I'm sorry," he said. "I didn't know. How can I help?"

"We're all right," she told him, her voice flat.

"New publishers taking care of you?"

"Not as well as you did. I haven't had much time. Tim needed nursing, and—"

"I know. I'd better tell you, Anne. I didn't know about the other book until it was too late. I liked it when I read it."

"Did you?" Some of the bleak look left her face. "Tim did too. He took it rather hard when it came back."

He nodded. There was nothing he could say, or do.

He stayed in New York that summer, as did Courtney. Both of them for different reasons were apprehensive. Matthew felt that the solid ground under the business was threatened. He could not escape the hysteria. Even his club was no longer peaceful. Closing stock prices were quoted on a board, and there were always men standing around it, half fascinated, half terrified.

"Look at Radio! Look at Electric Bond and Share! It's fantastic."

It was fantastic. But Courtney's anxiety was about his mother. All his arguments had been of no avail.

"Don't be such a pessimist, Court. I'll get out in plenty of time. Don't worry."

"What if there isn't time?"

"That's plain silly."

He had never told Ricky, but at the railroad station, seeing his family off on the train, he finally broke down.

"See here, I want you to keep your eyes on Mother," he said. "She's to get out when I send her the word, and no fooling."

"Get out? You mean—the stock market?"

"I do," he said grimly. "If it breaks, she's done for."

"She's in it, then?"

"Up to her neck," he said sourly.

Apparently everyone was in it up to the neck. One day after they had all gone to Maine Angela walked in and laid a bill on the desk in front of Matthew. It was for a set of needlepoint chairs, and he stared at it in stupefaction.

"What in God's name is this?"

"Chairs," said Angela smugly. "I think they went up to the country."

"Two thousand dollars' worth of chairs, for Maine?"

"I wouldn't worry, Mr. Wayne." She was still smug. "With things going the way they are—"

He eyed her with sudden suspicion.

"Look here, Angela," he said. "Are you in this market?"

"I've done pretty well. I was only getting three per cent on my savings. Not that they amounted to much, of course. Now I have a nice little nest egg.

It seemed to him he was seeing her for the first time in years. She had a new permanent, and on anyone else her dress would have been smart. As it was it was certainly expensive.

"So you're a fool like the rest of them," he said heavily. "Get out, Angela. Get out and shut the door. I don't want to look at you."

He paid the bill with a set face and sent the receipt without comment to Elizabeth.

With the servants in Maine he moved in with Courtney that summer. The house was cooler than a room at his club, but he missed his own bed and his familiar library. The summer was very hot. There had been no rain, and the city water supply was low. Even the small-scale fountain had to be shut off, and Elizabeth's planting in the small back yard drooped and began to die.

Courtney was not often home. He was very busy, holding meetings with the salesmen, getting ready for the fall. The list promised well. Even Matthew, studying the catalogue, could find no fault with it.

"Not quite so radical as you used to be, are you?" he asked Courtney.

"I hope I'm still a liberal."

Matthew chuckled.

"Remember when the Bull Moose crowd was attacked because it advocated the eight-hour day and woman suffrage?"

"Didn't it advocate Prohibition too?"

Courtney had fallen into the habit of lunching at the Coffee House Club. There would be a scattering of other young publishers, painters, architects, writers, with good talk over the table. Most of them were only academically interested in Wall Street or the financial frenzy. They talked politics, or ideas. If someone had a good story, he passed it on.

"Say, heard what the Indian said when he saw the mermaid?"

He found it a good place to take his out-of-town writers. They were impressed by the men they saw there, and it was easy to talk business unofficially.

"Well, how's the new book going?"

"Not so good. I've got the body in a room bolted on the inside. Now I have to get the killer out."

"No windows?"

"Only one forty feet from the ground."

"Looks as though you'd have to use a human fly."

For now crime and mystery were exciting popular interest, if not critical glory. They had always had a following, of course. Woodrow Wilson read them, and the justices of the Supreme Court. But George Mather detested them. It was almost over his dead body that Courtney was following the new trend.

"Ever read any?" he asked Mather.

"No, with the help of my Maker," Mather said piously. "I leave them to the morons on the staff."

One day when Ricky had been gone a couple of weeks he received another letter from Professor von Wagner. It looked as though, having retired, he had more time for correspondence. But it was as usual entirely friendly. He wrote of Elsa's boy and Hedwig's two daughters. Then he went on:

"The Germany I know is gone. The people are carried away with this man Hitler, with his rasping voice and his nails bitten to the quick. Imagine if you can a leader who nibbles candy constantly while he shouts about the heartlands, and that we are to grow and grow, to the East as far as India.

"Now we have secret police who watch everybody. Do you know our Luther? He said when a prince is in the wrong his people are bound to follow him. This 'princeling' of ours is in the wrong. But where he would lead us, make no mistake, we will follow. The new geopolitics is another word for war."

He showed the letter to his father that night.

"Just to lay an old ghost, Dad," he said.

Matthew put on his glasses and read it.

"What does he mean about another war? Are they going to start all over again?"

"That's German pessimism, Dad. They're like that. They have a saying that an optimist is someone who thinks the future is uncertain."

Matthew did not smile. He sat still, in the seersucker suit he wore in hot weather, to Elizabeth's annoyance, and surveyed his tall son.

"The future *is* damned uncertain," he said. "I think we've come to a showdown, Court. How far is your mother in this market?"

It was a relief to have it out. Courtney put the letter down and faced his father.

"All the way, I'm afraid, Dad."

"She sold her government bonds, I suppose?"

"Yes. I feel guilty as hell. The original idea was only to make enough to pay for furnishing the house. But once she was on her way—"

Matthew got up and shook down his wrinkled seersucker legs.

"I know your mother," he said dryly. "It's been my theory all my life that a woman had certain rights—but she has no right to ruin herself, or me either. We have the business to take care of. We have our emloyees and our writers. And I'm not touching my insurance. That's for her after I'm gone, and for you and the children. I'm going to Maine and talk sense to her."

Court saw him off a day or two later. He did not take a drawing room. He had a lower berth, and he lay awake for hours mustering his arguments. As the hours dragged on, however, he was less and less sure of himself. He realized how adroitly she had managed him all their married life, the move to New York, the big expensive house, the people they knew.

He loved her, of course. He could not imagine life without her. When she had wanted anything he gave it to her, quite simply and without fuss. She had never known how close he had been to trouble during and after the war, with wages skyrocketing and paper an incredible price when you could get it at all. He had lain awake then too, while she slept quietly beside him.

But he had never touched her bonds. They were hers. Even when he had had trouble paying the premium on his insurance, somehow or other he had managed. But his new Elizabeth, with her new smooth face—

It was almost daylight before he went to sleep.

24

He left the train at Ellsworth at six the next morning and looked around for the car. There was no car in sight, and the early morning was chilly. There was a fog in somewhere. He knew the signs. He had brought no overcoat, so he waited for some time shivering on the platform. Finally he lost patience and, ordering a local taxi, drove the eighteen miles to Bar Harbor.

Before they reached the island they ran into the fog. The bridge was shrouded in it, the mountains barely visible.

"Looks like a bad one," the driver said companionably. "Worst this year."

Now and then they passed another car, only dimly seen, but Albert did not appear, and the fog grew even thicker. Matthew was very cold by that time. He had had no breakfast, and the change from the city heat had been too abrupt. He began to shiver again.

"Damn good way to get pneumonia," he said crossly to himself. "Maybe Lizzie didn't get my wire."

It was still thick in the town when they reached it, and they seemed to creep along. The long winding drive from his own gate to the house was a milk-white sea. The driver took it carefully, and Matthew continued to shake. He was still shivering when they reached the house.

To his surprise the door to the porte-cochere was open, as was the one at the end of the hall that faced the sea. The furniture had lost its distinctness, and he almost groped his way to the service quarters. Here, however, the lights were on and a strong smell of coffee filled the air. The cook was at the stove, but she looked at him strangely. And Hilda was in the kitchen, a Hilda with swollen eyes and uncombed hair.

"What the hell's the matter?" he roared. "Where's Albert? Where's the car? And get me some of that coffee. I've got a chill."

The cook did not answer, and all at once Hilda was crying noisily, with her apron to her face and her shoulders shaking. Matthew was astounded. And suddenly frightened.

"What is it?" he demanded hoarsely. "What's the matter. Stop that blubbering and tell me."

"It's the children," she gasped. "They're gone."

"Gone? Where? What do you mean?"

"They're out in old Trimble's boat and nobody can find them."

He sat down abruptly, staring at her.

"When did they go?"

"Yesterday. The fog came in sudden-like, and there's been a big sea since the storm. The boats have been out all night, searching for them. Albert's with them."

"Where's their mother?"

"She's on the beach by the cove. We can't get her in. She's been there all night. I'm getting coffee for her."

"And my wife?"

"We got her to bed, Mr. Wayne. She'd been out to a party. She didn't know until we called her up. When she heard it they say she fainted. Anyhow she's taking it hard. We got the doctor for her. He's giving her something to quite her."

He did not go up to Elizabeth's room. He found an old overcoat in the hall closet and automatically put it on. Then he went out the front door and through the fog to the cove. Dimly he could see a woman's figure there. The woman was not moving. She was standing still, gazing out into the milkiness that covered the sea. If she heard him she did not turn.

It was Ricky.

He went to her and put a hand on her arm.

"You're not doing them any good here, girl," he said gently. "Better come back to the house."

"I can't," she said dully, still without looking at him. "I want to be here when the boat comes in—if it ever does."

"That's nonsense. Of course it will come in."

"So many things could happen," she said, her voice still flat. "The captain might have gone overboard. Or the engine might have blown up and burned the boat."

"Or the fog have caught them and they anchored where they were. Use your good sense, Ricky. Trimble knows his job. They're all right. They'll come in soon howling for breakfast. I know them."

But he felt inadequate and helpless before the sick bleakness of her white face. He knew the sea and its tragedies. In the past, when they went up in May, more than once he had watched on Memorial Day the ceremony of throwing from the village dock the memorial wreath for the men who had died in the sea. And he was shivering again.

"I'll bring you some coffee and an extra coat," he told her. "No use your getting sick."

If she heard him she did not speak. He left her there, staring out and listening, and he remembered one night in Canada when Court had gone out in a canoe and a sudden storm had come up. Just so had he and Elizabeth waited until from the woods behind them they had heard his cheerful voice calling to them. Elizabeth had turned and run to him, but he himself could not move. He had stood there in the storm and heard his heart start to beat again.

Albert had come in when he reached the house. He was standing by the kitchen stove trying to warm his half-frozen hands and looking exhausted.

"Sorry about the car, sir," he said. "One of the lobster men was sick, so I took his boat and went out."

"No sign of them?"

"Well, no, sir, not yet. They'll find them all right. Trimble's a good man, and his lobster pots aren't far from shore. He'll have made haven somewhere, maybe around one of the islands. Trouble is, if his engine went wrong the tide might have carried him out a ways. That's what they think's happened."

"Has anyone telephoned their father?"

"He's been out, sir. He wasn't in at two o'clock."

When Matthew went back to Ricky the fog seemed to be slightly thinner. He had brought a thermos of coffee, a blanket and a chair for her. She let him wrap her in the blanket, but she refused the coffee and he drank it himself. He felt sick and cold, and the chill was definite now. There was a sharp pain in his chest too, and he went along the shore and lost his breakfast.

They were both still there an hour or so later when the children came back. They could hear their excited voices.

"Captain Trimble was scared, Hilda. But I wasn't."

And Jeffrey's voice, held down to a shout.

"I'm hungry. How soon's breakfast?"

Matthew never forgot the look on Ricky's face when she held them in her arms. Only when they were warmed and fed did she look up at him.

"Someone had better call Court," she said. "He may be back by this time."

But Courtney was still not at home.

25

It had started simply enough. Court had seen Matthew off and found himself with an empty evening on his hands. It was still hot at seven o'clock when the train pulled out.

The station was filled with men carrying their coats, with sweating men and women and crying children. When he went out the street felt soft under his feet, and the house when he reached it empty and forlorn.

He took a shower and felt slightly better. But the long evening stretched ahead with nothing to relieve it. For the first time in years he was glad to hear Emmy's voice when she called him on the phone.

"What are you doing?" she inquired. "I'm slowly dying of the heat. How about dinner in a cool spot somewhere?"

"Is there such a thing?"

"I know a place on Long Island. Good food and drink, and a breeze from the ocean. How does it sound?"

He hesitated.

"What about the Country Club?"

"What about Central Park!" she jeered. "They're both jammed."

In the end he picked her up in his car. The place she had recommended was not cool, but it was less hot, and the food and drink were both above average. He felt grateful to her. After all, she had filled in an empty evening. And she was at her best that night. She made no sentimental overtures, although when she leaned over the table her round full breasts were visible below the opening of her neck. She did her best to amuse him, telling her off-color stories, and he found himself relaxed, sometimes laughing.

They drank a good bit, and it seemed only natural when he took her home to go up to her apartment for a final nightcap. He had no intention of staying, but the heat wave had broken with a heavy storm. He waited until the worst was over, taking off his white dinner coat to cool off, and when she offered him another drink, sipping it comfortably.

It was very late the next morning when he wakened, and Emmy was apologetic.

"I'm sorry, Court," she said. "I meant to wake you, but I went to sleep myself."

He felt better after she made him some coffee, but he was uneasy. His car was in the street downstairs, and when he left it he was in his dinner clothes. Apparently, though, no one noticed him. At the house it was different, however. He found Rosie in the lower hall, and she looked tired and as though she had been crying.

"It's all right, Mr. Wayne," she said. "The children have been found."

"What about the children?"

"They were out in a boat all night. They tried to get you on the telephone, but I didn't know where you were. I haven't been to bed at all."

He sent her to get some sleep, but when he tried to get Ricky at Bar Harbor he was told she was resting. The children were apparently none the worse for what had happened. But his father was not well. They had sent for a doctor.

He took the train that night, to find Matthew in bed with pneumonia, and a cool Ricky who did not ask him for any explanation but was completely passive under his kiss.

"I'm sorry as hell, darling. I was out with some of the boys. Poker game."

"It doesn't matter."

"But it does. To have you go through that alone—"

"It's over. Let's forget it."

Matthew came very close to dying during the next few days. Nurses and doctors came and went through the house and a tightlipped frightened Elizabeth hung around the hall outside his room, listening to the struggle for breath going on inside. Most of the time he was only semiconscious. Then one day it was over. Matthew roused from a normal sleep to see Courtney sitting by his bed.

"When did you get here?" he asked weakly.

"Been here all along, Dad. Think I was going to let you go through this alone?"

He held out his thin hand and Court took it and held it.

But he was a bad patient. He shuddered at the cost when he found he had three nurses, and let two of them go. But—possibly he imagined it—Lizzie's face was almost natural again. It had the old familiar lines once more. And one day as he was propped up in the bed he saw her looking in the mirror.

"I can take so much and no more, Matt. Look at my face! It's ruined."

"I love every bit of it."

"I did it for you, Matt. You know that. I didn't want to get old and ugly."

"Never ugly, Liz. Not to me, my dear."

The children were all right. Jeffrey had had a cold, but Peggy was her plump and rather boastful self.

"I slept all night," she would say. "Captain Trimble put his coat on me. It was nice and warm. I liked it."

One day they allowed Captain Trimble to see him, an apologetic and suddenly aged man.

"I just came to say I'm sorry, Mr. Wayne. That engine of mine has held up right along, and the children had been begging to go. When your missus said they could—"

"Oh, it was my wife, was it?"

"Nobody's fault, sir. It looked like a nice day. That fog—it came in fast. Then when the engine quit on me—"

"We're not blaming you, Captain. You kept them safe, and we're grateful. If you'll let me buy you a new engine I'll feel better."

The captain, however, refused the engine. He was New England at its best. He wanted nothing he did not earn. And this was in Matthew's mind when Elizabeth came in and sat down by the bed.

"I've been thinking, Lizzie. Trimble's just gone. I offered him a new engine, but he refused. Said he liked to earn what he got."

She looked at him suspiciously.

"What about it? If he wants to be foolish enough not to take a thing like that—"

"Is it so foolish? I've always worked for what I have."

"You've worked hard, Matt. I know that."

"Trouble is, a lot of people today are thinking they're making money without earning it. It just can't be done, Liz. It can't be done. Sooner or later it's a boomerang. It comes back and hits them."

She made an impatient gesture.

"I suppose Court's been talking. To hear him you'd think I've lost my mind. I haven't yet. I'm in the market. I suppose you know that. But I'll get out in plenty of time."

She went on. The men who summered at Bar Harbor were mostly businessmen. They didn't expect trouble. Look, they were going to tear down the old Swimming Club and build a new one. They had held a meeting and raised a lot of money for it. They ought to put in five thousand themselves. It was the least they could do.

Matthew shook his stubborn gray head.

He was worried about other things too during his convalescence. There was something wrong between Ricky and Court. When he learned Courtney was sleeping in a guest room he sent for him.

"Not my business, Son," he said. "I don't interfere between husbands and wives. But when the husband is you, and the wife is a girl I'm fond of, maybe it's time to speak up."

Courtney took a minute out to fill his pipe and light it.

"It's rather a long story, Dad," he said. "In a way it goes back to Germany. She found a letter from Elsa von Wagner—it was in my war trunk. I didn't know it was there—and I suppose it left her suspicious of me. I don't know. She was a good sport about it. But when she couldn't locate me the night the children were lost she—well, she suspected the worst.

"Where were you that night? Can't you tell her?"

"I've told her I was playing poker."

"She doesn't believe it, I suppose?"

"No. I hate lying to her, but what can I do?"

"I wish to God you'd grow up," Matthew said wearily. "I won't have Ricky's life ruined."

"I'd been drinking, or it wouldn't have happened. That's no excuse, but it's how it was."

Matthew's recovery was slow. It was a long time before he could get downstairs to sit on the terrace, a blanket over his knees and a nurse at hand. Behind him, in the big living room, were Elizabeth's needlepoint chairs and in front of him the fountain. Over beyond the flower garden men were mixing cement for the new swimming pool Elizabeth was building. But Ricky was seldom in sight. When he asked about her it was to learn that she was out somewhere, climbing a mountain or knocking a ball around the golf course.

He did not like it. It was as though she had turned the children over to Courtney and was going her way alone. There were even times during that shocked interval when she considered going back home, to her mother, perhaps also to Jay. She knew it was foolish and irrational. Her life was fixed. But there was cool deliberateness in her handing the children to Court.

Up to that time he had taken them for granted, been fond of them, found them amusing and sometimes irritating. Now she wanted him to get to know them, and to realize what he had almost lost.

As a matter of fact his latent paternalism had finally been aroused. He spent much of his time with them, until even the children themselves revolted.

"Why can't we go to the beach alone? We've always done it."

"I like the beach myself. Mind if I go along?"

They were polite. They accepted him, even in time found him acceptable. He let them alone, save for keeping a watchful eye on them. He would sit on a rock, smoking incessantly and not talking much. Watching the ocean, and sometimes remembering the last time he had crossed it, a heartsick boy who had left a little German girl behind him and was coming home to a wife he barely remembered.

"Daddy! Daddy! Come and look at what I found!"

He would get up and saunter over, to crouch over some bit of flotsam or jetsam.

"I want to take it up to the house. Can I take it up to the house? Daddy, please let me."

Now and then he took them out lobstering in the Trimble boat, but only on brief excursions. The captain would slow his engine, lean over his marker and begin to pull, his muscles standing out like whipcords. Then at last the slatted pot would appear. Old Captain Trimble would show its contents to Jeff.

"Can I take it out, Mr. Trimble?"

"Better watch me do it. Remember the time you got pinched?"

Out would come the lobster, not red at all but an ugly green. The captain would bait the box and drop it again. But before all this he would set the rudder so that the boat would move in a circle.

"Just playing safe," he would tell the children. "Suppose I fall overboard and she keeps on going! Then where would I be? This way she comes right back to me."

Not until the day Courtney left did Ricky have any real talk with him. Then she told him frankly what she felt and thought.

"I think it's time you made a choice," she said. "I've done

my part. Now you have to do yours. Just be sure of one thing. I'm not like your aunt Roberta. You can't come back to me from someone else. And don't try to lie to me, Court. I always know when you do."

"I told you about that night."

"I don't believe it. I never believed it."

"That sounds like an ultimatum."

"It is. Precisely that."

She stayed on in Maine after he had gone. She seemed unwilling to go home, and one day Matthew—now gaining strength rapidly—saw her sitting on the rim of the fountain and went over to her. In her white sports dress, with her slim legs stretched out in front of her and the breeze ruffling her hair, she looked like a girl. Matthew eyed the tall figure on top of the marble bowl. It always reminded him of the fountain in Brussels, but close examination years ago had revealed that the bronze gentleman was holding a fish, and that it was the fish that was spouting.

"Where do you suppose Lizzie found that thing?" he inquired. "It's ugly as all get out."

"She likes it, Dad."

He sat down beside her and took her hand.

"What's wrong, my dear? You can tell old Matthew, can't you?"

"I was just thinking. It's very wearing to build your life about one person, Dad. It's like walking a tightrope. If someone jerks the rope—"

"Still holding that night against Court, aren't you?"

"I don't believe he was where he says he was. He's a poor liar."

Matthew was silent for a moment or two, gently stroking her hand.

"Let's look at it, Ricky," he said. "Most men marry later than Courtney did. They've—well, they've been around. He hadn't. If there's a woman in this it needn't mean anything. Maybe he'd been drinking; maybe he was only lonely. God only knows why. I did it myself once, but Lizzie took me back. We've been very happy ever since," he added simply.

"It isn't the first time, Dad."

"It could be the last, my dear," he said. "He's in love with you. Whatever it was—and I don't know if it was a woman—he realizes he's acted like an idiot. But he's proud, Ricky. Probably you've hurt him too."

"I have some pride of my own."

"Of course, but you haven't done anything you're ashamed of. Maybe if you wrote to him—"

"I'm not sure I want to go back to him. I gave him all I had. If it wasn't enough I can't help it." She turned and looked at him. "What am I to do?" she asked. "I can't go home. Mother has no place for me. But I can't carry on like this either; live on his money, in his house. Not if there is someone else."

"There's no one else," Matthew said sturdily. "Go back and carry on, my dear. I'm counting on you."

"Give me some time, Dad. I'll try. It's a promise."

26

Back in New York Roberta learned the story of that frenzied night. She thought it over for a day or two, then on a rainy summer day she went to see Emmy Baldwin.

The rain had kept Emmy home. She expected no visitors, so she was wearing an old negligee and no make-up. At thirty-four she found late nights and bad liquor left their mark on her. Now she had covered her face with cold cream and with a highball beside her was checking her holdings against the market reports.

When the doorbell rang she decided there was no time to improve her appearance, and she opened the door. She was stunned to see Roberta outside, and to have her walk past her into the cluttered living room. Roberta was as wet as though she had been fished out of a well, but her dignity was unimpaired. Roberta was a lady. Very often a great lady. And Emmy felt cheap and not a little frightened.

"I want to talk to you," Roberta said, putting her dripping umbrella against Emmy's best sofa and sitting down. "I want you to let my brother's family alone, Mrs. Baldwin."

"I don't know what you mean. If it's Court you're talking about—"

"You know perfectly well what I'm talking about."

Emmy moved the umbrella to the hearth, where it ran in small rivulets onto the carpet. Then she sat down and picked up a cigarette.

"We're very old friends, Lady Truesdale. I knew him long before he knew his wife. I don't intend to give that up. Why should I?"

Roberta ignored her. She took off her gloves and looked down at her hands. They were slim and long-fingered. In their time they had handled dirt and wounds, blood and pus and stinking bandages. On her bony knees she had knelt on the straw in barns and churches and folded other hands across dead young soldiers' breasts. But today they were cold and unsteady. Her voice, however, was quiet, her clear English diction impressive.

"I am not interested in your personal affairs," she said. "I *am* interested in Courtney Wayne and his marriage. I came to tell you that if you continue to try to break that up I shall have to interfere."

"What do you mean, interfere?"

Roberta looked around the apartment and through the open door at the bedroom, the wide bed mussed where Emmy had been lying on it, the cluttered toilet table, the pink-shaded lamp on the side table. She wondered vaguely if her fastidious Arthur had put up with that sort of thing.

"You see," she said calmly, "you haven't a chance with him. A wife always has the advantage over any other woman, and I think Courtney is in love with his."

"I don't know what you're talking about."

Roberta remained unruffled.

"I happened to see him leaving here one morning not long ago in his dinner clothes. He was very indiscreet. He had even left his car out on the street."

Emmy flushed angrily.

"And what do you propose to do? If his wife chooses to go away for weeks at a time—"

"She remains his wife," said Roberta.

"All right. Tell her. Break up her marriage. See if I care!"

"I have no intention of doing anything of the sort," Roberta said dryly, and got up. "Don't hope for that. He has an established place, a family, and a business. He has no intention of losing any of them. I shall speak to him myself if it becomes necessary."

She got her umbrella from the hearth, straightened her incredible hat, and took a final look at Emmy's bedroom.

"A trifle untidy, isn't it, my dear?"

"It's the way I like it," Emmy said sullenly.

Not until she had closed the door behind her did Emmy recover sufficiently to go into a rage. She had been right in one thing, however. Roberta did not talk. But the effect on Emmy had been rather disastrous. She had no intention of giving up Courtney Wayne, and the moment she learned he was back in town she called him.

"Back from the wilds, I hear," she said gaily.

"I'd hardly call Bar Harbor the wilds."

But he was still rankling from that final scene with Ricky. He took Emmy out to dinner that night and went to her apartment with her. Back there, however, while he mixed drinks and she changed out of her street clothes, he had a feeling of revulsion. He was acting like a spoiled brat, he thought. After all, he didn't want her. Why was he here?

When she came back, in a thin nightgown and with her feet bare, even her slim ankles made him feel sick. He tried not to look at them when she curled up on the long sofa. To his surprise she was laughing softly. "I wish you'd seen old horse-face when she came here, Court!"

"Who is old horse-face?" he asked idly.

"Now who could it be?" she mocked him. "The aristocratic Lady Truesdale, no less."

He put his glass on the mantel and turned a horrified face to her.

"Are you saying Aunt Roberta came here?"

"I am, and she did, sonny boy. She walked in here dripping all over the floor, and told me to lay off you." She laughed again. "I wish you'd seen this place. The cleaning woman hadn't shown up and I was a sight. I'll bet it jolted her."

He still looked incredulous.

"How on earth did she know?"

"Saw you leaving here that morning in your dinner coat. I told her to get out and to mind her own business."

"O God," he groaned. He looked around him, at the gaudy bed in the other room, at the untidy sitting room, at the light on Emmy's bleached hair and pointed breasts, and he loathed everything he saw. As it must have appeared to Roberta, sitting there and gazing about her.

"I suppose you know where this leaves us, Emmy," he said.

"Where? The old girl won't talk. She wouldn't dirty that aristocratic mouth of hers."

When she saw him pick up his coat, however, her mouth set.

"You're not leaving me, Court. I won't have it. No man walks out one me and gets away with it."

"I don't know what you mean by that, Emmy. We've never pretended to be in love. If I hurt you I'm sorry, but that's the way it has to be."

"You don't mind cheating so long as you can get away with it," she said furiously. "If you're afraid of that mealymouthed wife of yours—"

"We'll keep my wife out of this," he said, and heard a glass crash against the door as he closed it behind him.

In the end it was Sheila who told Matthew the story; an embarrassed unwilling Sheila, up to Maine for a weekend, and trying to make light of the whole thing.

"I'm sure there's nothing in it, Uncle Matt. What if he does take her out now and then?"

"I can guess what, knowing her."

He went back to New York soon after Sheila left. He was a thin shadow of himself, and Angela almost wept over him. But there was nothing soft about him as he shoved aside the accumulated mail on his desk and sent for Courtney. He was sitting stiffly in his chair, his hands out on his empty blotter and his eyes cold.

"Just how long have you been intimate with the Baldwin

woman?" he demanded.

Courtney flushed.

"So Aunt Roberta's been talking, after all."

Matthew looked surprised.

"Roberta? What's she got to do with it? I still have my wits. So has Ricky, although she doesn't know who it is. Are you letting that hussy break up your home?"

Courtney sat down. The flush was gone. He looked rather white.

"It's over, such as it was. I haven't been keeping her, if that's what you mean."

"Do you want your wife and children back? Or is she to go home to her mother?"

"That doesn't need an answer, does it?"

"Then call her up, write to her, go up to Maine and get down on your knees to her. I don't care what, so you end this nonsense."

"She's let me know pretty plainly that she's through with me, Dad."

"Not unless you want it that way. Only don't lie to her, Court. She's too smart for that."

It seemed to him, after Courtney left, that life did curious things to people. For years he had realized that Ricky had given more to her marriage than Courtney had, more love, more of everything. Now, after watching his son's face, he wondered if the situation had not reversed. Courtney was badly hurt. However much he had deserved it, he was feeling Ricky's desertion deeply. Perhaps it always worked out that way. As a man grew older he depended more on his wife. He might wander, like Arthur Truesdale, or like himself long ago, but in the end he came home. Or wanted to.

Ricky did not come back until well into September. The heat continued and people stayed late that year. Things, as Elizabeth said, were still on the up-and-up, meaning the stock market. The new club was an assured fact. Yachts crowded the harbor, and in spite of herself Ricky found herself caught up in the excited whirl of cocktail parties and dinners. She was pale and thin. She slept badly and ate very little, but she was still reluctant to go home. At night she would go in to see the children before she went out, and Peggy would inspect her gravely.

"I have a pretty mama."

"I'm glad you think so, darling."

But Jeff, boy-like, would protest.

"Do you have to go out again?"

"Yes. But you'll be asleep."

"I like to know you're in the house anyway. Where's your necklace, Mother?"

"I thought I looked better without it."

She never wore Courtney's pearls now. If Elizabeth noticed she said nothing. Ricky would go down the stairs; the car would be at the door, Johnson waiting, the parlormaid waiting, Albert waiting. She would gather up her long skirt with its train and follow Elizabeth, to hear again the same talk of stocks and markets or golf scores, to play bridge for higher stakes than she could afford, and to go home to her lonely room and her unhappy thoughts.

She had had a letter from Courtney, but it had sounded stiff and constrained.

"I am sorry to learn from Dad that you are still angry, darling. I have already told you I am sorry. I am. But I think I have the right to know whether you really want to come back to me as my wife. We can't live in the same house if you do not. Don't misunderstand me, Ricky. I want you and the children. I am lost without you. But I cannot be on sufferance as I was before I left. I cannot feel you will merely tolerate me. Anything which might have come between us is over. I promise that. If you will meet me halfway. . . ."

She wrote that she would come back to him on his terms, but not at once. She still needed a little more time.

But time seemed the only thing she could not have. At dinners she sat next to members of embassy staffs, escaping the

Washington heat, and one and all they seemed bewildered.

"What a country you have," one of them said to her one night. "It's fantastic, unbelievable. It's great, of course, but I hope you'll forgive me if I say that just now it seems a little mad."

It was mad, of course: Capone and his gangsters, the racketeers moving into the labor unions with their "come across—or else." And the stock market. Always the stock market. She grew sick of the very words.

Courtney himself was feeling frustrated as the weeks went on. Not only about his wife, or his mother. He had begun to suspect that even the office boy was speculating, and one day he called a meeting of the office staff.

He sat at the head of the long table in the directors' room and surveyed them as they came in: the grave executives, and uneasy stenographers, even the girl from the switchboard. There were not chairs enough, so they stood uncomfortably about the walls. He felt rather foolish, but he had to go on.

"I have a few things to say which are not actually a part of this business," he said. "In the first place, I have to thank all of you for the work you have done. It's been fine. But these are uncertain times." He looked around the room, finding some faces blank and others alert. Only George Mather was looking amused.

"What I want to say is this," he went on. "The business is safe and we intend to keep it so. Neither my father nor myself is in the market. In case of trouble we should be able to ride out the storm. We may have to pass dividends. That's only common sense. We may lose sales. Nevertheless, the business is fundamentally sound."

"What's this all about, Wayne?" Mather said. "If we're riding high, wide and handsome, what's the trouble?"

"We're riding, George. I don't know about the rest. If some of you are in this market on a margin I think it's time to get out. There may be the devil to pay."

He went on. There had already been a warning. The year

before the price of call money had been raised, and even now there was a slight sag. But as he looked about him at their faces he saw they did not know what he was talking about.

When it was over he found Mather waiting for him.

"Well, where do you think that got you?" he asked.

"Nowhere, I suppose. I had to try it."

"You're a fine one to talk, Court. What about your mother?"

"She can wreck herself. She's not going to wreck this company."

But he felt rather foolish as September dragged on and still the market rose. Then one day he had a surprise visit from Anne Lockwood. He had come from a hospital where one of his authors had been sent after trying to finish a book on a combination of liquor and sedatives. He had sat beside him and watched his twitching fingers as he tried to hold a cigarette.

"I'm through, Mr. Wayne. I can't concentrate."

"You can't concentrate on liquor and drugs. What you need is to get out of this town. It eats people up. Go into the country."

"I hate the country."

He left feeling discouraged. He knew what New York did to some of the writing people. It exhilarated them at first. They would sit around the Players and other clubs, or in some speakeasy, talking their heads off. But when they went back to their desks or typewriters they would find themselves empty. If he could only lock them in their rooms, as one publisher had locked a Canadian author to force him to finish a book!

It was an agreeable surprise, then, to find Anne Lockwood sitting quiet in his office. She had put a box on the desk and she greeted him with a thin smile.

"I've brought a manuscript," she said. "It's not a romance. You may not like it at all, but I've fulfilled my other contract. If you want it you can have it."

"Of course we want it."

"Better read it first," she said, still with her strange

quietness. "It's not my book, really. It's the one Tim meant to write. I did it from his notes. In a way it's a bitter book."

"That's strange, coming from you, Anne."

"Is it? I lived ten years with a war casualty. I know what war does to men. I don't want another one. I've called it *The Drifters*. Tim always said that's what we are."

He read it the same night, sitting in his pajamas in his study; read it with increasing surprise. In a sense he could see that it was not Anne's book at all. It was the book of a man who had lived and suffered. But it was not really bitter. There was no hatred in it, no malice. It was Tim Lockwood's world as he had seen it from his bed, a floundering hectic world seen clearly by his dying eyes, a world where people loved and mated and gave birth, but still were puppets moved by forces they did not understand or try to understand.

Tim had believed that there would be another world war, greater than the last. For nothing had been settled. Greed and avarice had built a bonfire among the nations. Someday a spark would set it afire, and war was the supreme folly of man.

It was two in the morning before he finished it. He sat for a long time with the last page in his hands, thinking of Jeff, of the boy Ricky's mother had adopted, of all the roistering youngsters playing in the city parks or diving into the pool in Maine. And he remembered Dave, dying in the mud and now only a headstone, one of the long rows that stretched like marching men along the slopes of Arlington.

His impulse was to call Ricky, to say, "Come home, darling. Come and bring the children. Life is short and uncertain, and I need you." When he looked at the clock, however, he put down the telephone. They would be asleep, all of them. It could wait.

He wrote her something of the same sort the next day, and he gave *The Drifters* to George Mather.

"Read it and weep, George," he said. "You've got a boy of your own."

27

In spite of Courtney's letter Ricky had not come back at once. She could not, for Elizabeth had unexpectedly collapsed. She had fainted at a dinner party and had to be brought home.

It was not serious, Ricky told them over the telephone. She had been going too hard. Now she needed a rest. Neither of them was to come to Bar Harbor, but she was sending the children home with Hilda.

Matthew was alarmed. Elizabeth was never sick. He could not remember her spending a day in bed except when Courtney was born. Even then she resented it after the first few days.

"It's silly, Matt, I feel fine."

"Now, Lizzie, the doctor said—"

"Oh, damn the doctor. He's never had a baby."

He was not to see her, however. Nobody was to see her.

To Ricky the time that followed was highly trying. Not that Elizabeth was a poor patient. She seemed contented enough, looking out at the sea and mentally figuring the profits. But after the first week or so they were virtually alone. Even some of the servants had gone back to open the city house, and most of the summer cottages were closed. Carpenters put up the winter storm shutters, caretakers moved in to take down draperies and set traps against field mice, floats were towed away from private docks, and with the yachts gone and the pleasure boats laid up, the harbor looked deserted.

Only Captain Trimble remained in the cove. Matthew had

sent him a new engine after all and he was busy installing it.

By early October, however, Elizabeth finally rebelled, and they started home. Matthew met them with a wheeled chair, but she repudiated it indignantly.

"There's nothing wrong with my legs," she said. "Send that thing away. I'm walking to the car."

She did not look well. Her color was poor and after a time she took Matthew's arm.

"I guess I need a little support, Matt."

"Well, I'm here, girl. I'm always here when you need me."

The meeting that day between Court and Ricky was a quiet one. Both had a sense of guilt, both wanted to get back on the old footing again. It was not easy. There was not only the shyness between all married people after a long separation. There was the pact implicit between them. In the car he reached over and took her hand.

"I'm sorry, darling. Sorry as hell."

"Let's forget it, Court. Your father explained some things to me. They helped."

"You can trust me now, you know."

"If I can't, my world goes to pieces. Do you remember you said that once? About picking up the pieces?"

"Well, we're doing that now, Ricky. With God's help, and yours."

Then they were at the house, with the children screaming down the stairs. He took her in his arms before they reached them.

"Here come the pieces!" he said. "But for this minute you are mine. Only mine. Right?"

"Correct," she agreed smiling; and braced herself against the approaching onset.

She was very happy that day. Even the wall fountain did not bother her. After the children were in bed they sat in Courtney's study, and for the first time he unburdened himself fully about his mother. He sat, his head bent, his shoulders sagging, and told her the whole story.

"The original idea was only to get back what she'd sold to furnish this house." he said. "But she went on after that under her own steam. Now I feel damned responsible, to you, to Dad, and the kids. To the business too."

"We'll get through somehow, Court. You know I don't care about money."

"No." He looked at her. "I doubt whether you do, my darling. You've never liked this house either, have you? I wished it on you."

"I'm getting used to it, Court."

"Even the fountain?"

"Even the fountain."

It was like coming home after a long absence to hold her in his arms that night; as though she had been in a far country. He was very humble with her, but she gave herself wholeheartedly to him. Later he lit a cigarette and stared into the darkness.

"Want me to tell you about it?" he said.

"No. Never."

"It wasn't important, you know."

"Don't put too much of a strain on me, Court. I know it's over. That's enough."

He felt the next morning as though he was living again, the good smell of coffee and frying bacon, the shouts of the children getting ready for school, Ricky waiting for her bath until he had finished. He went over and kissed her as she lay in bed.

"I love you," he said. "Always and ever, my darling."

She put her arms around his neck and drew him down to her.

"We have so much, Court," she said. "Let's keep it."

But he was still worried about his mother. She had refused to tell even Matthew about her situation.

"You're a publisher, Matt. You don't know anything about finance. Let me alone."

"We'd better draw in our horns, Lizzie."

"Just why? And how?"

"Well, real estate is bringing enormous prices. This house

could bring a fancy sum."

"You mean sell it?" Her voice was shrill. "Have you lost your mind?"

"It's pretty big for us. And it costs a lot to keep up."

"Let me worry about that," she said grandiosely. "You stick to your books."

He did exact one promise from her, however. He told Courtney about it in his office one day. He had taken a cigar from his box and—after a glance at Angela's door—had lighted it.

"Your mother's promised to get out of the market by Christmas," he said. "It may last until then. If it doesn't. . . ."

Courtney looked at him. He had never entirely recovered from the pneumonia of the summer. He was still thin. His clothes hung on him. For the first time he looked an old man, and Courtney went around the table and put an affectionate arm around his shoulder.

"We'll weather it, Dad," he said. "If and when it comes. We've weathered panics before in this country, five or six of them."

"Nothing like this one will be," Matthew said. "Nothing in all the world like this one."

Yet the business was doing well, that October of 1929. *The Drifters* had been selected by one of the book clubs, and the fall list was a good one. There was nothing to warn anyone of what was to come so soon. The market merely slipped at first. Elizabeth sold some stocks that day on her broker's advice, but as prices went down still further she bought again.

"Only some steel," she told Courtney over the telephone. "It's a good buy. After all, everybody needs steel."

"Look, Mother. You get out, and get out fast."

"And take losses! Be yourself, Court."

"This is only the start," he told her. "And you don't actually own anything. Remember that. A sharp decline will wipe you out."

She refused, and when she did consider it, it was too late. As the week went on one by one her margins were wiped out, and her brokers were obliged to sell her out to protect themselves. But the time came when there was little or nothing to sell. She not only had nothing left; she found herself heavily in debt.

"I don't understand it," she said, bewildered. "How could they do such a thing to me? If they'd only held on—"

She was restless at night. Matthew would feel her stirring in the bed. And sometimes he went down to the basement kitchen and heated her some milk to put her to sleep.

Nothing had any value now, not even the house or her jewels or the cars. In five days billions of dollars in values had been wiped out, and both Matthew and Courtney spent long hours in the bank or at the brokers' trying to untangle Elizabeth's affairs.

Nor was it only Elizabeth. Angela Ellis was going about the office red-eyed and hysterical, her future lost. Some of the staff were involved too. Even Mather, that Rock of Gibraltar, was losing his house in Tarrytown.

Matthew did not reproach Elizabeth. By the middle of November he sat down with her quietly and told her where she stood. And where he stood too.

"The house will have to go for what we can get for it," he said, "and you'd better let me see what I can get for your pearls. Not much, I'm afraid. We'll have to put the Bar Harbor place on the market too. No buyers, probably. But one thing I'm holding on to, my insurance."

"That old insurance," she said bitterly. "It's kept us poor for years."

"It's all you may have when I'm gone, Lizzie. I'll be lucky to pay the premiums, but I intend to, if we have to live in two rooms."

It almost came to that in the end. Years ago he had put the house in her name. Now he found she had mortgaged it heavily, and the bank took it over. They might have stayed on there, paying rent, but Matthew refused.

"We can't have enough servants," he said. "We can't light and heat it, either. Get this into your head, Lizzie. We've still got the business, but outside of it we're back where we started. Only then we didn't owe anything."

Both Courtney and Ricky offered them their house, but Elizabeth refused it bitterly.

"We'll manage," she said. "That Frenchwoman walked out on us first thing, but Katie says she'll come back. We'll find an apartment somewhere. God knows there are plenty of empty ones."

But by some synecdoche of her own she blamed the debacle on everyone but herself, on her brokers, on Courtney, on the country itself.

"Court got me into this mess," she told Ricky one day. "Now it's up to him to get me out."

It was impossible, of course. The news was horrifying. The market continued to drop, and all over the nation men—and women too—were facing bankruptcy, or worse. Some refused to face it. There was suicide in the very air. Men they had all known were taking the tragic way out, through open windows, with long-forgotten revolvers, or in the automobiles they could no longer afford; getting in, shutting garage doors, turning on the motor, and making their escape into eternity.

Once more Wall Street was justifying its description, the river at one end and a cemetery at the other.

Courtney came home one night to tell Ricky he would have to mortgage the house if he could get a mortgage on it.

"I feel responsible," he said. "It will have to go into the general pool for Mother's debts. Both Dad and I will have to sell some of the stock in the firm too. We'll still keep control, but it's a blow for the old boy."

"Of course," she said simply. "Anything to help, Court."

It was Roberta who found the apartment for Matthew and Elizabeth, a Roberta who knew—who better?—what it was to lose a home. It was small, but it faced south and Matthew took it. Elizabeth protested, but in the end she accepted. For this was a new Matt, grim and gray of face; a silent Matt, always going over papers at night, figuring and calculating. One night when he did not come up to bed Elizabeth went down, her knees shaking with fear, to find him alone in his dismantled library, with no fire and with packing cases all around him. He looked up at her gravely.

"Can't you sleep, Lizzie?"

"Not with you down here, Matt. I'm frightened. You'd never leave me, would you? I mean, you'd never try—"

"Leave you? What are you talking about? Of course not."

"I'd be so lost without you," she said. And broke down for the first time. With his arms around her she quieted finally. She even told him her fears, and he patted her gently.

"I guess I'm still needed, my girl," he said. "We'll fight this out together. Anyhow," he added, with a return of his old quizzical smile, "anything like that would invalidate my insurance. They slipped in a suicide clause while I wasn't looking."

She was less resentful after that night, as though she had found something she had lost awhile. One day, clearing out the attic, she found her mother's old trunk. It was filled with moldering clothing, but on top was a small box.

Its contents were a surprise. There was an old Bible. On the first page in Papa's writing was an inscription: "Born August first, 1869, Elizabeth Anne Hilliard, our dear little daughter." There was also a cabinet photograph of Papa as a young man with a long mustache and his head held very stiff by the clamps to steady his neck.

There were clippings too, announcing her engagement to Matthew and later her marriage. And down in the bottom was a small envelope with a dark curl inside. Mama had marked it. It said: "Our baby girl's hair."

That day for the first time in years, Elizabeth wept for her mother and father, and perhaps for her own lost youth.

The day came when she stood by and watched her tapestries

and pictures being carried out for sale. She refused the cup of tea a maid brought her—Johnson had been gone for weeks—and her face was blank and still. Only when Fanny the peacock appeared she reached out and touched the dry old feathers.

"You brought us bad luck after all, Fanny," she said.

The moving man looked at her.

"Sure bad luck, them birds," he said.

28

It was the end of a cycle. Gone were the flagpole sitters of the nineteen-twenties, the Elinor Glyns and *It*, the dance marathons, even Harlem as a resort for the intellectuals. The country was sobered, but it carried on.

In New York the crowds on the streets were much the same, the shop windows, the movie houses. The crash, beginning at the top, was slow in reaching the masses. But the demand for goods was less, including books, and the vast new office buildings were largely unoccupied, their windows looking over the city like blind eyes.

Both Courtney and Matthew had cut their salaries sharply. And by the spring of 1930 Ricky had dismissed all the servants but the cook and Hilda.

"I rather like it," she said. "I feel as though I belong in the house now."

There was no questin of selling it. They could hardly have given it away.

There were no cars now, no chauffeur to tuck the rug around Ricky's knees. But the children were still going to their expensive schools. One night she suggested public school for them, but Courtney objected violently.

"All I can give them is an education, Ricky."

She smiled.

"I'm a public school product, Court. It didn't hurt me."

He agreed finally. He was very gentle with her now, as

though the panic had drawn them together. They were closer than they had been for years, and it looked at last as though they had built a marriage which would survive. But the house remained a burden. No one wanted to buy it. And a good bit of the housework devolved on Ricky. One morning Roberta dropped in to find her on her knees scrubbing a bathroom floor. After that Roberta came frequently. She would come in, put on an apron, find a duster and a carpet sweeper, and without removing her hat set to work. When Ricky protested she ignored it.

"Why not?" she said. "I've done dirtier work. And men I knew drove milk carts and even locomotives during the general strike in England. As for housework, when Arthur got too hard up I used to fire the lot and do my own."

She was there, as it happened, the afternoon Emmy Baldwin came to see Ricky. A determined, hard-faced Emmy, with her hair no longer brassy, and her make-up carelessly applied. Ricky herself admitted her. Roberta was not in sight, and Emmy said nothing as she followed Ricky up the stairs.

It was a long time since the two women had met. And Ricky was puzzled.

"Can I give you some tea?" she suggested.

"Tea!" Emmy laughed shortly. "No, thanks. I'm not making a social call."

"Then why are you here? I hope you're not in trouble of any sort."

"Trouble! Who isn't?" She sat down and took a cigarette from a box. "Except you and Court. You seem to be doing all right. Other people are out in the streets but you're smug enough."

Ricky had not sat down. She looked down at Emmy, puzzled and uneasy. There was a momentary silence, when the only sound was the splashing of the wall fountain in the hall. Then Ricky spoke.

"I'm afraid I don't understand," she said.

Emmy leered at her.

"You wouldn't," she said. "Women like you never do. Protected women! God, they make me sick."

She had been drinking, but there was something deadly about her. Ricky sensed it without understanding it.

"I'm broke," Emmy said. "Flat busted. If you don't believe me ask your husband about it."

"Court? What has he got to do with it?"

"He gave me a list of stocks to buy. Only he was smart. He sold out. I didn't. All I had," she went on, becoming slightly maudlin. "Every dollar in the world, and it's gone."

"I'm frightfully sorry—" Ricky kept her voice even— "but I'm sure he must have warned you. After all, you were old friends."

"If that's what you care to call it!" Emmy laughed, but there was no doubt of the malice in her voice. "It's nice of you to put it that way, but maybe Court—"

Ricky stiffened.

"I have no intention of asking Court about you or your affairs. I don't know why you are here, Emmy. I'm sorry you've lost your money, but if this is polite blackmail I'm simply not interested."

Emmy opened her mouth furiously, and then closed it again. Roberta was standing in the doorway, staring at her with cold, malignant eyes.

"I'll see this person out," she said. "Don't bother, Ricky."

She wore her hat and a checked apron, but there was nothing humorous about her. Emmy put down her cigarette and got up.

"All right," she said. "I can take a hint. I'm going, Lady Truesdale. How are Sheila and her bootlegger getting on?"

Roberta ignored this. She stood aside and let Emmy start down the stairs, but she followed at her heels. She was still there when Emmy reached the pavement. Roberta closed the street door behind her and reaching out one bony hand caught Emmy by the arm.

"So you're trying to make trouble," she said. "The English have a nice word for that. They would call you a stinker. I think the American one is better. I believe it is bitch."

Emmy was frightened. There was something alarming in Roberta's face.

"Let go of me!" she said. "What business is it of yours anyhow?"

"I'm making it my business," said Roberta inflexibly. "If you start any trouble between Courtney Wayne and his wife you will be sorry. Very sorry."

"Just what would you propose to do?" Emmy demanded, her voice unsteady. "If you're threatening me, I'll go to the police."

Roberta released her, with a curious smile.

"Why not?" she said. "I'm quite definitely threatening you. I am even willing to be very drastic if I have to. I've seen a lot of trouble and even death in my time. I don't seem to mind them much any more."

Emmy managed a laugh as Roberta finished speaking.

"You're crazy," she said. "You ought to be shut up somewhere."

But she knew Roberta was not crazy. There was complete cold sanity in her eyes. Emmy shrugged and walked away, but her knees were weak. She felt as though someone behind her was pointing a loaded gun at her.

Roberta found Ricky where she had left her. She was standing in front of the mantel, trying to light a cigarette. Except that both cigarette and match wavered, she looked much as usual. Roberta gave her tops for that.

"She won't bother you again, Ricky. She'd been drinking."

"That doesn't alter what she was saying."

She broke down after that. Her unnatural composure left her.

"If there had to be a woman, why one like that? She's a common tramp. It makes me feel dirty. Cheap."

She cried a little on Roberta's skinny shoulder, but when Courtney came home she was her usual calm self. She even met him with a smile, for the man who came back to her that night—and every night—was a weary man, looking older than his years, and with even a little gray in his heavy dark hair. But after Roberta had gone she went out into the hall and shut off the fountain. As though it had been a symbol of something that was lost.

Courtney saw no change in her. He was distracted, almost frantic at times. When he could not sleep he used the daybed in his dressing room. And the market continued to slide. By the summer of 1930 most of those who had managed to hold on were slowly being eliminated.

The business, however, was still carrying on. Matthew had thrown all his resources into the company, and so far they were managing. At night he went home to a bewildered Elizabeth in the small apartment they had taken, and Katie, back again after all, and Elizabeth eating little or nothing. Where had the money gone? She had had it, now she did not.

"It never was yours, Lizzie."

"But it was. I had a million dollars, Matt. More than that."

One day Courtney went into his office to find Roberta there. She still wore the same incredible hat. And because it was her habit, she still carried the umbrella that had dripped on Emmy's carpet. But—as was also her habit—she lost no time in preamble.

"I'm a little anxious about Sheila, Court," she said. "I've let her live her own life, like most mothers do today. But she's going around with a bootlegger. She says she's going to fix up an apartment for him somewhere, but I think it's more than that."

"You mean she's living with him?" he asked bluntly.

"No. I think she has had affairs. She came of age at a bad time, and apparently chastity isn't important any more. No, I think she's in love this time. You know him, Courtney. He was your mother's chauffeur years ago. His name is Walter. Walter Kincaid."

Courtney whistled.

"Walter!" he said. "Well, he used to be a decent sort of

chap. Matter of fact both Dad and I buy our liquor from him."

"Apparently there's money in bootlegging," she said calmly. "Or was. I suppose it will soon be over, if the wets can manage it. Only—it's dangerous, isn't it?"

"He seems to have managed all right so far, Aunt Roberta. She might do a lot worse."

He was grateful that she did not mention Emmy, or her visit to her revolting apartment. But he smiled too after she had gone. He thought Arthur Truesdale might be whirling in his grave.

Sheila and Walter Kincaid were married soon after Roberta's visit. Elizabeth had refused to be present, but Matthew was there, and Ricky. She and Courtney stood up with them, but the ceremony was a dreary one. The office was shabby and dusty, and the magistrate himself clearly bored. But there was nothing either dreary or bored in Sheila's face, or in Walter's eyes when he kissed her after it was over.

"I'll be good to her, Lady Truesdale," he told Roberta. "Don't worry about her. She'll be fine."

"She'll have you to worry about," Roberta said. "Better take care of yourself, young man."

Walter glanced at the magistrate, but he had pocketed his fee and looked completely disinterested.

"I'll manage all right," he said. "It won't be long anyhow. Then Shilly and I are going to have a farm somewhere."

It was odd to hear him call Sheila Shilly; odd and rather tender.

Courtney and Matthew went back to the office and their problems. Sales were steadily dropping. *The Drifters* helped, but it was not enough. And by the summer of 1931 it was clear that the depression was to be a long one. All over the country there was unrest and resentment. The dam had burst on the wise and the unwise, the poor and the rich. And to add to the general consternation the hunger marchers came to Washington, two thousand of them in a mass demonstration. They came in trucks, camped near the railroad yards, and carefully guarded by police, marched along Pennsylvania Avenue in a straggling but ominous line.

"Remember that fellow years ago," Courtney said to Mather. "To him there were only two thrills, sex and crime. Maybe we'd better add another. Revolution."

"I thought you were a liberal," Mather jeered. "Don't take it too hard, Court. Ever read what Walt Whitman thought of the men who were in the Congress after the Civil War?"

"I don't read Whitman."

"Well, I don't remember it exactly. He said they were pimps, for one thing. Also conspirators, murderers, syphilitics, spies and bribers. I forget the rest."

There was no talk of opening the Bar Harbor house. It had not been sold. For two summers now it had stood dank and cold behind its closed blinds, the pool empty and the fish on the fountain no longer spouting. And that summer of 1931 Ricky took the children to her mother's. They needed a change and so did she. Not only was she tired, she needed to get away, to get some perspective on her marriage after almost fourteen years.

Perhaps Courtney would be better without her for a while, too. The long strain was telling on him. Even the children angered him at times; the rough talk they brought from the public school, their noise and bad manners.

"Get up when your mother comes into the room, Jeff."

"Oh heck, I'm reading."

"Get up, I tell you."

Jeff would unfold his rangy length sulkily and stand. He was almost eleven now, and growing too fast. But he was headstrong and often recalcitrant. It annoyed him that Peggy tagged after him wherever he went.

"Mother, tell her to let me alone. I'm only going to the drugstore on Madison Avenue."

"He's going for a soda, Mummie. I guess I can walk there if I want to. The pavement's free."

At eight Peggy was losing some of her baby fat. She was a pretty child, with yellow curls and dark eyes, but Courtney spoiled her.

"How's my girl tonight?"

"All right, Daddy. What's that? Candy?"

Ricky did her best with them all, although at times the house itself seemed to bear down on her as a physical burden she could hardly carry. But it was sanctuary to Court, and she tried to keep it clean and quiet for him. At night she rubbed cold cream into her roughened hands, and crawled exhausted into bed to wait for him. But often she was asleep before he came upstairs, and on the night before she left with the children she wakened at two o'clock to find he had not come up at all.

She put on a dressing gown and slippers and went down to his study. He was sitting at his desk, his empty pipe in front of him and his head in his hands. He was not asleep, however. She put a hand on his shoulder.

"What is it, Court? Why don't you come to bed?"

He turned, startled, to give her a sheepish smile.

"Sorry I worried you, darling. I'll come in a minute."

"There's something wrong, isn't there? Is it anything new?"

He took a long breath.

"Not new, particularly. It's the same old story. I've got the interest on this house to pay and the taxes. And what little was left of Mother's stuff is about gone. This damned market is like a greased pig. You can't hold it."

"We can put down further. I can let Hilda go."

"No. You need her. God knows you do enough." He reached out and taking one of her chafed hands looked at it with a strange look on his face. "I was wondering—when you get home, Ricky, will you see how things are out there? Even what I send your mother counts up. It's little enough, I know, but if she can do without it . . ."

She sat down, rather breathless.

"Of course, if it's as bad as that," she said. "There must be some way to manage. Beulah's strong. They might rent some rooms. The house is big enough."

He got up and kissed her. Then he did an unusual thing. He

opened a drawer of his desk and took out the long dark braids they had cut off when her hair was shingled. They were in a box and he ran his fingers over them gently.

"I always loved your hair, Ricky," he said. "Do you remember when Peggy was born? You looked like a madonna that day."

She was deeply touched.

"I didn't know you cared about it, Court."

"Maybe I didn't know myself," he said heavily. "I do now, darling."

Some of the old warmth between them came back that night. She felt less frozen than she had since Emmy's visit. And Courtney looked rather desolate when he saw them off the next day.

"God, I'll miss you," he said. "And you kids are to behave. Your mother's worn out. Look after her. She's had enough of looking after you."

It was still daylight when they left. As they went through New Jersey Ricky realized what she had not understood in the city, the closed mills, the smokeless factory chimneys. There was something else that shocked her, the freights they passed with men and boys huddled on them, not knowing where they were going; only hoping that somewhere else would be better than where they had been.

It did not help to know that the depression was world-wide, the inevitable result of world war and the economic problems that had followed it. All she could see was boys, some of them not much older than Jeff, holding precariously to their perches on the moving trains.

29

Ricky was still more startled when she got out of the train the next morning. There were no cars in sight, not even the local taxicab, and the railroad spur leading to the factory was grown up with grass. Even the station agent seemed to move more slowly as he greeted her with his dour smile.

"Kind of different from the last time you were here, isn't it?" he said. "Place's as lively as an amputated leg." He glanced down at the children, who were eying him with bright-eyed curiosity. "These kids yours?"

"Yes. This is an old friend of mine, children."

Peggy made her small curtsy and held out a small hand. Jeff grinned.

"It must be fun around here. I like trains. But I'm going to fly a plane when I grow up."

"That's fine, son." He looked at Ricky. "Place is dead," he said. "Died overnight, you might say. They ain't even finished the new hotel. Never will now, I reckon." He seemed to take a macabre sort of pleasure in the situation. "Lots of wise guys around here got their comeuppance all right. Them and their new cars and fancy doings!"

He spat, to the children's delight, and Ricky was relieved when at last a taxi arrived and she could bundle them into it. Nevertheless, the town appalled her. It was as though a moving picture had abruptly stopped. She had the same sense of shock. And all over the country this was going on. There was the same blank dazed look on the faces of people, the same hopeless inertia.

It was a relief to find the house much as she had left it. Evidently Courtney's allowance had helped. The lawn was cut and the porch steps mended. But she was surprised when Beulah, opening the door, put her finger to her lips.

"She's sleeping," she said. "She got excited about your coming, and you know her. She had to have everything just right. I kep' her in bed. She don't sleep so well." She leaned down over the children. "So these are your babies! Come in, young miss and master. Beulah's mighty glad to see you."

They eyed her as they had the stationmaster, with the usual suspicion of all children for strangers. But Beulah had the gift of her race. In no time at all they were at home with her. That morning as she washed the train dirt off them she talked to them steadily.

"Now you're going to be quiet, because your grandma's not well. You and me both, quiet as mice. Lemme at that pretty hair of yours, Miss Peggy. Looks like there's been mice in it too."

She got heavily down on her knees to wipe their shoes, and Peggy inspected her gravely.

"Why's your skin so black?"

Beulah chuckled.

"Because the good Lord made it that way. He said: Some of my children's to be white, and some red and some yellow. The rest is going to be black, so the sun won't bother them none."

"Doesn't it? Bother you?"

"Bless you, no. I like the good old sun."

To Ricky's great relief, Pete and Jeff hit it off from the start. Pete had improved, in both speech and manners, although he occasionally let loose language which made her shudder. He was thirteen now, a tall boy who immediately patronized Jeff and took him in tow.

"Bet you never climbed a tree."

"I have too. At Bar Harbor."

"Where's that? Never heard of it. Come on, let's see you

do it."

From that time on she saw them only at mealtimes, when they would come in dirty and hungry. Only Peggy seemed at a loss. The little girls around made small uneasy advances to the city child.

"Can't you come over and play?"

But she was shy, shy and detached.

"No, thanks. I have to stay here."

They were slightly afraid of her, of her blonde curls, her socks and white sandals, her full fluffy dresses. When she did talk to them she did not help matters. Once Ricky overheard a bit of conversation. A child in rompers had wandered into the yard.

"This your house?"

"Goodness, no! I live in a big house. It has an elevator and everything. It has a fountain in the hall too."

There was no use scolding her, but sometimes Ricky thought she saw a bit of Elizabeth in her: the same quiet determination to have her own way, the same pride of place.

But Ricky was worried about her mother. That first morning when she had finally wakened, Mrs. Stafford was indignant at Beulah.

"Really," she said. "I'll have to get rid of her. The way she acts, as if she was head of the house. I had it all fixed to go to the station."

"I'm glad you didn't. The children were tired and dirty."

She asked after them then, but she was only mildly interested. Clearly her real love was given to Dave's boy. And Ricky, sitting beside the bed, was shocked to find how ill she looked. Her lips had a slightly bluish tinge, and she seemed more short of breath than when she saw her last.

One thing was certain, however. Courtney would have to continue to help her. There could be no talk of cutting her allowance, or of paying guests, or roomers. She was definitely a sick woman.

Ricky spent most of her time at home with her. People

called, putting on their best clothes and sitting in the parlor while she tried to make talk. But like everybody else, something had happened to them. It had left them unhappy and uncertain. The bank had failed, the factory had closed. In many cases their small savings had gone, they did not know why or where.

Not that they spoke of any of this. They were politeness itself.

"You have such lovely children, Mrs. Wayne."

"I think so. And don't call me Mrs. Wayne. I'm Ricky, just as I always was."

They still had their churches. On Sundays they sat in their pews and tried to think that all this was meant. They sang that there was a wideness in God's mercy like the wideness of the sea, but they still felt adrift. Ricky, marshaling the children to the old pew, was divided between pride and pity.

She had been there only two weeks when Courtney wrote her he was going to England.

"Father thinks I'd better see our people over there," he said, "and with you away it seems a good time. It's only a flying trip, darling, or I would take you along."

He was to be gone a month, but she felt lost and rather lonely when he left. He sent her a good-bye cable from the ship with love to them all, and he mailed her a check, for now she was paying all their expenses. Even with Courtney's allowance Beulah had barely managed.

"It's them doctor bills," she explained. "Not that they do her any good. She won't even take her medicine."

It was after Courtney's cable came that she saw Jay again. She had been marketing and was carrying a basket on her arm when he came across the street.

"Ricky! When did you get here?"

"A couple of weeks ago. It seems longer. I brought the children."

He took the basket and fell into step beside her, smiling down at her.

"And I had to choose that time to go fishing!"

"You look as though it had agreed with you."

"Nothing else to do. No business. I suppose this town looks like a minor tragedy to you, but it's real enough. It hasn't hit you, has it? I suppose people still buy books."

"We've saved our house. That's about all. Of course there's the business."

He glanced at her. There was a new note in her voice. It had no bitterness. It was merely that it lacked its old lilt. Something had gone out of it. Perhaps it was only youth. How old was she? Ony in her early thirties, and still lovely. Even lovelier than ever. But she was thin. Too thin.

"Well, everything passes. This will too. The wheel turns. Sometimes we're up on top of it, sometimes we're down under it. How about taking the kids for a picnic someday? They ought to know me. I'm their Uncle Jay. There was a time when I hoped I'd be closer than that. That gives me a claim of sorts, doesn't it?"

She found herself flushing.

"Of course. They'll love it."

He carried her basket home, claiming to have nothing else to do. If he suffered a small pang when he saw Peggy he concealed it. Peggy was on the pavement, balanced precariously on a pair of roller skates while a boy stood by watching her. Even then Peggy liked boys better than girls.

"Hello," Jay said. "And what young lady is this?"

Peggy eyed him critically.

"I'm Peggy Wayne."

"Well, well, who'd have thought it! Would you shake hands with your Uncle Jay?"

But Peggy, being Peggy, put up her face to be kissed. He looked slightly embarrassed.

"Do you do that with all the men you meet?"

"Only with the nice ones."

"God," he said to Ricky as Peggy skated off shakily. "I'd go nuts about a kid like that. I'd better go. You'll have me sobbing on your shoulder in a minute."

A few days later they held the picnic, the three children in the back seat of the car, Ricky and Jay in front. As they passed the abandoned Stewart farm Ricky thought she saw a woman by the barn. Whoever it was, she disappeared and Ricky promptly forgot her. There was a small wry quirk of amusement in Jay's face when he stopped at the old high school picnic ground.

"Don't use it any more," he observed as he lifted out the baskets. "They have dances instead, or go to the movies. We were a pretty innocent lot, weren't we, Ricky?"

They ate their lunch at a rough table. Jay cooked steaks over hot wood ashes at the open fireplace, his face intent and serious. And Ricky, laying out the paper plates and cups, found herself wondering what her life would have been had she married him instead of Court. Jay would have been faithful, she thought. Their lives might have been unexciting, but she would at least have felt safe.

When the meal was over Pete took the youngsters off, and Jay looked after them.

"How's Pete doing?"

"All right, I think. Mother adores him. Of course, a lot of him is Stewart."

"Considered pretty wild here in town," Jay said, and scrapped the subject. He lay back on the grass and looked at her.

"Rather fantastic, isn't it?" he said. "Here I am where I longed to be. Home is the sailor, home from the sea, and so on. And it doesn't mean a damn thing." When she said nothing he smiled. "All right, Ricky, don't let me worry you. I'm just Old Faithful. Don't mind my spouting."

"Why don't you marry, Jay?"

"Oh, I'm all right. I'm no celibate. I've got a girl in Columbus, I see her now and then. There's no sentiment in it. After all, what do we expect out of life? We can't live on mountaintops forever." He laughed. "Good God, I'm going netaphorical again."

The drive home was quiet. No one was in sight at the Stewart place, and the children were tired. She got them all to bed as oon as she could, and went in to her mother. Mrs. Stafford was wake. She was holding her Bible but not reading it, and she vas breathing heavily. Ricky put an extra pillow behind her nd, leaning over, kissed her.

"Pete loved the picnic, Mother."

"He's like his father. Dave liked the woods."

But any hope she had of discussing money with Mrs. Stafford died that night. They were just getting along. When here was a small margin—which was not often—her mother ad bought Pete bonds with it. He kept them in his room and vas very proud of them. He earned a little money for himself oo. He cut grass for the neighbors.

"He's as good as any of them," Mrs. Stafford said. "He's egitimate and this town knows it. I put it in the paper."

"Mother!"

"All I did was to announce Dave's marriage. It shut them up a hurry."

She was growing excited, so Ricky kissed her and left. She vent out on the porch and looked down on the lawn where long go her father had stood with the garden hose. Behind her was ne window where her mother had set a light, to bring David afely home from a war. There was no light there now.

She sat down in the cool darkness. From somewhere nearby ame the sound of quiet voices, and a slight cool breeze ruffled ne leaves of the vine that shaded the porch. Somewhere not ar away a plane was moving. She could hear the drone of its notors, but she could not see its lights.

She was still there when she heard a woman's voice from the orch steps.

"Hello, Mrs. Wayne," it said. "I've come to get Pete."

Annie Stewart came up on the porch. In the light from the all Ricky could see she looked half sick, and she coughed as ne sat down.

"What do you mean, you've come for Pete?" Ricky said incredulously. "To take him away?"

"Why not? He's a good-sized boy by this time. He can get a job, and when I'm better I can work too. We can stay at the farm for a while. There's nobody living at it. And there's some stuff in the house. We can manage."

Ricky pulled herself together.

"You wouldn't do that to him, would you? He has a good home here. And of course he can't work. He has to go to school."

"He could work part time," said Annie stubbornly.

"But you're not well yourself. Perhaps we could find a place where you could stay until you get better."

"I'm all right. It's only this cough. He's my own son. Just remember that, Mrs. Wayne. You folks have no claim on him."

"He's my brother's son too."

"Lot's of good that did him!" Annie said, her voice rising. "When Pop left, your ma grabbed him. It's kidnaping, that's what it is. And I want him back."

She was determined. Also she was frank. She had been in a house in Columbus, she said. The fellow she ran off with had left her stranded, and what was she to do? There had been good money in it at first, and on Saturday night and Sunday the millworkers crowded the place, sometimes standing in rows for admission.

"It was a cheap place, of course," Annie said matter-of-factly. "And a lot of those big bums treated a girl pretty rough."

But Annie had got along all right. She didn't mind it. She could sleep all day, and when she got up she didn't have to bother to dress. She just went around barefooted or in worn carpet slippers, in the nightgown she had slept in. But by night, of course, they were made up and ready, smoking their eternal cigarettes, dancing together to a phonograph or playing childish games until the men began to arrive. Now and then, of course, one of them became infected. The woman who ran the house paid their bills until they were out of the hospital, but she would not take them back.

That was what had happened to her.

"She gave me twenty dollars," she said, lighting a cigarette while Ricky stared at her incredulously. "That's how I got here. But she said I was still sick. That's a dirty lie. I'm all over it. It's only because times are bad now. She's a mean old bitch."

Ricky recovered her voice.

"Is that what you're planning to take Pete back to?"

"No, I'm all through. I'll get a job and he can work. He's mine. I'm his mother. I have a right to him."

Neither of them had seen or heard the boy in the hall. The cigarette had started Annie coughing again, and Ricky had risen to get her some water. He chose that minute to come up on the porch and close the door behind him. He waited, in his pajamas and slippers, until the coughing stopped. Then:

"Hello, Mom," he said, his voice a trifle stiff. "Where did you come from?"

"Pete! Is that you, Pete?"

He moved slowly toward her, and she began to cry. He did nothing about that. He stood by her, waiting for her to stop and glancing uneasily at Ricky. When at last Annie got a soiled handkerchief from her bag and dried her eyes he still made no move toward her. But he let her reach out and put an arm around him.

"I've been sick, Pete," she said. "Awful sick."

"Gee, I'm sorry, Mom."

"I haven't any money either, Pete. I want to go back home. You'll go with me, won't you?"

"To the farm? There's nothing there. It doesn't belong to us, anyhow."

"Then we'll get a room somewhere. You wouldn't leave me alone, would you, Pete? I'm sick. Maybe I'm going to die. I need you. I'm your own mother. You haven't forgotten me, have you?"

"No," he said slowly. "I remember you all right, Mom. I guess if it's like that . . ."

He glanced at Ricky, fairly desperate by that time.

"You can't do it, Pete," she said. "I'll see that she's taken care of. She needn't be alone at all. Think it over, anyhow. You've been happy here, haven't you? Think it over."

He drew a long almost gasping breath.

"She's my mother," he said. "I guess I belong with her."

There was no love in his simple declaration; no particular interest in the woman who claimed him. He was merely seeing his duty and intending to do it. But there was Dave's stubborness too in his mouth and young chin.

"I'd better go upstairs and pack," he said. "Don't worry, Mom. I'll come along all right."

He turned and went into the house. Ricky thought there were tears in his eyes as he went, but his slight body was erect in his striped pajamas. Annie regarded her with triumph.

"You can't do a thing about it," she said. "Not a thing. He's coming because he wants to."

"He's going with you because he's sorry for you," Ricky said contemptuously. "You've played a cheap dirty trick, but it won't work. Not if I have to call the police."

Annie, however, was not looking at her. She was gazing at the hall door. Mrs. Stafford was standing there, a hand clutched to her chest.

"What's wrong with Pete?" she said, her voice thick. "He won't speak to me. He—"

Then she saw Annie, and staggered.

"What are you doing here?" she demanded.

Annie smiled at her.

"I've come for my son," she said. "He's going away with me."

Mrs. Stafford did not answer. She drew a long strangling breath, clutched at the doorframe for support and then slid almost gently to the floor. By the time Ricky reached her she was dead . . .

Ricky did not cry until Jay arrived and took her in his arms.

"My poor girl," he said, and let her sob on his shoulder.

She cried her heart out, there with his arms around her. Something sternly repressed for a long time revived as he held her. He could have wept for her and for himself, for the years gone by, for his own frustration and her grief. "Don't cry, sweetheart," he said huskily. "She's at rest now." He hardly knew he was speaking.

Beulah was on her knees beside the dead woman, a picture of despair.

"I told her," she said over and over. "Her old Beulah told her, over and over."

Not until the doctor arrived did Ricky miss Annie. She released herself from Jay's arms and dried her eyes on his handkerchief. The doctor was bending over the still figure on the floor. He straightened slowly.

"I'm sorry, Ricky," he said. And to Jay: "We'd better get Mrs. Stafford upstairs."

Ricky could not watch them. She turned her back, listening to their careful footsteps as they carried her mother for the last time to her room. Beulah had gone ahead of them. She was alone, and it was then she realized that Annie had gone.

Only a few minutes later Beulah came lumbering down the stairs.

"That Pete!" she said. "He's gone, Miss Ricky. He's taken his clothes and all he had. And he's been at your pocketbook. It's on the floor empty."

They had escaped completely. Jay searching for them at the old farm the next day found no sign of them. The stationmaster had not seen them either, and he had to go back to Ricky with the news. She took it almost indifferently, though, as the shock of her mother's death had deadened her to everything else. It was a part of her grief that she had not loved her mother. But her mother had never cared for her as she had for Dave. Her whole life had been centered on Dave.

"He may come back," she said wearily. "Annie had been

living in a disorderly house. I'm afraid she got something there. If he finds it out he'll leave her."

Only of course there would be no place for him to come back to. Matthew had come out to help her, and he told her so after the funeral. He and Jay had taken hold of everything, and she had had a cable from Courtney sending his sympathy and love. But even Court seemed far away. If she was willing, they told her, the house was to be sold, and the furniture auctioned off. She agreed. What else was there to do? It took some time, however, to get ready for the sale. Matthew left her there and went back to New York, taking the children with him. They had been wide-eyed and excited over what had happened.

"Why do they put flowers on the door, Mummy?" This was Peggy.

"To show that the people inside are very sad, darling."

They were sent to a neighbor's for the services themselves, but their curiosity was endless.

"I touched Grandmother," Peggy reported. "Her hand was cold as ice."

She was glad to get them away, with Beulah preparing to go to her son Joe in the country, and while she counted sheets and towels and stacked the familiar china, she realized that one page of her life had been turned, finally and forever.

She saw a good bit of Jay during the time that followed. He was continuing his search for Pete, notifying the police, even advertising in the papers, but without result. He was unobtrusively helpful, wandering in to move the few things she wanted to keep or to give to Beulah.

"Going to sleep soft on that bed," he would tell the big colored woman. "Here, help me put it on the back porch."

Never, however, had they gone back to the night of her mother's death, but he told her one day that there would be a home for Pete if he came back.

"He's Dave's boy, Ricky, and I live alone. I'd like to have something that—" He checked himself. "I like boys. Maybe I could make something of him."

She thanked him gravely.

Once again the town called, sitting in decorous sympathy in the dismantled living room, talking in low voices, and going out wondering that she was not wearing mourning. It believed in mourning. It was a "protection." Also it was a decent tribute to the dead. But it did not forget that Jay was in and out of the house rather often.

"Always was crazy about her. That's why he never married. Where's her husband?"

When the day of the auction came Ricky could not face it. It was like selling her girlhood, like a rape of her past. Before the crowd gathered, she strolled out to the airfield where once long ago Court and Dave had drilled, had jumped trenches and jabbed their bayonets into straw-stuffed sacks, while a red-faced sergeant yelled at them.

"For God's sake, don't tickle them!" he would bellow. "You hate those fellows—they're Germans. They're trying to kill you. Get them in the guts, the bastards! In the guts!"

There was nothing to keep her now. She spent the night at the old hotel and the next afternoon before traintime she drove with Jay into the country. He was constrained and unhappy.

"I'll miss you, Ricky. You can't realize what these last few weeks have meant to me."

"I wouldn't have known what to do without you," she said gratefully.

He slowed down and looked at her.

"I wish I felt you were happy, darling. Of course I know—your mother's death, and Pete. But even before that, there was something, wasn't there? Something wrong?"

She had a wild desire to talk to him, to tell him her uncertainties, to get his own masculine point of view. But she could not be disloyal to Court.

"People have to build a marriage, Jay. I've had the usual problems, that's all."

"He's kind to you?"

"Always."

"I think I'd kill anyone who deliberately hurt you."

"He's never done that. Never. Naturally he's been worried. His mother was in the stock market, and it's made it hard for all of us."

He picked up one of her hands and looked at it. It was softer than when she came, but her nails still looked broken and chipped. He said nothing, however. He let it drop and changed the subject.

"If Pete comes back and I take him it will be for your sake, Ricky. I'll do my best to make him a man."

"I know that, Jay."

"And I'm always here," he said. "Good old reliable Uncle Jay to your kids! God, Ricky, how am I to let you go?" He stopped the car and put his arms around her. "Let's say good-bye now, darling. I don't mean to be bitter. It's just that I've been living too long on husks."

He gave her a hard kiss and let her go.

30

Courtney had not realized how fatigued he was until he got on the ship. It was his father's idea, and he had been pleased with it at the time.

"We might be able to jack up some of our British friends," Matthew had said. "We need them and they need us. Not for lectures, either. We can talk to ourselves. You might try the French too, although we never got anything worth a damn from them."

He sailed a few days later. The Atlantic was quiet, and he slept a good deal in his stateroom or on deck in his chair. Now and then he wandered into the bar for a drink, but he made no acquaintances on the voyage and the few people he knew he avoided. But England dejected him from the start.

"Why come to us?" their London agent said as they lunched at Boulestin's—at Court's expense. "We're looking to you for material. There's nothing here."

It seemed incredible. The country which had produced Wells, Swinnerton, Maugham, Galsworthy and dozens of others had no new writers and a few of the old ones were producing.

"What happened?"

"What's happened all over the world? Ever think you people had a lot to do with it?"

"I know we fought a war, if you English don't," Court said grimly.

"If you'd joined the League of Nations—"

"You could have had a European League without us."

The meal ended amicably, but he left England with little to show for his trip. Nor was France any better. His Paris agent was pessimistic. Not only about writers. He expected another war with Germany.

"So we build the East Wall!" he said resignedly. "We build the Maginot Line, to point all our guns at a front the Germans did not use before and will not use again. Perhaps if they had—" He smiled thinly. "Have you ever thought, my friend, that if the Germans had come that way and not through Belgium, the British would have let us fight alone? They had an agreement with Belgium. They had none with us."

Courtney spent only a few days in France. He took time out to see some of the battlefields, but he could not orient himself among them. Nature had put a protective covering of green over most of them, and the towns he remembered as flattened masses of rubble had been rebuilt. Only the vast cemeteries remained. But after the fourteen years Paris had not regained its prewar gaiety. The people looked sober and anxious. Even the prostitutes who accosted him had lost their insouciance. They looked shabby, and many of them were middle-aged.

He had not intended to go to Germany, but so far his errand had brought in very little. At the end of a week he took a plane and flew to Berlin.

Rudolph Hauck, their German representative, met him at the airfield. He was a Prussian, with the heavy build and short neck of his people. But he had a pleasant face and greeted Courtney with a smile.

"So," he said in his clipped Oxford English, which sounded so odd coming from him. "Look around you and see what we have done with your money!" He made a sweeping gesture over the vast Tempelhof airfield. "This is only a small part of it. You Americans have been lavish with us, Court. And you know us. We take all we can get."

Before this cheerful cynicism, Court found little to say. Hauck took him in a taxi to the Adlon, but he was not optimistic about manuscripts. He lowered his voice so the cab driver could not hear.

"What can you expect?" he said. "We are muzzled here, all of us. It is not safe to think, even less safe to write. And our writers have no martyr blood in them." He waved a hand out the window. "Great Berlin!" he said. "The third largest city in the world, the publishing center of Europe; and a year from now not even the bravest of us will be able to say what he thinks."

"There have been a few good German novels in the last ten years."

"Most of them by people who have left the country," Hauck said bitterly.

They dined together that night at a restaurant with a stage and floor show. But Hauck was in a dour mood. When a comedian, making an exit, dropped to his hands and knees, sniffed dog-fashion at a painted tree and then raised a leg against it—to wild applause—he grinned at Court.

"You see?" he said. "We are a delicate and fastidious people. That is our idea of humor."

"The French have worse."

"Only for tourist purposes. Don't listen to me, Court. My mother was a Jewess. I'm likely to be in the hell of a spot someday."

It was largely boredom that led Courtney to call on Professor von Wagner a day or so later. He walked there, stopping now and then at a bookshop. Some of the Wayne books were there, but they were old titles. At a stall he found *The Passion Flower* in a Tauchnitz edition, but the dealers all looked disheartened, and their stocks were small. He noticed that several of them displayed Karl Marx.

When he found the address it was a shabby house, reconverted into flats. The professor lived on the fourth floor.

The stairs were clean but not too firm, and his first sight of the old man shocked him.

He was definitely an old man now, his beard white and his hair thin. He peered nearsightedly from the door of what was both living room and bedroom before he recognized him. Then he held out both hands.

"Captain!" he said. "Captain Wayne! So you come to see me at last." He drew him into the room. "It is like old times, is it not so?"

It was not, however. The room was small and dark, and its poverty was only too obvious. But the old man was excited and pleased as he drew out chairs.

"So you did not forget?" he said. "I so often think of you and the days—" A shadow passed over his face. "I had my dear wife then, and my daughters. Now I sit alone much of the time. Of course I see Hedwig, who lives not far from here. She does my marketing for me. But Elsa—"

"I was wondering about Elsa," Court said as he sat down. "You wrote that she was in Munich."

"Yes. Perhaps it is as well she is not here. Time does strange things to us, Captain. We think we know our children. Then they grow up and go their own way."

"You said that she is married."

"Yes, she is married. Soon after you left. Now her husband is a Nazi. You know about them, of course. And she herself is of the party. She seldom sees me any more. I tell her of the S. S. men and the Storm Troops, that they are wicked and cruel, but she thinks I am a fool."

Court listened incredulously.

"It doesn't sound like her," he said. "She was a quiet girl, very gentle, as I recall her."

"A wife grows like her husband, always."

It was evident that the subject worried him, and Courtney let it drop.

The professor insisted on making him a cup of coffee on a

small gas stove. He explained that it was not mocha, but at least it was hot and stimulating. It was synthetic, so was everything else in Germany, but he made no complaints.

"I manage," he said. "It is not like the inflation. Then the mark went down until we carried our money in baskets, and workers were paid two and three times a day. It was not safe to wait overnight."

He was excited when Court offered him an American cigarette. He had not seen one for a long time, he said. He was even more pleased when Court gave him the rest of the package. And over the cigarette he reverted to the Nazis and to Elsa, who had married one.

"She has a son," he said. "How old is Otto? Let me think. He was born here in Berlin. He must be twelve years now. It is a shameful thing to say, but I am afraid to speak what I think before him. I do not trust him," he added, with the first touch of bitterness he had shown. "A fine tall good-looking boy, but he alarms me. It is what they teach him, at home and in the schools.

"Wait a moment, I have here a picture of him with his mother."

He rummaged in a drawer and brought out a photograph and while he fussed with the coffee Courtney carried it to a window.

Mother and son were standing together, Elsa in a white dress, the boy beside her. She had not greatly changed, Court saw. She was still small and slender. The boy was as tall as she already. But when at last he looked at the child he almost dropped the picture. Except for the clothes and the hair it was Jeff who looked out at him; the eyes, the young mouth, the small square chin were all Jeff.

He never remembered how he left that day. He got out somehow, and went down the stairs. So distracted was he that he bumped against a heavy-set woman wearing spectacles in the lower hall and made her drop the basket she was carrying.

Not until he had gathered up and replaced her packages did he so much as look at her. Then he recognized her.

"Why, Hedwig!" he managed. "You haven't forgotten me, have you?"

She regarded him unsmilingly.

"I am surprised you come here, Herr Captain."

"I am not a captain now. And why the surprise, Hedwig?"

"If you do not know I shall not tell you. But I think you do know."

There was antagonism in every muscle of her stiff body, every line of her face. Courtney stood staring at her, unable to find any words. And she went on, coldly and inexorably.

"You could have done something. She was alone and helpless. She even had no money. Can you imagine that, Captain Wayne? No money at all."

He found his voice again.

"I didn't know, Hedwig. I swear I never knew until just now. I saw his picture."

She had put down her basket. Now she stooped and picked it up.

"She had to marry at once, to marry a man she disliked. Can you imagine that too, Herr Captain? He thinks the boy is his. And so he is, Elsa's and his. You cannot take him away. He is a Nazi now. How do you like that?"

She did not wait for an answer. She climbed the stairs, a typical German housfrau, her legs heavy, her body thick and coarse. He turned and went out into the street.

Back at the hotel he went into the bar and took a drink. It steadied him somewhat, but in his room again he fell to pacing the floor. There was nothing he could do for his German son, or for Elsa. The secret had been well kept. Nevertheless, he was in a wretched frame of mind. There was a saying that old sins left long shadows. He knew now that they did.

But he could not stay in Germany. He wanted to go home to the security and peace of his marriage, to Ricky and his children; his other children, he thought, and felt faintly sick.

He got a ship at Bremerhaven a day or two later. It was a fast ship, but the voyage seemed endless. He felt as though he had not drawn a full breath until he saw Ricky on the pier. She looked exhausted, but she gave him a radiant smile. It was over, he thought. All over. In the taxi he took her in his arms and held her close.

31

By the summer of 1932 it became increasingly obvious that Hoover would be defeated. Matthew wired him frantically to support the anti-Prohibitionists but he failed to do so. And his Congress was sour and disgruntled.

For now the vast bonus army was making its so-called death march around the Capitol, and building its huts of tin and corrugated iron wherever it could find space. Labor was still a drug on the market, although now there was no Mr. Zero—as in 1921—imitating the old slave sales, and auctioning unemployed men to whoever would take them. "Here's a big fellow, strong and healthy. About a hundred and seventy pounds. Willing to do anything. Who wants him?"

There was talk that Hoover had wanted to close the banks, to prevent further catastrophe; that he had summoned a number of financiers to a secret meeting in Washington at Andrew Mellon's apartment. He had got nowhere. The men sitting in Mellon's vast rooms under his priceless paintings were unwilling to take so drastic a step.

Matthew was appalled at all this. To blame one man for a world depression was ridiculous. To blame the Republicans for it was plain wicked. He sat at his desk, roaring with fury.

"Why elect Roosevelt of all people?" he shouted. "Look at the condition this state is in! Look at its debt! The man's a spending fool. And he's a Brahmin, at that. How does he get that way?"

But at least the election of Roosevelt that fall meant the end of Prohibition. Not yet, of course. It would take time, and in the interval he still bought his liquor from Walter. It came disguised as china, or preserves, or anything but what it was. One day Walter delivered it himself, wearing overalls and driving a small truck.

"Had a driver knocked out last night," he explained. "He's in the hospital."

"Pretty dangerous job, isn't it? All this, I mean."

"Well, we get our knocks. But I'm making hay while the sun's still shining." And he added, "Don't worry about Sheila, Mr. Wayne. I've laid up quite a bit. She'll be all right."

"How is she? We don't see much of her any more."

"She's fine. She stays a lot with me at New Bedford. That's what you might call my base. Don't you worry about her, Mr. Wayne. My men are a decent lot. And we stick to our business." He smiled. "No slot machines, no stolen cars, no bawdyhouses. And we sure let the unions alone. We're not gangsters."

He hurried out, a businessman going about his business, which was no more lawless, Matthew considered, than his own drinking of forbidden liquor. What would happen to him when this fellow Roosevelt got in? Maybe they could use him somewhere. Useful man, Walter.

Now and then that fall Ricky had a letter from Sheila. They were ecstatic; almost exalted. Walter was wonderful. Her life was wonderful. She had even gone out one night in the boat with him, and they had been chased. It was fun, but Walter would not let her do it again.

"He was terribly scared for me," she wrote, "and for heaven's sake don't tell Mother. She would lose her mind, or think I'd lost mine."

But there was nothing in the letters about the long nights when she waited alone, walking the floor of the hotel bedroom while Walter was away, either in his boat or to see to the loading of his trucks in a small cove a few miles along a deserted beach, or even to take a truck himself. Of the agony of watching the clock hour after hour, and of seeing the sun come up without any sign of him. And then the almost hysterical relief of his footsteps in the hall, his hand on the doorknob, and his coming in and taking her in his arms.

"All over, honey! Everything's fine. Didn't worry, did you?"

Worry! As if that was the word for it! He would bathe and put on his dressing gown. And they would have breakfast together.

"How was it, darling? Any trouble?"

"No. The trucks were late. That's all. Sun almost caught us."

Sheila began to hate the sun.

That was how it had been until one cold night in December when the telephone rang by Courtney's bed. He reached over drowsily to answer it.

"Hello," he said. "Who is it?"

Ricky was sitting up in bed, her face frozen. She had never got over the feeling that a long-distance call meant trouble. And this time it did. A strange flat voice was saying:

"It's Sheila, Court. Can you come at once? Walter's been hurt."

"Hurt? How?"

"They tried to hijack a job. He was on the truck. I'm afraid—" Her voice broke. "It looks bad, Court. I—I can't take it alone."

"Where is he?"

"In the hospital at Hartford. I'm calling from there."

He would not let Ricky go with him. He had no car, and a hasty call to Grand Central told him there was no train at that time. In the end he hired a car and drove through the night, reaching Hartford at dawn. Even then he was too late. Walter had died just before he got there. And a gray-faced Sheila was standing at the window, staring out.

She turned slowly and looked at him.

"The sun's coming up," she said strangely. "Only it's not going to worry him now. Not again. Never again."

She did not cry then or later. There was something of Roberta's bitter acceptance in her attitude. Only one thing seemed to touch her. And that was the announcement in the local paper. "Bootlegger killed by hijackers." Merely another man dead, and a lawbreaker at that.

She went back to New York to find that Walter had left her comfortably well off. Her former occupation was gone, for there had been no decorating business since the panic. There was no place for her anywhere, and no life. One day she went to see her mother, her animation gone, merely a plain woman in a black dress and black hat.

"I'm going to England," she said. "I have to start life again somewhere. It might as well be there."

"You've been away a long time, Sheila."

"What does it matter?"

Roberta did not argue, and one day she stood on a windswept pier and saw Sheila off. If she felt she had nothing left to live for she never said so. She went back to her lonely apartment, to cook her small meals, to have a cup of tea in midafternoon, to help Ricky two or three times a week, and to take Sunday lunch now and then with Matthew and Elizabeth.

She did not like the way Elizabeth looked that winter. Her skin showed a waxy color, and she spent a good bit of time on the couch in the living room. She scorned the idea of a doctor, however, and both Courtney and his father were too absorbed to notice her failing energy.

For business was still bad. Matthew sitting over his books with a depressed and embittered Angela in her cubicle next door, realized that they had an enormous amount of money out in unearned advances to their authors.

"What the hell's happened to them?" he demanded. "We can't go on financing them forever."

"What's happened to the world?" Courtney retorted. "It's pretty hard to create when the rent's overdue."

Book sales were low, disappointing, sometimes as little as two or three thousand to a title, and many of the manuscripts coming in now had a radical tinge. But even Matthew was beginning to look with favor on the book clubs, and the royalties they paid.

"Never thought I'd come to it," he said. "But those fellows are lifesavers."

In all his worries that fall Matthew found his real relaxation with Courtney's children. Quite often he would drop in at the house on his way home in the evenings. He had his own whistle for the children, and they would come tumbling down the stairs to him. Occasionally he brought them things, a box of candy, a puzzle of some sort.

"Now see if you can do this one."

They would hang around him, both talking at once. Peggy was a tall slip of a girl now. She had put her dolls away and lived a secret life of her own, in books and at Saturday movies.

"How's my girl? Going to be a young lady before we know it, isn't she?"

She was older for her years than Jeff, less headstrong and difficult to manage. Over her books and in the movies she already dreamed romantic dreams, and Ricky, watching her, was often worried.

"I wish she'd be more practical," she said to Hilda. "She has her head in the clouds most of the time."

"What do you expect, with all these movies?" Hilda replied.

"I can't keep her away. All the other children go."

They were no longer in the public schools. With the death of Mrs. Stafford and the final payment of Elizabeth's debts Courtney managed to return them that fall to the schools they had attended before the debacle. But now they used buses. There were no cars, no chauffeur. In three short years the whole pattern of American life had changed.

Yet Ricky was happier than she had been for a long time. There had been a change in Courtney since his return from Europe. He was more gentle with the children, more tender with her. In his awkward masculine fashion he even tried to help her about the house.

On the cook's day out he would wander into the kitchen where she and Hilda were getting the dinner, and insist on loading the dumbwaiter for them.

"Ahoy there! Dinner coming up," he would call.

The children would be in the pantry above to take off the dishes and carry them to the dining room. When everything was ready Ricky would take off her apron, and arm in arm they would go up the stairs.

"Your mother's a fine cook, kids."

"I'll say she is."

But he still had his bad times, remembering the photograph and Hedwig. There were nights when he did not sleep but lay tossing in his bed until morning. Once or twice he even broke into a hot sweat. He would get up, dry himself with a towel and put on fresh pajamas, to have to explain them awkwardly the next morning.

"Spilled a glass of water over them," he would say. "Got pretty well soaked."

She was not suspicious, but now and then she saw him watching Jeff with an odd look on his face.

32

Elizabeth was still not well by the following summer. Matthew suggested she go to Bar Harbor, but she refused to make the effort.

"Let me alone, Matt," she said pettishly. "I'm only tired. Don't bother about me."

He did, of course. She had been the center of his life for almost forty years. But he had other things to worry about.

"Gradually America was accepting a new slogan—to spend its way out of the depression. Instead of a dole there was to be a make-work program. It sounded well. In some cases it was even to work well. But before long the people were to invent a word for it. They called it boondoggling, which meant useless spending.

In Germany Hitler had come into power, and was already drunk with it; strutting through his new quarters at the Chancellery and making his extravagant plans. He was to have great kitchens, a billiard room, even a hospital suite and operating room. He had had his parades and his bonfires. Now he had a nation to play with, and maps, and a dream inherited from Bismarck. Only a far more comprehensive dream.

"It's the same old idea," Rudolph Hauck wrote. "Bismarck's plan before him. After he has wiped out the Jews he will march east, and do not think he cannot do it. If I do not write again you will understand."

The East, however, seemed far away from America, that year

of 1933. After sixteen years Russia was still impoverished and down at the heel, the house roofs sagging, the people hungry and without work. The country people had wandered into the cities and stayed there, walking the streets aimlessly and hopelessly. When they fell dead they lay almost unnoticed until their bodies were removed.

Matthew watched this alien world with jaundiced eyes.

"Communism!" he snorted. "They entombed that in glass, with Lenin. Now we have two dictators over there. Well, I hope to God they fight each other. I'm like a woman whose husband was fighting a bear—I don't care which licks."

Elizabeth seemed a little better that fall. When Ricky went to see her she was often up and dressed, although her color was still bad. But there was nothing wrong with Elizabeth's mind, or with her sharp eyes.

"What's happened to Court?" she asked one day.

"To Court? Nothing that I know of."

"He seems quiet. I suppose he's had a hard time. They all have."

Ricky considered that on her way home. Perhaps life was being too dull for him. It was a long time since they had gone anywhere but the movies, and he often slept through them. But he only laughed when she asked him about it.

"I'm getting on, Ricky. That's all. I'm almost forty. Remember?"

There was, however, a small break in her rather monotonous life that winter. Jay had found Pete and was bringing him to New York.

"I need to consult you," he wrote. "The boy has had a bad time, and he is still suspicious of me. Of everybody, I imagine. I had thought of a good school, perhaps a military one. He needs some sort of discipline."

She met them at the train when they arrived. Jay looked much the same, and his face brightened when he saw her.

"Didn't expect you," he said. "We'll go to a hotel, of course."

"Nonsense. You're both coming home with me."

She looked at the boy. He was neatly dressed, and he was more than ever Dave's boy. He looked sullen, however, and he barely greeted her. Jay took advantage of a moment when the crowd separated them to caution her.

"Don't ask him any questions, Ricky," he said. "I'll tell you later."

She took them back to the house, and while Jay paid the taxi she put a hand on the boy's arm.

"Come on in, Peter. Jeff's at school, but he'll be home later. He'll be crazy to see you."

He shook himself loose.

"You can have me arrested if you want to. I don't care."

"Why on earth should I have you arrested?"

"We took your money, didn't we?"

But here a new and authoritative Jay took the situation in hand.

"Go in there and behave yourself," he said sternly. "This is your father's sister. Act like a gentleman, Pete."

She sent them up to the guest room to clean up, but when Jay came down he was alone.

"He found some of those toy planes of Jeff's," he said. "He's still pretty young, Ricky, and he's had a rotten time."

Pete was less stiff when he finally appeared, but he still acted rather like a trapped animal. He relaxed, however, when Jeff came home. They took his bicycle and went to the park, and Ricky watched them from a window.

"They're a fine-looking pair of boys," she said wistfully. "I wish Dave had lived, Jay. Things would have been different. He's never really had a chance. What happened to him?"

But Jay refused to tell Pete's story until that night when the children had gone to bed, and they were in Courtney's study with the door shut. Then he told it briefly.

"His mother died of tuberculosis last summer," he said. "She was no good, anyhow. I gather he didn't care for her, but he tried to look after her. I suppose somebody buried her; the welfare authorities probably. But after that he was on his own."

Courtney had listened gravely. He was sure that Jay was in love with Ricky, that he always had been, perhaps always would be. But he was soberly courteous.

"How did you find him?" he asked.

Jay glanced at Ricky.

"Well, that's a queer thing," he said. "I was in Columbus on business, and there were a lot of young hoodlums about that night. One of them jumped on the running board of my car and asked for a cigarette. I thought he had a knife in his hand. He hadn't, of course. Anyhow it was Pete, and when he reached in I grabbed him. We pretty nearly had a knockdown fight before I got him in the car. Thought I was taking him to the police."

"Poor boy," Ricky said. "No wonder he's afraid of me."

"He's afraid of everybody, in a way. When I found him he was sleeping in a flophouse if he had a quarter. If not—well, I had to damn near disinfect him that night before a hotel would take him in."

That had been two weeks before. Since then he said he had had him at home. Bertha had bought some clothes for him and between them they had tried to offset two years or more of bad food and worse company.

"He's not a bad kid, but he's still pretty wild," Jay said, pulling on his pipe. "I feel like an anxious mother most of the time. But you'd be surprised what an interest it gives me. I thought if you agreed I'd put him in military school. But I'll miss him like hell. One thing about him," he added, "he's honest. He doesn't steal and he won't lie. His mother took your money. I got that much out of him."

It seemed a good idea, the military school. Certainly Pete needed control. He was not vicious, but he was wildly restless. Even young Jeff was relieved when they had gone. Pete had turned on the wall fountain and flooded the floor, had taken over the elevator as his personal property and induced Peggy to get into the dumbwaiter and left her halfway between the two floors. Jeff gave him a black eye for that.

"What's eating you?" Pete said aggrievedly. "It didn't hurt her any."

"She's my sister."

"Oh girls!" Pete said with disgust. "What good are they anyhow?"

Jay was very careful during that visit. He was seldom in the house until evening, when Courtney came home, and never alone with Ricky if he could help it. Once or twice, however, she found him watching her as though trying to fit her into this new and strange environment of hers. He said nothing, and if Courtney noticed it he ignored it. But on the evening Jay and Pete left he closed the door behind them with a grunt.

"Well, that's over," he said. "Old sweetheart of yours, wasn't he?"

"Years and years ago, Court."

"He's not over it yet if you ask me," he said morosely.

Surprisingly enough Pete did well at school. Jay sent his reports now and then, and Ricky studied them carefully. But any effort on her part or Courtney's to help with the expenses was promptly negatived.

"I'm doing pretty well," Jay wrote. "Things are picking up a bit out here, and the boy gives me an interest I needed. Let me have my fun, and let me pay for it, please."

Things were picking up somewhat under the new slogan of tax and spend, and contrary to the expectations of the drys the repeal of Prohibition did not set the citizenry reeling and staggering along the streets. They seemed to go about their business much as usual; what business there was. But as time went on it was apparent that no miracle was being performed. The depression continued with its usual concomitants—strikes, unemployment, and continuing suicides. And the New Deal was costing money in vast sums.

Courtney, however, by 1935 was still riding hopefully with Roosevelt.

"He's doing all he can, Dad. Remember when men and boys

were panhandling all over the country?"

"What are they doing now?" said an unregenerate Matthew. "Panhandling on the government. That's what. Look out the window and watch those fellows pretending to move the snow."

But in some lines business was slowly improving. Books were selling rather better than since the crash. But George Mather watched with jaundiced eyes the enormous sales of *Anthony Adverse* continuing.

"Maybe we can do some business, if and when that elephant gets out of the way," he said.

But the success of Hervey Allen's book had made publishing history. It was followed immediately by a vogue for historical novels; as though, their own static world having failed them and the present one being in flux, the writers of the country found their only safety in the past.

"If you want to locate our authors these days," Mather commented, "look for them in the public library. You'll know them by their notebooks."

"Or down in Washington," Courtney said, "writing books for Roosevelt."

For now the Administration was subsidizing writers under various projects. Under the aegis of the government they were writing plays, histories of the forty-eight states, anything—or everything—to enable them to live.

"By God," said Matthew, "I can compete with the other fellow on his own terms, but I can't compete with the United States Treasury."

33

By the fall of 1935 Courtney decided that it was time to send the children away to school. Not even to himself did he admit that the youth movement in Germany with its emphasis on strong bodies and discipline had influenced him; but Jeff was a tall boy, inclined to stoop, and it made him impatient.

"Stand up, Son. What have you got a spine for?" he would say. "Get your head back and your belly in."

He was determined to do it now. New York was no place for them, Peggy's room was plastered with pictures of movie stars, and even Central Park had been infested by gangs of boys since the depression and the crime wave that accompanied it. Listening to his arguments Ricky agreed reluctantly, but it was like tearing something out of her heart. And Hilda shed tears as she packed the children's clothes and sewed tapes on everything.

"They come back," she said, sniffing, "but they're never the same, Mrs. Wayne. That's life, I suppose, but I don't have to like it."

So it happened that shortly before they were to leave Ricky took them to see Elizabeth. They had kissed her as she lay on the couch and then wandered out to Katie for the cakes and cookies she always kept on hand. Katie had met them with her usual buoyant Irish good humor.

"Well now, and look at the size of you both! It's a sweetheart you'll be having before long, Jeff."

"He's crazy about girls now," said Peggy, nibbling her cookie. "Don't let him fool you."

Katie eyed him shrewdly.

"They'll be liking you too, by the looks of you. That's nature, Jeff. It comes to one and all."

"Not to me." But he colored. Already he was aware of girls, of their slim young legs under their short skirts, of the small rounded breasts under their school blouses. Peggy, younger and with braces on her teeth, was still satisfied with a mute adoration of the heroes in moving pictures, or in the books she devoured.

"I hate boys," she said smugly. "They're noisy and dirty. And the way they talk!"

"Your time will come," Katie hinted darkly. "Just wait and see, young lady. There's no woman escapes."

In the living room, while Ricky sat beside the couch, Elizabeth could hear their voices, young and vibrant with life. She stirred uneasily on her pillows.

"I've been thinking, Ricky," she said. "I know you've done your best, you and Court. It's been hard on you, especially that house. I'm afraid it was my fault. You never liked it, did you?"

Ricky flushed.

"I'd been raised very simply, you know. It was rather overwhelming at first. I'm used to it, of course."

"So was I," said Elizabeth, in a burst of unusual honesty. "Very simply. We had a small house, and I can remember my father stringing morning-glories on the fence in the back yard. My mother was an ambitious woman, like me. Like Court too." She was silent for a moment. Then: "There's something I want to say, Ricky. I can't talk to Matt. He gets excited. But I'm not young. If anything happens to me I've left the Bar Harbor place to you. It's about all I have left."

"I wish you wouldn't talk about that," Ricky said uncomfortably.

"I'm sixty-six," Elizabeth said uncompromisingly. "That's getting on. The place in Maine will be valuable someday. I'd like to think if you sold it the money would go to educate the children. Or perhaps things will be better. You might like it yourself."

Ricky regarded her gravely. Her color was bad, and she was wrinkled and haggard. But she lay back on her pillows and smiled faintly.

"I've made a will," she said. "Don't look like that. Everybody makes a will, and it's really for the children." She hesitated, as though unwilling to go on. "There's something else I want to say. You've been a good wife to Court, my dear. I'm grateful to you for it. And you're still a beautiful person. I've always envied you your looks, you know. My poor old face. . . ."

She let that go. She knew her face had gone again, and there were still those faint scars behind the hairline. Not that it matterd now. Only the one thing mattered, the small nagging pain which kept her awake at night while Matthew slept, and which she never mentioned for fear of a surgeon's knife.

When the children came in again that day she made them stand up by the pencil marks on the doorframe, where each year Matthew had measured their height. They had commenced it in the old house, and when they moved had carried the measurements with him. They had grown enormously. Jeffrey was almost as tall as his father now, a second Court except for his adolescent thinness, and Peggy was tall too.

But Elizabeth did not keep them long. She lay back, after kissing them good-bye, and closed her eyes.

"Have a good time at school," she said. "And learn things. You have to be smart in this world to get along."

Ricky was uneasy on the way home. They passed the old house, with all its memories: the day she had stood at the drawing room window, when Elizabeth had said her marriage to Court had been ill-considered and hasty; the coming home from Newport News without him; the scene when she had demanded a home of her own. It was being made into apartments now. Mama's parlor was open to the street, and a man with a wheelbarrow was carrying out the hearth where the conch shells had lain.

She made a sudden resolution: she sent Jeff and Peggy on home and took a taxi to the office.

She seldom went there. When she did the girls looked up from their machines to smile at her, for she was popular with them. But on this Saturday afternoon the desks were empty, and Matthew was alone in his office. Even Angela was gone. He looked surprised when he saw her at the door.

"Come in," he said. "Come in and sit down, my dear. I was beginning to feel lonely. I'm used to a lot of noise."

She felt miserably uncomfortable. She got out a cigarette and lit it, while he indicated a manuscript on his desk.

"Court wanted me to look this over for possible libel," he said. But he chuckled. "Not much danger. As often as not the plaintiff turns out to be the defendant. Things come out he doesn't want aired.

"What is it, girl?" he inquired genially, match in hand. "Got some bills you can't pay?"

She found herself short of breath. She put out her cigarette and braced herself.

"Do you know Elizabeth has made a will?"

"A will? Lizzie? Why on earth a will? She's all right, isn't she? Maybe tired a bit. That's all."

"I don't think that's quite all, Dad."

"You mean she's really sick? I don't believe it." He was pleading for hope now, behind his spectacles. "She won't see a doctor. She's stubborn as a mule, of course. You know her."

"Perhaps she's afraid to see one. It might—it might be a matter for operation. I thought she was having some sort of pain today."

"Pain? She's never mentioned pain."

Ricky got up.

"I hated to come," she said. "But it wouldn't hurt to find out, would it? She may be worrying about something that isn't there. And it's never up to a patient to decide whether he needs a doctor or not. It's up to the family."

Matthew rose stiffly, his untouched cigar in his hand.

"I guess you know how I feel," he said heavily. "In a way she's all I have. Court's married. He has you and the children. But we've been together a long time. She's been foolish at times. Who hasn't? I—don't know how I'd manage without her."

He was going to have to manage without her, nevertheless. Over her wild protests came doctors, to consult gravely, to examine her and meet Matt outside in the small drawing room and to talk with lowered voices. She was barely civil to them.

"Just how long since you noticed this distress, Mrs. Wayne?"

"Who says I have any distress?"

"Well, how long is it since you noticed you were losing weight? You have lost it, haven't you?"

They had to draw the picture from her bit by bit. But it was clear as a photograph, her color, her thinness, and her pain. They told Matthew carefully, seeing his drawn face and shaky hands.

"Always best to look into these things, Mr. Wayne. An exploratory is not necessarily serious. Matter of fact it may relieve your mind. And hers."

But Matt was not fooled. He watched their faces as they met him after the operation. As regarded Elizabeth he was almost psychic.

"How long?" he asked, after they had told him. That was all he said.

"No one can tell. A year or so. She needn't suffer, you know. The operation will help, of course. She may have longer."

"Longer? For what?"

He had twenty-four hours before he saw her. He spent most of it walking the streets, and Court finally started out in search of him. He found him on a bench in Central Park, his hat drawn down over his eyes and his face gray.

"Better come back, Dad," he said gently. "She'll be needing you."

"I can't do anything for her."

"Oh, yes, you can. You can stand by. You always have, you know. She'll count on that."

They went back together to the hospital, to find Elizabeth conscious and watching for them.

"Well, here I am," she said faintly. "I can't boss either of you any more. It's your turn, Matt."

"You can count on me, Lizzie," he said humbly. "Always on me, my dear."

"And you won't let me suffer too long?"

"I promise that, before God," said Matt, his voice husky.

They brought her home from the hospital after a month or so. Now she lay in her bed in the apartment, bitterly resentful of what had happened to her. She blamed the operation for everything.

"I was better off the way I was," she would say. "Why not have let me die quickly and decently? This is horrible."

She hated her body; the small opening into her flat abdomen, the gauze and charcoal to absorb the odors, the humiliation of the dressings. She would close her eyes when the nurses changed them, her neat fastidious mouth set in a tight line. Now she kept an atomizer of cologne beside the bed.

"I didn't know it would be so filthy. Raise the windows, somebody. I can't stand it."

Now and then she asked for Jeff, as though she found strength in his youth. They would bring him from school for a weekend and when he came, standing awkwardly beside the bed, she would pretend to be getting well.

"I'm just weak," she would say. "How are you? What are you doing?"

"Oh, nothing much. Sure you feel all right?"

"Of course I do. I'll be up and around by Christmas."

She never asked for Peggy after the first time she came.

Peggy unfortunately had burst into tears and been violently sick in the hall.

Nevertheless, there was a real gallantry about Elizabeth as the weeks and months went on. Never once did she fool herself, or let them fool her.

"I know what's wrong. I'm not an idiot. Now let's forget it."

They kept her comfortable, or at least as comfortable as possible. Matthew, hanging around outside her door, saw to that. And at night after she had had her final hypodermic he would read to her, lowering his voice as she began to doze off until the room was silent. Once or twice she asked him to read from the little old Bible she had found in the attic, with the inscription of her birth in it. There must, she thought grimly, have been a religious streak in Papa, although she could not remember it.

One night he read: "Ask, and it shall be given; seek, and ye shall find; knock, and it shall be opened unto you." When he went to bed after that he always prayed, although he felt it was too late. Still there it was, a definite promise. But Elizabeth only gave a sardonic smile when she heard it.

"Ask, and it shall be given!" she said. "It doesn't work out, Matt. What have I got?"

"You've got me," he said sturdily.

It was a trying time for all of them. Courtney was short-tempered and sleeping badly. He was even curt with his editors.

"Well, get the stuff in. That's all I say. And don't ask us to type it. We have a right to expect a decent script. Oh, I know all that. Maybe Edgar Wallace kept three stenographers busy and Oppenheim two. This fellow doesn't happen to be either of them." He would apologize later.

And Elizabeth lived on. Ricky saw her only when she asked for her, but Roberta was there a good bit of the time, doing the marketing for Katie, seeing the rooms were in order. But as time went on Elizabeth paid little attention to what was around her. Sometimes she was back in the past, with Papa looking horrified when Mama sold the old rosewood furniture and installed a plush parlor set. She was back with Matthew too, to the old days in the office and the way he had asked her to marry him.

Even then he was not handsome. He was a solid youngish man, with steady eyes and an engaging smile. His proposal had been characteristic. He had dictated some letters. Then unexpectedly he got up and came around the desk to where she sat.

"I feel awkward as hell, Lizzie," he said. He had always called her Lizzie. "But I've got to get this over. Is there any chance you'd care to marry me?"

It had been as simple as that. When she nodded he put his arms around her and kissed her.

"I'll be good to you, Lizzie," he said huskily. "Always, my girl. Always and forever."

And so, with one break, he had been.

She lived on and on. It seemed as though she could not die. She made hardly a rise under the silk cover of her bed, but her vitality was incredible. When the children came to see her during their Christmas vacation she insisted on her best nightgown, and on having the window shades drawn so that the only light came from the rose-shaded lamp beside the bed. She insisted too on some lipstick for her colorless lips and a touch of rouge on her withered cheeks.

"No use letting me scare them into fits," she had said, undaunted. "I'm bad enough, heaven knows."

She had a hypodermic before they arrived, and she managed to put up a pretty good show.

"Well, hello!" she said feebly. "Good heavens, how you've grown up! How do you like school? Learning anything?"

They stood by the bed, uncomfortable and not a little alarmed. This Elizabeth had nothing to do with the one they had known best, a lively Elizabeth who somehow never had seemed old; who had wandered in and out of their young lives, bringing gifts and generally spoiling them. This was a flattish bulge in a big bed, surmounted by a made-up skull which managed rather horribly to smile.

"We're awfully sorry you're sick, Grandmother."

"Who told you that? I'm taking a rest. That's all," she said, with a faint return of her old sharpness. "I hear you've been playing football, Jeff."

"I'm trying."

"Well, don't let them break your nose. You have your father's nose, you know. It's a nice one. Let me see you, Peggy. Getting a figure at last, aren't you?"

Not very inspired, perhaps, for a last talk. Elizabeth the worldly had not changed, in spite of Papa's Bible.

She did not live long after the children went back to school. The time had come for Matt to fulfill his promise. The hypodermics were not enough any more. They only allayed the pain for a time, then it was back, like an enemy which did not know when it was beaten and kept on charging.

Roberta knew it. She was staying at the apartment now, helping Katie. She watched Matthew, but there was nothing she could do for him.

"Can't you eat anything, Matt?"

"I'm not hungry, Bertie."

She was always Bertie to him now.

But she did not know of the cache he had accumulated, tablet by tablet, from the nurses' supplies. Or of the nights when he walked the streets trying to gain the courage to fulfill his promise. Or of the prayers he said, that God would step in and save him from this last terrible step.

It was Elizabeth herself who determined the issue. The nurse was out, and he was sitting by the bed, holding her thin hand, the hand he had held for more than forty-five years. She opened her eyes and looked at him.

"I think it's time," she whispered. "You promised, Matt."

"I know, Lizzie. It's bad, is it?"

She nodded.

"I can't take any more, Matt. I want to go to sleep and not wake up."

He shivered, but who was he to give her a week or even a month more of torture? He felt cold and stiff as he got up, but he too had reached the breaking point. He was ready. He had promised, so he was ready. He sat down beside her bed with the hypo in his hand, and for a minute he buried his head on the pillow beside hers. Then he sat up, a sturdy undistinguished figure of a man who had loved one woman all his adult life.

"I guess maybe I won't be long after you, Lizzie," he said hoarsely.

"I'll be waiting, Matt."

All she ever said was a "thank you" as he plunged the needle. After that he merely sat there and watched peace return to her face. For almost half a century he had watched her face. He had seen it grown old, had seen it repaired, had seen it tortured. Now it was quiet.

He was still holding her thin hand when she stopped breathing. . . .

34

So long had Elizabeth been shut away that her passing changed very little, except to Matthew. He had no sense of guilt, but now when he went to the office he had no desire to leave it. There was nothing to go home to.

True, Roberta was doing her best, but there had been a long gap in their relationship while she had lived in England. In a way she was more British than American. He wondered too sometimes if she suspected how he had eased Elizabeth out of life. He had never questioned her intelligence.

But now when he paid his insurance premiums there was no meaning to them. Of course Court and his family would get the money. Would need it too, if things went on as they were. Matthew had never fooled himself. The New Deal had tried, but priming the pump when there was no water was useless. Fundamentally things were still bad.

Elizabeth had left the Bar Harbor house to Ricky, but it had been idle for several years, and the field mice were still in possession. They made nests in the mattresses and couches, and in Elizabeth's needlepoint chairs, and frolicked up and down the broad staircase. Moths ate the Aubusson carpets she had loved, and when it rained the gulls stood in the bottom of the fountain and waded in the rain water gathered there.

The country was still looking inward, at its own troubles; but a weary suspicious Europe was watching Germany, and from the fastnesses of the Kremlin both Communist agents and propaganda were invading America. Matthew had never been reconciled to the Roosevelt administration. Now in his new grief and despair he blamed it even for Russia.

"Letting the Reds in," he said angrily. "And the Reds taking over labor. The government too, for all I know."

"We'll never get communism here, Dad," Courtney said. "It grows out of discontent, and as a people we—"

"So we're contented!" Matthew said. "We've got a reign of terror here this minute, and I'm not saying where it stems from. Men I know are scared out of their senses. They're honest men, too—not criminals, nor economic royalists. Look at us! The way the revenue men go over our books, by God, you'd think we're headed for Atlanta."

"Perhaps it's our fault, Dad. If we've got a dictatorship, maybe we deserve it. Perhaps that's the only way to govern people anyhow. Hand it to the masses and you have mob rule."

"Changed a bit, haven't you?" Matthew said dryly.

Courtney flushed.

"I was pretty wet behind the ears," he acknowledged. "I'm still a liberal, only I'm darned if I know what that is these days."

Only seldom did Matthew bother to argue. Since Elizabeth's death he did not really care much either way. And he had aged perceptibly. Courtney, struggling with taxes, with warehouse strikes, sometimes even with his own staff, kept all possible anxieties away from him. But the strain was telling on him. He came home one evening during the Easter vacation to see Peggy going out. Her young cheeks were rouged, and her mouth heavily painted. He caught her by the arm and inspected her.

"Just where the hell to you think you're going, looking like that? Take that stuff off your face."

"Let me alone, Father. All the girls do it. I'll look silly if I don't."

But his mouth was set. He dragged her to the lavatory and soaping the end of a towel washed her face thoroughly. Off came the rouge and lipstick, to the accompaniment of tears and rage.

"You're a brute," she told him, "a complete and utter beast."

His life had changed in other ways. He had not seen Emmy for a long time. He had heard she was reading for another publishing house. It meant nothing to him, however. And one day he realized that the young effervescent groups of his early days had disappeared. They were all growing up. Perhaps other and younger men and women had taken their place, sitting on the floor in badly lit rooms and drinking vodka while they tore down the world and built a new one.

He was in his forties now, and outside of his mother's death his life had settled into a pattern, more or less comfortable. The house was too big for them, with the children gone, but he was still proud of it. He was proud of Ricky too, still lovely with her short skirts and soft short hair. But although there were still times when passion flamed, there were now long intervals when it was dormant, when they lived together in companionable affection.

He was enormously proud of his children; of Jeff, hoping to go to Harvard the next year, and asking his permission to smoke since "all the fellows do." Beginning too to fill out and hold himself straighter. And of Peggy, home for the holidays and one minute a little girl wandering unself-consciously in her pajamas or lying on the floor on her stomach, reading with the radio going full blast; and the next a young lady, with a curious dignity all her own.

The house was very quiet without the children. Sometimes when he came he would find Ricky at the window looking out toward the park.

"Remember when Jeff took his first sled over there?" she would say. Or: "Peggy used to take her turtle there for exercise. She really loved that turtle."

"I used to find the little beast in my bathtub. Whatever did she do with it?"

"I think she turned it loose in the park."

It was hard to tell whether business was better or not by 1937. Paying the soldiers' bonus had helped, but the slogan of tax and spend confused everything. Nevertheless, Wayne and Company was doing fairly well. Courtney bought a small car, and Adele George, bringing Courtney the morning orders, would look cheerful. One morning, however, she looked puzzled as she carried in his letters. On top was a photograph of a boy. She put it down in front of him.

"You'd think it was Mr. Jeffrey, wouldn't you?" she said. "There's a note with it. I'm sorry I opened it."

Courtney stared down at it. It was a picture of a tall boy in Luftwaffe uniform and flying helmet. He was standing very stiffly, with his chin up and his eyes cool and level, as though he dared the camera to do less than its best. He turned it over automatically. On the back was written "Otto Reiff, 1937."

He looked at the letter that accompanied it. It was brief and cold.

"My father died a month ago. As you know, his political opinions were not popular. I enclose photograph which you should have. Hedwig."

As though it was of no importance he shoved the picture into a drawer of his desk and took up the other mail. But he was profoundly shaken, not only by the photograph but by the implication of Hedwig's note. So those devils had killed the old professor, perhaps by torture. There were rumors of torture by the Gestapo. Perhaps Otto his own grandson, had reported him. The professor had said he did not trust him.

Probably he would have destroyed it, or at least have hidden it in his private file. But Mather brought in a manuscript just then, and he dropped it into a drawer of his desk.

"Thought you might like to read this," Mather said. "Out of our line, but the fellow knows his stuff. It's about airpower in the next war."

"What next war?" Court said truculently.

"Ours. Yours and mine, my boy. You don't think we can

keep out, do you?"

"Why not?" Court said. "Let those fellows over there settle their own troubles this time. You were in the last war, George. Now you've got a boy. Want him to go through the same thing you did?"

Mather eyed him.

"No," he said. "I'd hate it like hell. But I hope he'll have the guts to take it, if he has to."

Courtney took the manuscript home that night, but he did not show it to Ricky. The author made plans, and he was a flier himself. He made a good argument, and Court sat up late to read it. He went to bed, to lie awake until almost morning, but the next day he told Mather they would publish the book.

"I think he's an alarmist," he said. "Still, if it's a matter of defending ourselves we'd better do our two bits' worth. Any use trying to get the army behind the book?"

"Those dodos!" Mather jeered. "They're still back fighting the battle of Gettysburg. Look what they did to Billy Mitchell. Know how many planes they've got?"

"No."

"Neither do I." Mather grinned. "But you can bet your bottom dollar it's plenty few. This guy Graham says as much."

The book worried Court. Jeff was almost eighteen. In a few months he was to enter Harvard. He did not fool himself. If a war broke out after that, Jeff would want to go. Yet war seemed far away. What did it matter that Germany had marched into the Rhineland, over the desperate protests of France? America was safe, would always be safe. We had the navy, didn't we?

"The book was called *War in the Air*, and he showed it to Matthew. Matthew thought it was nonsense.

"We've got the navy, haven't we?" he demanded. "That's one good thing Roosevelt's done. Likes ships. I suppose."

They published the book, however. It had a moderate success, and one day that fall he had a visit from Eric Graham. He breezed into the office, a brisk, good-looking man about

Court's own age who walked as though he were on springs.

"Name's Graham," he said. "You've done a book of mine on fighters. Remember?"

"Certainly I remember." Courtney got up and shook hands. "It's a darn good book too. Sorry it didn't have a better sale. Sit down and have a cigarette."

"It's a start. It's a start." Graham lit his cigarette and squinted through the smoke. "We Americans are a hard people to scare, Mr. Wayne. But we're moving. Remember the box kites we flew in 'seventeen and 'eighteen? We're doing a lot better nowadays."

"So I gather. Not well enough, I suppose, to satisfy you?"

"To an airman there never is enough. I'm on my way to Washington. The army is beginning to want planes. So is the navy. But Congress is still clutching the dove of peace instead of the eagle. Maybe it will turn around and bite them someday. By the way, I understand you have a son. Going to make a flier of him?"

"God, no," Court said fervently. "Not after that book of yours!"

Graham laughed.

"It wasn't intended to have that effect. On the contrary!"

There was something attractive about him, as of wide open spaces and wind-swept air. Court felt a little flat, looking at him. Graham was no younger than he was, if as young, but he was not anchored to a desk. The whole world of adventure was his, a world where in the air a man might feel himself a king.

In the end he asked him to dinner that night. He accepted cheerfully, but Court was not prepared for his expression when he saw Ricky.

"So it's you again!" he said. "Who says there's no such thing as coincidence? Remember me, Mrs. Wayne? Out in Ohio?"

"Of course I do. I read your book. You're Buddy Graham."

He grinned at her.

"It's a long time since anyone called me that," he said.

But the evening was hardly a success. War was brewing in Europe, and America could not keep out. Ricky was pale when she excused herself and left the two men to talk. Hours later Court found her in bed. She was holding a copy of Housman, and she had evidently been crying. When he picked up the book he saw she had marked a verse:

> Oh stay at home my lad, and plough
> The earth and not the sea.
> And leave the soldiers at the drill
> And all about the idle hill
> Shepherd your sheep with me.

He sat down on the bed beside her and took her in his arms. He was beginning to feel the terrible dependence of a man on a woman after years of marriage. And—like Matthew the occasional helplessness.

"He'll be all right, my darling. Jeff will be all right. After all, this talk of war doesn't mean we'll be in it."

She went to sleep finally, with his arms still about her.

Probably he would have destroyed the photograph the next day, but something intervened, and when he next looked for it it was gone.

The "something" was a long-distance message from Jeff's school. He had appendicitis, and they were going to operate.

Once again, as when the children were born, it was the same waiting in a hospital, the same watching each time a nurse appeared, or a doctor. Only now Ricky was with him, white-faced and silent. Afterward Courtney could only remember her speaking once. She was standing outside the door of the room, waiting for the stretcher to come from the elevator. She was standing—she would not sit down—and she turned a desperate face to him.

"It's a dreadful thing to bear children," she said. "One dies a thousand deaths."

Jeff was up and around in a couple of weeks. Back at school and slightly boastful.

"Want to see my scar, you guys?"

"No. What's a little old scar? Want to see where I was vaccinated?"

35

The children were growing up. What Elizabeth had called Peggy's figure was fairly definite now, her small breasts high, and she had apparently exchanged her movie heroes for a series of pimply boys. And Jeff's voice had changed. When he came home he retorted to an exasperated Hilda in a masculine tenor.

"What on earth happened to your clothes?" she would demand. "Where's your dinner jacket?"

"No idea. Some other fellow borrowed it, probably."

"Why on earth don't you lock your door?"

"What's the use. There's a transom."

He was constantly on the go. Ricky complained she saw him only now and then. And he was like a puppy. His extremities were large and awkward.

"For God's sake, Ricky," Courtney said. "Did I ever use my hands as if they were hams on the end of a stick? Or fall over everything in sight?"

"I'm sure you did, darling."

She was very happy while the children were at home. There was a sort of radiance about her, like a second blooming. At night when they were all safe in bed she felt like a mother hen spreading her wings over her chicks, and in the morning she would go about, picking up their clothing where they had flung it, Peggy's little silk panties, Jeff's damp shirt, Court's socks, and with each garment she felt she was holding them to her.

She always turned on the wall fountain when they were at home, and one day Courtney heard it splashing as he came up the stairs.

"So all's well with the world!" he said quizzically.

She colored.

"What does that mean."

"Our little barometer, isn't it? When things are right, you can take it. When things are wrong, off it goes. Like that old peacock of Mother's. Dad used to say its tail drooped when Mother was upset."

Fanny the peacock! It was years since she had thought of it.

Now and then they saw young Pete Stafford. He was a good-looking, tough-fibered youth of twenty or so. School had improved him. Now he was at a small eastern college, and highly discontented.

"Know what he wants to be, Dad?" Jeff said to Court. "A test pilot."

Pete grinned.

"Sure," he said. "Everything's going up in the air. People, freight, the whole works."

"I see," said Courtney. "You'd do away with the railroads, I gather?"

"They'll carry the heavy stuff, like coal and iron. For a few years anyhow."

He amused Courtney, his young cocksureness, the almost patronage with which he viewed the earth-clingers.

"I suppose the idea is to save time?"

Pete eyed him suspiciously.

"Of course. Why not?"

"And what," said Courtney smoothly, "will people do with the time they save?"

Pete smiled. He looked younger when he smiled.

"I don't go that far, sir. Maybe I've been shooting off my mouth too much. I guess I get excited."

He and Jeff got along well together. Jeff expected to go to Harvard the next fall. He was as tall as Courtney now, a big handsome boy who smoked a pipe around the house and seemed to receive incredible numbers of letters from girls. Apparently he never answered them, however, or even his invitations for the holiday dances and dinners. Ricky took this over finally, using the telephone.

"I'm terribly sorry, Mrs. Babcock. I just found your card. You know how it is. They're simply swamped with parties and the time's so short."

And Jeff would turn up at the party, or not turn up, as it fitted into his personal plans.

Peggy was less trouble. When she went to dances now she wore long dresses, and Court no longer washed the make-up off her face. She merely laughed when he suggested that Hilda go with her.

"Don't be a goop, Dad. They'd die laughing. Nobody has a chaperone any more."

So she went alone in a hired car, dancing cheek to cheek with the youth of the moment, being kissed in odd corners, rousing young passions and perfectly aware of it, wearing her fingernails as long as claws and painting them odd colors—once they were black until Hilda saw them—and still remaining young and virginal and increasingly lovely.

"Getting to look like your mother," Matthew said. "What do you want for Christmas? Don't push the old man too hard."

It was always a dress. She would show herself to him, wearing it.

"Like it, Grandfather?"

"Kind of low in the neck, isn't it? You're pretty young, you know."

"Low! You ought to see the other girls."

Now as Matthew watched them there was a reason for the insurance again. It was not the same. Nothing was the same without Lizzie. But coupled with his love for them was a small nagging fear. Like Elizabeth's pain. At night he and Katie sometimes discussed it.

"Fine world we've made for them, Katie. First we blow up a

balloon and stick a pin in it. Now the Germans are blowing up another. And when it explodes—"

Life, however, went on as usual, although it seemed to Ricky she saw very little of her children during the holidays, except on the staircase or in the elevator. They were eternally rushing in, changing their clothes and hurrying out again. In the mornings they slept late, waking only in time to dress for a lunch somewhere, and after being out all afternoon getting back to dress for a dinner or dance.

Once she caught Jeff literally by the coattails as he passed her in the hall.

"I'm your mother," she said. "Remember me?"

He gave her an apologetic grin.

"I'm the hell of a son, aren't I? What am I to do? All these people on my neck."

"All the girls on your neck, you mean."

Before they all left that winter of 1937 she gave a small supper-dance at the house. The drawing-room carpet was lifted, and she rented a juke box for music. It seemed to be a great success. The youngsters ate enormously, drank her mild punch, and danced zestfully to the new rowdy blaring music. Rather surprisingly the boys from Jeff's school called him Jigger.

"Jigger!" Courtney said. "Where on earth do they get that?"

"Didn't you have a nickname at school?"

"Sure. They called me Chut. Short for chutney. There was some sense to that."

She smiled at this masculine reasoning. They stood side by side on the stairs, watching the rest below.

"They make me feel as old as God," Courtney said. "Shall I grow a beard, darling? A long white beard?"

"Don't. I feel like a nice old lady myself."

He put an arm around her.

"Then thank heaven for nice old ladies," he said, and kissed her. "Tell me, my ancient crone, did we ever behave like that?"

"I don't remember spiking the punch with gin."

"Good God, is that what they're doing?"

Pete was a huge success that night. He had had no dinner jacket and Ricky had told him it did not matter. Nevertheless, he had come downstairs properly attired.

"Borrowed it from a waiter," he said proudly. "Cost me two bucks. He threw in the spots for nothing."

Hilda managed to clean him up somewhat before the crowd came, but he danced all evening in a gentle aura of gasoline.

When the party was over, Ricky and Court stood together in their wrecked house. Jeff and Peggy had gone on somewhere for scrambled eggs and sausages, and they were alone. Court was scowling.

"Who put the gin in the punch?" he said. "Was it Jeff?"

"I don't think so. I locked the liquor closet. Court, were we ever as young as that?"

"Young! Some of those kids knew the facts of life before they were weaned."

"Not Jeff! Not Peggy, Court?"

"I wouldn't like to bet on it," he said dryly, and began putting out the lights.

At four in the morning Pete brought Jeff home. Courtney heard them going up in the elevator and climbed the stairs. He found Jeff on his bed, and Pete trying to get him out of his clothes. Jeff did not move. He had passed out completely. He was a waxy white, and Pete looked up apologetically.

"Guess he's not used to much liquor," he said. "I'm sorry, Mr. Wayne. He'll be all right tomorrow."

Pete had been drinking too, but he was not drunk. He took off his rented coat and hung it carefully over the back of a chair while Courtney stared down at his son. Jeff's big body was sprawled, but his face looked young and somehow helpless.

"I don't want his mother to know about this, Pete. Where did he get it?"

"Well, the crowd sort of moved around after we left here. I didn't notice him much."

"Think you can handle him?"

"Sure. Don't worry. He'll be all right."

Courtney turned and went out. He felt rather sick. He had seen plenty of drunkenness, had drunk too much himself more times than he liked to remember. But Jeff was only eighteen. For the first time he wondered about Peggy. Peggy was tucked away in her bed, however, sleeping sweetly.

When he went downstairs he found Ricky awake and the light on.

"There's nothing wrong, is there?" she asked.

"Nothing. Just seeing they were all in." He forced himself to smile at her. "After a night like this I don't know whether I'm being a flat tire or a jitterbug," he said, "but I wish you'd get some sleep, darling. The—the kids are all right."

Jeff was a sick boy the next morning, and a very sheepish one. Courtney said nothing to him until evening when he appeared in the study.

"I guess I made a fool of myself last night, Dad," he said. "I've felt like hell all day. Does Mother know?"

"I haven't told her, but she has eyes to see."

"She hasn't said anything, has she?"

"Not to me."

Jeff lit a cigarette—apparently a pipe was too much for him—and wandered about the room. His father watched him, trying to think what to say. This thing of raising a boy these days was a problem. He remembered an incident in his own youth, and what Matthew had said at the time.

"A gentleman drinks like a gentleman," he had said. "He doesn't make a hog of himself."

He told Jeff the story, and the boy gave him a faint grin.

"I'll bet no hog ever felt the way I did this morning," he said.

Later that night he had a talk with Pete. Pete disclaimed any credit. He had had as much to drink as Jeff but he could carry his liquor better. Anyhow he had done nothing but bring Jeff home. Yet the incident was to have repercussions of some importance. It developed that Pete was fed up with college and with having Jay support him.

"I'm not the college type," he said. "I like to work with my hands. And Burton's not doing so well. Law business in a small town doesn't pay much."

"What do you want to do, Pete?"

"I'd like to get into an airplane factory."

He put up a number of arguments, and Courtney suspected he was right. The boy had his father's charm, but he was tough and in deadly earnest. After he had gone to bed Courtney called Jay on the long-distance phone. It required some argument. In the end, however, Jay agreed, with the result that by the first of the year Eric Graham received a visit from a tall blond youth at a factory on Long Island.

"So you want to learn this business?" he said.

Pete eyed him. Eric was wearing overalls, and his face was streaked with grease. He was not impressive at the moment.

"I'd like to, sir. Of course I don't know anything about it."

"Well, thank God for that much," said Eric, and put him on the payroll as the equivalent of a day laborer. Pete did not mind. He managed to live on what he earned, did his menial jobs cheerfully, and kept his eyes open. Eric Graham watched him with interest. One day, about to take up a new ship, he told him to hop in. The boy was crowded in the small cockpit, but there was something in his face which impressed Graham. Pete watched every move he made, too.

"Like it?" he said, when they came down.

"It's wonderful, sir."

"You know your size is against you, Pete."

"For a fighter. Not for a bomber, sir."

So that was the way the wind blew. Eric went back to his office, to his desk littered with blueprints, to a typewriter clattering in the next room. After a while he picked up the telephone and called Ricky.

"This nephew of yours wants to learn to be a pilot," he said. "It's up to you, of course. I don't run a school, but he can learn a bit here. After that—"

He heard the hesitation in her voice.

"It's really up to Jay Burton," she said. "I do wish our boys would keep out of the air, Eric. It frightens me."

"It scares me to cross Times Square."

In the end Pete got his way. From the beginning it was evident that he was a born pilot. There was a dash of reckless courage in him, but he was careful too. He left the factory and enlisted in the Army Air Corps that year, a force now beginning slowly to expand. He sent his picture in his uniform to Ricky, and she kept it on her dressing table.

Now and then she stopped to look at it.

"I couldn't help it, Dave," she thought. "He's your boy, and you were a fighter too."

36

Roberta was very lonely after Elizabeth's death. Matthew hardly seemed to know she was there, as though the dead Elizabeth was more real to him in the apartment than she was. On good days she went to Central Park and sat on a bench there. She rarely heard from Sheila, who had taken a job in the Admiralty now and was very busy. But one letter from Sheila rather amused her.

"I saw the old house the other day," she wrote. "It looks rather run down. Nobody has much money. But I went to tea there and they have a new bathroom! They boast like anything about it; or rather, being English, they merely mention it casually, which is their way of making the hell of a fuss."

Roberta smiled dryly at that, remembering the time Arthur had had to choose between a new bathroom and a new lady.

But Roberta's England—and Arthur's—had apparently disappeared. She had liked young Edward, but now he had abdicated his throne for a twice-divorced American woman. She was a cheerful person, singing her gay little southern songs, even cooking for him now and then the Baltimore dishes she had learned in America. Perhaps he had never wanted to be a king, or perhaps he felt inadequate for the job of ruling a great people. But there it was. He had loved her, he had wanted her, and he had got her.

The summer before Sheila had sent Roberta a silver cigarette box from London. It had been made for his coronation, and it had his face on the lid in colored enamel. On the card she wrote "De mortuis nil nisi bonum!" which was the epitaph of Davy, as his family always called him.

Roberta had no home of her own now. She had closed her apartment and put away most of the things, including the picture of her own presentation dress. It had been a silver brocade, and Arthur had been proud of her, with the three plumes in her hair and a train which almost threw her as she backed away after her curtsy.

Worth had made the dress, and she and Arthur had owed him for it for years. She still had it, packed away in storage in London, with its train lined with real lace flounces. That was over, of course. Beauty and elegance had gone out of the world and the cult of ugliness had come in; paintings which were hideous, poetry without rhyme, and women like this Gertrude Stein, who was either a poseur or a lunatic, and possibly both.

So she sat on her hard bench in the park and watched the children. Then she went back to a silent Matthew, to an elderly Katie, and to her own fears.

Then one day in the spring of 1938 Ricky came home to find her seated on the drawing-room couch before the unlighted fire-place, with her gloves off and her long thin hands in her lap.

"I came to ask you something," Roberta said, without preamble. "If I go back to England would you take Matt here? I can't leave him alone."

"If you go back to England." Ricky was astonished. "But why, Roberta? Is it Sheila?"

Roberta shook her head.

"Sheila's all right," she said. "She likes to live her own life. No, but I think I may be useful again, Ricky. I'm not too old. I'm still active. They'll need all the help they can get before long. And Matt doesn't need me."

Ricky looked at her.

"So you think there will be a war, after all?"

"After all what?" Roberta demanded. "After we've sat on

our backsides and let the Germans get ready to conquer the world! Of course there will be a war, sooner or later. Don't you read the papers?"

"And England will be in it?"

"Everybody will be in it."

She got up, pulling on her gloves. She belonged to the school that would as soon have gone shoeless as gloveless on the street.

"Then you would take Matt here?"

"We'd love to have him, Roberta. You know that."

Ricky went down to the door with her, and in the lower hall Roberta hesitated.

"I don't suppose you ever see Emmy Baldwin, do you?" she asked.

"Emmy! No. I heard she had taken a government job in Washington. Why, Roberta?"

"I merely wondered about her. She's not a nice person, Ricky. Keep away from her."

Ricky flushed.

"That's over long ago, if there ever was anything." Then she smiled. "Court's not like your Arthur, darling. He would always choose the bathroom."

Roberta sailed soon after. Matthew had sturdily refused to give up his apartment, but he insisted that she go if she wanted to.

"You'll like England again," he said. "After all, it was your home for a good many years, my dear. And it looks as though they're doing domething, after all. This Chamberlain . . ."

Roberta said nothing. She had a very low opinion of Mr. Chamberlain, coming back from his conferences with Hitler looking like a terrier who had just buried a bone. She suspected that the bone was the British Empire. Only the year before there had been the coronation with all its pomp and ceremony, the coaches and jewels, the peers in their robes, the Yeomen of the Guard, the Indian rajas, the admirals of the Royal Navy uncomfortable on horseback, and the terrifying solemnity of the service in old Westminster Abbey, with the new king trying not to stammer when he spoke.

Now they needed friends. Not only the royal family. All of England. It was a small and lonely island. Behind it was only the wide Atlantic, and driven from it they could only become lemmings, swimming out to inevitable death.

She packed determinedly, taking only her clothes and selling the furniture she had stored from her apartment. Courtney tried to dissuade her, for now he knew trouble was coming. She was firm, however.

"If there is a war Sheila may need me, or if she doesn't others may. If there is no war I'd like to go back anyhow. I always liked London," she added, almost wistfully.

They all saw her off, loading her stateroom with flowers and fruit and the latest Wayne books. As the ship moved out it was easy to see her tall thin figure in its eternal black. They waited until she was out of sight, and Ricky turned to see tears in Matthew's eyes.

"Got a lot of spunk, Roberta," he said huskily. "She's going into trouble, and she knows it."

Yet war still seemed far away from America. Courtney had a letter that fall of 1938 from Rudolph Hauck, who had managed to get to Vienna.

"Were you ever here?" he wrote. "Or perhaps you were too young. If not, do you remember the Bal Tabarin and the other night spots. The cocottes in the boxes, almost buried in flowers? The sweetish champagne? The Hungarian orchestras, and New Year's Eve, with the ritual of the chimneysweep carrying a little pig, to be touched for luck?

"Well, we have the pigs, but they are two-legged ones, and there is no such thing as luck, unless one manages to get over the border. If this reaches you a friend of mine has succeeded and I will try. In that case—only in that case—I may see you again."

It had, not surprisingly, been mailed in Switzerland.

They were somewhat gayer that winter. Now and then they went out to dinners. Ricky would come down the stairs wearing the pearls Courtney had not allowed her to sell, her figure still slim and young, her long dresses sweeping about her. She was letting her hair grow again. Already it made a loose knot on the nape of her neck, and Courtney, waiting below, would see in her the girl he had married so long before.

"You're lovely tonight, sweetheart."

"You're looking very fine yourself."

It was all right. Everything was all right. She would get into the car and he would tuck the rug around her. "Warm enough?"

He was a man, of course. He still liked a pretty woman, and women liked him. He took that all for granted, and without vanity. He did not even realize that he had moved to a conservative position politically until some of his editorial staff recommended a book by a member of the New Deal. At the next conference he sat with the manuscript before him and looked around the table.

"Maybe some of you still believe all this," he said. "That you make money by throwing it away, or have more by producing less. I don't. Let this fellow take his alphabet soup elsewhere. And I hope it chokes him."

He was still hopeful that the foreign situation would clear up. After all, the Japs had been in China for seven years, and life still went on there. And look at Italy, hadn't Mussolini cleaned it up? Apparently it was a pleasure to go there now, the cities were so clean. And no beggars, either. Well, hardly any beggars. As for Abyssinia, what did it matter? Italy deserved something after the last war, and why bother about a lot of savages and a little king who was reported to eat raw liver and had only three paved miles—or was it five—on which to drive the royal automobile?

Only Matthew remained pessimistic, that winter of 1938.

He was an old man now, was Matthew. He still wore the black band on his sleeve, still—sometimes in bitter cold—made his weekly pilgrimage to Elizabeth's grave, and still sat behind his desk in the office, smoking his two cigars a day under Angela's watchful eyes. Now and then he saw one of his old authors, however. One day Anne Lockwood came in. She had been on her annual pilgrimage to Arlington, and she kissed Matthew's wrinkled cheek.

"New book's not finished," she said. "Try raising and educating four youngsters and see where it gets you. I've got a boy in college now."

Matthew inspected her. She was older and heavier, and her hair was almost white.

"We'd like another, Anne."

She looked down at her hands, the nails cut short for her typewriter.

"That was Tim's book," she said quietly. "There will never be another Tim, Mr. Wayne, so there will never be another *Drifters.*"

"You do all right, my dear. You'll always sell. I'm old enough to like young love myself. I'm proud to have published you, Anne. Always remember that."

She smiled.

That was all. She left soon after, and he sat still after she had gone. He had known very little about her, outside of her work. Now he wondered how much he had really known about any of their writers. For years they had come and gone, sitting across the desk from him, hopeful or discouraged, successful or failures. Outside of these casual contacts they were merely rows of figures on the books, and of recent years not even that to him. Yet they were the material on which Wayne and Company was founded.

It was wrong somewhere. They were real people, spending hour after hour at their desks, or bent over their machines. It must be like penal servitude, he thought, to be shut off like that. Like the Children of Israel, making bricks without straw.

He sent for a copy of *The Drifters* and ran through it carefully. So Tim Lockwood had expected another war, and that America would be in it. He put the book down and sat for a long time looking at nothing.

37

Adele George was very proud of her position in the firm. She liked standing by Courtney's elbow and blotting checks as he signed them. In the mornings she dusted his office and filled his inkwell, and now and then when he was out she cleaned the drawers of his desk.

She had not much time, however, for business was good that winter of 1938-39. Perhaps the wild spending of the government was at last having some effect. True, the national debt had grown until it was enormous. True, too, that race prejudices were growing, that class was rousing against class, and that the pump priming had still essentially failed. But there was a definite improvement. Even in publishing, American incentive had at last refused to be held down by repressive measures.

They had published a book the fall before called *Before the Drums Beat.* It was a warning against the country's being dragged into the coming war. And both Matthew and George Mather had been in favor of it. Courtney had been uncertain.

"How much of your feeling about it is because you have a son, George?"

"Well, I have a son. So have you. So have millions of other people."

The pacifists had welcomed the book, but much of the country resented it. Courtney, finding himself classed with the isolationist crowd, was indignant and short tempered. He would snap at Adele.

"Where the hell is that jacket sketch? It was here yesterday."

"I think the art department has it."

She knew he needed her, but that often he was scarcely aware of her. She would sit patiently, her book on her knee, while he looked at her and through her, as if she was not there.

"Take this, Adele. Let's get on with this job."

She was surprised one Saturday in January when Emmy Baldwin called her on the telephone.

"Hello, kid," she said. "Boss working you to death as usual?"

She had always admired Emmy. Emmy had always called her "kid." She had almost had a quarrel with Angela Ellis in the women's lavatory when Matthew fired her.

"I'm glad that trollop's gone," said Angela. "She's a mischiefmaker if I ever saw one."

"I liked her," said Adele stoutly.

"Just because she took you out to lunch once or twice!"

"That's not true. And she's not a—a trollop."

"Listen, girlie," said Angela. "She's not only a trollop. She's so crooked you could screw her into a cork."

When Emmy called her one day and said she had taken a job in Washington she felt that something exciting had gone out of her life. Now Emmy was on the phone again.

"I'm in town for the weekend," she said. "How about lunch at the Ritz, kid, and a movie later?"

Adele could hardly speak for excitement.

"I'd love to. It's Saturday and we close early, but I'm hardly dressed for—"

"Don't be silly. You always look smart. One o'clock all right?"

Of course it was all right. It was wonderful. Adele spent fifteen minutes after the office closed at twelve fixing her small rather pretty face, and draping her old fox fur around her neck. She had never been inside the Ritz, but when she went in there was Emmy, smiling and brassier than even. She even kissed her.

"Glad you could make it," she said. "Let's have a cocktail before we go in."

Adele found her timidity going with the drink, and with the second one she was talking a mile a minute. She was not used to cocktails. She apologized, but Emmy smiled.

"Go ahead," she said. "I like to hear about the old place, even if they did fire me."

"You had a dirty deal," said Adele hotly, her face flushed with alcohol. "A filthy, dirty deal. They've never had as good a reader as you since you left."

"They seem to manage," Emmy said. "How's your boss?"

"He works too hard, Mrs. Baldwin. His father hardly does anything now. To see the airs Angela puts on you'd think he was the whole business, but he isn't."

The lunch was very good. Adele had never eaten such food. She became more and more expansive. The office gossip flowed out. George Mather, she said, was a pacifist and one of the girls in the art department was an out-and-out Communist.

"Well," said Emmy philosophically, "I suppose it's like sticking buttons up your nose. Most kids try it once."

But always somehow the talk veered back to Courtney, to the children, to Ricky and back to Courtney again.

"I think he liked the Germans," said Adele. "Some of them anyhow." She bit daintily into her French pastry. "He's got a photograph from Germany too. That's a funny thing, you know. I opened it, and if I hadn't seen the uniform I'd have said it was Jeffrey Wayne. It looked awfully like him. Maybe he's a cousin or something."

"Very likely," said Emmy indifferently. "What did he do with it? The picture, I mean. I'd like to see a German uniform. Down in Washington they say they're pretty snappy."

"It's still in his desk," said Adele. "I saw it there the other day. What heavenly coffee!"

It was quite late when they left the movie. They wandered

down Madison, Emmy window-shopping and Adele entirely happy. When she saw a bag she admired Emmy went in and bought it for her. It was that sort of day. And when Emmy suggested she would like to see the office Adele agreed joyously.

"We've got another floor now," she said. "I'd like you to see that one too."

No one disputed their entrance to the building. Adele had her own key and Emmy duly admired everything, including the photograph.

"It does look like young Jeff, doesn't it?" she said. "So that's the German air uniform. It looks practical. Could I have a glass of water, kid? Martinis always make me thirsty."

When Adele came back with the paper cup Emmy was closing the desk drawer and picking up her bag.

"Well, I'd better be moving on," she said. "I need a fresh wave if I can get one. I'm out to dinner tonight."

Courtney did not miss the picture, nor did Emmy use it. She was content to know she had it. She remembered when Court came back from the occupation. She had asked him once if there hadn't been a little German fräulein over there, and he had flushed painfully. But she was having a good time in Washington. It was filled with men, officers and civilians, and more were crowding in.

For now there was no question of Hitler's plans. In the fall he had taken the Sudetenland. In March of 1939 his fleet moved into the harbor at Memel, and Courtney offset the bad effect of the pacifist book with others presenting the opposite side. But the isolationist label stuck. In the club at lunch some men avoided him, while others undertook to argue with him.

"For God's sake get this through your thick heads," he would explode. "I'm not a pacifist. Have you read only one book? Publishers don't necessarily take sides. They try to inform their readers."

By late spring, however, he had taken a beating. Ricky, watching him anxiously, suggested going to the Bar Harbor house that summer, and he finally agreed. The decision pleased Matthew, although he refused to go with them. The place had too many memories for him. But once again the storm shutters came down, the field mice fled, and the sea air blew away the mustiness of long disuse.

The change did Courtney good. It was his first real holilday in years. He would play thirty-six holes of golf, come back, take a shower, and look ten years younger.

"Feel like a fighting cock," he would say to Ricky. "How about some cocktails before dinner?"

He was not drinking much, however. When he and Jeff stripped for a swim in the club pool they were both flat bellied and narrow hipped. And he could still outswim his son.

"You're the hell of a parent!" Jeff would gasp. "Didn't you see my girl watching?"

There was always a current girl now.

But one bright afternoon a plane from the field at Trenton flew low over the water in front of the house and someone seemed to be waving from it. An hour or two later a triumphant Jeff walked in on them.

"Did you see me?" he said. "Boy, was it fun! What do you bet I fly a plane of my own one day? It's easy. No wonder Pete's crazy about it."

There was nothing Ricky could do, or even say. It became almost a daily matter to hear the little plane droning overhead. She would not even look up, but on the day Jeff came home joyfully to announce that he had made a solo flight she took him in her arms and held him there, to his considerable embarrassment.

"Great Scott, Mother! Are you crying?"

"No, Jeff. I just— Only it seems such a short time since you were a baby."

She wanted to tell him all the little things she remembered: the time Courtney had bent over him as he lay naked in his crib and he had wet in his father's ear; the time his steam engine blew up; his first bicycle, and the time outside the operating room at the hospital when he had his appendix out. She did not, of course. She went back to darning Elizabeth's needlepoint chairs, and managed to smile up at him.

"I suppose boys have to grow up," she said. "I'm glad, if you're happy."

That was all she wanted for any of them, to be happy. Happy and safe. O dear God, keep them safe. Take care of them, always and ever.

By the middle of August Courtney went back to New York, leaving Ricky to worry about Jeff now flying every day, to pack picnic lunches for Peggy or to press her dresses for the club dances. Peggy was still playing the field, sailing with this boy, motoring or mountain climbing with the other. Her body was filling out now at almost sixteen; her swelling breasts embarrassed her.

"I'm going to look like a cow, Hilda."

"A cow's a useful animal."

There was always a lovelorn youth somewhere in the offing. Jeff maintained they lived in the shrubbery and came out, like cockroaches, at night. Once he overheard one of them telling Peggy she had soulful eyes. After that she was Soulful Eyes to him, later corrupted to Eyes. But Hilda only snorted.

"Soulful eyes my foot," she said. "I know that look of hers. She's only wondering whether there's ice cream for dinner."

They were still in Maine when on the first of September Hitler's forces rumbled up from ships in the harbor at Danzig. He found a partially evacuated city in which to fire the first shots of the second World War. But he found an unexpected resistance. A garrison of two hundred Poles held out for six days and at the end only seventy-one remained to surrender.

Nevertheless, Poland was doomed, and the British, pledged to its protection, found themselves at last at war. Roberta was alone when she heard it. She had stayed only a month or two in Sheila's flat. If she missed American plumbing she did not mention it. She learned to light the geyser in the bathroom and to bathe without fearing it would blow up. She grew accustomed—after twenty years—to the traffic moving in the wrong direction. But from the beginning they had differed over Sheila's calm assumption that the United States would let England fight alone.

"Of course the American will come in," Roberta said. "They can't afford not to."

"Why should they?" Sheila demanded. "Just because the King and Queen ate hot dogs with the Roosevelts? Be yourself, Mother. They don't like us and we don't like them."

This was a different Sheila, a sober and now thoroughly English one. She would never again be the shy mousy girl who had gone to America, nor the wildly happy woman who had tossed everything away to marry, and to have her man die in her arms. She was even a little hard.

"That fool of a Chamberlain! As if you can appease a tiger with a lump of sugar!"

One thing was certain; she did not need Roberta, nor even want her much. When she came home at night she was tired. She would eat her dinner and go to bed, and Roberta began to feel not only superfluous but rather foolish.

She walked the streets during the day, while Sheila was away. Except that the faces of people looked strained, London seemed much as it always had been; the buses as crowded, the shops doing business as usual. And she made one or two small pilgrimages to Hyde Park, where so long ago Arthur had drilled an awkward squad, his long lank body sweating under the August sun.

Twenty-five years. One day at that time she had seen a short youth with a snub nose watching. He had spoken to her.

"They don't want runts like me," he had said, without bitterness. "But I'll get there."

The next day she had seen his picture in the paper. "Peer's son enlists as army cook." But even army cooks had a hard time in those days. The time came when she saw him among the casualty lists as killed in action.

She went, too, to look at the house in Cadogan Square. It

looked old and battered, as Sheila had said. A royal prince and his wife lived near it now, in a house almost like it, and she wondered vaguely what they had done about bathrooms.

She took a small flat of her own one day, and going to the warehouse got out as much of her furniture as she needed. Among her things she found the old case she had carried in the last war. It was fully loaded, hypodermics, drugs and all, and out of sentiment she took it back with her. But there still seemed no place for her in this new England, anxious and waiting. At night she crawled drearily into her bed to keep warm but the very sheets were damp.

The few attempts she made to reach her old friends were not very successful. Some of them lived out of London. To those who remained and who asked her for an occasional cup of tea the mere fact that she was American born made her more or less suspect.

"Of course it won't be your war, Roberta. When are you going home?"

"I'm staying. I was rather useful before, but perhaps you don't remember."

A few of them did remember. Only this time they said it would be a different war. It would be in the air, where she couldn't go. Naturally, if the Germans moved west, as they had before— But of course they wouldn't take France. The French were wonderful fighters. Look at the army they had! And the Maginot Line!

She listened to them, sitting with her hands folded in her lap, trying to understand them, trying to reorient herself seeing their rooms cluttered with odds and ends from all over the world, where their sons held together the vast empire. Sitting by the fires that warmed nobody; holding her teacup in her long thin hands, watching their handsome highbred English faces and hearing their confident voices.

"I suppose America will be too busy to come in."

"I think it will help us. But of course it's not really their affair, is it?"

They would be cold and silent after that. And they would not ask her again. When she told Sheila she was impatient.

"For heaven's sake, Mother! Why make enemies like that? What good does it do?"

"It's the truth," Roberta said stoutly. "If it takes constant wars to keep a balance of power over here, there has to be some place left on earth where people can survive."

She was alone when Sheila came in the night war was declared. Sheila looked exhausted, but she had come with a purpose.

"It's the beginning of the end, Mother," she said. "I want you to go back to New York. You'll be safe there," she added bitterly.

"I'm staying here, Sheila."

"Suppose they bomb us?"

"I'm still staying," said Roberta.

Poland was only the beginning, of course. There was nothing to stop the Germans. And at last America was aroused. Lend-Lease now, with fifty old destroyers to Churchill, now Prime Minister in England. Mussolini and the knife in the back. Norway, Denmark, Holland, and Belgium gone. "Again and again I say—"

"I don't believe him," Matthew said stubbornly. "Roosevelt wants a war. Only way to get the Democrats out of the mess they're in. It's Wilson all over again."

"It's a world war," Courtney told him. "We can't keep out. Sooner or later—unless we're too late, Dad."

It looked as though it would be too late. Nothing so dramatic and so terrible had happened in the world's history, nothing so fast. The German army moved as no army had ever moved before, its troops in trucks, its tanks behind them. They followed the old encircling movement, like the jaws of pincers. And what they pinched off, dead or alive, was theirs.

At night Courtney would find Ricky hunched over the radio, or with an atlas in her lap, studying a map. Then one day he came to find her in her room, instead of waiting for him as usual downstairs. He knocked and went in, to find her standing by a window with a letter in her hand.

"It's from Jeff," she said tonelessly. "He thinks we'll go in. If we do he wants our permission to enlist!"

He went over and stood beside her. Outside the streets were snowy, with a cold wind blowing. A few children were scurrying home, their nurses behind them. He took the letter from her and read it.

"He's nineteen, Ricky. Pretty soon he won't need our permission."

"He's not even a man yet," she said bitterly. "Do I have to hear all this again? I saw you go. Isn't that enough?"

"It may not be enough, my dear," he said somberly.

She stared at him.

"I think men are crazy," she said. "They want wars. They like them. It doesn't matter about their mothers or their wives. Give them a gun and a uniform and they're off."

"I didn't want this war, darling. It's here."

"But you'd go if you could. You'll let Jeff go."

"Let's wait until it happens, darling."

He was very tender with Ricky after that. At night when she could not sleep he would go down to the kitchen and heat milk for her. As Matthew had once done for Elizabeth. Or, knowing she was awake, he would reach out to her bed and hold her small cold hand in his big one.

"Want me to come in with you?"

"No. I'll be all right, Court. You need your sleep."

38

Roberta was still in London when in the summer of 1940 the Germans attacked it from the air. Two hundred German planes were shot down, and in September began what was to be a three months' siege. Streets were blocked with debris, fires were started, the death lists were enormous. So wild was the panic that policemen were killed by crowds rushing for the safety of the underground.

Toward the end Sheila was bombed out. She appeared at Roberta's one night, tired but unruffled.

"My place is gone," she said. "If you don't mind putting me up, Mother . . ."

It was a long time since Sheila had needed her. Now her girl had come back to her. She made tea, fixed a bed for her, and when at last Sheila was tucked away—in one of her own long-sleeved nightgowns—she stooped awkwardly and kissed her.

"I'm glad you weren't home."

"It's a mess, isn't it? I haven't a thing but what I had on."

But in the morning when she wakened her mother was gone. Only later did she learn of Roberta's activities during the interval of hell; of her moving about from one stricken spot to the other, carrying her old leather case and looking like nothing on earth.

"I have morphia here, if you need it."

"Need it! I'll say we do."

But one night a surgeon, looking up from the broken body

on the ground, glanced at her sharply.

"I've seen you before, haven't I?"

"I don't know," said Roberta. "Have you?"

"Well, thanks anyhow, Mrs.—"

"Truesdale, Lady Truesdale. I hope the morphia is all right. I've had it for years."

"Truesdale?" he repeated. "There was a woman in the early days of the last war named Truesdale. I ought to remember. She brought some morphia to a first-aid post when we were out of the stuff. Never knew how she got there."

"She walked when she had to," Roberta said dryly, and moved away quietly.

Matthew was horrified by the whole situation. Roberta did not even reply to his cable demanding her return. All she ever said was that she was well and busy, as indeed she was. But he still believed it was Europe's war.

"Been doing it for centuries," he said with disgust. "But Roosevelt's itching to get in. Why in God's name doesn't he look after his own country? This kowtowing to labor until it's too big for its pants makes me sick."

He was astonished as well as relieved when Hitler without warning gave up his plan of invading the British Isles and turned to Russia. This was something like it. What did it matter if German tanks and trucks raised clouds of dust as they raced along the Russian roads? Or that German planes dropped bombs on cities with unpronounceable names? Or that the Communists were being murdered, and their towns burned over their heads? Or even that across the Pacific a group of little yellow men, having got into power by assassination, were dreaming of Asiatic domination? It meant a breathing spell at least for America

They spent that summer again in Bar Harbor, but Jeff had no more flying lessons. His instructor was in Canada teaching the Canadian Air Force to fly. And when they finally persuaded Matthew to go for a rest, he went unwillingly. He had not been there since the summer the children were lost in the fog and he had had pneumonia. He missed Elizabeth, and he found the town greatly changed since the boom era. The brokerage office had long been closed, the old race track was almost obliterated, and some of the houses he had know best had been either torn down or were vacant.

The place did not belong to him now. It belonged to Ricky and the children, and he felt like a visitor. Once Ricky found him gravely inspecting the damaged needlepoint chairs in the drawing room.

"Lizzie was proud of them," he said. "What happened to them?"

But like Roberta years before he spent most of his time on the terrace, looking out at the sea. The fountain was running again, but he could see past it to where just over the horizon Mount Desert Rock light was guiding the convoys on their way to Europe; the ships edging along, and death only too often under the blue surface of the sea.

Both the summer colony and the town were quiet that summer. At the club the children had taken over the pool, the children and the older people, for many of the young men had already enlisted. Even the golf course looked deserted, and Jeff was sulky and impatient.

"Pete's in it already, Dad," he protested. "I feel like a damned slacker."

"Pete's older than you."

"What do you want me to do? Sit around and chew my fingernails?"

Perhaps it would be as well to let him go. When he had spoken of it to Ricky, however, she had looked sick. He turned back to the boy.

"There will be plenty of time, Jeff. This is a long war. It may last ten years or more. You're not twenty yet."

"You don't want America in it, do you?"

"I don't want us in until we have something to fight with. When we're ready—"

"Oh, ready! I'm sick of the word."

The problem solved itself that fall, however. Jeff was still sulky and at a loose end when he went back to college. He had been there only a few days when the Selective Service Act was put into effect, and a day or so later Courtney arrived early at his office to find him there standing by the window and looking out. He looked defiant as he turned.

"Well, here I am," he said. "What are you going to do about it?"

Courtney said nothing until he had shed his hat and overcoat. He sat down behind his desk and eyed his son.

"I think I'd suggest a bath," he observed. "You look as though you needed it."

"I sat up all night in the train. No berths."

"I suppose this is a more or less polite way of saying you've left college?"

"I'm not going to be dragged into the service by the neck. Anyhow they've kicked me out. Call up the dean if you don't believe it."

"I see. Suppose you sit down. Don't stand there glaring at me. What have you done?"

"The charge was drunk and disorderly. I sure was disorderly." There was the faint sign of a grin on his face. "I broke a few windows and knocked down a policeman. I spent night before last in the hoosegow. Yesterday they expelled me."

Courtney lit a cigarette. He did not offer Jeff one. He blew out the smoke deliberately.

"So it was an act," he said. "I must be the hell of a father! Why didn't you come home and talk it over with me? It all sounds a bit drastic, Jeff. Did you hurt the officer?"

"Not much. He banged his head on the curbstone. I didn't mean that, Dad. He got pretty rough with me, so I—" Behind the grin he looked rather pale. Evidently things had gone further than he had intended. "They took him to the hospital. But he's all right."

"I suppose you hadn't been drinking?"

"No. Just enough to smell of liquor."

Courtney got up.

"You'd better go home," he said. "It will hurt your mother, so go easy with her." He picked up his overcoat and glanced at his watch. "Tell her I'm flying to Cambridge this morning. I'll be home tonight."

Jeff looked startled.

"Cambridge? Why?"

Courtney jammed his hat on his head. His face was stiff.

"I've seen you through a lot of things, Jeff, but I dislike being pushed around by my own son. If you're out you're out. I had about decided to let you enlist anyhow. But I'm no easy mark, and this whole thing stinks."

There was nothing much to do in Cambridge when he got there. The dean was polite but firm. Jeff had not stood well scholastically for the past year or so, and this last escapade had finished him.

"Deliberate or not, Mr. Wayne, he's lucky to get off as he has. I gather he wants to get into the service. Many of our boys do."

"That seems to be the general idea," Courtney said shortly. "He wants to fly."

For the first time the dean ceased to be a dean and became a human being.

"I don't blame him for that," he said. "I flew myself in the last war. I cracked up, or I'd try for this one."

Courtney left a check for the police officer and spent a little time wandering around the Yard. The old elms had gone, but the new ones were flourishing. Before he left he found himself under Professor Copeland's windows. Old "Copey" with his books and his open fire, serving coffee to his old students and distinguished visitors. Old Copey in the classroom, satiric and dry. "The writing of a book, gentlemen, consists of a mixture of backbone, hands and brains. This third constituent, however, may be entirely lacking. The mere matter of words, printed on paper and neatly bound, does *not* make a book."

He wondered what Copey would say about some of the books he published.

But the college depressed him. The students he saw looked incredibly young, and he felt old beside them, old and worn. Now Jeff would go into the Army Air Corps as he had hoped, and it meant the breaking up of the family. A man struggled to get ahead, to raise his children. He worked and planned, and then they grew up and life took them away. Or a war.

There were no tapes to sew on Jeff's clothes this time when he went away. The army attended to that. And Ricky held her head proudly when she said good-bye to him. She even managed to smile.

"Just come back, darling," she said. "We'll be waiting."

The house was quiet after he had gone. It had a new and rather dreadful stillness. Now and then Jeff wrote brief enthusiastic letters. He was having to unlearn all he had known about the air, to start again. But it was great. The men were wonderful. Everything was wonderful. Maybe he would get home for Christmas. If he did he would like a new wrist watch. He had smashed his old one.

Neither of them dared to ask how he had smashed it.

But Courtney found himself restless that winter. It was not the sight of Jeff, resplendent in his new uniform, dashing in and out during his brief holiday. It was the thought that men older then himself were in the new growing army. He took to making trips to Washington, flying down and back, but the results were always the same. He would sit for hours in a waiting room, to be at last ushered into an office where a man sometimes in uniform, sometimes not, would look up patiently from a crowded desk.

"My name is Wayne. I've been hoping in case war came I could be useful somewhere."

"I see. Sit down, Mr. Wayne. Of course we hope there will be no war, but who can tell?"

He would inquire into Court's record. Sometimes he would ask if he had been wounded and if he had any permanent result from the injury. But inevitably he asked what he was doing now. Court grew to know what the answer to that would be.

"I see. Books. Well, of course we will need books, Mr. Wayne. We need them now in the camps. Aside from that we want an informed public. Not propaganda, you understand. Understanding."

One and all they took his name, and one and all they promptly forgot it. It was the brush-off, and he knew it.

One day in the summer of 1941 he met Emmy on the street. The strong Washington sunlight was beating down on her pitilessly, and in the heat her usual make-up had disappeared. He was shocked at her appearance. She looked older than he would have believed possible. But she had the same gamin smile when she saw him, as though the past was past. As of course it was.

"Well, for crying out loud!" she said. "If it isn't Court Wayne in person!"

"Hello, Emmy," he said awkwardly. "How are you?"

"About the way I look, I expect. This heat is killing me. How about coming to my place for a drink? I've got an apartment, thank God."

"I only have until six. What about the Willard? It's nearby."

She agreed, and at the hotel she disappeared to repair her damaged face. When she came out Courtney had a table and she sat down across from him.

"How's the book business managing without me?" she inquired.

"How am I to answer that? If I say it's good—" She laughed, and he relaxed somewhat. "Aren't you out early? It's not half past four."

"This town works only until four. After that it enjoys itself."

He looked shocked and she laughed again.

"Oh, some of the top boys make a job of it. But the rank and file take it easy."

"How do you get along?" he asked her curiously. "No night clubs and only a few bars. Must be quite a change for you."

"I manage," she said, rather dryly. "Where's the family? How did you get away? You're still pretty domestic, aren't you?"

If this annoyed him he ignored it.

"Jeff's in the Air Corps. He seems to like it."

"And that old harridan of an aunt of yours? Lady Truesdale?"

"She's in England. So is Sheila. I wish they were here."

The mention of Lady Truesdale, however, had cost Emmy her good humor. So too perhaps had Courtney's cool detachment. She sat back and surveyed him with a mocking smile.

"I met an officer a few days ago who was with you in the occupation," she said, inventing rapidly. "You must have been a bit of a lad over there, from his account. His name was Boyle. He was a lieutenant then. He's back in the service now. Got a desk job."

"We were all pretty cheery in those days," he said cautiously. "I don't remember anyone named Boyle. What did he tell you?"

She smiled over her drink.

"It seems you had a little affair with a German girl over there. He didn't remember her name. Said it was all good clean fun." She was watching him with shrewd malicious eyes, and to his fury he felt his color rising.

"That's a long time to remember."

She was enjoying herself. She had taken the photograph from his desk purely on impulse. Now she almost told him she had it. She did not, however.

"Of course you remember. Was she pretty, Court? Some of them are."

"Forget it, Emmy. It was kid stuff. She's been married for years."

"Oh! So you kept track of her!"

"Her father was a friend of mine. He wrote at intervals. The Nazis got him finally. I'd rather not talk about it."

Well, she'd been wrong, of course. It was sheer coincidence about the picture. But some of the amused interest died out of her face. She looked what she was, a woman in her forties, no longer thrilled by the man across the table, or indeed by any man. She seemed slightly deflated when he glanced at his watch and said he had to go.

"Well, good luck, Court."

The same to you, Emmy."

Nevertheless, he was uncomfortable on the way home. He was not afraid of Emmy. What could she know? He more than suspected her of a shot in the dark. He remembered no Boyle. She had been fishing, and he had fallen for it. He was furious with himself and with her, but to be on the safe side he determined to get rid of Otto's picture. It had been lying around long enough.

He looked for it in his desk the next morning, but he could not find it. He was puzzled rather than worried when he buzzed for Adele.

"I had a photograph here in the desk," he said. "A boy in uniform. I can't seem to find it."

She stared at him; she had gone very pale.

"It's been gone a long time, Mr. Wayne. I thought you took it."

"You didn't throw it out?"

"Oh, no. I would never do that."

He watched her go out of the office. Something had upset her, but he had no idea what it was. Nor had Angela, finding her later in the washroom crying her eyes out.

"What's the matter, child? Boss cranky today?"

"No. I just—lost something."

She did not say that what she had lost was more than a picture. It was her confidence in a woman she had believed in and liked.

39

One afternoon, in the fall of 1941, Peggy made a small informal afternoon debut. She was a tall girl now, taller than Ricky, and she had finished school the June before. But she did not want to go to college. She had indeed no plans for herself, and so Ricky decided to bring her out.

"She ought to meet some really nice people," she told Court. "This café crowd she knows is cheap. All it wants is publicity in the gossip columns; it doesn't care what."

"Really nice people can be pretty dull," Court teased her.

"They have children, and grandchildren. She's been away from New York too long."

Peggy looked very pretty that day, standing beside her mother in her long pale-blue dress, her hair cut to shoulder length, her cheeks flushed with excitement, and her flowers wilting in her hot young hands.

"You remember Peggy, don't you, Mrs. Robbins?"

"I certainly do. But she's a young lady now. Good gracious, how time flies! How are you, my dear?"

They moved on, staid and dignified New York, facing a bewildering existence which had not only cut their incomes to the bone, but had forced them to abandon many of their charities and even taken away the city they knew. Now it was crowded with refugees who seemed incredibly rich, who filled the hotels, jammed the best shops, and shoved and elbowed them on the pavements.

But they were kindly folk. They smiled and welcomed Peggy to their own lost world. And she smiled back, not realizing that it was lost.

Jeff had got leave for the party, and Courtney was proud of his family that day. Proud of his house, his wife, his children. He moved around in his morning coat and striped trousers, shaking hands, seeing the champagne was being passed, and keeping an eye on the hired butlers.

"Better ice another bottle or two."

"Certainly, sir."

The champagne was Matthew's contribution, but Matthew himself did not come. He was not well, and at his age crowds tired him. He sent her instead a gold bracelet hung with minute gold toys. "With love from your grandfather," he wrote in his shaky old hand.

Abroad things were looking rather better. America was making its vast contribution, of armament, of food, of supplies of sorts. True, the Germans still held most of Europe, but at last the Russians were battling back. Who would have thought it? That rag-bag country, and now Stalin actually holding a parade in Red Square; a short tubby man, standing on top of Lenin's tomb and defying the oncoming hordes, almost jeering at them.

Now Matthew had new maps. Courtney would find him studying them.

"Better keep an eye on the Japs," he said. "They've been in China ten years. What's the use of Roosevelt telling them to get out? Talk's cheap."

He was having lunch at Courtney's the day of Pearl Harbor. Peggy was out somewhere, and they were having coffee in the drawing room when the news came. Pete Stafford was there on a brief leave, and it was Pete who turned on the radio. An announcer was talking rapidly. The raid was a fact. No one knew yet the amount of damage, but it was considerable. The Japanese . . .

No one stirred. Ricky was very pale. She had given one

glance at Court, then she was staring again at the radio, as a man in the electric chair might wait for the switch to be thrown.

Pete got up, unfolding his big body slowly.

"Well, I guess this is it," he said. "I'd better be on my way."

He looked at their stunned faces, gave them a sort of salute and was gone. Court went over to Ricky and put his arms around her.

"It's war, isn't it?" she said.

"I'm afraid so, darling."

"Then Jeff—"

"It's his job, Ricky."

Matthew was raging up and down the room, his face bleak. How in hell had it happened?

"My God!" he said. "The dirty little buck-toothed bastards! What were we doing out there, to let them attack us? Where was the fleet?"

The fleet of course was either on fire or lying in the muddy bottom of the harbor. Nobody knew it then, however. Court, his arms still around Ricky, realized she was shaking and offered her some brandy, but she refused it.

"I don't need that sort of courage, Court."

She was busy the rest of the afternoon. She had no time to think, for the waitress had collapsed in the pantry and had to be taken up to bed. Ricky sat with her for a while, stroking her small work-hardened hands.

"We was to be married his next leave."

"He'll be all right, my dear. Wait and see."

"I've been saving for my wedding dress. Now—"

"You'll still need it. I'll give it to you myself. What would you like? White satin?"

Courtney and his father were talking gravely when she went downstairs. No one mentioned Jeff again. But late in the afternoon an excited Peggy arrived. She burst in on them like a hurricane.

"I've just heard it," she said. "What price a girl in this war?

I'm not going to sit it out on my fanny—that's sure."

"We'll need you here," said Court.

"Some place else may need me more," she said.

It was strange after that to find life in the city going on much as it had before; no uniformed men, the theaters and movies crowded, the streets and avenues rivers of flowing cars. Behind the scenes of course, there was enormous activity. But the country was slow getting under way. Matthew, taking a bus on Sundays and walking over the rough streets behind the piers and docks, found them as deserted as though the whole nation had gone on strike. On Mondays he would go irritably to the office, to blame Roosevelt for everything. And Angela, who thought him the savior of the world, would resent it.

"He wanted a war," Matthew would say. "Why the hell wasn't he ready for it?"

"He did all he could, with everyone against him. Look at the navy he built."

"Look at the navy he lost!"

He knew it was foolish. There was real fervor in this Angela. She actually loved the man.

"At least he's done his best for the poor. You can't deny that, Mr. Wayne."

"Sure I can. Everybody's poor now."

The sparring went on for some time. Then one day Matthew almost lost her.

"Well, if he wants excitement he's got it. Any man who's tied to a wheel chair and can play with millions of other men—"

Angela got up, notebook in hand.

"I'm sorry, Mr. Wayne," she said. "I've taken a great deal. I've been here for thirty years. But when you say a thing like that about a man who is doing his best for all of us, I'm through."

There was a certain stiff-spined attitude in her as she left the room. He felt sheepish and in the wrong. Not that he believed she would go. She was as much an office fixture as his desk, he went to the door.

Angela was crying. He went over awkwardly and put an arm around her thin spinster's shoulders.

"I'm sorry, Angela," he said. "You're right. And I'm wrong. Leave if you want to, but don't go hating me."

She did not go, but little by little during the following months he felt the foundations of his life giving way. Not only Jeff, happily training now for actual combat. One by one the younger men in the office drifted away. Anne Lockwood's oldest son went. So did George Mather's boy. Watching Courtney he realized how difficult it was to carry on the business, with his associate editors all gone, and even the salesmen.

There was a difference too in the manuscripts that were coming in. There were no romantic treatments of war, as there had been during the first World War. These books were hard, factual and uncompromising. They pulled no punches. And the British were writing nothing of any importance. After all, how could they?

But no one could complain of the city's inertia now. It was the nerve center of the country. Long-empty office buildings were opened, their windows lighted all night. The East and North River piers were the scenes of wild activity, and the streets were crowded with trucks. Before long, too, uniforms began to appear, only a few at first, but more to come. Millions to come.

But Matthew still hated Roosevelt and the increasing dictatorship in Washington.

"We started wrong," he said bitterly. "We gave those fellows their heads, with their doctrines of scarcity, their alphabet soup, and all the rest of their nonsense. Now we've got what we deserve. Maybe that's the way to govern a people anyhow. This fellow Stalin seems to be doing all right."

Now and then he heard from Roberta. The blitz was over, but bombs were still falling. Her letters, however, were calm. She was working in a canteen. Sheila was well but working too hard. It was a relief to know America was in, and he was to give her address to Jeff in case he got to London. Nothing about the shortages of everything, or the exhausted people, or the ruins everywhere. But she did ask for shoes, for both of them.

It rained a good bit that spring of 1942, and Courtney limped rather more than usual. Perhaps it was a form of escape, for he had made a final attempt to get into the service and failed. Nevertheless, he was very busy. Already he had helped to form the Council on Books in Wartime, an agency to act as a liaison between the government and publishers. All the publishers belonged to it, for according to the government books were weapons. Now as time went on he found it took a good bit of time. When the army or the navy wanted a book published, the council met and put their names in a hat. The firm whose name was drawn got the book.

It was a nonprofit organization, and at first Matthew thought it nonsense.

"Books!" he said. "I've lived through two wars and nobody ever fired a book that I heard of."

He changed his mind about that later, although he was never entirely reconciled to the small pocket-size editions, two columns to a page, which came out under the council imprint.

"Call that a book!" he jeered. "Some fellow spends half his life writing it, and it comes out like a squeezed lemon!"

To Courtney the days were too short for what he had to do. Now when he came home late he would undress carefully, not to waken Ricky, and once again sleep in his dresing room. He seldom thought of young Otto, but one day he saw where the Germans had made another air attack on London, and he asked Adele about the photograph.

"Ever come across it?" he inquired.

He had again the queer feeling that the question troubled her.

"No, I haven't, Mr. Wayne. Is it—was it—important?"

"I don't understand what happened to it," he said, "that's all."

He had no idea she would worry about it, or that she would translate her anxiety into action; that on the following Saturday she would go to Washington and confront an astonished Emmy with blazing eyes.

"Why, hello," said Emmy, finding her waiting downstairs in the apartment house. "What brings you here? Looking for a job?"

"I'll tell you when we get upstairs."

Emmy laughed.

"What's wrong, kid? Found a German spy under your bed?"

"I came for the picture you took out of Mr. Wayne's desk."

Emmy's eyes narrowed.

"Oh! He's looking for it, is he?"

"No. He says it isn't important. But you took it. I want it back."

"Rather late, isn't it, kid? How do you know I still have it?"

"Why did you steal it?"

Emmy did not answer. She wanted no scene in the lobby with this excited girl. Already there had been complaints about her, of late drinking parties in her apartment, and even worse. She took the elevator with Adele behind her, and inside her sitting room she closed the door and mixed herself a drink.

"Did Courtney Wayne send you here?" she asked at last.

"Certainly not."

"I'd give a good bit to know why you want it."

"It wouldn't occur to you that I'm a trusted employee, I suppose. I'd be after you if you'd taken a two-cent stamp."

Emmy felt better after her drink. She kicked off her slippers and sat back in her chair.

"I think it's in the desk over there," she said. "I haven't seen it for months. Who is it anyhow?"

"It's the picture of a boy whose grandfather was a friend of Mr. Wayne's. The old man was killed by the Nazis, if that means anything to you."

"Not a thing," said Emmy. And when Adele gazed at her in astonishment, she added: "Take it if you like, and then get out.

I have to dress for dinner."

It was late when Adele got back to New York. Her first idea was merely to put the picture back in the desk. She was still excited, however. The next day was Sunday, and she could not wait. She took a taxi to the house and rang the bell. Courtney was still out, but Ricky was up. She opened the door and looked at the girl with surprise.

"Why, Adele!" she said. "Is anything wrong?"

"No. It's all right. I just brought something for Mr. Wayne. He missed it out of his desk, and I—just found it."

"Well," Ricky smiled at her, "why not leave it with me? I'll see he gets it. He's out just now. Won't you come upstairs and have a glass of sherry? You look weary."

"I'd like to," Adele said faintly.

Upstairs in Court's study she relaxed over the wine and a cigarette. She began to laugh.

"You'd never guess where I found it," she said. "I knew Mr. Wayne was worried about it, so I flew to Washington today and—well, I guess I hijacked it."

She reached into her coat pocket and got out the photograph. Ricky, however, did not take it.

"In Washington?" she said, puzzled. "I'm afraid I don't understand."

Adele held it out.

"It's a photograph of a German boy. Probably you know about it. He looks a bit like your Jeff. But why that Baldwin woman wanted it I'll never know. She took it out of Mr. Wayne's desk."

Ricky felt as though all the blood in her body had left the surface and gathered around her heart. For a moment she was literally unable to speak. She put down her cigarette and took the picture from Adele's outstretched hand. It might have been Jeff himself who looked back at her, only an older and harder Jeff. She turned it over. "Otto Reiff" was written on the back.

She never doubted who it was, or that Courtney had treasured it, had kept it in his desk and missed it when it was gone. She knew too why Emmy had taken it. But her hand was steady as she held it out to Adele.

"It's the son of a family Mr. Wayne knew in Germany years ago," she said. "I'm sure he would be sorry you went to all this trouble. It isn't really important. Why not just tell him you found it somewhere, Adele? Why drag in Mrs. Baldwin?"

Adele stared at her.

"Just put it back?" she said uncertainly.

"Why not? Mrs. Baldwin is an old friend. I have no idea why she took the picture. Perhaps she thought it was Jeff."

It was a badly confused and rather deflated Adele who went back to her room that night. She took off her high-heeled shoes and rubbed her tired feet. She could slip the picture into the files somewhere on Monday and pretend to find it, but she could not forget Ricky's face as she saw her out of the house.

It had looked somehow drained. Not of course that she used that word.

40

It was daylight before Ricky slept that night. Courtney came home late from a meeting of air-raid wardens, for now he had taken over a downtown zone in addition to his other work. When he saw her transom dark he did not go into her room. She heard him, however; heard him undressing and later the heavy breathing which told her he was asleep.

She lay wide-eyed in her bed, going back over the long years of her marriage. She never doubted that Courtney had always known about his German son. He could have told her, and she would have tried to understand. It was the long years of deceit she could not forgive. Had he been supporting this boy during the long interval when every penny counted? When she had worked to make and keep a home for all of them? And a Nazi at that. She found herself shivering, and getting up found an extra blanket. A Nazi and an airman, perhaps even now dropping bombs over some innocent sleeping population.

Yet she could not tear down what she had so carefully built. Not with Jeff about to go to a war, or with Peggy going into the WAAC, now the age limit had been reduced. There must be something stable for them to remember and to come back to.

She did not see Courtney before he left the next morning, and when he came back that night she met him much as usual. Only after they sat down to dinner she told him she had taken a war job. He raised his eyebrows quizzically.

"A war job? What sort? Going to run a lathe?"

"Driving a car for the American Women's Voluntary Services."

"Whose car? If I may ask?"

"Ours," she said calmly. "You can use a bus or taxi, can't you? I'll be careful of the car. You needn't worry."

"Of course," he said shortly. "It looks as though I'll soon be the only one in the family not in a uniform. You make me feel like a slacker."

After that they were seldom in the house together. Courtney was in Washington a good bit, a Washington building an air-raid shelter for the President and issuing gas masks to his staff. And Ricky was driving officers about, meeting trains, even taking ambulatory cases to hospitals. When she drove down the East River Highway she could see the antiaircraft guns there, surrounded by sandbags, to protect the Navy Yard across the river. They looked small and inadequate, she thought. Now and then a ship passed her, on the way to the Sound and a rendezvous with its convoy.

It would be heavily loaded, and the decks were lined with men. When she waved to them they waved back, as though the salute was for each of them, making them individuals again, not merely cogs in a vast and growing war machine.

But now they carried books with them, little books to fit into uniform pockets, to while away the tedium of the sea or the later tedium of the war itself. The books were being made in the millions, Armed Services Editions, as they were called. And they went all over the world, along with the shoes for the front-line trenches, along with anything that would take them.

The work helped Ricky. For months she had been living on her nerves, even before she had learned about young Otto; watching for Jeff's letters, listening to the radio with its news of a still victorious Germany, even shivering a little as the new huge war planes passed overhead. Now she at least had little time to think.

If Courtney found a change in her relationship to him, he laid it to fatigue. He had moved permanently into his dressing room, so as not to disturb her. Sometimes he was out almost all night, for he found his visits to the posts in his zone helped the morale of the tired men and women who sat alerted wherever they might be stationed.

He walked miles during those nights, from basement rooms to mortuary parlors, from garages to hotels and exclusive clubs; any place where some small space could be found for the watchers against enemy attack from the air.

He felt rather foolish sometimes, covering the zone while the sky above was starlit and peaceful, and the great sleeping buildings about him were empty of their daily quota of workers. But the work had to be done, and he realized that his wardens watched for his arrival and went back to their dreary vigils with renewed enthusiasm.

"If you'll wait a minute, Mr. Wayne, we'll have some coffee for you."

He would drink his coffee, out of a glass, out of a cracked cup, sometimes out of a tin one. Sometimes it was good, sometimes horrible, but he always drank it.

"How are you getting on here?"

"Well, this neighborhood ain't so good, sir. Couldn't wake it up. Last blackout some of them wouldn't put out their lights."

"Get the police after them."

"We did. By the time the cops got there the blackout was over."

But there were a good many times those nights when, going from post to post, he felt as though he was playing at war, that he was fooling himself into thinking he was useful. It was difficult too to arouse the population. He held meetings and demonstrations. The people came, as they would to any free show. Then they went away, and there would be the same lighted windows the next time. Or some man or woman would decide to take a walk instead of taking cover during a blackout. Courtney came across one himself one night.

"You should be inside somewhere," he said. "You know the law."

"So what?" the man said truculently. "You telling me I can't take my dog for a walk?"

"I'm telling you."

"Why, you God-damned self-important jackass! I'll walk my dog whenever I please."

He made a pass at Courtney, which was unfortunate, for when he came to he was in a cell in the precinct station house, with a lump on his jaw and his dog tied to a chair by the sergeant's desk. Behind that incident lay more than Courtney's indignation and resentment. There was his own sense of frustration, that Jeff, and other and still younger men, were fighting the war for him.

He was at home very little. When he was, it was to eat dinner and start out again to his various posts, to the little Italian's near the East River which was a family affair, with always a pot of coffee on the stove, to the one in a mortician's parlor, where often a grieving group was mixed up with his wardens, or to the one in his father's old club which had given him a large donation for equipment and telephones.

One day he found the photograph of Otto back in his desk, and heard Adele explain she had found it in his files. He looked at it with distaste before he tore it up. How lightly a man sowed his seed! A moment in a woman's arms! But the seed might become dragon seed. Was dragon seed. This hard-eyed German boy in his flier's uniform was dragon seed indeed.

He had little time to think, however. If the air-raid warden work took most of his nights, he was still a publisher by day. Now when he flew to Washington no patient officer brushed him off. He was even speaking over the radio, for radio was a part of the council's work. When a Wayne book was dramatized for the air he sometimes introduced it. He would sit or stand at a microphone, with his speech in his hands, and a quiet-voiced man beside him.

"Now just be calm, Mr. Wayne. Forget the people listening in. You are talking to me. Be as matter-of-fact as you can. And of course don't rustle the paper. In three seconds now . . ."

He was not nervous after the first time. And in Washington one evening Emmy heard him when she happened to be at home. She got up and mixed herself a stiff drink.

Occasionally he and Ricky had an evening together. They would go to the newsreels, to see the released movies of London burning. But they had little to talk about. It was as though their paths had diverged more and more.

"What sort of day did you have?" Court would say.

"About as usual. I don't know how long the tires will last. I put on the spare today."

It did not occure to them to sit down and analyze what was happening to them. They were too anxious, too exhausted. One day Ricky, driving down Madison Avenue, saw a young naval officer walking with a girl. The side of the face he kept toward the girl was apparently all right, but the one Ricky saw was hidiously burned. He was walking with his chin well up, as though defying the people who stared at him. She had carried mutilated men before, men who bore the loss of limb with apparently cheerful philosophy, but she looked away quickly, as though she could not bear it.

It was fall when Roberta's letter came. She had sent it to Ricky, and Court coming home found her with it in her hands. Sheila had been killed.

Roberta wrote with her usual directness.

"Perhaps you had better break this to Matthew. He was rather fond of her, I think. And tell him it was very quick. Perhaps we had all grown a little careless. One does, you know, and the shelters are so horrible. My poor Sheila loathed them.

"As I think back I am glad she had her short time with Walter, and I don't think she minded going. Not really. She took all sorts of chances, and sometimes I thought she wanted to go to him—if there is such a thing."

There was nothing about herself. She did not mention that she had been bombed out and was living in one room, or that she was working to the limit of her strength day and night. There was a good bit of the stoic in Roberta.

Court took the letter to his father that night, and Matthew sat for a long time with it in his hand; remembering Roberta in the house at Cadogan Square, sitting behind her tea tray, pouring tea with her long hands, and her full face brightening when Arthur came into the room. That had been a love affair, he thought. "Stuck by him through everything," he considered. "Other women, gambling debts, the whole mess. Then she lost him after all."

Now she had lost Sheila.

"Never was lucky, Roberta," he said, his voice bleak. "She has nobody now. Plenty of spunk, though. Stuck to Arthur through thick and thin. Mostly it was pretty thin."

The two men were silent after that. Courtney was remembering Sheila, the night Walter died; how she had turned away from the rising sun as though she hated it. Well, there would be no dawn for her now, unless she wakened into an existence where everything was bright, and perhaps Walter would be there, smiling at her.

"I knew you'd come, old girl."

"It seemed so long, Walter. Is it safe here?"

"Very safe. You needn't worry any more."

He roused to find his father's eyes on him.

"Noticed Ricky lately?" he was saying.

"Noticed her? What do you mean?"

"Looks tired. Pretty thin too. Can't you get her out of that damned job of hers? Plenty of younger women to do it."

"It gives her something to do. With both children gone—"

"She has you," said Matthew stubbornly. "Or maybe she hasn't. Seems to me you don't see much of each other nowadays."

Courtney considered that on his way home. His father was right. One way or another he felt he was losing Ricky. There had been a change in her for months, only he had been too busy to notice it. He went back, determined to make up for any failure on his part, to try to get back on the old basis of love and tenderness again. As often happened, however, she was out and he did not hear her when she came in late that night.

Then unexpectedly Ricky lost her job, and with it her escape. The car broke down on a country road. She was alone, and by the time she had made what repairs she could she was hot and perspiring. She had a violent chill that night. She called Hilda, and Hilda wakened Courtney. But it was pneumonia, and when she recovered the doctor forbade her going back to work.

She was vague about it all later. She could remember Courtney's anguished face. He seemed to have been always in the room. And once she was sure she saw Jeff in the doorway. She called to him weakly but he had gone, and she relapsed into her coma.

Only when it was over did she realize how ill she had been.

When she was strong enough she took up her life again as best she could, standing in line at the schoolhouse for ration books, and fighting the losing battle for food, for stockings, for shoes, for everything. When she came home her first look was at the hall table for a letter from Jeff, or from Peggy, now a Waac apparently loving it. "Although I wish you could see me, flat heels, uniform and all . . ." she wrote. "I am hideous. At the moment I am going through something they call indoctrination. If that's a word for standing on your feet for hours, or marching, or learning to salute some detestable female who looks as though she hated your guts, that is what I am having."

It did not sound like fastidious Peggy, Ricky thought; Peggy with her bath salts and perfumes, her mascara and rouge and lipstick. She felt as though she was living in a strange and frightening world. As of course she was.

One day to her sruprise she came home to find Matthew standing by the fire in Court's study. He seldom came during the week and never during office hours. It alarmed her.

"Is something wrong, Dad?"

"That's what I came to ask you, Ricky."

She put her parcels on the desk and sat down. Her knees

were still shaking.

"I thought it might be Jeff," she said. "He's still all right, isn't he?"

"So far as I know. Ricky, has anything come between you and Court? I have eyes, my dear. You're not the same girl you were a year or so ago. What is it?"

"We've both been busy, Dad," she said evasively.

"Sure it isn't Court? He cares a lot for you. You know that. He was as nearly frantic as a man can be when you were sick."

She looked at him. In spite of his age he still looked solid and dependable. Perhaps if she told him—"

"It's like this," Matthew went on. "A man of my age gets to a place when all he can count on is the happiness of the people he cares for. He can't face any more trouble. He's had enough. I don't want you to let Court go, my dear."

"I'm not letting him go, Dad."

But Matthew was still not satisfied.

"Most men make fools of themselves one time or another," he said. "If Court did it's over long ago."

She faced him bravely.

"Yes," she said. "Of course it would be over. All over, Dad. I'm sorry I've worried you. I'll do better now."

She was always glad she told him that, for he died not long after. One morning Katie telephoned the office, her voice frightened.

"It's your father, Mr. Courtney," she said. "I can't wake him up this morning."

"You don't mean—"

"He's breathing all right. Only I don't like the look of him. He opens his eyes and then goes off again."

"Get the doctor," Court said briefly. "I'll be there in fifteen minutes."

He found Matthew awake in the big double bed. His thin old body looked shriveled, but his face had not lost its pugnacity nor his voice its strength.

"What the devil's the matter with everybody?" he roared. "Just because I go to sleep that fool Katie has hysterics. I'm not seeing any doctor."

"Katie got excited. That's all, Dad. You know the Irish. They're an emotional lot."

"I'm getting up after I rest awhile."

"Sure you are."

Almost instantly, however, he was asleep again, in that pleasant coma where not even dreams disturbed him. He was still asleep, with Courtney by the bed, when the doctor arrived.

"How long has he been like this?" he asked sternly.

"He's never been like this. He's slept a good bit lately. He'd doze off at the office. I've wanted him to see you, but he refused. You know how he is."

Matthew roused to the crowning insult of a needle in the vein of an arm, and after a moment of incredulous fury tried to jerk his arm away. That proving impossible he lay back on his pillows and told his God his opinion of all medical men, especially one, and of the Irish in general and Katie in particular.

After which he went to sleep again, leaving the doctor to cork a small bottle of bluish blood and to tiptoe out of the room.

"Looks like his kidneys," he said to Courtney. "I'll get a report for you as soon as possible."

"Anything we can do?"

The doctor hesitated.

"I could talk your ear off about diet and that sort of thing. But, frankly, what's the use? If it's what I think, it's too late. Just keep him comfortable, at least until we know."

Matthew was an obstreperous patient during the weeks that followed. The report was bad. For years his kidneys had been slowly poisoning him. "Blood's like a sewer," the doctor put it. Now there was nothing to do. He had his good days when he sat in a chair, and his bad ones when he slept almost round the clock and insisted the calendar had gone crazy.

He would not have a nurse.

"Do you think I want a strange woman giving me a urinal?" he shouted.

So as fast as they came he fired them. Not ungently, however.

"Now look, my girl," he would say. "You're a pretty creature and I expect you're a good nurse. You look in my wallet over there and get twenty dollars. Then get the hell out of here and stay out."

He did not mind Katie. It was Katie who looked after him, brought him the urinal he loathed, on bad days; even managed to give him a bed bath now and then. It was Ricky, however, on whom he depended.

"You bring your knitting or whatever you like and sit with the old man. I like to have you around."

She went every day. Sometimes she read to him. Sometimes she was merely there, for him to see when he roused out of his increasing drowsiness. She brought the children's letters too, and he watched as she read them, her still face, her quiet voice. Better even than Court he realized the terror she so carefully concealed. One day in the strong sunlight he saw some gray in her hair.

"How old are you?" he asked abruptly.

"I'm almost forty-four, Dad."

"You don't look it," he said and closed his eyes.

Courtney stayed with him at night, although Matthew did not know it. It seemed incredible to Court that his father's indomitable spirit and vitality should be reduced to this heavy-breathing silent figure. Going away to college, and Matthew at the train. "The Waynes haven't done much in this world, Court, but they've always been gentlemen." Matthew at his wedding, refusing to wear the morning coat and striped trousers Elizabeth had ordered packed for him. "This is a small town, Lizzie. How many men here have an outfit like that?" The cold day on the dock at Newport News after the war, looking down from the ship and seeing him there, ruddy and excited and pretending the wind had made his eyes water. Then, year after year, at his desk, forceful, shrewd and in his later year irreconcilable. "These damned New Dealers! What's wrong with them? Giving labor its head so it can run away with the country!"

There was nothing Court could do at the last. Now and then he wiped the cold sweat from Matthew's face, but Matthew never knew it. Katie hovered in the doorway. There was no priest to administer the last sacraments, so she prayed for his soul; that it be somehow received where it was going.

Thus died at three o'clock in the morning Matthew Wayne, publisher, citizen, father and grandfather. He had represented an era which was rapidly passing. Now he himself had passed.

Court got up, his face frozen.

"I'd better call my wife," he said, and went out.

Ricky received the news quietly. For almost a quarter of a century Matthew had been a part of her life, something stanch and solid behind her. Now with him gone, and with the children away, she felt lost and drained. Only Court was left. When at last he came home he found her waiting, and took her in his arms.

"It was easy, darling. He slept away."

"But he's gone, Court. I'll miss him so."

"You still have me," Courtney said sturdily. He did not know it, but it might have been Matthew himself speaking to Elizabeth long ago.

41

Matthew's will was like Matthew himself. His estate was left to Courtney with the caustic mention of "what remained after taxes." There was an annual allowance to Ricky, "his beloved daughter-in-law," and there were also many bequests "to the charities my government has made it impossible for me to support during my lifetime."

Courtney, hearing it read, thought his father must have enjoyed signing it.

Matthew had died in January of 1943. Neither Jeff nor Peggy had been able to come to the funeral. But in the spring of that year Jeff wrote an urgent letter asking his father and mother to come to Florida.

"We may be breezing off before long," he said, "and I don't know if I will get leave before then or not. Anyhow a fellow likes to see his folks."

Peggy wrote them before they left.

"Kiss the big bum for me," she said, "and tell him to remember he isn't playing games over there. You know how he is."

Ricky was very quiet during the trip, as though she was bracing herself. The train was filled with soldiers, restless and constantly on the move. It was almost impossible to get into the diner. When they walked through the coaches it was to find them jammed with the men's bulky luggage, and to stand in line for hours before they could eat. Court watched her anxiously.

"All right, darling?"

"I'm all right. Fine."

They were not surprised to find Eric Graham at the field when they went there, a smiling, cheerful Eric, looking distinguished in his colonel's uniform.

"He'll be in in a few minutes," he said. "Can't stop training for parents, you know."

The size of the field surprised them both. The planes were coming and going. And the air overhead was full of them, now flying out over the Gulf of Mexico to shoot at a trailing target, or practicing over and over the maneuvers which were—hopefully—to make the pilots into fighting airmen.

Ricky stood staring at the sky.

"He's up there?"

"Sure. Where did you expect him to be? He's a good boy, Jeff. Got the making of a flier. I can't say that about some we've got."

She did not even see his ship come in. She was still gazing at the sky, the blue incredible Florida sky, when he taxied toward them and crawled out, grinning.

"He wanted to fly a fighter," Eric said. "He's pretty big for one. Another inch and he couldn't make it."

But Ricky did not hear him. Here was Jeff coming toward them, hugging them both, saluting Graham, asking about Peggy and about Matthew's death. It was a few moments before anyone could talk. Then Court told him he had ordered dinner at the hotel in town, and Jeff suddenly looked self-conscious.

"Mind if I bring a girl?" he inquired. "You'll like her. *I* like her. A lot."

If they were disappointed they said nothing.

"Sure. What sort of girl?" Court inquired.

"Pretty nice," Jeff said. "Comes from a small town like you, Mother. Sister's married to a captain here. Fine people. You'll like them."

He had unfastened the chin strap of his helmet and taken it off. His heavy mane of hair was gone, but the grin was pure Jeff.

"You're going to be a blow to her, Mother," he said, his eyes bright. "She's expecting a gray-haired dame with a bosom."

That the girl was Jeff's girl was evident that night. He hardly took his eyes off her, and Courtney realized that this was no boyish infatuation. His training had matured him. There was a furrow from his nose to his mouth, as if too often his jaw was set tight. But the girl surprised him as Jeff's choice. She was obviously in love with Jeff, but she was silent and shy. He decided she was a pretty little nonentity, and said as much to Ricky when they were going to bed.

"Do you suppose he's really serious?" he said irritably. "Just a small-town pretty girl. If he can't do better than that—"

"I imagine that's what your mother told your father about me when she saw me."

"Good God," he said irritably. "You had brains and looks. Everything. Do you want him to marry that—that child?"

"She's twenty. She told me."

Jeff *was* serious. He told Court the next day, when he had a few hours off. They took a walk along a sandy road lined with dreary cabbage palms, where small lizards ran and hid and everything, even the grass, was dry and prickling to the touch. At first they talked of flying. Jeff loved it. There was something about it—well, you had to do it to understand. And Graham was wonderful.

That finished, however, he became awkwardly silent. He scuffed his feet in the gray Florida dust, squinted up at the sky where the sporadic shooting was going on, and stopped to light a fresh cigarette. It seemed to give him courage.

"How'd you like Audrey, Dad? You and Mother?"

"I thought she seemed a trifle young," said Court cautiously.

"I'm not so old myself," Jeff grinned. "But I guess I'm old enough to know what I want."

"And that is—Audrey?"

"Yes." Court said nothing, and he went on feverishly, "I'm

twenty-two, Dad. That's being a man these days. And I've been pretty decent. Oh, well, at college once or twice. It didn't mean a thing. You know how it is. I don't go into town like most of the fellows here. And since I've met Audrey I don't even want to."

"I suppose you've thought it over," Court said gravely. "This is a war, and a bad one. You'll take your chances with the rest, Jeff. To leave a young wife—"

"You did it yourself, Dad."

There was no answer to that. For a moment Court was back in the camp in Ohio years ago, anxiously walking with Matthew along a muddy road and putting his own case.

"I'm a man, not a boy, Father. I want something to come back to. You and Mother have been fine, but this is *my* life. I'm the one who has to live it."

"Yes, I did it," he said finally. "It was the best thing that ever happened to me. You know that. But my family knew something of your mother's background. You don't know anything about—Audrey, do you?"

"You haven't seen her sister. They're all-right people. They haven't very much, but who cares these days? That stuff's all gone."

Court eyed him.

"Just what does that mean, Jeff?

Jeff flushed uncomfortably.

"Her father runs a grocery store, if it's important."

Well, probably it wasn't important. It was the girl who mattered. Her name, it developed, was Cowan. Audrey Cowan, and they came from western Pennsylvania. Also it was evident that asking his consent was a pure formality. The boy had already decided.

"You're of age, Jeff," Courtney said. "You don't need us to give our consent. I'd like to talk to your mother, of course. When do you want to be married?"

"As soon as we can. I'll be going overseas pretty soon now. I'll get some leave first."

Which of course was what decided them both, Ricky and himself, talking it over in their small uncomfortable hotel room, with the distant pop-popping of the fighters out over the water and the buzzing of myriad insects beyond the screened window. Anything he wanted for this boy who was going overseas pretty soon. Anything, the moon, the stars, their own lives if necessary, if he wanted them.

He brought Audrey in to see them the next day, and they welcomed her warmly. Ricky kissed her, and Courtney put his arms around her. He felt her young body trembling as he held her.

"Now see here," he said, "we're nice people. We don't bite. We don't even bark. If you like this boy of ours and he likes you, as he says he does, it's all right, my dear."

"You don't really mind? We're such plain people, Mr. Wayne."

"Has Jeff been boasting about *his?*"

"Oh, no," she said, shocked. "But everybody knows who you are." She forced a smile. "I read your books, you know."

"What more can we ask?" he said, and kissed her.

She showed more character than they had expected, too. She did not want a wedding dress, or anything elaborate. Jeff might not have much time. Anyhow she could not afford one, and she did not want them to buy it. Or buy anything, it appeared.

"What's the use?" she said. "I'll be going back home when Jeff leaves. I'll have to. My mother's dead and my sister's going to have a baby in the summer. They'll need me there. I'll get along all right until"—her voice broke—"until Jeff comes back."

They had to leave it at that. No chest of silver, no gifts at all except a check which she took reluctantly only to bank against Jeff's return. Both Court and Ricky felt slightly repudiated, as though nothing they could do or give her mattered to her. Except their son, of course. Except their son.

They stayed for two weeks. Long enough to see Audrey on

her brother-in-law's arm walk up a church aisle in a plain short white dress, to see Jeff in his uniform stand and wait with his heart in his eyes, to see the little church crowded with officers, and to say the inarticulate prayers of all fathers and mothers at such times.

They held a small get-together afterward at the hotel. Grocery store or not, the bride had a dignity of her own. So did her sister, a quiet girl with dark tragic eyes; as though even then she were looking ahead to years of loneliness and anxiety. So did her captain, a smallish man with a short pugnacious nose and a stubborn fighter's jaw. There were a few women, not many. The room seemed crowded with cheerful flying men who drank incredible amounts of domestic champagne, ate hugely and obviously liked the bride.

"Got a kiss for me, Audrey? You haven't kissed me lately, you know."

She would blush hotly.

"I never kissed you. What are you doing? Trying to make trouble already?"

"All right. Here goes. Watch this, Jigger."

To Court and Ricky's surprise he was Jigger to them all. The name had stuck.

They saw them off later, a cheering uniformed crowd at the railroad station, with someone ringing a cowbell and parading along the cars shouting, "Hear ye! Hear ye! In Drawing Room A, Car Sixteen, is a bride and groom. Make it pleasant for them, folks. Make it pleasant. Make it pleasant." When the train moved out it left the voice echoing behind it.

Ricky stood on the platform. Years ago she and Court had started on their wedding journey to Cincinnati; and Dave had thrown an old shoe after them. It had struck Court, and poor Dave had almost collapsed because he had hit an officer. She looked at Court, staring after the train. What did the boy in Germany matter? They had built their marriage, and it still endured. They had to hold it. Soon, for a time at least, it would be all they had.

Jeff sailed for England soon after his short honeymoon. At first they only knew he had gone because his letters ceased. Now it was telegrams they watched for; coming home, looking at the hall table and drawing a long breath when there was nothing there. It was easier for Courtney than for Ricky. Publishing was becoming constantly more difficult, although it was less and less necessary to bury their mistakes on the remainder tables. "As doctors bury their mistakes in the cemetery," he told Mather, with a wry grin.

One day he went to one of the big printers to talk over the problem. There was still newsprint, but book paper was almost disappearing. He sat in the office on an upper floor, feeling the building vibrate from the motion of the great flat-bed presses.

"It's not only paper, Wayne. We're losing labor fast to the armed forces."

"We're already making smaller books. I don't know what more we can do."

Along with the shortage of paper the demand for books was rising, however. Never apparently had the public been reading more avidly. The sales department had to turn down orders or postpone them indefinitely. It puzzled George Mather.

"What's happened?" he said. "There's more excitement and tragedy in a five-cent newspaper today than anything we can print."

"No gas for cars, for one thing," Courtney told him. "Maybe we're at last becoming a literate people."

So they faced more demand, less paper, and even fewer authors. For now many of their writers were fighting, or doing war correspondence abroad, or in the Office of War Information in Washington or elsewhere. The company did its best, but Courtney missed his father during those trying days. Matthew's code had been simple. He had believed in serving his reading public, but he had held integrity above everything else. He had liked romance but never trash. If he had done a certain amount of prestige publishing he had also brought out books for the sheer pleasure of it, without thought of profit. And while he had published English and European books, his real encouragement had gone to American writers.

Perhaps for the first time he realized that Matthew had loved his country.

Peggy was somewhere in the Pacific by that time; washing her clothes in anything handy, and taking a shower under a gasoline can with holes bored in the bottom. Taking atabrine too, and developing according to her a tan which looked as though the sun had turned green. "Which same sun," she wrote, "is too damned close here anyhow."

By summer Audrey was still in her small Pennsylvania town. She wrote often, but she could not leave home. Her sister's new baby was a boy. Why were so many boys born in wartime? And a baby meant work. Ricky would have liked to have her with her, but she did not insist. Now, on her way to and from the Red Cross, or the endless struggle to feed the household, she would stop in some open church, to sit there quiet, or to drop to her knees and say a little prayer for her children, and for Pete, also somewhere in the European theater of war.

Courtney wakened one night to find her gone from the room and to discover her on her knees beside Jeff's bed in her nightgown. He stood there quiet. She had not heard him, so he went away, to lie awake until later she came back to crawl carefully into her bed.

It was after that she placed the lamp in the window of Jeff's room. She did not speak about it, but Hilda told him.

"It burns all night, unless there's a blackout. It burns then too, but she closes the curtains."

"A light?" he said blankly. "What sort of light?"

"A little lamp; one of his. Sailors' wives used to do that," said the coast-born Hilda. "To bring their men back from the sea."

The next night, coming home late, he looked up and saw it there, a small beacon of hope, and perhaps a prayer. He never mentioned it to Ricky, but he took to watching her more closely. She missed her former job, he knew. She was listless at times. Yet she was doing her best. He would come back from the office to find her waiting for him, bravely smiling and with the fountain splashing in the hall. Pretending everything was all right, talking about the news, about the business, while he mixed her a cocktail and watched her shove her food around her place at the table.

"Look, darling, you must eat."

"I'm all right. I'm not hungry."

Jeff's peril had wiped out everything else, even her resentment over the picture Adele had brought. He thought they were closer than they had been for a long time. Now sometimes it was she who crawled into his bed.

"Put your arms around me, Court. I'm cold. I can't seem to stop shivering."

The old scar was healed at last, or at least forgotten for the time. And Jeff was still safe, still in England, or at least in the British Isles. Once he got leave and went to London.

"Aunt Roberta is wonderful," he wrote. "She looks like nothing on earth, and she's living in one room, with no bath and the w.c. at the end of the hall. She has a little pot under the bed, poor thing. I got her cigarettes and some things to eat. I imagine she's half starved. But she is the same valiant old girl, working her head off at some canteen or other. She did not talk about Sheila at all. Funny thing, the old house at Cadogan Square is gone. She took me to see the ruins. They *did* have a bathroom. I saw the tub in the street."

So Roberta's last tie with her past was gone, Ricky thought.

Courtney had very little time now. Not only the business and settling of Matthew's estate. The war began to invade the office itself, and the first gold star appeared on the office service flag. Mather's boy had been killed in Italy.

Mather came back to the office a day or two later, his mouth bitter, his face set. Since Matthew's death Angela had become his secretary. He buzzed for her and gave her a hard look.

"What's over is over," he said. "I don't want any sympathy. I can be sorry for myself. Bring in my mail."

Still the struggle went on, endlessly, almost hopelessly. But now at last Russia was turning on the Germans, retaking Kiev, women as well as men fighting. The rag-bag country was saving the world. For the Germans at last had lost the offensive, and with it eventually the war.

But Courtney still shared his father's distrust of the Russians.

"They're playing their own game," he said. "God knows I'm grateful for them, but if we don't watch out we'll end with a Soviet Europe."

Nevertheless, the big blond Russian peasants now were trudging westward over their devastated country, living off it when they could, or fed by their makeshift service of supply, meager rations carried up by farm cart, by truck, by anything which could move. And America was behind them. Into their ports already was flowing such war material as they had never dreamed of, locomotives, guns, tanks, trucks, the whole machinery of war. It went through the Persian Gulf and the Caspian, through Murmansk and the frozen arctic. But the Soviet Union allowed no Allied planes to land inside its borders, and no man to know its secrets.

The Americans were scattering all over the earth. They had the finest equipment the world had even seen, and along with them went the little books, millions and millions of them. They passed from hand to hand, dog-eared and dirty, often with pages missing.

"What the hell happened? The last chapter's gone."

"They got married. They always do, don't they?"

"That's not the way I heard it!"

At the office they carried on, but once or twice Mather tried to find forgetfulness in liquor. He had always been an abstemious man, but there were times now when he could not face his wife. Angela would look after him when this happened. She made coffee in the restroom and carried it to him at his desk.

"Here, drink this. You need it."

He would look up at her with heavy despairing eyes.

"Am I as bad as that, Angela, old girl?"

"You're stinking. You can't go home like this."

He would pull himself together and get on with his work. But once she had to take him home and put him to bed in her spinster flat, while she slept on a couch. When he wakened the next morning she was making coffee for him. He sat up and grinned at her.

"Nice story to get out," he told her. "What will the neighbors say?"

"They'll probably think I waited a long time to get what I got," she said dryly.

42

Only those who saw even a part of it ever realized the vast and majestic power of America as it moved into the war. Fifteen ships lost? What did it matter, in an armada of a thousand? A jeep in a ditch? Get another. Get a dozen more. A hundred. Planes went across the Channel and did not come back, or wobbled into their landing strips, props feathered, rudders gone, sometimes to blow up and burn. But others were now rolling endlessly off the assembly lines at home. The airmen tried to ignore the empty chairs at mess after a raid.

"Shove me the catsup, Jim."

"Here goes."

Nothing in the history of the world had touched what the Americans were doing, fighting two great wars, supplying their allies, using up their irreplaceable reserves of oil, of iron ore, of copper. Impoverishing themselves for centuries to come. And most of all, losing their men.

America, the last free country, the final stand of opportunity and freedom, was spending all she had, and more. Even Matthew, had he lived, would have had to admit that Roosevelt was fighting a magnificent war, whatever he was doing to the country at home.

But as the war abroad was to the soldier a matter of his own small group, so to their families it was concentrated on the men and women who were fighting it. It was hard to believe that these were their children, the babies they had nursed, the toddlers they had taught to walk. So it was with Court and Ricky Wayne when one day a letter came from Peggy, somewhere in the South Pacific.

"Dear Mother and Dad," she wrote. "Don't faint when you read this, but your little girl is now a married woman, married with a ring made out of a silver quarter, with fifteen copies of everything—except the groom. There is only one of him—and according to the laws of God, General MacArthur, the district of [cut by the censor] and the United States Army.

"You would think this would be enough, but Terry says we are really living in sin, since his own letter of permission didn't turn up in time. If so, I don't mind. He is wonderful. Big and strong and gentle and with no background whatever. But who cares? He had a share in a garage in California, and did the repairs himself. So if ever you come out there and you need gasoline I'll probably sell it to you!

"He is still a sergeant, but he has all sorts of medals. And what a wedding! I washed my underclothes and myself in a pail, wore my only decent uniform, and was given in marriage by a colonel who had begun celebrating an hour or so too soon. It took, however. We had four days before Terry had to get in his plane and go places. I don't even know what places.

"He doesn't know anything much about me, except that he likes me. When I told him Dad was a publisher he merely said it sounded like a good job. My love to you both. Devotedly, Peggy. P.S. His name is Shane. Did I tell you? He's a sergeant in the Army Air Forces."

The letter came at breakfast time, and Court read it aloud. It was hard at first for them to grasp it. Peggy married and talking about running a garage. Fastidious Peggy, turning up her nose at anything less than the best. Out of sheer bewilderment they stared at each other.

"For God's sweet sake!" Courtney said finally. "I hope the kid knows what she's doing."

"She always has known, Court. At least he sounds like a man."

It was only one of the readjustments they were obliged to make. Even Rosie had gone at last, to earn fabulous sums in a factory somewhere. The car was laid up, and taxis and buses jammed. To add to Courtney's problems Washington was proving obdurate. The services would permit books, only to have censorship hold them up indefinitely.

"You'd think we were fifth columnists," he said disgustedly, "trying to tell the Germans what they are doing. As if they didn't know it themselves!"

With Courtney away most of the time the house seemed to echo with silence; a watchful waiting silence, which at any moment might be broken by the ringing of the doorbell and Hilda's step on the stairs with a telegram. During the day Ricky worked at the Red Cross, but the evenings were unbearable, and one day she told Court she had become an air-raid warden at the local post.

He looked at her. She was very thin, and even the slight makeup she used did not disguise her pallor.

"Sure you're up to it?" he asked anxiously.

"Of course. You're out a lot. It's only two evenings a week, anyhow, Court. It's something to do."

She did not say she had volunteered for night duty.

"It might relieve someone who really needs rest," she said to the harassed young man at the post. "I don't do much, and I can't sleep anyhow," she added, with her disarming smile. "I have a boy overseas."

"You don't look old enough for that," he told her. "But if you would take from nine to twelve on certain nights it would help. We don't like to keep women on after that."

It was arranged within a day or two. She went to her precinct station house where an officer in his shirt sleeves interrogated her and took her fingerprints, and a few days later she got a card with her photograph on it.

After that for at least two evenings a week she escaped the empty house. Sometimes she sat alone in her small room, with the stretcher in a corner, the emergency dressings in their box, the list of telephones on the wall over her head in case of an alert. But occasionally other wardens wandered in and out, or now and then a stray dog, and even once a drunken man. She put him on a sofa and let him sleep there. When he wakened she made coffee on the small electric stove and sent him home, sober if not rejoicing.

But there were times when, sitting there alone, she thought of the Allied bombers flying over France, with their cover of fighters above them, and imagined Jeff over some such sleeping city, with flak all about him and searchlights picking him out. She would look at her equipment, laid out before her, the screwdriver to open the base of the street light and so turn it off, her police whistle and the flashlight, its lens covered with blue paper. And she would wonder if other women in other lands were doing the same thing. And why. Always why.

Then one night she had a visit from Jay Burton. She looked up from her desk to see him in the doorway.

"Why, Jay!" she said. "What are you doing in New York?" Then, seeing his face, "Is anything wrong?"

He came in and put down his hat.

"Pete's been hurt," he said. "Nothing I can do, of course. He's lost a leg."

She stared at him.

"Oh, no, Jay. Not Pete!"

He nodded and sitting down ran his hands through his thinning hair.

"I thought maybe if I talked to you— At least he's alive. I suppose I have to be grateful for that. But it's hard to think of him like that. His nurse writes he's very cheerful. Says he doesn't need two legs to build planes. Just the same— In a way he's all I had, Ricky."

After a while he sat back and looked at her. She was different, he thought. Her mouth looked tight and strained, even a little hard.

"I suppose Court's all right?"

"Yes. He's busy, of course."

But her voice had subtly changed. She got up, as though aware of the strong light overhead, and sat down near him on a sofa. Impulsively he reached over and took her hand.

"There's something else wrong, isn't there?" And when she nodded: "Can't you tell me? Is it Courtney?"

"Yes."

"It's not another woman, is it, Ricky?"

"There have been. Not now. Not for a long time."

Of course there had been, he thought. Courtney Wayne would always be attractive to women. Queer how some men had that quality, while others—

"It might help to talk about it," he suggested.

She hesitated.

"I don't know. It seems so foolish. But I've always been able to tell you things, Jay. I suppose it's because I've known you so long."

"Maybe it's because I've loved you so long," he said steadily.

She nodded again.

"I know it's not rational. I've fought it all I can. But Court had an affair with a German girl while he was there after the last war. I've just learned he had a son there now, a flier. Like Jeff."

To her own shocked surprise she found tears in her eyes. All Jay's resentment at her marriage had returned, his long frustrated love for her. But she needed help, not anger. He got out a handkerchief and put it in her hand.

"Tell me about it," he said. "You can trust me, darling."

She dried her eyes and tried to smile.

"I'm sorry," she said. "Don't blame Court, Jay. It's a long time since it happened. He didn't even know about the boy until not long ago."

She told him then, the unpacking of Court's war trunk and finding the letter, the assurance on his part that there was no child, and later the photograph. Manlike, he showed no surprise at the Elsa affair, nor, he thought, did she greatly resent it after all this time. It was the fact that the boy was flying against Jeff and his kind that was unbearable.

"Of course," he said, as quietly as he could. "It's sheer nonsense to think the two of them would ever meet. Use your common sense, Ricky. The real issue is between you and Court. Has it changed your feeling toward him?"

"I don't know, Jay. I really don't know."

"If it has," he told her gravely, "you can count on me. I have never asked very much, but I have the right to look after you if you leave him. You know that, don't you?"

She nodded.

"But I don't think you will, my dear," he said, still gravely. "There are too many ties to hold you: the children, the habits of years, all the little things. Even that house you live in. It's filled with memories, Ricky. You can't escape them."

She knew he was right. Only, if anything happened to Jeff—

He left her soon after. Other wardens drifted in. The small room was crowded and filled with smoke. He shook hands with her finally, and she smiled at him.

"I'm carrying on," she said. "Thank you, Jay. You've helped me."

She did her best after his visit to bridge the gap between Courtney and herself, and to hope. The lamp still burned, but now for a long time there had been no letters from Jeff. She would go home, from the Red Cross or from her eternal attempts to buy food, to look at the table in the hall, and to try to avoid Hilda's desperate face.

"He's busy, you know. And the mail is so uncertain."

When Courtney came home it was the same thing. She would hear him stop, and then come slowly and heavily up the stairs, to avoid her eyes as she avoided Hilda's.

"How about a cocktail, darling? I've had a hard day."

But he was away now more than ever. After dinner he would put on his old trench coat and start out again on his nightly rounds; as though he could not endure the empty house any longer.

One day she saw he had gone very gray. And his big body was gaunt. On impulse she went to him and kissed him.

"It will be all right, Court," she said. "It has to be all right."

Only of course it was not.

43

Late in 1943 came the word that Jeffrey was listed among the missing. They had been to church, for even Courtney went now when he could, as though he realized at last that having done his best the rest was up to the God he had so long ignored.

The telegram was on the table when they went in. All through the house was the faint odor of cooking food, the Sunday roast beef, increasingly hard to get, and the Yorkshire pudding Jeff had loved. Ricky only stared at the envelope. She would not touch it, and it was Court who picked it up. He did not look at her. He read it and put it in his pocket.

"Nothing important," he said. "Want a drink before dinner? I could stand one."

She did not believe him. His voice was forced, his face rigid with the effort to control himself. She did not move toward the stairs. Instead she stood stiff, holding to the newel post.

"Is it Jeff? Or Peggy?"

He gave up the effort. Sooner or later she would have to know.

"It's Jeff," he said. "Apparently he's had to bail out somewhere."

"Bail out! He was shot down?"

He had recovered somewhat. He went over and caught her in his arms.

"Look, my darling," he said. "He's almost sure to be all right. Even if it was over enemy country a lot of them turn up later."

"How do you know he got down at all? What's in the message?"

He gave it to her at last. All it said was that Jeff was officially reported missing, and he stood by helpless while she stared at it.

"He hadn't even lived," she said dully. "A little happiness was all he had. He must have been alone, Court. All alone, up there."

"Stop it, Ricky. Don't torture yourself," he said hoarsely. "Don't torture me. I tell you there's a chance. A good chance. He may be a prisoner. He may be—"

"I think he is dead," she said very quietly. And slid to the floor at his feet.

He carried her to the elevator and took her up to their room. There he put her on her bed and sat down beside her, his face as colorless as hers. Before long she opened her eyes and looked at him.

"The sins of the fathers, Court," she said, her lips stiff.

"Now listen, Ricky, I tell you it's not final." Then the possible meaning of what she had said dawned on him. "What sins? What are you talking about?"

"Suppose it was your German son who shot him down?"

He said nothing for a moment, then: "How did you know?" he asked heavily.

She only shook her head. It did not matter now. Nothing mattered save that somewhere Jeff was lost to them. She had no hope. It was as though all her life had been pointed toward that moment, and that all of it had been useless.

Later he tried to tell her the story, sitting there by the bed, sending away a weeping Hilda and holding her cold hand. That he had not known about the boy until years later, how fatherhood meant nothing to a man unless he reared a son. He doubted if she heard him, or that it registered if she did. Behind his words, however, lay his own racking torturing grief. All at once he was shaken with dry convulsive sobs.

"O God, darling!" he said, and put his head down on the bed

beside her.

He slept as usual in his dressing room that night, if it could be called sleep. He knew that to hold Elsa's son responsible for Jeff was fantastic, but a man was responsible for his own action. Whether he lay with a girl in a barn, like David Stafford, or in a German bed, if there was a child it was his.

Once he heard Ricky moving about and went in. The room was empty. He knew she was in Jeff's room and when she came back he went up there himself. Jeff's things were all about, as he had left them, his college pictures, his school banner on the wall. But the lamp was still in the window.

It relieved him to find she had left it there.

At dawn he gave up trying to sleep. He got up and putting on a dressing gown went down to the kitchen to make coffee. Twenty-four years ago he had done the same thing, going down to the empty kitchen, and Katie finding him there.

"Why, Mr. Courtney, what are you doing at this hour?"

"Habit, Katie. The army believes in getting up early."

He wandered to the kitchen window while the coffee was in the making. The yard beyond was neglected and dreary. But he did not see it. He was remembering what the professor had said in Berlin about his grandson.

"It is a shameful thing to say, but I am afraid to speak what I think before him. I do not trust him. It is what they teach him, at home and in the schools."

He drank his coffee standing. The day was before him, but it meant little to him now. There had been a time when he had felt he was building the business for Jeff, as his father had built it for him. That was all over now.

There was nothing he could do. He had called Audrey on the long-distance telephone the day before, but she had already got the word. Her voice sounded as though she had been crying.

"What does it mean, missing?" she asked. "Was he shot down?"

"We don't know, my dear. We can only wait and hope. They have parachutes, of course. He is probably safe enough."

She was silent, as if she was fighting for control.

"I took that chance when I married him," she said brokenly. "Only—I wish I had a baby. I—it's lonely without him."

Lonely without him! Good God, of course it was lonely. He had to steady his own voice.

"Would it help if we all waited together? Why not come on and stay with us? We are lonely too."

But she would not come. She was busy there. Her sister wasn't well. She had had no word from her husband for months, and there was the baby to care for.

In a sense he was relieved. She was Jeff's wife, but she had only had him a brief time. What was her emptiness to theirs, who had loved him all his life? Youth was vulnerable, he thought as he hung up, but it had something older people outgrew. It had hope. There was always tomorrow. For the others it was too often only today, or yesterday.

There was no further news. They could only wait and hope. But he was increasingly aware that what should have drawn them together was keeping them apart. Ricky had withdrawn into long silences, and there were times when he found her eyes on him, so full of tragic bitterness that once he got up abruptly and confronted her.

"Why can't we talk this out?" he said. "If you're blaming me about Jeff it's nonsense. It's—it's not normal."

"I'm not blaming you. Can't you allow me a little decent grief?"

"Grief! How do you suppose I feel? He was my son too. Can't you remember that?"

She was alone at home when the parcel containing Jeffrey's effects arrived. What little hope she had had died when she opened it. She took it up to his room and put the things away. There was a bundle of letters from Audrey, but she did not touch them. When Courtney came home that night she told him quietly. It was a moment before he could control his voice.

"To us? Why not to his wife?"

"He must have wanted to save her that."

She went to the window and stood staring out. It had been raining, and the park looked gray and gloomy in the twilight.

"I wonder if it's raining over there."

His nerves were at breaking point. He was afraid to speak. He went to the portable bar in his study and poured himself a drink. When he came back he was steadier.

"I wish you'd stop this morbid thinking, Ricky. If he's alive, he's under shelter. If he's not—"

"If he's not, it makes no difference. Is that what you think, Court?"

"I'm trying not to think at all."

There was a short pause. He wanted to shake her, out of sheer despair. But she went on, her voice still a monotone.

"I've been thinking about Mother," she said as if she had not heard him. "She wanted Dave brought back. And Roberta too," she went on. "Do you remember how she wanted your father to find Arthur's grave?"

"Oh, for God's sake!" he almost shouted. He finished his drink and slammed out of the room and out of the house.

They both tried to do better after this explosion. They were donating blood now, sitting in a room with other donors holding their cards, having their blood pressure taken. Sometimes they went together, to lie side by side on the narrow cots, to feel the prick of the needle, to watch the smiling nurse when it was over as she put a bit of adhesive over the perforation.

"Here's your coffee. It's not very good, but you need fluid."

There was another anxiety too, for Peggy's letters had an undertone of anxiety.

"Mail is slow out here. I haven't heard from Terry for ages. I expect he is all right. He keeps moving, of course."

It was after such a letter that Ricky broke the long silence between herself and Court.

"All these boys," she said. "I've been wondering how it is when—the end comes. Do they just go to sleep, Court? And never wake up? Or is there something else? I'd like to thin there is. Something interesting and active, you know. They'd like that. A young man's heaven."

"Maybe there is," he told her, his voice tired. "Maybe there s. Even the other's not so bad, my dear. Remember that. To sleep and not even dream . . ."

She was not well. He could see that. She slept very little, and at night he could hear her stirring. Once he had got up, to find her in the big chair by the empty fireplace, an unlighted cigarette in her hand, and her face bleak when he turned on the light.

"Can't I help, darling? Maybe if I rubbed your back . . ."

He had done that before. He had good hands, big and strong and gentle. But she shook her head.

"I'm all right, Court. I'm just—waiting."

He went about in a sort of quiet desperation: about her, about Jeff, about Peggy. But the business had to go on. First copies came to his desk and he would be irritable: "What's the matter with these end sheets?" Or: "Look at this front flap! Who wrote that jacket copy?" Also the number of strikes was increasing. He blamed Roosevelt for that, for playing into the hands of labor, for failing to give the employer an equal chance with the employed.

He had opposed the fourth term. The President was obviously a sick man. It was sheer bravado, his driving around New York in an open car in the rain surrounded by heating pads while his thin exhausted face smiled at the shouting crowds. The man had guts, even if his Secret Service had no heating pads; had, as a matter of fact, a good chance of pneumonia. But he had been re-elected. Evidently the people liked courage.

The first thin ray of hope for Jeff came that winter of 1944. came when at last they had accepted his loss and were both struggling out from the black pall of misery that had almost separated them. Yet it was not much. It came from Eric Graham.

"Dear Wayne," it said. "I have been in another theater of

the war, so I have only recently learned about Jeff. As soon as I heard I got in touch with the men of his squadron and this is what I was told.

"When his plane was hit he was seen to bail out. It was certainly Jeff, as he was not carrying an observer. What is more, one of the other men saw his chute open. Things were pretty rugged just then but this man insists he got out all right

"He was a smart flier. He was an ace, as you may know. He had got five German fighters and two not corroborated. Bu this is a war, Wayne, and a dirty one. All I can say is if he reached the ground there is a chance for him. Quite a few o our fellows are turning up, sometimes after many months Don't hope too much, but he was a smart boy as well as a fin fighter. Here's luck anyhow. Yours, Graham."

He took it home that night, but in the bus he felt depresse rather than cheered. He was seeing Jeff in the little cockpit o his plane, with a fiery hell below and death all around him. An then bailing out. What hope was there, even if his parachut had opened? Those beasts shot helpless men swinging to th cords of their chutes.

But there was none of this in his face when he gave Ricky th letter, or when she looked up at him with her old radiant smil

"I can hardly believe it," she said. "It's wonderful, isn't i Court?"

"Very wonderful, darling," he said, and put his arms aroun her for the first time in months.

Their relations were better after that. The little leaven hope had helped them both. And they both knew now that the marriage itself was at stake. There were nights when she cre into his bed to cry a little on his shoulder, as if somehow the must keep close together.

Yet there was still no news as winter changed into sprin with the trees in the park showing their new fresh green a once more the procession of children going there to play. Th carried different toys now, small tanks and cannons and t planes. There were fewer nurses and governesses and mo

·oung mothers with them.

In April Courtney went out to see Jeff's young wife. He had ıot seen her since her marriage. Both he and Ricky had written egularly, but she had always refused to visit them. Now he ɔund her in a neat white-frame house, with a baby crying omewhere, and her hands red and moist. She was surprised ·hen she saw him.

"I was doing the baby's wash," she explained. "We can't get ny help at all. Come in, Mr. Wayne."

She led him into a small unused parlor. Some attempt had een made to smarten it. There were cretonne hangings at the ·indows and an unskilled hand had tried to make slip covers ɔr the furniture. But she apologized for nothing. She was erself and the house was her home. Courtney liked her for it. evertheless she looked as though her interest in life had gone. er eyes were sunken, there was a droop to her young mouth.

"I suppose there's still no news?"

"No. Not since I sent you Colonel Graham's letter. But that oesn't mean anything. If he went down in French territory ıe underground might take care of him. Even if he's in a erman prison—"

"The Germans torture prisoners, don't they?"

"Not necessarily. Probably not airmen, or officers. Anyhow ɔn't think things like that. I came because—well, you ɔuldn't come to us. And you're Jeff's wife, my dear. We'd like think you're well and comfortable."

"I don't want money, Mr. Wayne, if that's what you mean. e get along very well. We don't need much. You can see at."

"Just the little extras," he urged her. "I would like to think : are doing it for Jeff. You can understand that, can't you?"

She shook her head, but there were tears in her eyes.

"All I want is Jeff himself," she said.

Later she suggested he see her father. She took off her ngalow apron and they walked a few blocks to the store. It s a neighborhood grocery, very clean although scantily

stocked. Her father was there, but there were no customers a
the moment. Mr. Cowan was a short stocky man, neat in hi
white coat, and he came around the counter to shake hands

"How are you, Mr. Wayne? Glad to see you. Maybe you ca
cheer my girl here. She's been pretty low in her mind."

"We're still hoping. You saw Colonel Graham's letter?"

"Saw it! I guess I prayed over it."

He left Audrey to watch the store and took Courtney back t
a small cluttered office, where he offered him a cigarette an
took one himself.

"This used to be a good business," he said, "but wit
shortages the way they are—Audrey is taking this hard, Mr
Wayne." He sighed. "I haven't much hope myself, I'm afraid
I was in the last war, like you. It looks like a gentlemen's wa
compared with this one, doesn't it? At least we weren't a
killing civilians."

"If it's bad enough it may end all wars."

Cowan shrugged.

"We had no radio then, Wayne. Now we not only kno
what's happening; we know it before it happens. It stirs peopl
up. Ever think how easy it is now to influence the world? And
will be worse after this war."

"How do you figure that out?"

"These Communists! Freedom of speech was all right when
man could get up on a soapbox and shout. Maybe fifty peopl
heard him, or a hundred. Now maybe he gets ten million t
listen, or fifty million. Don't make any mistake, Wayn
They're out to get us."

It might have been his father, Courtney thought.

He ate lunch at the Cowan house. Audrey's sister was ther
with a now smiling baby in a high chair beside her. He
husband was in the thick of the fighting, but she heard fro
him now and then. Nevertheless, there was tension over th
meal Audrey had cooked. He thought she had been cryi
again.

When traintime came she walked with him to the statio

"I haven't given Jeff up," she said bravely. "He was a onderful flier. Everyone said so. And he was smart. He could et out of a tough place if anyone could."

He kissed her when he left her, remembering the time when hey had once before parted at a railway station; only then it as she who was leaving, she and Jeff. Jeff waving and grinning om the window of the train, and the boy with the cowbell nnouncing their departure to the smiling passengers.

"Good-bye, Audrey, my dear. You're worth coming back to. pray to God Jeff does."

Then again there was nothing to do but wait. Fortunately ley were busy, and Mather had rallied from his boy's loss. He as still bitter, however.

"Sure we're publishing war books," he said. "Let the people now it for the filthy useless business it is, not a cheap thrill at e movies."

Courtney too felt his nerves were going. In the office he was ort-tempered and impatient and it took a good bit of Scotch put him to sleep at night. He wakened feeling rotten.

"Where the hell's that jacket design?"

"I thought you had it, Mr. Wayne."

"It's not your business to think. You ought to know."

He sounded like Matthew at such times. Except that he was ller, he even looked like him. And he found himself resenting e young men he saw on the streets safe and sound, even the es in uniform. Then one day in a bus he sat next to a youth o was softly whistling to himself. The sound rasped his rves, and he put down his paper.

"Can't you stop that noise?" he said irritably. "And why en't you overseas?"

"Just back, sir," said the boy, and smilingly showed him an pty sleeve.

Courtney took him home for a drink and an apology, but he alized that he was losing control. He would have to watch mself. One day he asked Angela about Matthew.

"What about my father during the last war? Did he take it in his stride?"

"I wouldn't say that," said Angela primly. "When the news came you'd been hurt he went stark raving crazy. He walked in and fired me, just like that. Of course I didn't go," she added. "He needed me, if only to keep him from jumping out the window."

It had never occurred to him that Matthew had gone through something of his own anxiety.

But he had little time to think. The office had become a madhouse. Manuscripts about the war were pouring in; some smuggled bit by bit, others written on scraps of paper, in notebooks, anything handy. They came from Africa, from Italy, from the Pacific, and now of course from France. For the invasion had begun the year before. The vast Allied might had moved across the Channel, and little by little the men worked their way to the shore under the German guns. American boys who had never left their farms and villages died on the beaches. But the conquerors moved on. Never had France seen such tremendous power, such prodigality of men and armament, of food and supplies. The people were dazed as it moved along, sweeping up the Germans or brushing them back. The wealth of America was there, destroying itself as well as the enemy. It had to be seen to be believed, and even then it was unbelievable.

They swept on. Summer turned to fall, and fall to winter. It was costly, of course. Tanks rumbled along the roads, dispatch riders hurried to and fro on motorcycles, and men pushed ahead, their faces dirty and exhausted under the weight of their equipment. And the Germans fought back, with their 88s blasting viciously, their planes dropping the drifting flares, in false deadly moonlight, and following them with bombs onto the men below.

At night now Court and Ricky sat over the radio, often with Hilda there, quietly knitting.

"They're driving ahead, darling. Before long they'll be in Germany."

That was their hope, of course. The Allies in Germany, and Jeff found and released. They clung to it tenaciously, studying maps, hoping against hope. Neither of them was prepared for the setback when it came.

For the Germans were defeated but not finished. There was no one to warn the Allies that they had combed their army for English-speaking soldiers, had put them into Allied uniforms and formed them into a special brigade to infiltrate the American positions, as spies and assassins. They learned it the hard way, in December, when von Rundstedt got the weather he wanted, and Germans poured back in torrents into the snow-packed Ardennes.

So unexpected was the attack that men were killed before they knew an enemy was within miles of them. Whole divisions were surrounded. Communications were cut. A new murderous short-range German rocket was let loose, and for six days the Allied planes were grounded by fog and snow.

Then—in time for New Year's—came clear weather. Thousands of Allied planes swept over the German bulge and the enemy began to take its punishment. It was the last offensive, and all it had gained was the rows of white crosses over the graves of men who had said, "This far and no farther."

The war was ending, and still there was no word of Jeff.

44

During the early spring of 1945 they learned of Roberta's death. The news came from one of her old friends. Apparently one of the new buzz bombs had come over and the house she lived in had collapsed and burned.

"She has been wonderfully useful," the letter said. "We will all miss her. But she was not young, and I like to think she is with Arthur again. He was the great love of her life, which always surprised me, since he was flagrantly unfaithful to her. Still as she said he always came back to her, and in his own way really cared for her."

Year by year the family circle had been growing smaller. Now there were only the two of them left. Like castaways on a life raft they had to cling together, even to hope together, in order to survive.

Then without warning Roosevelt died. Even those who had hated him felt the shock of his going, and Courtney, who had followed him, first with hope and then with doubt, wondered what would happen to the country. For twelve years it had been under a more or less benevolent dictatorship. Now it was turned loose, on its own again. Could it survive, in a world where freedom was under constant attack?

"Don't fool yourself," his father had said. "People don't rule themselves. They *are* ruled, and that means leaders." Yet Matthew had frankly detested Roosevelt. He had never believed in democracy. His credo had been the Republic, and rule by justice under law. "Democracy can mean mass rule. Even mob rule, Son. Don't forget that."

But the country survived even the shock of Roosevelt's death.

Out in the Pacific the war was moving fast, and no word had come from Peggy for a long time. She had written not to worry if this happened. "The mails are slow and uncertain, and I'll be moving about." They did not worry, of course, although they had no idea that by early in 1945 she had been on her way to a still-burning Manila, washing out of a helmet now or not washing at all, ducking bullets from Japanese snipers, getting little drinking water and not much food. And still waiting, of course, for one Terry Shane who had a garage in California, and meant to return to it if he had to kill every Jap between himself and Tokyo.

Then one day Ricky had a visitor. She had gone to the park to sit on a bench there and watch the children taking advantage of the first bright day to sail their boats in the small lake. For now she was living largely on her memories, on Jeff trailing his small sailboat on a string, of Peggy riding her first velocipede, her legs fat and chubby.

She had gone without a hat, and the wind had blown her hair about her face and given her some color. When she reached the house it was to find a very big young man in uniform on their pavement, looking up at the number. She stopped and got out her key, to find him beside her.

"Excuse me," he said, touching his cap. "Is this the Wayne house?"

She saw his air insignia then and put a hand against the door-post to steady herself.

"Are you—have you any news? About my son?"

He looked at her, evidently surprised. She was too young. It didn't seem possible. Yet there she was, asking about Peggy's brother.

"I'm sorry, Mrs. Wayne. I've just come from the Pacific. I'm—well, I guess I'm your son-in-law. Name's Shane," he added awkwardly.

She stared at him.

"You're Terry?"

"That's my name." He grinned down at her. "Invalided out. Malaria and a busted eardrum. Hard luck, isn't it?" he added, and held out a big hand.

She was still dazed as she led him into the house. Peggy's husband! This strange rugged-faced young man, his skin yellow from atabrine, who seemed almost too large for his uniform and who smiled at her with bright Irish-blue eyes.

"I promised her I'd see you if I got back," he said. "I suppose she's all right? I haven't heard from her for a long time."

"We haven't heard either," she said worriedly. "Do come up and have a drink."

She settled him in Courtney's study and brought him Peggy's letters to read. He perused them hungrily. He did not even touch his highball until he had read them all. Then he drew a long breath.

"She's a great girl, Mrs. Wayne. I kept thinking about her when my plane went down. It kept me swimming. I had something to swim for."

He was on his way to a hospital in the South for treatment, he explained, and could not stay. But before he left he wanted to see Peggy's room and Peggy's father, if he could. She took him upstairs: to where the room was as it had been left, Peggy's toilet things and perfumes on the dressing table, the rows of small shoes in the closet, the dresses covered with sheets.

He moved around quietly, for all his size. Now and then he touched something gently, as he might have touched Peggy herself.

"I'll never be able to give her anything like this, Mrs. Wayne."

"Do you think that matters?"

"Not to me. It may to her."

"You've read her letters, Terry. You know it won't."

But he was sure Peggy was safe. "They take good care of our girls out there." And he even gave her some assurance about Jeff. He told her of men hiding from the Japs for years, to come out safely; of fliers who like Jeff had bailed out and been reported missing, and who had turned up after all hope had been abandoned.

"If he got down, he's likely to be all right," he said. "Even the Krauts take prisoners, especially airmen. The Jap doesn't."

Before Court came back from the office he asked awkwardly what he should call her.

"You're too young to be my mother," he said. "I'm thirty. What do you suggest? I can't go on calling you Mrs. Wayne."

"Why not Ricky? It's my name. Peggy and Jeff often do it."

Courtney liked him at once. He was wholesome and cheerful, although it was evident that he resented being sent back. He had wanted to get to Tokyo.

"You think we'll get there?" Court asked.

"Get there! The Jap's finished now, no shipping, no more armament, nothing to eat and no place to go—unless he's the hell of a good swimmer. Sure we'll get there."

When he left they let him go reluctantly. It was as though for a few hours he had brought Peggy back to them, and even—just possibly—Jeff too. Yet nothing more seemed to happen. The Allies were battling their way into Germany, MacArthur was at Okinawa. When Easter came Ricky received a huge box of flowers, with a card. It said: "To my dearly beloved wife." And he had added "with admiration and hope." For surely Easter was the time for hope, Easter and the spring. Easter and the Resurrection.

Court went on to the office from the florist's that Saturday morning. As usual it was almost empty, and in the past he had liked these mornings alone. They gave him time, a perspective on the work past or ahead. And he liked opening his own mail. Matthew had done it for years against Angela's protests, until it got beyond him. One of his early memories as a boy was of going with his father to the office on Saturdays. It was open in those days, but he could still see Matthew settling himself behind the desk and picking up the sharp letter opener.

"Well, Son, let's see what's here."

There was considerable mail that morning. He lit a cigarette and glanced over it. He put the business letters aside and picked out one which had come through Switzerland. Probably from Hauck, he thought, and was relieved to think he was still alive and safe.

It was not from Hauck. It was not even a letter. What he pulled out was the snapshot of what looked like a newly made grave, with a wooden cross above it, and an airman's insignia on the cross. There were other similar crosses around it but this one stood out, clear and unmistakable.

When he could move he got up and opened a window. He was finding it hard to breathe. And he felt sick with a deadly sickness. It was the end of waiting, the end of hope. How could he tell Ricky? How could he destroy what young Shane had brought, the bit of reassurance to which she had been clinging ever since?

He sat down and put his head on his outstretched arms on the desk. He was not even aware that Mather had come in and was staring at him, a Mather who looked puzzled and considerably alarmed.

"What's wrong, Court?"

"We've lost Jeff," he said, not lifting his head. "God knows how I'll tell his mother."

There was a brief silence. There was nothing Mather could say. He knew how it was. He put a hand on Courtney's shoulder. Then:

"How do you know? Had official word?"

Court moved then. He shoved the snapshot at Mather, who took it, looked at it, turned it over and saw what was written on the back.

"Who is Otto?" he said, puzzled. "What's he got to do with it?"

Courtney could not believe it. He took the picture back and

stared at it. It was a moment before he could speak.

"Otto!" he said thickly. "Otto is my German son. Or was, poor devil. This is to tell me he is dead."

He told Mather the story that morning, and Mather was understanding and kind.

"Come out and have a drink," he said. "You look as though you need it. What fools we men are, anyhow! Well, forget it, Court. It's over."

Courtney did not take the picture home but very gravely that night he told Ricky Otto was dead.

"I never knew the boy. I told you once a man is not a father merely by the act of conceiving a child. He has to rear it. And Otto was a Nazi. He and his kind have cost us—" He stopped there. "I can't grieve over him, my dear. You understand that, don't you? He meant nothing to me. He never did."

He saw with surprise that there were tears in her eyes.

"Not only for him," she said. "For all the boys who have to die in a war. For all the crosses all over the world. It's such a waste. Such wanton waste."

She held out a hand to him, and he went over and kissed her. The barrier between them was almost gone. . . .

Only through the newspapers did they know anything of the war as it had moved on through the winter and spring: the Germans falling back and the roads along which the Allies moved bottlenecks of snarled traffic. Early in March it was the bridge at Remagen that had to be taken. But the enemy was determined to destroy it first. There was a story of three German officers, loaded with explosives, who had dropped into the icy water to blow it up, and were themselves exploded before they reached it.

It was only one of many such stories, for the enemy was fighting with the courage of despair. Now and then a correspondent got through a human interest story, and the public seized it avidly. But there was no correspondent near to tell the tale of the two American privates who lost their way in one particular hell.

They were driving a jeep loaded with bazooka ammunition, and trying to make a detour around a bottleneck of troops, arms and guns. But they found themselves getting farther and farther away from the battle. It was very cold. Their hands were half frozen, and the road rutted. One of them lit a cigarette and put it between the blue lips of the driver. Then he lit one himself. He looked puzzled.

"Where the hell are we going, Bill? To join up with the Limeys?"

"You tell me. I'd like to know myself."

The road was muddy. The jeep jolted and bumped along. The men argued as to whether to keep on or turn back. The noise of battle was far behind them now and growing fainter. When they reached the top of a hill they saw a small village below them and stopped.

"Suppose there are any Krauts in it?"

"Not unless they're dead."

The village was a typically French one, the road providing its main street, with a small inn built around a courtyard and the usual heap of manure, and some distance beyond an imposing church. Bill drove grimly on, the other man clutched his rifle. The place seemed deserted. It had come through its share of war. Part of the inn was roofless, and the spire of the church was a leaning hollow shell.

Then they saw a man. He was leaning against a stone wall, and a homemade crutch was propped up beside him. He was tall, and the shabby French coat was too small for him. So, too, were the ragged blue jeans which barely covered his calves.

He did not move as they stopped near him, but there was alert suspicion in every line of his thin face. Bill had got out his phrase book and was studying it.

"Où est la route—" he began slowly. But the other man was impatient.

"For God's sake hurry up, Bill. Why now show him the map?"

Then for the first time the young man grinned. He picked up

his crutch and hobbled toward them.

"Either of you guys got a cigarette?" he inquired.

They stared at him, and Bill slowly produced a package of Chesterfields.

"Christ!" he said. "You a Yank?"

"What do you think? How about a match, brother?"

"Bum leg, eh?"

"Flak," he said, inhaling the smoke and releasing it carefully, as though reluctant to let it go. "Where are you going?"

They told him. He took their map and set them right. And when they offered to take him along he nodded.

"Got to say good-bye to these people," he said. "They've been hiding me and taking care of me for a long time."

He disappeared into the house, and was gone for some time. The two men waited, talking.

"What's he mean by flak, Bill?"

"Antiaircraft stuff, you damn fool. He's a flier."

"He *was* a flier."

"Yep. Looks like it."

When he came out a woman and her daughter came with him. The woman regarded the jeep and its helmeted occupants stoically. She was beyond surprise. For months the Germans had come and gone in the village. Now it was this casual pair in their queer green car. C'est la guerre, she thought. The girl, however, was crying. She was a pretty girl, full-breasted and black-haired. The men surveyed her with interest.

"I could go for that dame."

"Not so bad. I've seen better."

The lame man had no luggage except his crutch. When he reached the jeep again he looked faintly embarrassed.

"I don't suppose I could borrow some money?" he asked. "These people are poor. I owe them a lot. Including a leg," he added grimly. "I'll pay you double whatever you've got. I have a lot of back pay coming to me."

They were uneasy. Flier or no flier it was easy to lose touch in this man's army. Finally, however, they produced sixty dollars. He took it and counted it.

"That's a lot in francs," he said. "Thanks. Don't worry. I'll fix it. Got any paper? I'll write a couple of IOUs.

He wrote them standing beside the jeep and balancing on his crutch. When he hobbled back with the money the woman seemed surprised and mollified. But the girl was still crying. He put a hand on her shoulder and spoke to her in French.

"It is all right," he said. "Soon the war will be over and your husband will be back. And I'll never forget you. Be sure of that."

He shook hands with them both and, putting his crutch carefully into the car, hoisted himself into it. As Bill let in the clutch he smiled and waved to them. Then he turned and inspected the bazooka ammunition with interest.

"Take the dirt road by the church," said Lieutenant Jeffrey Wayne. "Looks like they need this stuff over there."

45

One day in the fall of 1945 Ricky got out of the car and spoke o the big young man at the wheel.

"Put the car away, Terry, and don't be late for dinner. Hilda ;ot a steak somewhere, and you like it rare."

He smiled and put a finger to his bare head in salute, perhaps o the steak.

"I'll be back. Don't worry. Maybe you'll look in the hall irst. There may be a letter from Peg."

There was a letter. She brought it out and gave it to him. His ace glowed.

"Hell of a thing," he said, ripping it open. "I'm here living n the fat of the land and Peg's out there still. I don't feel half a ıan."

"You've been sick, Terry."

"Yeah. I got shot at one million times, and then a mosquito ites me and lays me out!"

She left him to his letter and stood for a moment looking up t the house. For the first time in years it looked friendly again. t was shabby of course, like most things now. It needed paint, nd inside it bore the scars of years of living. Sheila's chintzes ad faded, there were cigarette burns on the Adam mantel, cars on the stairs where the children used to slide down the ail. Even the elevator was not working. It needed a new motor, nd there was none to be had.

Long ago she had ceased to dislike the house. Now she

realized she loved it. It was her home, hers and Court's. And now Jeff was on the way back. He might be in any time. And before long Peggy would come too. Not to stay. She would go to California with Terry, a Terry still given to occasional attacks of what he called the shakes, but otherwise solid and substantial. They had not been too grand for him. He had simply accepted them as Peggy's family and let it go at that. But he wanted to get back to California and to his job there.

"I can keep her all right," he had said. "We don't need a lot. If she starts to crave the things she used to have, I'll get her an old helmet to take a bath in!"

She did not go in immediately. Once again, as it had been twenty-six years ago, when Courtney came back, it was a raw day in November. She could see the trees in the park, their bare branches moving in the wind, and a few nurses herding their children as they crossed the avenue. They looked cold, children and nurses alike, and the women looked irritable. Here and there a dejected dog pulled at a leash, and when a policeman put up a hand, they all stopped as if they had abruptly run down. Like machines. Like robots.

When she went in, the house felt warm. She slid off her coat in the hall and went back to the kitchen. There were still practically no servants to be had. Perhaps there never would be again. But Hilda was there, flushed from cooking and the heat of the room, and Ricky sat down at the table.

"If the water's boiling I'd like a cup of tea, Hilda. I'm frozen."

"I'll make you a bit of toast too. All this excitement—"

"I still can't believe it. Better make an extra cup, Hilda. I'll take it up to Audrey. Has she been out at all?"

"Not her. She's up in her room. I see you got your hair done. You'd think she'd be getting a wave or something," Hilda went on.

Ricky was not listening. She was still back in the big house with Elizabeth saying the same thing to her; a small domineering Elizabeth, sitting in the drawing room, running her fingers over the keys of the piano to see if they were dusted, and regarding her with impatience. She could even remember almost exactly what she had said.

"I do hope you're not going to be difficult, Ricky."

And her own reply: "I think perhaps I'm a little frightened."

"Frightened?" Elizabeth looked annoyed. "I don't understand you. I thought you were both too young when you married. I still think so. People change as they get older. They want different things. But I'm sure Courtney will do his part, if you do."

It had been wrong. She knew that now. Marriage was not a matter of duty, but of love. Love and compromise and understanding.

Hilda poured out the tea and buttered a slice of toast. Ricky dropped a slice of lemon into the cup and waited for it to cool.

"It's not easy, Hilda. I remember how it was with me. It has been so long, and I was like her. I was young too. I was scared to death. I'll carry her tea up to her. I expect she needs it."

Hilda said nothing. She fixed a small tray with tea and toast, and Ricky picked it up.

"We must try to understand her," she said. "It may take some time. After all, they were married only a short time. And I understand he's very lame. He'll hate that. It will be hard for him too."

"The more reason she might have had her hair done," said Hilda stubbornly. "He'll get in any time now. Unless his plane crashes," she added dolefully.

Ricky smiled.

"They don't crash these days," she said. "Not on the transatlantic trips, anyhow."

She carried the tray carefully out to the stairs. She missed the elevator. She had been using it more and more often the last few years. Even Courtney had used it now and then. And Jeff would need it. She sighed as she climbed the stairs. She was somewhat winded when she reached what had been the nursery floor, and she hesitated a moment before she rapped at

Jeff's door. Perhaps she was foolish. Perhaps the girl wanted to be alone. But she must somehow make her feel one of them. She had only arrived that morning. She rapped, and Audrey's voice said to come in.

When she opened the door the room was dim with the early fall twilight. She could barely see her. She was standing by a window, looking out, and Ricky felt for a table and put the tray on it. She did not switch on the lights.

"I've brought you some tea," she said briskly. "Do you want a light?"

"I'd rather not. Thanks for the tea. I'll drink it in a minute."

Ricky sat down and lighting a cigarette offered one to the girl, but she declined it.

"I've smoked all day," she said. "My mouth's dry. I guess I'm scared. After all, it's been three years. Plenty of time for him to forget me."

"Plenty of time for you to forget him too. He's probably as worried as you are. Or more. He limps quite a lot, you know, Audrey."

"As if that makes any difference to me," Audrey said scornfully.

Ricky sat down and looked around the room. She had known Jeff would want it again, and except for the double bed in place of his single one it was unchanged. She and Court had argued about the bed, and Court had won.

"They have a big gulf to bridge," he had said. "Put them together, Ricky." And he added: I remember how I missed you when you first moved out on me. I'd throw out my arm to touch you and hit the damned table between us."

She looked at the clock beside the bed. By its radium dial she knew the plane was not in yet. Courtney would still be waiting in the cold at the airport and staring at the sky. Audrey had gone back to the window. Silhouetted against the fading light she looked small and young, and Ricky's heart ached for her.

"I think I know how you feel," she said carefully. "I remember the state I was in before Court came back. I la awake all night, scared to death. He had been gone a long time too. Like Jeff."

The girl turned to look at her.

"And it was all right?"

"It was still all right. Of course it took a little time," she said, still cautiously. "We had to get used to each other again, to being married."

"Jeff's always said you were the most perfectly happy people he'd ever known. He said the Waynes were one-women men. It's queer you were afraid. I never think of you as being afraid of anything, somehow."

Ricky put down her cigarette and laughed. If it was forced the girl did not notice it.

"My dear, my whole life has been one fear after another. And I'd been married in such a hurry. I was sure Court wouldn't love me when he came back. I pretty nearly lost him too."

"Lost him?" Audrey's voice was startled.

"I certainly did. I was so sure he'd forgotten me that I—well, he walked out on me in Washington, and I don't blame him. I should have been spanked," Ricky went on evenly. "I was a little fool, of course."

"I'd never act that way with Jeff. I couldn't."

"Then let him know it, my dear. Let him know it the minute you see him, that you love him and want him."

Down below the front door slammed and they heard Terry coming up the stairs. He took them two at a time and banged into Peggy's old room

"You see," Ricky went on, "I keep thinking about my mother-in-law's house, and about her. It was a very grand house, bigger than this, and it was filled with servants. She had a room she called Mama's Parlor, with a stuffed peacock in it. And there was a butler named Johnson. He scared the daylights out of me. I know Mrs. Wayne meant to be kind, but I don't think she liked me much at first. She was not a very understanding woman."

"No one can say that about you," Audrey said warmly.

"I hope not. But there was something else I wanted to tell you. You see, Court was her only son. When he came back she wanted us to stay with them, and we did try. Only it didn't work."

Audrey was definitely interested now. She walked over and turned on a lamp, the same small one which for so long had stood in the window. Then she lit a cigarette and looked gravely at Ricky.

"You're trying to tell me something aren't you?"

"Only that your lives are your own, Audrey; yours and Jeff's. Your marriage is your own too. Yours to make and keep. Always remember that."

For the first time since she had known her, Audrey came over and kissed Ricky warmly.

"We'll manage. I'll see that we manage. It's a promise."

She had done her bit, Ricky thought, as she went rather tiredly to her own room to dress for Jeff's arrival. At least Audrey would not make the mistake she had. She sat down in front of her toilet table and surveyed herself carefully in the mirror. By leaning forward she could see a trace of gray here and there in her hair, but she thought she had not changed greatly since Jeff went away.

She slipped off her clothes and took a quick bath, but she was still uneasy. What if Jeff came home resentful at being crippled? Or what about the nurses who had written his letters for him while his leg was being reset, and before he was able to write for himself? She put the thought away. She was reading her own past into his return, and it was silly. She dressed, and after a survey in the mirror used her lipstick and added a touch of powdered rouge to her cheeks.

She was still there when she heard Audrey running wildl down the stairs.

She opened her door and listened, her heart beating fast. Bu she waited. If it was Jeff, his wife had the first right to gree him.

It was Jeff. Standing on the stair landing she heard the excited voices below. Courtney and Jeff and Audrey's. Even Hilda's. For a moment she felt left out, as though none of them needed her. Then Jeff shouted.

"Hi!" he called up the stairs. "Haven't I got a mother somewhere?"

It was all right. She found herself running down, like Audrey, like a girl. And there was Jeff, his arm around his wife but his face lifted, looking up at her on the stairs.

"Hello, beautiful," he said. "Come and kiss the family hero."

He had no crutch, thank God. He was simply Jeff. Jeff, her baby of long ago and now a man. He released Audrey and caught her in his arms. Then he held her off and inspected her.

"Just a rag and a bone!" he said. "I thought you'd be a buxom old lady by this time."

But he was fatigued, although he scouted the idea of having his dinner in bed. He limped too, rather badly. He was conscious of it, she knew. He grinned at Audrey but his eyes were weary.

"Mind if we use the elevator, old girl?" he said. "You've got a cripple for a husband, you know."

"I've got my husband back," said Audrey stanchly. "That's all I care about. And the elevator's not running. Come on. We climb!"

They watched them going slowly up the stairs and when they were out of sight Ricky smiled at Courtney.

"It's all right, isn't it?" she said. "Do you remember when you came home from the other war?" she asked. "What a little fool I was!"

He looked rather blank.

"Should I remember? It's a long time ago, my darling." Then he laughed. "Of course! At the Shoreham, wasn't it? You didn't want me to stay with you. And was I sore!"

Dinner was very gay that night. Terry and Jeff took to each other at once, squabbled about their respective services, and ate enormously. There was all the news too, Roberta's death, Pete's losing a leg, Peggy's experiences and their hopes for her early return. But on his escape from the Germans his months in hiding he was unwilling to elaborate. He had made a bad landing on a field outside a village and had lain there all night, wrapped in his parachute. His leg had been bad. He couldn't even crawl. And there were Germans in the neighborhood. Once he had heard a patrol passing.

No one saw him until dawn the next morning. Then a middle-aged Frenchwoman, seeing the parachute in the field, came over to retrieve it.

She had been startled to find him beneath it. He told her in French that he was an American, and somehow she and her husband had got him to one of the outbuildings belonging to the inn. They did not trust the townspeople, however. And the Germans were in and out. Once for weeks some officers stayed there.

It was the curé of the church who had attended to his leg, coming at night to do so. It had been hard on the family. If he had been discovered they would all have been shot. Toward the end, the woman was anxious to get rid of him, for the Germans were destroying the farms and towns as they retreated. The man had already gone to join the Maquis. But by that time his French patois was good enough for him to pose as a nephew of the family. They found some clothes for him and let him out of the loft in the stable. He had even helped them with the work.

He grinned and looked at a breathless Hilda, standing in the pantry doorway.

"Need any help with the dishes?" he inquired. "Or how about a little laundry work? They thought I was pretty good at both."

Courtney listened and watched. Not once had Jeff mentioned the French girl, yet she had been there. One of the first letters he wrote in a rather shaky hand from the hospital had been one to Courtney himself, asking him to send clothes for her as well as for her mother.

"They took a lot of chances, Dad, and the girl was tops. They need everything. Maybe you can send the stuff with one of our fellows. Nothing fancy. They're peasants. But warm. And God knows they need food too if you can get it to them."

He had not told Ricky about the girl. He sent Angela to do the shopping, and knew she would not talk.

But when after dinner he had maneuvered Jeff into his study and closed the door, he remembered something. Just so, after his own return years ago, had his father sat at the desk in the library of the old house and sharply interrogated him.

"Look here, Court, you haven't made a fool of yourself over some girl over there, have you?"

"We were ordered not to fraternize, Dad."

Matthew had grunted.

"That meant a hell of a lot!" he said. And dropped the subject.

He was not going to make that mistake with Jeff. For a while he talked politics. With Roosevelt dead the country was milling about without leadership. And the national debt—

He caught himself up sharply. Jeff was not listening. Cigarette in hand he was wandering about the room. He came to a stop across from the desk and stood looking down at his father.

"About that girl in France, Dad. I want to tell you about her."

"I see. Go ahead, Son."

"She was good to me. She's the one who saved me. Her people didn't want me. I was a danger to them every minute."

"Is that all, Jeff? About the girl, I mean?"

Jeff hesitated. He put out his cigarette and dropped it in an ashtray.

"If you mean was I in love with her, no, I wasn't, Dad. But if you're asking me whether I slept with her or not, the answer is yes. I did." And when Courtney waited he went on: "She was married. Her husband was dead, I think. She didn't know. Anyhow, that's how it was."

Courtney moved in his chair.

"I didn't tell your mother about your letter," he said. "She might have worried."

Jeff nodded.

"Right," he said. "She would. But Audrey's different. She can take it."

"You're going to tell her? Is that necessary, Jeff? Why hurt her?"

"Better now than later, Dad."

Courtney glanced up at him sharply. Did the boy know about Elsa? Had Roberta told him over in England, perhaps to warn him against the same sort of entanglement? He did not know. Perhaps he never would know.

"Times change, you know," Jeff said quietly. "Girls understand a lot more than they used to. And things looked pretty rugged for a while. I didn't expect to get away at all. Now I'm back I want to start with a clean slate. Audrey's a lot like Mother, you know. She'll stick."

He smiled and picked up a new Wayne book from the desk.

"I haven't asked you. How's business, Dad?"

Courtney pulled himself together with some difficulty.

"Still going strong. I suppose war books will be out soon. People are fed up with war."

Jeff glanced at the book in his hand.

"Well, I guess we'll manage," he said cheerfully. "I see we have a new Lockwood."

He had laid no emphasis on the "we," but Courtney felt a sudden relief. The old imprint would carry on after all with Jeff, and perhaps Jeff's son after him. They would publish honest books, would follow Matthew's example of integrity and essential simplicity. And Americanism.

"I'll be mighty proud to have you in the firm, Jeff," he said huskily.

Later when the others had gone to bed he still sat in his crowded room. All around him were Wayne books, and he remembered what Matthew had said, that he had never heard of a book being fired out of a gun. But books had been ammunition. They still were.

He did not fool himself. The fight was not over, in spite of two wars. The struggle was still going on, not only between two ideologies. Intolerance and hatred were still to be fought, and freedom still to be won. Rather grimly he dedicated himself to that battle.

He mixed himself a whisky and soda and went back to the desk again. Now the house had become quiet, and he listened to its silence, broken only by the splash of the wall fountain in the hall. It was old and comfortable and shabby, but years of living had made it into a home. His home.

It was hard to realize it was all over, that the tumult and the shouting had died. He ran a hand through his hair, thinning on his forehead. He was over fifty, and he had had enough. It was time he sat back and let the new generation take over. Perhaps they would make a better job of things.

He put down his drink and picked up the latest Lockwood. It was not very good. How could it be, with Anne's boy with a bullet wound in his chest, now lying where Tim had lain so long, on the porch of the little house? But at the office they had done their best with it. They had used eleven on twelve Baskerville, which he liked. He opened it and glanced at the final paragraph.

"So it was finished. Behind them lay the years of separation. Now the reckless passions of their youth were over. All they asked was peace and security. But together. Always together, please God."

It was pure Lockwood, of course, but he gazed at it thoughtfully for some time. Then he got up and putting out the light, slowly climbed the stairs.

Ricky was at the toilet table in her room. She was in her nightdress, brushing her hair. He went over and leaning down, kissed her.

"Love me again, darling?"

She gave him a radiant smile.

"I never stopped, Court. I know that now."

He rather doubted it. He did not say so, however. He straightened rather stiffly and began to take off his coat. Who said passion passed with youth? It was a lie. A man at fifty was still a man, could still love his wife and want her. He hung his coat in the closet and sat down in his big chair to take off his shoes.

It was very comfortable. He leaned back and closed his eyes.

"It's been a big day," he said, yawning. "God, I'm about played out. Waiting for that plane to come in . . ."

He opened his eyes, but Ricky was not there. She was in the bathroom. The splash of the water was soothing. It reminded him of the wall fountain below. Ricky had not liked it for a long time, but now it was all right. Everything was all right. He grunted and closed his eyes again.

When Ricky came back a few moments later he was sound asleep. She stood smiling down at him. Then she tucked a blanket over his knees and got into bed, as she had so many times before. Alone.